ASHES AND ENTROPY
Edited by Robert S. Wilson

First Trade Paperback
Color Edition

Nightscape Press, LLP
http://www.nightscapepress.pub

All regional spellings have been kept intact in order to preserve each author's particular voice.

TABLE OF CONTENTS:

THE GRAY ROOM
by Tim Waggoner

You pull your beat-up Chevy Malibu into a parking space in front of an old two-story apartment building. You kill the engine and turn to Liza, sitting in the passenger seat beside you.

"This looks shady as fuck," you say. You try to sound cool, like you're amused, but you can't hide the nervousness in your voice.

She laughs, or at least tries to. It comes out more like a chuffing sound, a noise produced by the cancer-ridden throat of someone who's been smoking for decades. But Liza doesn't smoke. She has a far different addiction, one you've come here to feed.

"You can't buy this shit over the counter at your neighborhood pharmacy," she says. She pauses, thinks a moment. "I'm not sure you can buy it anywhere else."

Anywhere else in town? you wonder. Or does she mean anywhere else in the world?

She was beautiful once. At least, she looks like she might've been. There's a remnant of blue in her dull gray eyes, an echo of gold in her dingy straw-like hair, a touch of faded pink in her dry, cracked lips. You try to imagine what it would be like to kiss those lips, and you feel a shiver of disgust.

She opens the passenger door and steps outside. You hesitate a moment longer. Do you really want to do this?

It's beyond any high you've ever imagined. Beyond sex, love, life, death — *and more.*

That's what she told you at the bar last night, when you tried to match her shot for shot and ended up drunk off your ass while she seemed perfectly sober. It's the *more* that really caught your attention, the hook that sank deep in your flesh. What could be more than life and death? What would that more feel like?

She smacks the flat of her hand against the driver's side window, startling you.

"You coming or are you going to puss out?" she demands.

She's wearing a Rancid T-shirt and faded jeans that look at least two sizes too big for her. She's using an old piece of rope for a belt, and her bare feet are so dirty, at first glance it looks as if she's wearing a pair of black slippers.

You smile at her, trying to look like you do this kind of thing all the time, but it feels strained, and you fear all you've managed is an uneasy grimace. Still, she steps away from the door and you get out.

It should be dark, should be the dead of fucking night, but it's two in the afternoon. Although as much as you drank last night, it still feels way too early to be out of bed. The sunlight stabs your eyes, sets your head to thudding. A sudden dizziness hits you, and you put a hand on the car roof to steady yourself.

When you first pulled up in the front of the building, you thought it was old. But now that you take your first good look at it, you see it's downright ancient. The brick might've been red once, but the years have leeched away most of the color, leaving it almost white. It looks soft and porous, as if on the verge of crumbling to dust. The windows are cracked, the glass so grimy it looks as if it's been whitewashed from inside. Whatever color the shutters once were is impossible to tell. The paint flaked off them long ago, leaving behind only weathered gray wood. The roof is missing a good number of shingles, maybe as much as half. It's as if a huge storm blew through her recently, stripped the shingles away, and no one's got around to replacing them. There's a sidewalk in front of the building, and a small set of concrete steps that leads to a door. The sidewalk is cracked and broken, as are the steps, and the door – gray wood like the shutters – hangs slightly askew, its metal handle covered with rust. The ground surrounding the building is dotted with patches of dead grass but otherwise is bare, the soil hard and lifeless, the color of diseased bone.

An odor hangs heavy on the stale air, a rank foulness that reminds you of the time you were mowing your parents' back yard as a teenager and you ran over the flattened, desiccated corpse of some small animal – a squirrel, probably – that had died and remained out in the summer sun for days. As the chewed-up pieces of bone and leathery hide were ejected from the mower's discharge chute, a greasy stomach-turning stench had filled the air. The air around the building reminds you of that smell, only worse.

But all of this – the building's appearance, its smell – is nothing compared to how the place makes you *feel.* You're instantly on edge, jaw tight, teeth clamped together, eyes narrowed. It's as if there's a sound just outside your range of hearing, like the almost inaudible hum of electronic equipment. It worms its way into your ears, making you feel as if thousands of tiny insects are walking across the folds and ridges of your brain.

"Not much to look at, is it?" Liza says.

She tries to sound flippant, like she's aware of the effect the place has and is unaffected by it. But you can hear how uncomfortable she is, and for some reason, this bolsters your courage. You suppose it's good to know Liza's not as tough as she pretends to be. It makes you feel less alone.

She starts toward the door, and as she mounts the steps, concrete crumbles to dust beneath her feet. You follow, and you feel the steps sag beneath you. You're slender and Liza is close to emaciated, but even so you expect the steps to collapse entirely beneath your combined weight. But they hold, and when Liza opens the door—which is surprisingly silent given its condition—and holds it open for you, she smiles, revealing sore, bleeding gums and soft gray teeth. You could turn around. It's not too late. You could run back to the car, get inside, and drive the hell away from Liza, this place, and whatever waits inside. Last chance. Going once . . . Going twice . . .

Gone.

~

She finds you in the parking lot of Bottoms Up, a dive bar on the west side of Ash Creek. You're sitting in your car, windows down, head back, eyes closed, listening to the heroin's sweet, sweet song. Except the song isn't as sweet these days, is it? It isn't as loud, either. More and more often, it seems to fade into the background, and sometimes it falls silent altogether. You've become habituated and need stronger doses to get you where you want to go. Problem is, you're not exactly raking in the dough working in the kitchen of a twenty-four-hour hamburger joint, the kind of place where the patties are small and square and taste like used condoms. So you buy the best you can afford, but it's not enough, not anymore.

"Enjoying the ride?"

You slowly open your eyes and find yourself looking into Liza's face, although you don't know her name yet. Her hands – small-fingered, nails bitten to the quick – grip the edge of the window, and she's crouched down so she can look inside.

The smack in your veins might not be hi-test, but it's made you mellow enough, so you don't make a face upon seeing her. Her skin is sallow and drawn so tight to her skull she almost looks like an animated skeleton. At first you were afraid she was a cop who thought you'd OD'd and was ready to give you a shot of Narcan. But you can see she's only another addict looking to whore herself out so she can afford her next fix. The town's full of them. You're not an addict, though. You're a *user*. Big difference.

Her breath is foul, like the stink from an open sewer, and you turn your head slightly to move your noise away from the stench, but it doesn't help.

"Not interested," you mumble, the words barely audible even to you. She has no trouble hearing you, though.

"How do you know? I haven't offered you anything yet."

You have to admit she has a point. But you just want to be left alone.

"Fuck off," you say, voice raised to show you mean it.

The woman doesn't go anywhere. She continues looking at you through the open window. She smiles, the movement making her dry lips crack and bleed in several places.

"You've got a problem. I've got a solution." She pauses, then adds, "If you've got the balls."

She hasn't said so directly, but you sense that she knows precisely what your problem is. Who knows? Maybe she can smell it on you. Takes one to know one, right?

"Come inside with me. We'll do some shots and talk about what we can do to get you where you want to go."

You look at her for a moment, considering. Then you say, "What the fuck?" and get out of the car.

~

The entryway is short and narrow, two apartments on the top floor, two on the bottom, and four rusty metal mailboxes set into one wall. The baby-shit brown carpet is frayed, torn, and dotted with suspicious-looking stains. Dead insects line the baseboards, and at first you think they're cockroaches, and there *is* a superficial resemblance, but these insects have too many legs, each of which ends in clawed toes. Fliers plaster the walls, held in place by yellowed strips of tape. They're printed on different colors of paper – blue, pink, yellow, and, of course, white – and they advertise services or make announcements for things that you've never heard of, some of which are downright enigmatic.

HAVE YOU SEEN THE REST OF ME? CALL followed by a long string of symbols unlike any numbers you're familiar with.

TWO MINUTES OF DARKNESS! LOWEST PRICE IN TOWN!

COME EXPERIENCE THE GREAT DISMAL.

DELICIOUS CANNIBALS – FIFTY PERCENT OFF!

The smell in here is even worse than outside. It's like an overfilled dumpster baking in August heat – spoiled fruit and rotten meat slathered in piss and shit. Your gut convulses and stomach acid sears the back of your throat. You don't throw up, though, even if your body wants to. You haven't put anything in your belly besides booze for days, and there's nothing to bring up. A small mercy.

Liza leads you to the ground floor apartment on the left. A few meager flakes of pale green paint cling to the door, and a symbol has been crudely carved into the wood in place of a number, a lopsided circle with an X over it. The door across the hall has a zig-zagging line running downward from left to right.

Liza doesn't bother to knock on the door with the circle and X on it. She takes hold of the rust-caked knob and turns it. She pushes the door open and grins at you, displaying her soft gray teeth once more.

"After you," she says, gesturing for you to precede her.

There's something seriously fucked up about this building, about the whole goddamned situation. How badly do you want this? You don't, you decide. You *need* it.

You enter and Liza follows, pulling the door shut behind her.

~

Sometime after your first couple shots, but way before your last, Liza asks you a question.

"Why do you do it?"

She doesn't specify what *it* is. She doesn't have to.

You shrug. "Because it feels good, I guess."

"Just good?"

You grin. "Okay, it feels goddamn fan-fucking-tastic."

"But not like it used to."

"No. I wish it did."

"What if I told you I can hook you up with something that's a hundred times better? Hell, a *million* times."

"I'd say you're full of shit."

She continues, taking no offense, "What do you imagine the ultimate sensation would be?"

You have to think about that for a time before answering.

"Dying," you say.

She purses her lips in disapproval. "Dying's no great trick. Everything dies, even the universe. It's just dying so slowly compared to us that we don't really notice."

She's starting to irritate you by this point, and you're thinking of leaving after one more shot. Or three.

"So what *is* the ultimate sensation?" you ask.

"To *feel* the universe dying." Her dull eyes seem to brighten a bit as she speaks these words. "To know what it's like to be in the throes of death for billions of years, with billions more yet to endure. It's . . ." She breaks off, searching for the right words. "Rapturous. And that's what you've been searching for, isn't it? The same thing we're all searching for. To escape these sacks of meat we're trapped in –" she slaps her chest for emphasis – "even if only for a short time. Doesn't that sound better than heroin?"

Until tonight, you haven't given much thought to the reasons why you use drugs. But Liza's words resonate with you. You're such a small person, living such a small life. To touch something so big. . . to know what it's like to be *everything* – even if that everything was dying. . . That would be the ultimate, wouldn't it?

"And there's a drug that can make you feel like this?" you ask.

She nods. "And I know where to get it."

~

There are no lights on in the apartment. There's a window on one wall and a glass patio door, but both are covered with sheets affixed to curtain rods with wooden clothespins. The sheets are thin, though, allowing enough light to filter through so you can see. The walls are the sickly gray color of diseased mucus, and the floor is covered with taped-together sheets of plastic that wrinkle with each step you take. There's no furniture, at least not in the main room – the gray room – which is all you can see at the moment. But the room is far from empty. The space is filled with some manner of bizarre sculpture made from bones lashed together with rusty barbed wire. Arm bones, leg bones, spines, ribcages, pelvises, skulls. . . all arranged in haphazard fashion, none of the pieces connected in anything remotely resembling a natural way. You recognize some of the bones as human – from both adults and children – but others appear to be from animals. Dogs, cats, birds, cows, horses, large reptiles like alligators or crocodiles . . . But some of the skeletal pieces are. . . different. Skulls with one eye socket, three, or even more. Two mouths, no mouth, a circular orifice where a mouth should be. Twisted spines with serrated fins protruding from them, pelvises which are all sharp angles, rib cages that are curved outward instead of inward, the ends of the ribs sharpened spear points. After the initial shock of seeing this lunatic construction, you realize it's made of more than just bone and wire. Thin plastic tubing runs throughout the thing, coiling around bones, running in and out of eye sockets and mouths, threading through ribs. . . The tubing isn't empty, though. Something thick and dark moves through it, and you can almost hear the moist sound of oozing sludge.

Like the outside of the building and the entryway, there's a strong smell inside the apartment, but it's different than the others. It's the smell of dead, lifeless earth, of a desert so barren it's incapable of sustaining even the hardiest form of life. With each breath you take, it feels as if you're losing moisture, drying up inside a little bit more, and you wonder what would happen to you if you stayed here too long. Would you become a shrunken, dried husk, nothing but parchment skin draped over dusty bones?

"Oh, hello, Liza. I didn't hear you come in."

You turn toward the voice – a mild and not unpleasant tenor – and see a man enter the gray room from small hallway that presumably leads back to an equally gray bedroom. Although from what you've seen of the apartment so far, it might be best to avoid making such assumptions.

You expect the man to look strange, perhaps even inhuman, but he appears perfectly normal. Middle-aged, balding, medium height, clean-shaven, dressed in a long-sleeved white shirt with the collar buttoned, black slacks and black shoes. But then you notice that what hair he does have looks as if it's been painted onto his head, and his shirt is preternaturally white, so much so that it almost glows in the room's dimness. And his pants and shoes are so black it's as if they're a void, drawing in the surrounding light and snuffing it out.

He smiles as he sees you and makes his way carefully around the bone-and-wire construction to greet you. He's still smiling when he gets there, and you see his teeth are as white as his shirt, so white it hurts to look at them directly. You also notice that every tooth is exactly the same size and shape –

perfect little squares aligned in twin rows. His eyes look normal enough, except that they give the impression that they have no pupils, but rather small openings that, if you wished, you could fit the tip of your pinkies into them.

He extends his hand for you to shake, and you hesitate a few seconds before doing so. His flesh is cool and rubbery, and the feel of it causes you to shiver with disgust. He gives no sign that he notices. Instead he releases your hand, smile still in place.

"Please forgive the plastic," he says. "The Spiritus Mori leaks sometimes. You are . . .?"

You give him your name. He nods, continuing to smile, as if it's a very fine name indeed.

"I'd give you mine, but I'm afraid I don't have a name. Never had any use for one, I suppose." He claps his hands together and rubs them vigorously. They make a sound like two snakes sliding against one another. "Let's get down to business. You've come to sample my wares, yes?"

You nod. "How much?"

The man looks offended. "I don't charge!" Then his expression turns sly, and he adds, "Not the first time."

He turns to Liza.

"And you wish to partake as well, my dear?"

Up to this point, Liza has seemed confident and relaxed, completely in control. But now she bows her head, almost in supplication, and when she speaks her voice is plaintive, as if she's begging.

"Yes. I've brought the first half of my payment." She gives you a quick glance before turning back to the man in the too-white shirt.

"So I see. Are you prepared to pay the remainder?"

"Yes." She whispers the word.

"Excellent!" Another hand clap followed by more sliding snakeskin. The man walks over to the Spiritus Mori and taps the head of a tiny bird skull, once, twice. He then holds his right index finger up to the skull's beak and a single drop of a thick, tarry substance emerges and falls onto his finger. He quickly switches hands and catches the second drop on his left index finger. He then returns to the two of you. Whatever the substance on his fingers is, it doesn't drip or slide off. It remains on his skin like a pair of black beads.

"This doesn't have a name either, I'm afraid. Not the best marketing, I'll grant you, but then again, my product sells itself. Put your tongue out."

This situation has long gone past the point where you can tell yourself that none of this is real, that it's all some elaborate practical joke. You may not understand exactly what's happening, but you damn well know that it's real, all of it. You can feel it in the core of your being. And whatever that black goo is, you know it will deliver the experience Liza promised. All you have to do is open your mouth and stick out your tongue.

So you do.

The man in the too-white shirt places the drop on your tongue, but before he can place the second on Liza's, she grabs hold of his wrist and shoves his index finger into her mouth. She sucks on it, sucks *hard*, as if she's trying to pull the meat off his finger, too. The man's lips purse in disgust, and he places his other hand on Liza's head and shoves her backward. His finger comes free from her mouth with a wet schlurp, and she stumbles backward, almost falling. She doesn't care, though. She's too busy laughing.

You watch this happen, but it barely registers on your consciousness, for the drug has already been absorbed into your tongue and is beginning to do its work. The first thing it does is shut down your senses. Sight goes first, followed swiftly by hearing. The drug left a sour tang in your mouth, but when your taste goes, the sourness goes with it. The apartment's dead earth odor cuts off as your smell dies, and then your nerve endings follow, and you can no longer physically feel anything. It's like you no longer exist, except you're still conscious, still *you*, but you're nowhere and nowhen. This non-sensation should be the opposite of a high. After all, it's nothing. But there's an almost euphoric feeling of deep peace, and rather than your sense of self being diminished, it instead feels enhanced, strengthened. You are, after all, the only thing that inhabits this noplace. That makes you God, doesn't it? You wonder what would happen if you said, *Let there be light.*

If this was as far as the experience went, if it was all the black drop had to offer, it would've still lived up to Liza's promises. But it's only the beginning, a mere appetizer for what's to come.

You feel yourself begin to expand rapidly, growing at a rate beyond comprehension. You become aware of the physical world again as you grow, becoming larger than the building, larger than the city, the state, the country, the continent, the hemisphere, the world . . . and still you continue growing, expanding outward in all directions, past the moon, the sun, the other planets in the system. And then, although you wouldn't have believed it possible, your growth accelerates exponentially, and soon you encompass hundreds of star systems, millions, then this galaxy, then the neighboring ones, then *all* the galaxies until you are everything that was, is, or ever will be. You are All.

It should be too much for a single human mind to withstand, and your tiny limited psyche should be obliterated by the experience. You're overwhelmed, to put it mildly, but that's okay. You can handle it, with the drug's help. And you think this – *this* – is the ultimate, that there can be nothing beyond this. How could there be?

And then you feel it, feel reality dying. It's been happening since that timeless instant everything came into being, an inexorable process, unimaginably slow but constant, like the dripping mineral-rich water that over centuries forms stalactites on a cave ceiling, or the trickling stream that over millennia carves out a vast canyon. You are All, and you can feel yourself dying, giving forth an endless moan of pain and despair that is the true song of existence, a discordant symphony of glorious hopelessness, of absolute and utter futility. The universe was born to die. It has no other purpose, and knowing this, *being* this, is truly the ultimate drug.

Then you're shrinking, even more rapidly than you grew, and with a dizzying rush and a hard jolt, as if your mind has been thrown back into a cage, the door slammed shut and locked tight, you are you again. Small, limited, and oh so empty.

You open your eyes, see the man in the too-white shirt smiling at you, see Liza standing close by, looking even thinner now, little more than a skeleton, really, but with an expression of bliss on her skull-like face. Then her eyes, now sunk deep in their sockets, open and she lets out a despairing sob. You know just how she feels.

The man looks at her, eye holes growing wider, the darkness within them roiling. But when he speaks, his voice is not altogether without sympathy.

"Are you ready, Liza?"

You can sense she isn't. Who would be?

"Does it matter?" she says.

"Not in the slightest," the man replies. Then he opens his mouth and inhales deeply.

Liza remains standing for a moment, unaffected, but then bits of her begin to flake away like ash and drift toward the man, who's still somehow drawing air into his lungs, though they should've been filled by now. The man breathes the pieces of her into himself, only a few at first, but then more and more, faster and faster. Liza is being dismantled, pulled apart, as if she's a dying flower whose petals are falling away one by one. Her face is halfway gone when she looks at you, and the remnant of her mouth attempts to say three words. No sound emerges, but you think she says *It's worth it*, but you aren't certain, and then she bursts apart into thousands of tiny fragments which swirl and tumble as the man in the too-white shirt sucks them in. When the last piece of Liza passes between his lips, he closes his mouth and gives a contented sigh.

You don't know what he is, only that he's a terrible, awful *thing*, but still you step toward him, moving slowly on legs that are thinner than they were before, plastic crinkling beneath your feet. You reach out and grip his arms with hands that are weaker than they used to be, look into the dark holes where his pupils should be, and speak a single word in a tremulous voice.

"Again."

It's a demand as much as a plea. You'd do anything, sacrifice anything to experience the Dying All again. Absolutely anything.

"Easily done," the man says. "All you must do is leave here and came back with a friend, just as Liza did. Then you have to pay the same price. Sound fair?"

It sounds more than fair, sounds fucking *excellent*, in fact. You smile, showing your new teeth, now soft and gray, and your hands drop away from the man's arms. You turn and head for the door, already thinking about where you can go, who you can make your sales pitch to. You have no doubt you'll find someone who'll buy what you're selling. There are lots of fools like you out there. And after all, the first one's free.

THE HEAD ON THE DOOR
by Erinn L. Kemper

May 5, 1986

Trevor had only been on the job a few days when he spotted the head on the door.

He and Greg were taking a break after being on the scaffold all morning in full sun. From up there they could see the Berkeley Hills dropping down into the morning fog of San Francisco Bay. A scattered jigsaw of old paint littered the grass in jagged pieces. The edges of the flakes showed a transition from red to white to yellow and back to white, like geological stratum that held the secret history of the earth.

Trevor leaned against one of the porch's cool stone posts. Dusty pencil taste coated his mouth. A long toke on the joint and a gargle with Coke just made it worse.

Greg came around the corner, Van Halen thumped from the boom box he carried on his shoulder. "You got more of that?"

Trevor tossed him a can. Greg caught it, put down the boom box, and held his hand out for the joint.

"I can't believe you like Hagar. Seriously, if you had a choice between them, who would you want for your front man?" Greg said, continuing the debate they'd been having all morning from the top of the scaffold. "Diamond Dave. No fucking doubt."

The argument held for a moment while the painters passed the joint and squinted at the house. A classic three-story Victorian on a street of classic Victorians. The houses here had big yards—big for the area anyways—picket fences and sculpted hedges. With gingerbread bargeboards, multi-paned bay windows, and a spired turret, the restoration was going to take a while.

The porch wasn't even half done. It had been rebuilt, years ago, but being sheltered from sun and rain, the paint still adhered. All they'd managed to scrape totally clean were the big oak double-doors. The coating of jelly-soft stain had sloughed off in easy clumps. Trevor took another drag and admired the bronzed sheen of the bare oak through a haze of smoke.

"Hey, check it out. There's a head there, on the door."

"The fuck you talking about, man?" Greg took the joint back, pinched it for a long hit, tipped his head back and held his breath.

"That knot. Right door, close to the top hinge. Kinda looks like a face."

~

The street was usually quiet. That's why he liked living here. Why he kept this house, right through the recession and the realtors coming by working their angles. There'd been work on the old house years before. But that had gone quickly. He'd worried that the family who owned the house were planning to come back, but they didn't. The house stayed empty.

Moving would be complicated. And he wanted to stay close.

He peered through the curtains at the young painters across the street. Splattered work pants, long hair, thin mustaches. *Crazy drugged-out hippie musicians.* One lifted his leg and played it like a guitar in time to the brittle squeal that came from their ghetto blaster. Music that sounded more like metal being ground to pieces, sharpened to points.

He let the curtain drop and went back to the kitchen to prepare lunch.

~

"John says the gig's been moved to Friday. Gonna have to do a short day at the house to fit in showers before sound check." Trevor raised his voice to be heard over the after-work bar crowd. He set the beers down and sat on a spindly wood chair, bumping the table, sending everything sloshing. "Could be worse, I guess. Could be Sunday."

"Yeah, or we could get bumped for that guy with the toilet plunger on his dick. Fuckin' hate that guy." Greg took a sip of beer. "Hey, is Cheryl gonna come for the gig?"

"Nah. She's in Ohio, at her sister's. Says she still feels weird. Weak. I honestly don't know if she's coming back."

"Bummer." Greg leaned forward, his expression one of wary concern. "You know, life's long, man. There's tons of time to do it all. Now we focus on the band. Live the dream. Later we do the kids and little league thing."

"Don't really feel like talking about it, Grego. Thanks, though. We'll just see how it goes."

Trevor tipped back in his chair and watched the happy hour crowd. Office workers, ties pulled loose, students in tight little groups, the occasional all-day drinker. One old dude sat on the corner stool at the bar, swaying to his own groove. Was he drinking to forget, or drinking just to drink? Trevor hoped it was the latter.

The TV over the bar played the local news, the anchor's face blurred red, radiated. Greg focused on the screen, burping between long gulps of beer. He sat up straight, excited, and pointed at the monitor.

"You see this? They found that guy. The poet who left his Plymouth by the Bridge in the 50s and vanished."

"Where'd they find him? Roswell? A corn field?" Trevor couldn't help but mock Greg and his obsession with conspiracies and crop circles.

"Turned up dead in Mexico. Down there painting folk art, they're saying."

"So, not aliens? Too bad."

~

Three knots marred the façade of the house, so far. The one on the door, another next to a bay window, and the third on the inside of one of the jig-sawn spandrels that decorated the space between the tops of the porch posts. Not remarkable for the wood to have knots. But whether Trevor and Greg were straight, or stoned out of their gourds, they saw heads: Faces, ears, specific hairstyles.

"Fuck me." Greg was reading the newspaper. The house kept getting deliveries, and they were saving them up to tape to the window glass when it was time to paint. "Listen to this. They just found that milk-carton kid. The first one. He was on his way home from basketball and pulled a runner or got kidnapped or whatever. Turned up in Kansas. He's, like twenty-five now. Our age."

"Weird." Trevor only half-listened. Most of his attention focused on the music coming from the boom box. Joe Satriani was back in town for a few shows and Trevor was getting geared up for a wicked tribute during their gig Friday. A nod to the great guitar man.

Greg was flipping through the box of newspapers. "Not weird, man. *Fucking* weird. Check it." He held up the picture of the kid. Then the photo of the poet they found in Mexico.

"So?"

"So—look." He held the poet's photo next to the head on the door.

Trevor squinted, tilted his head a little to the side.

"And this!" Greg's voice had taken on the fevered tremble usually reserved for his alien abduction and crop circle theories. He went over to the other side of the porch, climbed the rail and held that day's paper in front of the spandrel. "It's definitely him."

"Okay. I see it." The dark patches matched hair, eyes, nose. A crack near the center of the knot matched the grim line of the mouth. "What about the one up there?"

"We just scraped her out today. Guessing from these other two, she'll probably be in tomorrow's paper."

~

He waited until dark to take a look. He checked the road for cars before he turned on his penlight. An envelope in his hand from the cable company, delivered to his house by mistake, his excuse for going over. With the small circle of illumination he scanned the front door of the house until he found the spot that had drawn the painters' interest.

A knot. That was all? Crazy guitar-hippies.

He turned to leave and something crinkled under his feet. It was the newspaper the blond hippie had been flapping around. He picked it up and scanned the front page: *Recession Recovery Brings New Development; Good Day for the Bay—Athletics take Jays, 17/3, Giants over Pirates, 7/2; Poet Found Dead in Mexico.*

There was a picture of the poet. He held the paper next to the knot, like the painters had done. Looked from one to the other and considered what it meant.

~

"The fuck are you doing?" Trevor got to work first and found a woman, mid 40's, dressed in overalls and a tattered men's shirt, scraping the side of the house.

The woman stood up, brushed her hair back from her forehead and bit her lip. "Helping?"

Then she went back to scraping, the blade stuttered along against the wood grain, leaving gouges in the siding.

"Whoa, whoa. Hold 'er there." Trevor reached around the woman and pulled the scraper from her hand. "You can't do that. You one of the owners?"

The woman shook her head. "I'm sorry. I heard about the heads. A friend of mine was at Dave's Bar yesterday and called me. I want to help."

"You can't, lady. Two reasons. My insurance doesn't cover you, and you're doing it all wrong. You'll add weeks to the job scratching the wood up like that."

Tears welled up in the woman's eyes and she looked down at her feet. "It's my son. He went sailing a few years ago and he never came back. He was sixteen."

"What the hell does that have to do with—" Trevor stopped when he remembered what went down at Dave's Bar the previous night.

When the news had come on Greg made Suzanne, the barkeep, turn up the volume. He squawked in triumph when they reported a young woman's bones found by a river in Kansas. The photo looked a lot like the bay window knot. Greg had informed the bar in his drunken foghorn voice that the house they were working on was psychic. Most people laughed, someone bought him a shot of tequila, but clearly some had believed.

"I'm sorry, ma'am. About your son. But I can't let you help."

"Can I stay and watch? I'll bring coffee? Maybe this is all coincidence." She waved dismissively at the house. "But it's something. You can't imagine what it feels like to lose your kid."

Trevor thought about Cheryl. Sitting at the living room window in the buttery morning sun, hand on her belly. Then a few weeks later pale in the oncoming headlights, towels stacked under her, fussing about staining the car seat as he ran red lights all the way to the hospital.

"Fine. Just don't get in the way."

Her name was Ellen. She was the first of the hopefuls.

~

So many people coming to the house. At first two, then six. They sat in the yard. Some in fold-out chairs, some on blankets. They sat all day and watched the painters, at times getting up to inspect a newly cleared section of siding.

Each knot they uncovered sent them rushing forward, *en masse*, to examine it in silence. One after another shoulders fell in disappointment, and they turned and shuffled back to their seats. After a few minutes the chatter would begin. Speculations as to who it was. Which news story, which person found.

From his front lawn where he stood watering his roses he felt a tingle of apprehension. He had to be really careful now. With so many people around. He went inside.

In the kitchen he poured two glasses of Coke, waited for the hiss of the bubbles to fade, then took them down.

~

A woman crossed the street and paused at the end of the walk. The hopefuls had been passing around a thermos of coffee and cuttings from newspapers—both from original news stories of those they'd lost, and recent ones of those who'd been found. Conversation guttered into silence as they saw her standing there. She walked slowly up the cobbled path to the house. The first of the hopefuls, Ellen, jumped up and gave her the tour. Without speaking she led the older woman from head to head, then brought her to one of the fold-out chairs, kicking a 'missing husband' hopeful onto the lawn.

"Who is she?" Trevor took the cold can of Coke from Ellen at break time. Good to her word she'd been supplying the painters with coffee, soda, sandwiches, and keeping the rest of those gathered from interfering with their work.

"The War Widow. Joyce Freeman. She lives over there." Ellen pointed to a house across the street and three doors down. "She's been watching us. I'm glad she came over."

"Huh. Never heard of her. She got a missing person?"

"I'm surprised you don't know the story. I guess you were a kid when it happened." Ellen spoke quietly so he had to lean in a bit. She looked good today. Eyes clear. Not so sad. "Her husband was in 'Nam. Big war hero. Fifth Special Forces Group out of Fort Bragg. He died rescuing a trapped patrol."

"Man. That sucks." Trevor looked at the woman, her eyes glazed over with years of grief and solitude, her grey-white hair pinned in a loose bun. "But I don't get it. He's dead. Not missing."

"She's not here for her husband. She was pregnant when he went to Vietnam. Her family is one of the first families of the area. Inherited money. She moved into that house so her parents could help her take care of the little girl. Poor thing, five years old, was playing in the yard and vanished."

"The fuck? Poor woman." Trevor broke the tab off his Coke can and flicked it into a waste bin. "Some fucking people."

~

Police at the house. The two painters and the woman who came every day spoke with them. One officer snapped some photos while the other took a few notes. They shook their heads as the woman's arms rose and fell with her desperate pleas, her mouth and shoulders tight at their refusal. He couldn't hear what they said, but he imagined the police's skepticism. Their denial.

When the police car pulled away a few minutes later, he exhaled.

He didn't know what to do. Any move could lead to problems, questions. He could go away for a bit, but he didn't know how to do that cleanly.

So he would do nothing, for now, but watch.

~

Oakland Tribune, May 7, 1986
Psychic House: Hope or Hoax?
House in Berkeley Hills predicts 'Missing Persons' Found
The past week has seen five cases of missing persons solved. First it was the discovery of the body of poet Weldon Kees in Mexico. Kees went missing in 1955, leaving his Plymouth Savoy parked near the Golden Gate Bridge, keys in the ignition. Then there was Bobby Stewart, who vanished on the way home from basketball practice, and Janette Anderson, who disappeared from the Bay area after pressing abuse charges against her husband in 1973. A startup company will be able to recover some of their lost profits from Albert Winger, who turned up in Los Angeles living under an assumed identity and has been arrested for embezzlement and fraud. Yesterday a scuba diver discovered a leg bone from what is suspected to be the remains of either Theodore Cole or Ralph Roe. The two famously escaped from Alcatraz in 1937.
House painters Greg Brand and Trevor Tremblay of the Oakland-based band *Rock Encounters* uncovered unique shapes in the wood siding of a Victorian house...

~

"Check it out, man. They mention the band!" Greg fanned the paper at Trevor's face.

"Let me see." Trevor grabbed it and scanned the article. "So that last dude was one of the Alcatraz guys. Huh."

The painters were taking apart the scaffold and moving it to the back of the house. The hopefuls were moving too. Coolers and lawn chairs, blankets and sun-umbrellas. Up on the platform Trevor felt like he was at some weird kind of festival, the spectators talking in hushed tones about who might be next. If their loved one would be found alive, or if a bundle of bones was all they'd get back. Something to lay to rest.

"Have you noticed how they're divided?" Greg loosened a bolt on the metal tubing. "Over there you have the parents. That side you've got spouses. And those are the siblings and kids. I hear them talking, too. Some of them think they know what they're gonna get."

"Huh?"

"You know, a live one or a body."

At lunch Ellen delivered sandwiches. Meatloaf. Trevor's favorite.

"So. Does she have a feeling about her daughter?" He nodded toward the war widow.

Ellen tightened her lips, a grimace more than a smile. "Alive, she thinks. Says she can feel her. But a lot of us believe that until they call us to identify the remains. Not me. I know my son's dead."

~

She's out there every day. The widow from down the street. They've moved behind the house, so he can't see anymore. Each night he goes and looks for heads. They've done the front, the West side. Nearly done the back. Each missing person they find is closer. He's been mapping the discoveries. Mexico. Kansas. LA. The Bay—closer each time.

He climbed down the stairs to her room.

Some days she hid from him. He would play her game—look under the bed, behind the candy-colored dresses in the wardrobe—then leave her to her mischief, his chest heavy with disappointment that he hadn't seen her. Today she sat in the middle of the room in front of her mirror. Dressed in yellow, radiant like the first day he saw her, drawing him, even now. She didn't move, so he placed the glass beside her.

He had brought the mirror to her as a birthday present. He liked watching her comb and braid her hair. He didn't like how much attention she paid to the mirror, to the person she saw there. But when he took it away she screamed and screamed. An endless wail that he heard in his sleep, even though no sound could escape this room.

"How are you feeling, my girl?"

"Tired. But we'll feel better soon. It won't be long now." She smiled at her reflection.

"What won't be long?"

She didn't answer.

He sat on her bed—a four-poster with a flowing pink canopy—his heart pounded, an ache sliced forward in his head. The sandwich he'd brought days before sat by the lamp, and its moldering stench made his stomach tighten. He stuck his hand in his sweater pocket and twined the lock of hair around his fingers until the nausea passed. So soft.

~

"Joe fucking Satriani."

Greg was still obsessing about Friday's gig on Monday morning. Trevor felt a little numb. He'd almost bailed on the tribute solo he'd planned, but in the end he took a deep breath and went for it—sliding from the riff in Satriani's "Not of this Earth" into the bridge from "The Enigmatic" before hitting the solo from *Rock Encounter's* own track, "Alien Warship." Satriani, sitting in a booth near the back, had joined in the applause. Trevor was disappointed at the end of the night when he couldn't track the great man down.

"Tomorrow we're on to the last wall." Trevor changed the subject. "Ellen said the cops came again on the weekend. But they're still not buying it. Said people see what they want to see. Besides, how do the heads help the cops, really?"

"What was she doing here on the weekend? Not messing with the siding again?"

"Naw. Checking in on the widow from up the street. Apparently she sits on the porch here a lot. Says she feels closer to her daughter." Trevor scanned the group sitting on the lawn. "Surprised there are still so many hopefuls here. What are the odds we'll find one of theirs?"

Greg shook his head. "You suck at this kind of thing. We're only finding people who went missing from the Bay area, man. A lot of these people moved here after their person went missing. But they come anyway. Misery loves company, right?"

A tension slipped through the crowd when the painters broke down the scaffold at the end of the day. They'd only uncovered one head on the back wall. An old guy in round glasses. A couple in their 50s clung to each other as the man held up their picture with a trembling hand, making sure.

"Oh my god. It's Dad. We're finally going to know."

The man had told Trevor about his father, who had Alzheimer's and had wandered from the senior's home just down the hill. Tears coursed down his face and he smiled.

"Whatever it is, I just want it to be over."

~

He had to do something. They were almost at the end. Each missing person from closer, closer…he couldn't let them finish.

He went to the gas station and bought four jerry cans of fuel, and a lighter.

The wait for darkness was agony. He sat at the window while the painters packed up for the day. The small group of watchers dispersed, each one pausing to hug the couple who'd found their person's head.

When he was ready, and night had come, he went downstairs to see his girl.

"Mommy's going to find out what you did." She said, sitting primly in front of her mirror. Her dress in ruffles that swirled around her chubby knees.

The fabric gleamed, the same yellow as the dress she'd worn that day in her yard. A sun-kissed dream picking dandelions and watering tomatoes with a pink plastic glass. The breeze had danced around her, the flowers strained toward her, everything was pulled by her magic. He couldn't resist.

He wanted to touch her now, her feather soft hair, to rest his fingertips on her chest, spider light. A shadow flickered across her eyes and she looked away from him. The last time he'd touched her had ended badly. So much noise. So much mess to clean up. Now was not the time.

She pulled herself closer to the glass, cross-legged now, eyes closed, fingertips pressed against reflected fingertips, so lightly they left no mark. She whispered. Her breath too delicate to cloud the glass.

"We're here, we're here, we're here, we're here…"

He closed the door and locked it. His heart thudded. He wound his fingers in the lock of hair as he whispered his own prayer. *They can never find her. She's mine. My girl.* It was a risk, but he had to finish it.

He made two trips across the street. No one saw him. Taking a chance he poured one of the cans of gas across the front of the house and up the stairs. Around back he cracked the window next to the kitchen door. The trim was dry, the glazing putty crumbled, easy to lift a few shards out, reach in and unlock the door. He brought the jerry cans inside and splashed gas around. He worked from the bottom up, emptying one can per floor. Giving the rickety stairs a good douse on his way up.

A sound from below. He listened. Nothing. He moved into one of the bedrooms and let a torrent of fuel spill across the wood floor.

A creak on the landing inside the house. "Hello? Is someone there? I heard something break." A female voice, shaking and high. The stairs creaked again. "That smell. Is there a gas leak…what's going on?"

He froze, unsure of what to do. She stepped into the bedroom. His neighbor, the widow.

"Bill? What are you doing here? Why are you—" She looked at the plastic canister he held up-ended over the floor. Then she looked at his face, her eyes black in the unlit room.

"Joyce—" There was nothing he could say.

Her mouth opened, stretching wider and wider in horror. He waited for the scream. Then her jaw snapped shut and she rushed at him, feet skidding on the slick floor.

"It was you! You took her."

Fury and raking nails. He tried to push her off but lost his footing and they fell.

"Where is she? Where is she?" She screeched, louder and louder, right in his ear, fingers ripping at his hair.

He scrambled free of her, and got to his knees. Gas dripped in his eyes, almost blinding him.

She rolled over onto her stomach and crawled toward him, panting, teeth bared.

He looked for a weapon, something to hit her with. On the floor in front of him lay the lighter.

It was over. He knew it. He had to.

He picked up the lighter, and for a moment she didn't notice, her glare intent on his face, his guilt. He flicked the flint. It caught on the first try. Yellow. Bright in the darkness.

"My daughter—" Her scream cut short as the flames washed across the floor between them.

He closed his eyes and pictured her, waiting for him, beckoning. *My girl.*

~

Greg came around the side of the building, a ladder under one arm, the red plastic top melted beyond repair. "Some of the scaffold looks okay. I talked to the rental company and they're fine with a little scorching, as long as the metal's still sound." The police had given them the okay to recover their gear. "The rest of it we can maybe sell to the metal recyclers. I don't know about our insurance. Man, this sucks."

"What the hell was she doing here?" Trevor stared at the house in shock.

All the windows were shattered, the siding above black where flames and smoke had poured out only hours before. Half of the roof had collapsed, and the whole block reeked of death and burning.

"She who?" Greg sifted around on the porch for any more of their equipment.

"The widow, man. Get a freakin' clue."

"Chill. You're right. She shouldn't have been here. And the other body. Who the hell was that? I'm sure the cops'll have the whole story soon. We can grab a brew at Dave's and wait for the report. Talk about our next gig. I got a tip there's a California Bungalow in Frisco needs a good tune-up."

Trevor wasn't sure if there would be a next gig. Cheryl had called, said she was staying in Ohio. Said her brother had a construction company and could give him a job. Then she'd said in a low, sad voice that she missed him. Wondered if maybe they could try again.

He knew she meant more than just their relationship, and he'd been overcome with conflicting emotions. A warm anticipation and the gnawing fear of the hospital, the blood, and another potential snuffed out before he'd cradled it in his arms. He squatted and looked up at the charred remains of the house.

"Hey man, what are you doing?" Trevor frowned as Greg climbed up onto the front porch. The burnt timbers creaking under his weight.

"Wanna check and see if that dude's face is still on the door."

Greg pulled back a section of roof that had fallen in front of the oak door. The wood was burnt to charcoal black, in some places it had crisped to ash— white flakes that shivered in the breeze. A few boards in the porch collapsed under him. Flailing and calling for help, Greg tried to pull his legs free. Trevor rushed up to the deck, hooked his arms under Greg's and hauled him out. Under the weight of both of them the porch cracked, then gave, and Trevor fell back into the cavity below.

"You all right, buddy?" Greg had managed to grab a joist and peered down from above.

"Yeah. Just a sec." Trevor rolled over onto his stomach and pushed himself up. His hand brushed against something cool, smooth. "Move out of the light. There's something here."

Sun trickled into the dirt-floored crawl space, pale dust-blurred beams of light that fell on the ground and the thing half-buried there.

Trevor moaned, the air forced out like a blow to the gut. There was a pale rounded mass curving up from the ground. A skull. Small, unbroken, clearly a child. And beneath it two bird-boned hands laid across the cage of the skeleton's chest. A torn dress, ruffled and stained brown with age was folded around the remains. He knew who she was. One last missing, laid to rest under her mother's funeral pyre.

FLESH WITHOUT BLOOD

by Nadia Bulkin

When all this is over, there are going to be stories printed about Claire. Somebody's going to find out that she set a state high school record for the 3,200 meters and got a full ride to Rosewood and ran into traffic in her sophomore year. Somebody's going to find the hospital records – medical and psych – and they're going to paint a picture. She'll be just another girl-runner who couldn't handle the realization that she could no longer keep up with the best no matter how hard she trained or how thin she got; who decided it was better to die than to fail.

I'm sure they'll take a long look at our parents – stoic dad, high-strung mom – and write some mumbo-jumbo about *sky-high expectations* and *pressure to be perfect*. Never mind that our parents weren't athletes, that they never understood the look on Claire's face when she ran. They always thought she looked driven by an invisible whip, and I'm sure they'll quickly clarify for any journalist that asks them: "a whip of *her own* making." Because sure, they were proud of us – we were the *Kessler kids*, known for collecting those plastic trophies that you can buy for two dollars but mean so goddamn much because it's about the fact that you *placed*, you *rated*, your name was going down as having risen above the rest, even for just one Saturday afternoon – but they didn't make Claire the way she was.

Claire was born like that. Claire didn't need to be taught to *never give up* or *be the best you can be*. She just knew there was no other way to exist. I wrestled in high school, so I knew it too – knew life was all about domination, all about winning. I never gave up my position on the mat, and Claire ran hard, vacant, brutal, and definitely not driven by any whip. She ran in hunger, because she was always starving. Proteins. Lean meats. Sweetbreads. That didn't change once we were adults. Our parents made me go grocery shopping with her once and I remember those eyes glazed over at the butcher's counter, hands twisting every yogurt carton in the dairy aisle to find the nutritional content. I told our parents Claire was fine. At least she was eating, I figured. In college – when she had her "accident" – she was running on celery sticks and coffee.

"Is she running again?" they whispered. That's how they put it: not *depressed* or *suicidal* or even *in trouble*. Just *running again*. As if running, the thing that had made Claire "Claire" since she won her first little plastic trophy at age twelve, was the monster here.

I could tell she was indeed running again — the shoes were a dead give-away, even though she hid her tracksuit under layers of sweats — but I decided not to tell our parents. Two weeks later they called again, because Claire had stopped answering her phone. "It's not like her to go dark," they whined, and I thought of her sneaking out of the house at 4 a.m. to run around the quarry before school. I went with her a few times — felt like it was the right thing to do, as her big brother — but she was so much faster than me. She would just vanish, weightless, into the night.

Her office said she'd taken a leave of absence, so I went over to Claire's locked apartment on Saturday and got the building manager to let me in after convincing him the Barons were going to win that night and Marcus Hayes was going to have a forty-point game. I wasn't sure what I expected to find. Claire in one of her gloomy squalls, probably, or possibly — a small, shriveled possibility that sat rotting in my brain like a smashed squirrel on a highway — I would find dead Claire, tucked under the covers to bury herself, a smear of medicinal vomit on her lips.

The bedroom was empty, and the entire apartment felt lifeless. Just a carton of expired skim milk in the fridge. Bed made, toothbrush gone. I checked the hall closet — no running shoes. Even though we shared a city, I hadn't been to Claire's apartment since I helped her move in. I know how that sounds, can already guess what they're going to write about me: *absent older brother Chris*. But Claire wasn't much of a hostess, and I might have bailed on her a few times — nothing I could do about midnight deadlines, or the fact that the last thing I wanted to do after getting out from under a midnight deadline was sit on a futon and listen to my sister breathe.

The only thing that carried a pulse in that apartment was an uncomfortably large print in the living room — a painting of a smiling girl-gymnast with silk angel wings, arms outstretched on a balance beam, rainbow colors bleeding off her and then melting into a dark expanse. I guess it was supposed to be inspirational — *Through Me All Things Are Possible*, it said in flamingo pink script — but the glow in the girl, the pitch-blackness of her eyes, gave me vertigo. Like looking down through a bridge of glass onto the Milky Way.

Someone started coughing behind me. The building manager, the anxious Barons fan.

"I saw her leave with a duffel bag on Tuesday," he said, which would have been helpful to know before climbing up three flights of stairs. "I thought she was going on vacation."

"Claire doesn't go on vacation." I texted her again: *You out of town?*

"So you're sure we're gonna win tonight, huh?"

"The Bobcats are the worst team in the division," I said, scrolling up through our texting history for Claire's last message: *ran 5 miles, felt like dogshit.* "No way we don't win. No way."

But we didn't win, because life doesn't work that way. Marcus Hayes, the guy we paid a hundred million for last year, the hottest draft pick of his generation, our hometown hero, had a thirty-point game in front of his own crowd. Every time Marcus missed a three-pointer, screams of anguish ricocheted through the poor insulation of my building; when Marcus turned the ball over the third time, I threw the remote against the wall so hard the batteries popped out. With two minutes left, I was standing there screaming at the television – me and everyone else in the city, I could see lights flickering in the apartments across the alley – "Level up! Level up!"

Before you ask, only once did I scream *"Level up"* at Claire. It was the state championships, her senior year of high school. She was a half-step behind the leader, a girl she had beaten before, and I knew she would have regretted it if she didn't give it her all. And here's the difference between my sister and Marcus Hayes: Claire got it done. Claire leveled up.

~

I was hardly ever the most talented wrestler on the mat. I wasn't like Claire or Marcus Hayes – I wasn't born with an athletic physique or perfect hand-eye coordination or great balance or boundless stamina. But I always tried. I showed up at practice early, I put in double the work. I never complained about binging or purging to stay in the right weight class. I may not have had the most impressive win-loss record but I made the varsity team, Coach said, because I had the biggest heart: I was Mr. Overachiever, the one he could count on to put his body on the line every time, to play every match like it was life or death. *One of these days you're going to hit the wall,* my father said, but I never met a wall I couldn't breach. When Coach yelled *level up, Kessler* when my stance slipped or my lift faltered, I always *tried* to push my muscles into a louder scream. Because unless you're actively bleeding, and sometimes even then, you've probably got something more to give.

~

Claire had never been good at making friends, only competitors – the girls on the high school track team were always thinking of ways to slip each other laxatives right before a race, steal each other's salt tablets. Claire was too single-minded even for that; she ran inside a dark tunnel, blind to anyone else's jealousies and fears, deaf to their whispers. The sort of self-centeredness that all true champions have. But she had marked herself as "Going" to a bunch of get-togethers hosted by a group called Roughshodders (*Serious Runners Only*), so I figured those were the snakes she'd decided to slither with for now.

Of course none of those long, lean, gamey bastards in their aerodynamic track suits claimed to know where Claire was. They sneered and snorted and shook their heads, hands on their hips, slick polycarbonate eyes looking through me to some invisible finish line. "Nah, man. I have no idea." "Nah, man. She never really talked much." Bunch of bullshit. Claire was a champion, could outrun a lot of men even, and they were probably just happy she was gone. People aren't there for each other. That's something you learn, before the end.

I'd almost given up — the race through Centennial Park was about to start, and I know how runners get when they're waiting for the whistle, like a bull that's seen a flag — when finally, one lady-Roughshodder about Claire's age with a suspiciously cheerful grin tapped me on the shoulder and asked if I was the guy looking for Claire Kessler.

"Claire's on a spiritual quest," she said, popping the cap of her water bottle. "I don't think she wants to be found."

As she drank I thought of Claire, ten years old, running her thumbnail between her teeth during Christmas Eve service at Second Presbyterian as if thumbing her nose at the pastor, whispering to me that "if there is a God, I bet He hates us." I thought for a long time that she meant our family, but now I realize she probably meant the human race.

"Claire doesn't go on spiritual quests," I muttered.

The lady-Roughshodder pursed her lips mischievously. "Depends on what's at the end of the rainbow, doesn't it?"

Out of nowhere, the after-image of that girl-gymnast in Claire's apartment started to pulse in my vision — arms outstretched like a crucifix, leaking color. Like a prism. A rainbow.

"She found some radical detox program," the girl was saying, "Supposedly they have some way to squeeze every drop of potential out of you. Purge everything that doesn't matter. Total body transformation. Got a weird name: Holy Star, something like that." She shrugged. "I told her it was probably bullshit. They don't even have a web site. But she said Lee Sheridan joined it three years ago and… do you know who Lee Sheridan is?"

Suddenly I saw myself as she probably saw me — an out-of-shape worker drone slouching toward middle age, pasty and pallid and an embarrassment to his high-performance sneakers, an unworthy, a weakling — and the urge to grab her by her elastic shoulder straps and scream at her that I had made the varsity wrestling team, I had once been rated a superior physical specimen just like her, washed over me like a wave.

"Yeah, I know who Lee fucking Sheridan is," I said, because who doesn't? Local IT nobody who suddenly turned into a nationally-ranked triathlete, got written up in a bunch of regional press, competed at the World Championships last year. A bit of a weirdo, but hard to mistake the look of punch-drunk ecstasy and disbelief in his photo finishes. Hard not to envy it.

He went from spending his life chained to a desk to suddenly being a motherfucking *doer*, the apex of what a human body can be.

"Then you can guess how excited Claire was to have found the people who made him over." The lady-Roughshodder swiveled away – she had a race to run, after all, and who the fuck was I? – but not before throwing me another smart-ass remark over her shoulder: "Hey, if that Holy Star detox worked for Claire, will you let me know? Name's Emma."

Under my breath, I hissed "no."

Emma was right that they didn't have a web site, although the phrase did pop up on a few fitness forums, mostly desperate people looking for information that nobody had. But one local bodybuilding nutjob did swear that there was a Church of the Holy Star on the shitty side of the city, so I drove over while listening to the guys on Metro Sports Talk swear that the Barons were going to turn the season around and His Royal Highness Marcus Hayes was going to pull his head out of his ass and start delivering. The Prince that was Promised was just having some growing pains, they said. By the time I parked next to a basketball court adorned with a Christ-like mural of Marcus Hayes holding a basketball like a divine lamb, I was muttering – to myself, to Marcus, to the whole city – "Level up. Level up."

It took me a while to find it in the half-light, but eventually, on a door to what looked like a basement apartment in a run-down walk-up, I saw a white star. The paint was faded but I knew just by laying eyes on it that this was the place. I leaned my ear against the door and heard a sea of nothing, so I was surprised when my knock was immediately answered by a little old woman, as if she'd been waiting on the other side for me.

"Ah – hello – is this the Church of the Holy Star?"

Her face showed no reaction. Barely a breath. Certainly no blinks.

"I'm looking for Claire Kessler. I'm her brother, we haven't heard from her in two weeks…"

"You aren't ready," she said, and shut the door. And I was locked out, left out, eighteen years old and hearing that *St. Sebastian's University regrets to inform you that we will not be able to offer you an athletic scholarship this year.*

~

Marcus Hayes lived in a mansion outside the city, for tax reasons. He also had a penthouse downtown, for "entertaining." Everything he wore – everything that touched his skin – cost at least a grand. He traveled either first class or by private jet, decked his family in diamonds. Hundred million dollar contract, remember, and that's not counting the endorsement deals: sneakers, soda, headphones, cars, computer chips, pizza. He spent more time filming commercials than he did training. And this isn't jealousy. I was a jock in high school; I know that there are perks to being a hero, because nothing brings a community together like a championship. None of this would be a problem if he just *won* his games, if he *made* his shots and *led* the team. If he *did* his fucking job. And yes, I know, I know: one man can't do everything. But for a hundred million dollars – for two dozen murals across the city, for the beating hearts of two million people – can you blame me for expecting just a little bit more?

~

For the next month I went to every race in the greater metropolitan area and waited for Claire to cross the finish line. She never showed up on entry lists, but I figured she wasn't competing under her own name. Even when Claire didn't show, I got to watch other self-imposed catastrophes: at the Race to Beat Cancer, someone got heat stroke; at the Rock 'n Roll Marathon, someone fractured their leg; at the Spartan Invitational, the leader collapsed five hundred feet from the finish line and was nearly stampeded by everyone else.

"Heard that's what happened to Lee Sheridan," the guy next to me said as they carried the fallen runner away, and I realized I hadn't heard anything about that lucky IT motherfucker since he placed third at Worlds. I figured he peaked, but maybe he joined senior management at the Church of the Holy Star. Maybe he took up recruiting. "Overtraining. It's a killer."

"He retired?"

"More like went dark. Disappeared. Nobody knows."

Something else kept popping up, too: the white star on the door of the church that ate Claire. It was on track vests and water bottles and protein bars being handed out by men and women who seemed to be part of an unofficial cheering squad for a few of the very best runners. I thought they were Scientologists at first – they had that creepy, unblinking, plastic look – but I once got close enough to hear them urgently whisper about *glory* and *the astral divine* and *Saint Sasha the Star* to a victorious runner. Before they noticed me and shut up, that is, then proceeded to watch me from the trees until I pulled out of the parking lot.

It wasn't until the Sioux River Run that I found Claire. She still braided her hair the way she did in sixth grade, but I could immediately tell that everything else had changed – that her body had been taken apart and remade into something at the very upper limit of muscle-to-fat content. Having broken away from the rest of the pack, she came into focus first, looking like she had enough in the tank to keep going for another 5,000 meters. The Kessler inside me wanted to start hollering, because Claire hadn't won any race since sophomore year of college, and for a second I imagined our parents standing with me at the finish line, our mother squeezing my shoulder and our father holding up his fist in triumph. I saw us happy again. *Claire's Comeback.*

Instead she was immediately greeted by a Holy Star contingent, and I remembered that all of that was gone. All of us were gone. Her church friends gave Claire a bottle that she guzzled and lovingly patted her shoulders, her biceps, her quads – had she ever been that well-sculpted? – and Claire was shaking her head, grinning, saying, *"I can't believe this."*

I couldn't believe it either. I shoved aside two Holy Star missionaries, intent on scolding Claire for a lot of things: joining a New Age cult, making our parents panic, sending me on a wild goose chase when I had my own fucking problems that she couldn't even imagine because she had refused to grow up and accept that she *wasn't good enough to win anymore.* But all that anger melted away when it was just me and her, the Kessler kids, with nothing else between us. Claire's aura knocked me back. You have to understand: she was *infused* with strength. Even after that 5k she stood so straight, so powerful. As another human being you can't help but crumble in front of something so perfect. Just looking at her made my muscles wither.

It worked. Whatever that church was doing, it worked.

"Chris, I won," she giggled. It was like she was fourteen again and getting her first taste of the ambrosia that is winning, although I had to admit there was a hollowness in her laughter. A hunger that was even stronger than before. Something about her was still starving, despite all that muscle, despite her energy reserves, despite her finally-perfect runner's body. "I did it!"

"Yeah. That's great. I don't get it. How?"

The Holy Star folks tried to cut in with some bullshit about recovery time but Claire sent them away. "They're just protective," she explained to me. "Most people don't understand."

"Is that why you haven't been picking up your phone? Mom and Dad are making themselves sick worrying about you. If they knew you were running again..."

She rolled her eyes. "That's why I'm not picking up. They don't understand. They never have." Then she cupped my face in her hands, and I felt like I'd just stuck my finger in a light socket. "But I know you get it. Chris, this is the closest I've ever come to God."

You'd better believe my heart was pounding. I didn't want to understand, but I was flashing back to the way my legs trembled after my first varsity-level victory, like I was both weightless and unshakable. The only time in my life I could even pretend that I had scraped a fingernail against the sublime was when I managed to overpower a competitor. When I got thrown into the pit, and emerged the survivor. When I won.

Still, I tried to resist. "Please just call Mom."

"The Church of the Holy Star brought me this far, by the grace of St. Sasha," she said, and I realized what it was about her that seemed so different now: her skin was barely thick enough to contain a human soul. And underneath she was all flesh, no blood. Pulseless meat on a butcher's block. One of those preserved cadavers propped up in a science exhibit, calf muscles forever engaged, a display of the naked wonder of the human body at full gallop. "I can't quit now. I need to repay them." She squeezed my arm, and I winced. "I hope I see you again."

I couldn't have stopped that thoroughbred if I'd tried, no more than I could've caught a comet. Claire moved through the sea of sweat and polyester toward her fellow Churchgoers, who were preening over some prodigal preteen girl-runner — some little Claire — who'd beaten most of the adults. Stroking her hair. Pinching her chin, as if measuring… something. The prodigy turned her head toward me and smiled, with a mouthful of teeth.

~

I used to be a Marcus Hayes apologist. I used to say, *we've got to give him time,* and *the pressure on him must be off the chain.* I used to find excuses because I wanted to believe he was going to save us, and that when he did, it would be like I had saved us too — with my belief, if nothing else, my faith in his innate superiority and superhuman abilities. But then I realized that he was just another entitled asshole who didn't deserve his talent, too selfish to be a hero. He'd been handed everything since he hit his first growth spurt, glided through high school and college without breaking a sweat, and now that things weren't coming so easy, he was struggling. Because he never knew the meaning of *hard work,* because he didn't understand *effort.* It was ironic — *enraging* — because everybody thought he was a god among men and he didn't even know how much of a god-with-a-capital G he could have been if he had just *tried.*

~

I figured out who "St. Sasha the Star" was: Sasha Spell, a seventeen-year-old Olympic gymnast who disappeared during a famine in her home country across the sea. She used to fill stadiums, heart and soul of the people, face on every billboard. What kind of government lets a national asset like that starve, I had no idea. They dedicated the Olympic flame to her at the next Summer Games; her father, a reverend, went insane. The most famous picture of Sasha? You guessed it: arms outstretched on a balance beam, grinning ear-to-ear. *Through Me All Things Are Possible.* I went back to Claire's apartment to make sure it was the same girl in the poster, and ended up sitting on the floor staring up at St. Sasha with my mouth open for three hours.

After that, I tried to put Claire and the Church out of my mind. Things were on fire at work, and I didn't have any spare mental space for dead gymnasts or missing triathletes or whatever the hell had happened to my sister. But whereas I was usually able to tuck Claire into a bottom drawer and forget about her — because it's not like she'd been our *Claire* anyway, not after her breakdown; she was just Claire's angry, sickly, broken ghost — after I watched her win the Sioux River Run she refused to be hidden away. She snuck into my bedroom and leaned over me as I slept; she perched on my desk in her ultra-responsive running shoes and watched me type. Sometimes she had skin on. Sometimes not. But never any blood.

"Level up, Chris," she'd whisper. "Dig deep. Power through."

And I'd whisper, hands over my eyes: "Shut up, shut up, *shut up.*"

The more I thought about her, the sicker I felt. Numbers and dates slipped through my fingers. I was losing sleep, losing time. I missed two meetings, fell asleep in another. At one point I caught myself standing in front of the water cooler with my thumb on the handle, water overflowing onto my hand. Wasn't too long after that – though I don't remember exactly when – that my boss called me into his office and asked what the hell was wrong with me. He was one of those CrossFit freaks, and started yelling at me over his half-eaten salad, pointing the fork at me every other sentence.

A lot of words were being thrown my way, like "unacceptable" and "irresponsible," but I couldn't keep my eyes off the television in the corner, flanked by motivational posters of men rowing toward waterfalls, climbing cliffs, running up hills. *Determination. Commitment. Endurance.* ESPN was reporting that Marcus Hayes, the Prince that was Promised, hadn't shown up to practice that day – *lazy shithead*, I was thinking.

"Chris." That I heard. "Level. Up."

But I didn't know how. When I tried to dig deep for some reservoir of energy, some crawlspace of strength, I found my body hollow. Cleaned out. Decimated. I had hit the wall that I was sure I'd always be able to barrel through, and I slinked out of his office with my head down. Because once you can't level up – once you fail yourself – once you let your weakness win – what good are you? What worth do you have?

As you can imagine, I wasn't in the best of moods getting on the highway that night. It was raining, and I was starving. Some fucker cut me off and I chased him because the sea of angry bile churning inside me didn't know what else to do – missed my exit, followed the guy into a gas station parking lot and then just sat there, shaking, because as soon as the fucker got out of his car I knew he would have killed me and an animal side of my brain that I had never wanted to acknowledge – a meek prey animal – paralyzed me.

I had nowhere to go but home. My shitty, empty apartment; my shitty, empty body. And then, as if she'd been waiting for me to sink to my lowest, Claire finally texted me back: *Watch it.* I thought at first it was a warning, but when I picked up the mail, a flash drive was perched on top of *Sports Illustrated* – a little silver flash drive with a white star on it. In that moment, you have to understand, that star looked like a lighthouse in a storm to me.

On the flash drive was a janky video, maybe a decade old. And on the video was a man: some Norman Rockwell type with cracked-out eyes and a bad suit, sitting behind a desk with a bronze statuette of a human figure in a back-breaking curve, arms holding up an orb that was the world. "Hello," he said to the camera, to me, "I'm Dr. Richard Kettle, Professor of Religious Studies at Rosewood College. If you're watching this, congratulations. You've taken the first step toward overcoming your human limitations and realizing your full potential. As you begin your journey toward greatness, I'd like to tell you the story of Saint Sasha the Star."

Apparently, Sasha Spell didn't starve to death. Apparently, she sacrificed her body to feed her father's flock. And because she was *touched* – because the *astral divine* had blazed into her body when she was still in the womb, a random turn of fortune that could neither be predicted nor earned – her flesh kept them all alive. Not just alive: thriving.

"Saint Sasha, in her infinite grace, understood the gift that she had been given," said Dr. Kettle. "She knew that her ultimate act of glory – beyond any medal or trophy – would be sharing her bounty with those who had always believed in her, thereby refracting that holy white light into a thousand magnificent colors."

There was an uncomfortably long pause as the camera crept toward Dr. Kettle's unblinking eyes as if trying to find a spark, and then an abrupt blackness. I felt numb, but also weightless – no more knot in my stomach, no more grip on my shoulders – not because the pain was gone, but because my whole body seemed to be. Out of the corner of my eye I saw a light: Claire had texted me again. *Did you watch it?* I could barely feel my fingers as I replied: *Yes.*

~

Since he transferred back home, every article about Marcus Hayes uses the word "community" about twenty times. Have you noticed? *Gives back to the community. Welcomed by the community. Boost for the community.* And there'll be a picture of him at a pediatric cancer ward or shaking hands with disabled veterans or showing star-struck kids how to shoot a free throw. As if he's doing us a favor by slumming it in our shithole city when he could be living the good life in Miami, L.A. Except we made him here, in this shithole city. He went to our schools, walked our streets, drank our heavy metal water, inhaled our smoke. He's ours. And if he really wanted to "give back," if he really wanted to repay us, then the least he could do is give us a taste of what it feels like to win. I want you all to remember that, when you write your eulogies. Remember that none of these trophy-hogging superstars would have their big glass houses if it weren't for all of us. Remember that we made them. Remember that they're ours.

~

This time, the door with the white star was open, because this time, I was ready. Claire stood in the aisle, her bulging muscles glowing by candlelight and the unearthly gleam of the Holy Star, and took my hand. Her little hand had grown so calloused while I wasn't looking, strong enough to break mine. "I'm so glad you came," she said. "I knew you understood."

We walked past two dozen pews filled to capacity with true believers. The prodigal girl-runner from the Sioux River Run was there. So was the old woman who'd greeted me at the door and told me I wasn't ready; this time, she was nodding. I looked around for Lee Sheridan, but Claire gently whispered that having reached his full potential at the World Championships last year, Lee had already given his body to the congregation. "I ate first," she said sheepishly.

At the front of the church was a man in a tweed jacket who I recognized as Dr. Kettle, looking not one day older than he had on that video. In front of him knelt a wriggling, handcuffed body with a sack over its head. Claire urged me on alone with a few claps and a pump of her fist, like I was seventeen again and headed down to the mat.

Looming above everything was a gorgeous twelve-foot statue of St. Sasha the Star. A hole had been carved where her heart would be, and a prism placed there – a ray of white light shot in from the back of the church, and her heart splintered this light into a brilliant rainbow of color that teemed out over the pews. She was beaming up at a ceiling that was painted a thick, palpable black to represent the unknowable universe. Not the universe they show you in a planetarium, full of tiny needle-prick stars arranged into animal shapes. That's an illusion. It's got nothing to do with what lurks out there, bestowing gifts, stretching possibility, sounding drums. Death is a drummer, they say, but what hides in that darkness is beyond life or death.

I knew who was being offered even before Dr. Kettle took the sack off. I recognized the ripple in his calves, the ridges in his biceps, his Galatians 6:14 tattoo. *Through which the world has been crucified to me, and I to the world.* I had prayed for those muscles to contract correctly during a lay-up, to extend at just the right angle to make the basket. Prayed for that high-octane body to hit the peak performance levels it was made for. Sometimes I don't know if he realized how perfect he was. Innocence, I suppose.

Marcus Hayes was sobbing, which shows how little he understood the gift he'd been given. He looked older up close. I could see acne scars and bags under his eyes and shaving nicks. For the first time *he* stared at *me* and warbled, "Why are you doing this? Why do you hate me?" As if we didn't all love him so much that it made us shake to watch him, as if our hunger wasn't the ultimate expression of our love! And then: "I got money. I can give you money." And he said other things, too, but it all dissolved into static.

Dr. Kettle held out a boning knife. "I've heard a lot about you from Claire," he said, and I remembered her screaming my name at a high school wrestling meet – louder than our parents, louder than my friends, because Claire understood what being a champion meant. "She'd really like you to be here to witness her ascension, when her time comes."

You know what they say: some are born great, some achieve greatness, some have greatness thrust upon them. And some of us — the believers, the doers, the never-say-diers — seize greatness by the throat and wrestle it into submission.

I didn't use the knife to take Marcus' life. I didn't have to. I put him in a chokehold, one we learned how to do in high school even though it was illegal to use in a match. For one sublime moment, it was just me and him, locked in struggle, and when I pressed my skin against his I could feel the fever-burn of the Holy Star, the blessing of infinite possibility, passing from him to me. And then Marcus went limp and fell forward nearly onto Dr. Kettle, who offered me the knife again. That time, I took it and sliced a three-inch chunk of flesh off his calf.

You'd think I'd be shaking, pissing myself — but I wasn't. I was completely calm, calmer than I'd been in years, as if some enormous force that I guess you'd call God was holding me safe in its cloud of arms. That was how I knew I'd made the right decision. You have to obey your gut, when you're in pursuit of excellence. That's what mediocre people don't understand. You have to answer your hunger. Holding back from the bounty is an affront to the divine.

When I put that raw star-kissed flesh on my tongue, I shut my eyes and saw Claire. She was bathed in a white coffin of light, floating in darkness, holding a platter of meat carved from her own body. It was only a matter of time — years, months, weeks, who knows when you're going to hit the wall — before it was Claire kneeling before St. Sasha the Star, freely giving of herself. Bloodless and heartless and triumphant.

Dr. Kettle was starting to chant, and I could hear my sister behind me, and the parishioners behind her: "Through him, all things are possible. All hail the Holy Star."

I imagined how proud I was going to be, and swallowed greatness whole.

SCRAPS

by Max Booth III

The diner door chimes and by the time I turn around, coffee pot in hand, the boy's already standing next to the PLEASE WAIT TO BE SEATED sign. All thoughts of taking my 2:30AM lunchbreak and smoking a cigarette in the alley while scrolling through my dead wife's Facebook account vanish. My brain freezes at the sight of him. For a second, I swear to god I'm staring at my son, but that's impossible. Muddy hair hangs past his shoulders, his body skeleton-thin, his skin pale, his eyes dark. He's young—ten, eleven max. A rank odor rises. A garbage smell. A death smell. The boy had dragged the stench in from outside.

I set the coffee pot—freshly brewed—down on an empty table waiting to be busted and rush over to the checkout counter, slowing as I get closer, afraid of spooking him away.

"Holy shit, are you okay, kid?"

The boy wears a plain T-shirt that had probably once been white but is now mostly black and jeans with more holes than a drive-by victim. He's barefoot, and judging from the dirt and blood smeared across his toes, he hasn't owned shoes for quite some time now. A thin jagged cut runs across his face, from the right side of his forehead down to the left of his jaw, skipping over his blackened eye, sloping over his crooked nose, and digging through his lips.

He licks those lips now. "Hungry."

I gently touch his shoulder and lead him across the diner. "Of course, come sit down, I'll bring you something. Are you okay?"

"Hungry."

Once he's seated in an empty booth, I race into the kitchen in search of something to bring him. On the counter next to the sink in queue to be tossed in the trash is a plate of fries and a half-eaten burger. I fill up a clean glass with tap water and bring that and the plate back out into the dining area. The boy's head rests against the Formica tabletop and for one terrifying moment I'm convinced it's too late and he's already dead. Died of hunger, died of the smell attached to his presence, died of whatever caused him to be here, right now, at 2:30 in the morning, who the hell knows. I stand above him and clear my throat and wait. The boy stirs and raises his head. When he sees the food in my hand, his dark eyes widen.

But they do not brighten.

I place the plate and glass on the table and the boy dives into it, ravenous. I watch him feast, unsure of what to do with my hands, eventually settling on folding them behind my back. "So, uh, what's going on with you? Should I...call the police? Do you need an ambulance? Are you hurt?"

The boy shakes his head as he chews. "No police. No ambulance."

"Are you alone? Where are your parents?"

"No parents."

"Okay, uh…" I scratch my head, wishing like hell I knew what to do. "Maybe you have some kind of other family I can call. Someone who could come get you?"

"No family." The boy shakes his head again then swallows what was in his mouth and meets my concerned eyes. "Call no one."

I lean forward, afraid to disturb the boy's eating. "Can I get you anything else, at least?" The question comes out in the form of a timid whisper.

The boy nods enthusiastically, crumbs falling from his dirty mouth, and points at the plate. "More."

"Okay, sure." I return to the kitchen and bump into Beth, the manager-on-duty, waiting for me by the sink. Bitch is eager to pounce, like she's been hiding in the back watching the whole time, just waiting for me to screw up.

"You care to explain what's going on with that...kid?" She grimaces at that last word, like it physically disgusts her just having to say it. Beth works the night shift because she is the only manager who doesn't have a family waiting for her at home. The other managers, they all got loved ones who depend on them. But Beth. Beth's more like me. Neither of us has got a single soul other than our own. She goes home every morning to an empty apartment and eats junk food while watching some dumb shit on Netflix then falls asleep on the couch. If she never wakes back up, the only person who will feel anything at all is the poor sap who ends up having to cover her shift. And I'm no better.

"I don't know who he is." I gesture to the dining area, keeping my voice low. "He just came in here. Saying he was hungry."

Beth sighs and rubs her hands through her hair. "Everybody who comes in here is hungry, Owen. That doesn't explain why you're feeding him trash. Or why you even gave him a seat. He smells *awful.*"

"What was I supposed to do? Make him leave? He's just a kid." It's then that I realize for the first time who he reminds me of. Of course I'd known it the second he walked inside the diner, but a wiser part of me had refused to acknowledge the similarities until now.

If I'd never gotten behind the wheel that night, back in 2013, Bobby would be about this kid's age now.

Jesus Christ.

"He's not our responsibility. If he can't pay, then he has to go. Call CPS if you have to, I don't care, just make him leave." She pauses, cheeks swelling like she's swishing wine. "And besides, given your history, do you really think it's a good idea to be...*socializing* with children? Especially the way you look right now. I mean, *God*."

She's talking about my fading black eye, my broken left pinkie still in a splint, yes, but she's also talking about much, much more.

Right fist tightens at my side. Teeth grind against teeth. Flashes of cuffs, flashes of my P.O. shaking his head and telling me I blew it, I blew everything. Fist loosens. Teeth remain grinding. I turn and stomp back out into the dining area, back to the kid who looks like my son, but isn't my son, can't be my son. I lean over the booth and whisper into his ear, ignoring the rancid stench clouding so close to his face.

"Sorry, kid, but my boss says you got to leave or she's calling the cops. You got some place to go?"

The boy does not respond, only stares down at the table as if still expecting more food to appear.

I reconsider, feeling Beth's eyes on my back, mean and acidic. "Tell you what. Go out the front door, then walk around back, in the alley? Hang out there, by the dumpster. I'll meet you in a couple minutes with something else to eat. Cool?"

The boy nods, stands, leaves.

"There, was that so hard?" Beth says, suddenly right behind me, breathing down my neck.

I sidestep away from her and head for the timeclock. "I'm going on my break."

~

The boy's waiting by the dumpster, just like I told him to. Arms at his sides, back stiff, face blank. The wind's picking up and I start shivering as soon as I step into the alley, but the boy doesn't seem the slightest bit bothered. The homeless, they get used to the cold. They learn to adapt. I met plenty ex-hobos during my time in Centralia. A lot of them there on purpose, terrified of freezing to death out on the street, would rather commit a sloppy B&E than wonder whether or not they'd wake up the next morning. Chicago winters are a gamble nobody wins, except maybe Satan, and that motherfucker rigged the game from the get-go, anyway.

"Hungry," the boy says as I approach him, hoping like hell Beth doesn't get any wise ideas and peek her head out the back door. I hand him the brown paper bag I'd brought from my apartment. We're allowed to eat the food at the restaurant, but management makes us pay for it, and the discount's an embarrassment, so I just bring my own lunch. The boy rips the bag from my hands and tears it open, devouring the peanut butter sandwich within seconds. I light up a cigarette and take long, slow drags as he nibbles on the apple.

"Where'd you come from?"

No response.

"You all alone?"

"No."

"Who else is with you?"

The boy hesitates. "Friends."

"Friends your age or older?"

No response.

"Okay. Where are they, then?"

"Hiding."

"Hiding from me?"

He nods.

"Because they're afraid?"

Nods.

"Well. They don't need to be. I'm not gonna hurt them or nothing. But you all should be careful about the places you walk into. Almost got the cops called on you."

"No cops."

"Yeah, I know."

"Afraid. Afraid of the Bad Man."

"The bad man?"

Nods.

"You mean me?"

He shakes his head no.

"Then who?"

No response.

"Did someone hurt you, kid?"

"Hungry."

"Sorry, kid. That's all I got tonight."

"Tomorrow." It's not a question.

I shrug, weirdly uncomfortable with denying his request. "Yeah, sure. Just wait out here, though. Don't come in. Beth sees you again, she'll call the cops herself."

"Friends."

"Yeah. Bring your friends. Sure."

He points at me. "Friend?"

"Me?"

Nods.

"Yeah. Okay. My name's Owen. And I'm your friend."

The boy steps forward and hugs me and I wait until he leaves the alley before crying.

~

My apartment door is ajar when I get home later that morning and I stop in the hallway thinking *fuck, not today*, but thoughts like those didn't help Becky, nothing helped her, so I clear my throat, making my presence more obvious, and the hands of my intruders reach through the door crack, waiting for me, always waiting for me, and grab my shirt and drag me inside the apartment. The door slams shut a second later and I'm flying, not an inch of me touching the floor, then all of me's slamming down—going *bang* against the hardwood and skidding forward—another victim of gravity, another idiot of stupid, terrible decisions.

I flop like a fish until I'm on my back. Standing above me: Kenneth and Mallory Noble, sixty-eight and sixty-three, faces dripping of tears, bodies trembling, determination fierce in their gaze.

The parents of Nancy Marie Noble Matilla.

Once upon a time, before I killed their daughter and grandchild, I'd been their son-in-law.

Kenneth stomps his boot in my face and my nose crunches and warm blood pours into my eyes, my mouth. It tastes like pennies. I drink it all in, telling myself I don't deserve to spit it out. Mallory raises a cane and slams it into my ribs and I curl into a ball as more blows strike. Everybody's sobbing, including me, but not because of the pain. As blood and snot choke my lungs I try to scream, "I'm sorry! I'm sorry!" but they can't hear me. It doesn't matter how loud I say it. They'll never hear me.

Fifteen minutes later, once they're both exhausted, we clean up the blood from the floor and I take a shower and bandage my new wounds. When I get out, they're sitting on the couch, three cups of coffee on the table in front of them. I sit on the floor, Indian-style, and sip at the cup closest to me. My body throbs. My nose is caved into my brain. My teeth ache. My innards moan. But it's okay. This is the way it's meant to be. This is the only way it *can* be.

They ask me if I'm okay and I tell them no and I ask them the same question and they echo my response.

Conversation evolves to other topics. How's work? Work is fine. How's your parole officer? A hardass. Are you doing okay on money? I'm doing fine. Will it ever stop hurting? No, it won't ever stop hurting.

I consider telling them about the boy I met last night and how much he reminded me of Bobby, but my body's not ready for another beating, not yet, not now. We hug and say our goodbyes and I watch them leave down the hallway, toward the elevator. I don't bother locking the door as I turn and search for safety within the blankets on my air mattress.

Sleep does not find me for several hours.

~

Before heading out into the alley, I grab the trash bag I'd stashed under the sink earlier in my shift. The boy's waiting in the same spot as last night, next to the dumpster. A group of children similarly aged hide behind him, cowering in the shadows. They all stare at me as I approach, filthy, emotionless. The boy who looks like Bobby but isn't Bobby says, "Hungry," and I hold up the trash bag in my hand. He reaches out to take it but I pull away, lift the index finger on my other hand.

"Not yet. You want to eat, you gotta answer some questions first."

The boy's brow bends into a V. "Hungry."

The kids behind him all step forward, staring at me, and the boy shakes his head no and the kids return to the shadows.

"Hungry."

"What's your name? Tell me that, and you can have some of what's inside."

The boy hesitates, and for a moment I don't think he understands the question, then: "Nameless."

"Nameless?"

The boy nods.

I wave my free hand at the kids behind him. "And what about the rest of you? You all nameless, too?"

They don't budge. Continue watching my every movement. Cats hunting flies.

"Okay. Where are you from?" The question's for all of them, any of them.

"Nowhere," the boy who is not Bobby says.

"What does that mean?"

"Nowhere."

"You haven't always been in this alley. Where do you live?"

"Everywhere."

"What are you? Runaways?"

Nothing.

"What about the bad man? Who is he?"

They all flinch and look over their shoulders, as if expecting to find the bad man waiting behind them.

"Bad Man is bad," the boy says. "Bad, bad, bad."

"But who is he? Why is he bad?"

The boy reaches for the bag again. "*Hungry.*"

I sigh and surrender the trash bag. The boy takes it and rushes behind the dumpster with the rest of his group. Camouflaged by shadows. Loud, wet chewing noises. A desperate feast of leftover pancakes and rolls. I shuffle my feet in the alley, shivering and lighting a cigarette, and try to remember the last time I've actually eaten. My stomach growls. Ignore the emptiness. Ignore the ache. Everything hurts just as it should.

I wait, hoping they'll come back out and talk to me a little more, but my break ends before they're done eating, so I flick my cigarette butt on the ground and head back inside the diner, wondering if I should do something more, if I should call somebody. Then Beth stomps toward me and shoves a plunger against my chest.

"Someone clogged the shitter."

~

Every night I feed the kids, their group seems to expand. I lose count at twenty. How the hell do they get here without being noticed? Twenty kids can't travel in a group around Chicago at 2:30 in the morning without drawing some kind of attention, yet they somehow manage to move around the city undetected. Sometimes people, they choose not to see things they don't want to be involved in. Sometimes it's easier to ignore a problem than to try solving it. The homeless are masters of stealth. Thinking about them makes people sad and angry, so they just don't think about them. It's easier that way. But I can't ignore these kids. I can't be that kind of person. I can't.

"I was thinking about maybe contacting a shelter," I tell them one night as they devour old hamburger patties behind the dumpster. "You know. A place you can all stay. It's too cold to be sleeping outside. Once the snow hits, you'll freeze to death. I'm surprised you haven't already."

The boy who is not Bobby steps out of the shadows and shakes his head. "No shelter."

"But where will you go?"

No response.

"You know, I can't just keep feeding you guys like this. Someone's going to notice all the missing food soon. I...I can't get in trouble. I used to be in jail, and if I get in trouble for something like that, they might send me back. Back to jail. And besides, don't you guys want to do something else besides just eat trash every night? You never talk to me. What do you do all day? Where do you go?"

Where do you hide? I almost ask.

And the boy cocks his head, expressing curiosity for the first time since we met. "Jail?"

I retreat back, embarrassed. "I don't want to talk about that."

He continues staring like that isn't a good enough answer.

"It was...it was a bad time in my life. I'm trying to do better. Like by helping you guys. But you gotta let me, first."

The boy's face goes blank again. I'm not going to win this. These kids are stubborn. They're used to living out here on their own. They don't want to change their lifestyles. They just want someone to feed them.

"Listen." I raise my hand like I'm going to place it on the boy's shoulder, then think better of it. "I won't be here tomorrow. It's my night off. So don't freak out when I don't show up, okay?"

"Hungry."

"I know. I'm sorry."

"Hungry."

"I'll be back in two nights, okay? So not tomorrow, and not the night after, but the night after that, I'll be back. You'll be...okay, right?"

Of course they won't be okay, but they're not going to die because I take two nights off from work. They survived long enough before finding me, and they'll survive long after I'm gone.

(after I'm gone)

If the boy understands what I'm saying, his facial expression doesn't alter to show it. Sometimes when I talk to him, I get the feeling he doesn't exactly know English, only bits and pieces he's picked up over the years while living on the streets. But he doesn't seem to have an accent. When he speaks, his voice comes out in a monotone.

"Where will you guys go?" I ask, not expecting an answer.

But I get one, anyway:

"With you."

~

I tell them they're nuts, but they either don't understand or don't give a shit. I try to make them see things my way. How weird and suspicious it'd look, me, not only a grown-ass man but also an ex-con, being trailed by two dozen small children who are obviously homeless. People are going to have a lot of questions, I tell the boy who is not my son. They're going to intervene. Society just doesn't work like that.

And the boy says, "It fine."

I still don't agree to the idea, but there's no way for me to prevent them from following me on their tiny dirty feet as I walk to my apartment a little over a mile from the diner. It's seven in the morning and the sun hasn't quite decided to rise, which I get the feeling the children are grateful for. I've never seen them during the day and when I try to picture it in my head I get nauseated. I don't know why. But maybe I do, maybe I know exactly why.

This morning the city is surreal. Usually, walking home at this time, the sidewalks are crammed with other people, students and workers and joggers, everybody. But today the sidewalks are empty, as if reserved for me and the kids. And, while there's an odd car driving past every now and then, the normal busy traffic does not seem to be present, and those who do drive our way don't even look in our direction. Like we're under some kind of cloaking spell, invisible to the public eye.

There are far too many of us to fit in the elevator, so we take the stairs up to my apartment. Again, we pass nobody. Once inside, I lock the doors and show them around. It isn't much, not by any stretch, and with them all in here there's barely any room to breathe, much less move around. Some of them cram together on the couch, and others sit on the floor, taking up all of the living room. I stand in the kitchen and they all stare at me, expecting something.

"Well, this is my home. You're all welcome to stay here as long as you wish. I know, there's not a lot of room, but it's all I got. Just...try not to make too much noise or draw attention. I don't think my lease allows for so many people to live here at once. But, uh, if you need to shower, feel free. I'll try to stop at Goodwill later and pick up some clothes that might fit some of you. Uh. There's not much food here, I'm sorry to say, but you can help yourselves to whatever you find."

The boy who is not my son points at a framed photograph of my actual son hanging from the living room wall. "Who?"

I ignore the question, pretending he hasn't spoken, but he continues pointing at it, waiting, so I swallow and try to remain calm. "That's my son. His name's Bobby."

"Where at?"

"He. Uh. He's dead. My son is dead."

"Dead?"

"Yeah."

The boy lowers his hand, doesn't say anything else.

My cell phone starts ringing, and all the kids flinch in unison. The caller ID says it's my parole officer. Fuck.

"Okay, guys, don't say anything, all right? I have to take this. Seriously. Don't make any noise." I don't know why I'm telling them this. I've never heard any of them even speak besides the one who originally showed up inside the diner. The rest of them, it'd be difficult to tell they existed if not for their odor.

Gonna have to buy some candles if they're staying here. Some Febreze and shit like that. Money I don't have.

I answer the phone. "Hello?"

"Owen. I was starting to think you weren't going to answer."

"Yeah, sorry. I just got home from work."

"And how is your job doing?"

"Oh. You know. It's okay. It's a job."

"Beats a cell, huh?"

"Yeah…"

"Anyway, I was just calling to remind you of our appointment this morning. Wouldn't want you to be late."

"Appointment?"

"Don't tell me you've forgotten, Owen."

"What time was it at again?"

"Ten, Owen. The appointment's at ten. You *will* be here, correct?"

"Is there any way we can re—"

"No, Owen. That's now how this works."

"Okay. I'll be there at ten."

"Good. That's what I like to hear. See ya then, Owen."

I tell the boy who is not my son that I'm going to be gone for a couple hours, that they should just stay in my apartment and try to relax. I wish I had a TV for them to use. Instead I show them my collection of paperbacks I've been slowly scavenging from Goodwill. I don't know if any of them can read, but if they can they're in for one hell of a treat.

Before I leave, the boy who is not my son tells me they're hungry again.

"I know. I'll try to bring some food home on the way back, okay? You like Ramen?"

And the boy just stares, face blank. "Hungry."

Hungry, hungry. They're always so goddamn hungry.

I can't feed them all.

~

The parole officer doesn't have much to say. It's the same conversation every time. How are you adjusting? Fine. How is your new job? Okay. Have you been in contact with family? Some. Where do you see yourself in five years? I don't know. Have you attended your required Alcoholics Anonymous meeting for the month? Not yet, but I will before the month ends. Have you had any alcohol since your release? No. Have you desired any? Yes. How often? Every second I'm awake. What stops you? The fear. The fear of what? Of hurting someone else. Of going back to jail. Of fucking up my second chance. Do you still think you deserve a second chance? No. Why not? I don't know. You don't know? No. Will you pee in this cup? Yeah, I'll pee in that cup.

~

On the way home, I stop at Goodwill and purchase a large assortment of children's clothing. There's not much money in my checking account and I'm holding my breath as I insert my debit card into the chip reader. Miraculously it goes through. I try my luck again at the Dollar General next door and buy a basket-full of Ramen noodles. Again, it goes through. What the hell. Things are actually on my side this morning. Even my parole officer was mostly pleasant. These kids, it's like they're some sort of good luck charm. I ought to keep them around, see what happens. I already fucked up one child's life. Maybe this "second chance"—as my P.O. calls it—is a lot more significant than I realized. Maybe I was released from Centralia to help these kids, to save them. Feed them. Shelter them. Take care of them. Be the dad none of them ever had.

I walk into my apartment with a smile on my face, and I'm only two steps inside before the smile vanishes forever.

Kenneth and Mallory Noble.

Sitting on my couch.

Fuck, not now. Oh shit oh shit. NOT NOW!

The kids sitting on the floor around the couch all turn to me, faces stained red, as if asking, *What? What's wrong?*

I rush forward, stumbling for the right excuse. "Look, it's not what it looks like, okay?"

Still in denial about what I'm looking at, about what's happened while I was gone.

"You have to leave," I whisper, although I don't know who I'm saying this to. Kenneth and Mallory. The kids. Myself. Someone, anyone. We all have to leave. Leave and never come back again. This is a bad place. The kids have made it so.

I refuse to acknowledge reality until I'm up close, practically on top of them. Although Kenneth and Mallory are sitting and staring in my direction, they do not see me. Where eyeballs once rested, their sockets now remain black and empty, as if scraped clean and sucked dry. Their clothing is ripped to shreds and hundreds of tiny bite marks trail up and down their bodies. Their mouths hang open in a perpetual scream. Neither still possesses a tongue.

I back away, trembling. The kids don't move. The red on their faces. Of course I know what it is. And they know I know. They want me to know. The boy who is not my son stands from the floor and slowly approaches me, one hand out, fingers stained vermillion.

"Friend?"

~

The next morning the bodies are gone. I don't know what the kids did with them and I don't want to know.

Nobody complains about being hungry.

Later, the boy who is not my son tells me about the Bad Man.

The Bad Man wants to hurt the kids. Wants to kill them. Has *already* killed some, will surely kill more. The Bad Man is evil. The kids try to hide but the Bad Man always finds them, no matter where they go, how far they run. The Bad Man travels in people's shadows. He's not human. He's everywhere and nowhere at once.

The boy who is not my son tells me about the Bad Man, then he tells me where the Bad Man lives.

"Help," he says. "Help. Help. Help."

~

The Bad Man lives in a motel across the city. Come dusk, the boy leads the way, the other kids hanging back at my apartment. We take the train. No one seems to notice either of us. The boy already knows what room he's staying in. I ask the night clerk at the motel for an extra key, claiming to have lost mine at a bar. The clerk, annoyed I distracted him from whatever he's watching on his laptop, barely glances at me as he programs a new keycard and tosses it on the front desk.

"Have a good night," he mumbles, sitting back down.

No one's in the motel room when we slip inside, which is probably for the best. Gives me time to look around, get a feel for who this Bad Man really is. The room's a disaster. Empty fast food bags littered across the floor. Discarded clothes here and there. Thick tomes with strange symbols on the covers. On the desk in the corner of the room, I find a large crossbow. It's loaded with an arrow, ready to go. *Why does he have this? Why does he have any of this?*

On the wall, above the motel desk, a corkboard hangs with dozens of photographs and drawings tacked within its borders. Printouts of maps laying out the streets of Chicago. Newspaper articles with headlines emphasizing grisly murders and strange disappearances. Photographs of random children. Photographs of murder scenes. Many, many pencil drawings of kids. Kids with black eyes and long fangs. Kids without faces. Kids with—

A noise outside the room. Footsteps. Heavy breathing.

I freeze. The boy who is not my son hides behind the bed. Someone inserts a keycard into the door lock. A click of acceptance. The handle turns. The door opens. A tall obese man in a fedora and trench coat stands in the opening. The brown paper bag falls from his grasp at the sight of me.

"What are you doing in my—" He pauses. "Did they send you?"

I don't respond.

"They did, didn't they? They sent you. They were too scared to do it themselves, weren't they? So they found someone else to do their dirty work." He laughs. His throat sounds clogged with phlegm.

"Who are you?" The words barely leave my lips.

"Who did they say I was?"

"The Bad Man."

Again, the laugh. "Well, they aren't wrong."

"You have to leave them alone. You have to go far away."

"I'm not going anywhere. Not after all the work I've done. Fuck that." He gestures to the corkboard, then stops. Sniffs. "One of them is here now, aren't they? I can smell the fucker. Where is it?"

As if on cue, the boy who is not my son stands from behind the bed, but this time when I look at him he is no longer the boy who is not my son but is instead my son, my Bobby, my poor dead beautiful baby boy, and he is so perfect tears burst from my eyes at the sight of him.

The Bad Man grins. "Yeah, there you are, you motherfucker. I'll never forget that smell."

He reaches inside his trench coat, and I realize he's going for a weapon.

A weapon to injure my boy.

No.

I pick up the crossbow and aim it at the Bad Man and pull the trigger and an arrow shoots out and penetrates his gut. His hand falls from his trench coat, a pistol hitting the floor. The man groans and steps back, eyes wide and focused on me standing across the room, still holding the crossbow. I drop the killing device on the desk and move toward him. Fear and panic glow like electricity across his face. Both of his hands caress the arrow in his stomach but he doesn't pull it out, he doesn't dare.

I follow him out to the second-story landing, him still backpedaling until he bumps against the stair railing.

"You don't understand," he whispers, wincing and groaning. "You don't understand what they are."

But he's wrong. I understand exactly what they are.

"They're mine," I tell him, and push his chest with both hands. He stumbles back, reaching for air, and crashes down the stairs, rolling and flipping and screaming.

By the time he reaches the bottom, he's silent again.

On the way back home, Bobby tells me he's hungry again, and I rub his hair and tell him he can have whatever he wants, anything at all, and he smiles and holds my hand and says, "Daddy?" and I smile back and nod and say yes, yes, yes.

YELLOW HOUSE

by Jon Padgett

You'll find it on Old Shell Road between the docks and the park. It is asymmetrical and L shaped and includes several octagonal rooms and a kind of attic-tower with curved windows. It is excessively ornamental with fish-scale siding. It is three stories tall.

I live in the yellow house with my grandmother. Each morning she hobbles downstairs from her room in the side attic-tower. My grandmother is bent over so that her torso is nearly parallel to the floor, head straining forward, a crooked smile playing on her face. Her rheumy eyes appear addled.

"Where did my Millie run off to?" she might ask on one of her more lucid days. Millie is her daughter and my mother.

Grandmother calls me her heart before turning around and trudging back upstairs. My grandfather, a small but fat man who resembles a walking roly-poly, may or may not accompany her. He doesn't recall that he died many years ago. I remind him sometimes, at which points he sits down in an old easy chair in the living room and stares at the hutch where his television used to be.

The woodwork is gaudy in the front sitting room of the yellow house. Its bay window overlooks the park. Stare through that window at your own risk. If it's raining outside, you may get stuck inside the glass. It's thicker than it looks. The glass is old and warped. Through it, a huge, storm-ravaged magnolia appears to be a water spout hovering over brown, undulating leaf-water.

I'm forgetting something.

Maybe this: grandmother hates my mother for getting pregnant with me out of wedlock. That makes me a kind of bastard, grandmother says sometimes.

I don't know where my mother is, but I think about her every day.

No, that's not what I'm forgetting.

The yellow house backs up to Dunnstown Bay. There are waves during storm season, sometimes as high as ten to twenty feet, crashing on the dingy shoreline. The bay is unclean. There is a decaying boardwalk that runs along the shoreline. During storm season the filmy, rainbow-sheened water often threatens to flood the bottom floor of the yellow house.

In the distance, through a sliding glass door in the kitchen, you can see a line of gargantuan, steel, electrical pylons marching diagonally across the bay. The closest one appears impossibly tall. I sometimes pretend it's a giant, skeletal doll in the form of my grandmother as she once was—erect, hands flung up in an attitude of eternal, shocked rage. The next pylon is further out and appears from my vantage point like a much smaller skeletal doll. Sometimes I like to imagine it is me as a child, impersonating grandmother's attitude, connected to her by multiple metal wires.

"I wonder where mother went," pylon-doll-me says.

"God knows where that whore has run off to this time," the pylon-doll-grandmother in my head might reply. "Rutting like a cur in heat with only hell knows what."

"Don't profane my mother," I imagine the smaller pylon figure responds. By this point I find my eyes drawn further across the bay, beyond the smaller of the two pylons, into the distance where a third pylon stands. This one, I imagine, is my skeletal-doll-mother running away. From my vantage point, the lines between pylon-her and pylon-me are invisible. It appears there is nothing at all connecting her to us. I smile, imagining my mother in mid-escape, almost out of reach, nearly free of the yellow house. It feels like part of me is on the verge of being set free as well.

I imagine grandmother dislikes these smiling thoughts. I can feel the giant pylon-doll form glaring down at me through the sliding glass doors and, simultaneously, through the floor of her tower-attic behind and above me. Grandmother reminds me that the pylon-doll is in fact still connected to us, no further off than she ever was. Waiting to be reeled in. Not that I can hear grandmother saying these words exactly, but I can sense them through every board, each yard of old plaster and petrified wood in this yellow house.

I also sense she wants me to close my eyes again, but I've learned to never do that.

See, whenever I close my eyes for any length of time, the yellow house changes. When that happens, it is no longer a glorious three-story but a lowly single-story. I could be anywhere in the yellow house—in the guest bedroom or kitchen or foyer. But as soon as I close my eyes for more than several seconds, I am sitting in a low ceilinged, ranch-style living room. I have spent so much time in this phantom house, and I can never remember how to open my eyes when I'm there. I stumble around, feeling the walls, the floors, the cheap but locked hollow doors for some escape route until, days or weeks later it seems, all at once I'm back in the fully restored, three-story yellow house again, eyes open.

If only I could remember what I've forgotten.

Maybe it is this: there is an intercom system that grandmother had installed many years ago throughout the yellow house so that she could monitor every word that was spoken within it. Each room still contains a plastic, louvred square on the wall. On each square is a brown switch that may be pressed to contact and speak with other individuals in the house.

Many years ago, I spent the night with my grandparents while my mother went out. They were arguing about her, and while they screamed at each other over who was to blame for my mother's rebellious and self-destructive nature, I dismantled the intercom system's central control panel on the living room wall. When I was caught in the act soon afterwards, I told grandmother I had only been curious. She replied that the devil in me was to blame.

"Go fetch a switch," she said. Of course, I brought in the flimsiest twig I could find. Grandmother grabbed me, marched me outside and made me strip a long, sharp piece of wood from a boardwalk piling. Then she struck my bare, right leg with it over and over until my skin was a mass of splintered gore.

There were other severe punishments over the years, always aimed at that one, poor leg. She never explained why it was the target of her reprimands. I wonder if she thought that's where the devil in me lived. Following these beatings, grandmother called me her heart and pulled me close, squeezing me too hard as I bawled.

"You got book learning but no horse sense," my grandfather would observe, not unkindly, when grandmother walked me back through the sliding glass door of the yellow house.

As years went on, I developed a permanent limp from grandmother's attempted exorcisms, but I guess the devil never left me. And her intercom system never worked again.

There is still something I'm forgetting—not the intercom system nor the switchings.

Perhaps it's only this: these days, in spring and summer, I sit in the kitchen overlooking the ruined boardwalk and pray for storms. I start by imagining I can make the bay-wind change direction. Just gradually at first. After pretending that I'm moving the branches of a tall, skinny pine out back, I set my sights on the clouds above the murky bay. I begin concentrating on pulling them towards the yellow house. Then, if I get that far without interruption, I imagine those clouds darkening and building. All the while the wind seems to pick up. And sometimes it storms.

My mind, at these moments, is focused on one goal: to see this yellow house demolished. I want to see it in ruins, even if it means an end to me and grandmother and the befuddled ghost of my grandfather. Don't misunderstand. I love my grandparents, regardless of how they may or may not feel about my mother. But my loathing of this place outstrips all affections. I want the yellow house razed.

And one summer, late in the storm season, I came so close to success.

I had mastered the winds, slowly, quietly, sweet talking the puffy white clouds into massive thunderheads—far off over the bay so that there was only yet a whisper of the storm that was to come. Grandmother was quiescent, the floorboards creaking in time with her napping snores. As the minutes of my concentration ticked by, I coaxed five little fingers of dark purple cloud into the now churning bay.

To my delight and astonishment, the funnel clouds soon became full-fledged waterspouts, dwarfing even the closest electrical pylons in size. They swirled and howled in the water, the catastrophic winds producing waves big enough to crash upon the boardwalk itself, smashing many of its rotten boards to pieces, even hurling a switch-sized sliver of piling through the kitchen window.

The crash woke grandmother, who immediately rushed into the kitchen and seized me. No old man or woman, bent over and ancient, should ever move that swiftly.

"What have you done to us, wicked heart?" she asked, shrieking into my ear. The wind shook the yellow house to its foundations.

"Nothing at all, grandmother," I replied, quivering with fear and victory.

She twisted my wounded, right leg with a gnarled hand, making me squawk.

"You have so much to feel guilty about, my little bastard-child. Now close your eyes and make it all better."

But I refused to shut my streaming eyes for a moment, screaming and laughing while she pinched my leg harder. One of the waterspouts, now a powerful tornado on shore, angled towards us in the storm-gloom, and all light vanished. I could feel the hum of the fish scale siding sloughing off the house. I tried to keep my eyes open, but the agony in my bad leg made my eyelids squeeze shut.

And the hum becomes the world, and the top of the world blows off.

Now I am sitting, blind,

in my long-dead grandmother's ranch-style house – the living room, if I could see it, would be full of bright greens (the curtains), yellows and reds (the colorful faux-Turkish carpeting). The creamy, bumpy, low ceiling always appeared delicious once to my child-self, as if it were covered in ice cream on the brink of dribbling down onto the high-backed, Victorian looking chairs and couch, upon the coolness of the marble end tables, upon the colorful carpet, upon my grandmother's miniature organ. I am staring (had my eyes been open) at that organ, which I haven't seen in thirty years or more but that I can feel crouched across from where I sit as if it is alive—an instrument that smells of burning wood in autumn suffused with the pungent, synthetic florals of an old woman's perfume and soap. I get up, turn to where I know the open dining room is with its long, dark-wooden table, its room-wide mirror, brilliantly lit by a chandelier, crystals meticulously clean and sparkling. I turn back to the organ, walk to it, sit down upon the smooth, lacquered bench, flip the power switch on the organ's face, red light I know beginning to glow upon my face, a familiar, electric hum filling the room.

And I (who have never taken a music lesson in my life) play that organ, deftly switching the gray rocker switches from one sound—bells—to another—pipe organ— switching from upper to lower keyboard, feet pumping, playing the most intricate, harmonized melodies, which vibrate through the living room, throughout my body, with that underlying, electrical hum. I feel tears of relief pouring down my cheeks as I finish.

But when I try to pull my fingers away from the organ keys, I can't. My fingers are stuck. It's as if the organ keys have grown claws as sharp as needles, which hook the skin of each of my fingers, into the meat, and out again. I try to get up from the bench, but it also feels like it has sprung claws that hook inside my thighs and buttocks, and I am held fast in my grandmother's phantom, ranch-style house, eyes fastened shut in the living room full of bright green curtains I cannot see, the yellows and reds of imagined faux-Turkish carpeting, the ceiling bumpy with petrified ice cream, but now it seems like something is about to erupt from all those little imagined bumps, as if something is shifting, ready to dig itself out, upside down, within them, like funnel cloud fingers from a thunderhead, maybe to bloom, the artificial floral smell of old women's perfume and soap smells more like smoke and the miniature organ begins to shriek and something is burning inside it, and then all at once I am sitting again on the high-backed faux-Victorian chair sitting across the room from the miniature organ, which I know glowers at me like a predator, its red eye shining through my lids, its electrical hum purring, its keys ready to hook their claws into me, hungry for the connection.

Then I hear her voice.

"That was just lovely, my precious heart. Now tell me where Millie has run off to. She's coupling with some crook in the Indoor Swamp, I'll warrant."

"Don't profane my mother," I almost say, but I'm exhausted and want only to be unmolested by that crooked, deranged voice and grandmother's many grasping fingers.

When I open my eyes at last, I'm sitting in the yellow house again, on the kitchen bench, and there is no sign of my grandmother.

The house now seems undamaged, most notably the recently broken kitchen window, making me wonder if I dreamed the storm. But the boardwalk, I can see now, is gone, leaving only long splinters of itself on the dingy shore.

I look out onto the bay at the electrical pylons and smile.

The first two—the giant-pylon-grandmother-doll and the smaller-pylon-me-doll—still stand, connected as always to each other, but the pylon I always imagined as my mother is gone completely. Not even the wires remain. A dark fog is moving in over the bay towards the yellow house.

And then all at once I remember what I'd forgotten.

I walk to the living room and sit in my grandfather's old easy chair. I become quite still and stare at the hutch where his television used to be.

WHAT FINDS ITS WAY BACK

by Damien Angelica Walters

When they were children, Keira and her sisters buried their secrets in the woods behind their house. She and Ava and Amanda would run between the trees, hands linked, one of them with lips clamped tight, drawing as close to the stream separating the old woods from the new as they dared. Together, they'd dig a hole and one would bend low, pressing lips to waiting dark, whispering the secret into the exposed dirt, their voice like drifting feathers, and the three of them would cover it up as fast as they could and run back home, not speaking until they were clear of the tree line.

By the time they'd finished grade school, the ground was thick with secrets—*Jennifer Smyth is a jerk; Mrs. Halloway isn't as pretty as she thinks she is; I hate Stephan Gregory and wish he would die*—all trapped in place by the self-righteous fury of childhood.

The woods on the other side of the stream held other, darker secrets.

~

Keira's hands tightened on the steering wheel as she turned down the narrow, winding driveway leading to her childhood home. It was the first time she'd been back since Nana passed away a year and a half ago, and she had the same pit in her stomach now as she did then. She'd already stopped at the sheriff's office, and Sheriff Banks told her exactly what she expected him to say. Amanda was an adult and her note made it clear she left of her own accord. "I guess she decided to follow in your footsteps," he said, his goodbye perfunctory, his smile tight-lipped.

As the house came into view, she eased off the gas pedal. Time and the environment had dulled the green siding on the two-story Craftsman and weeds had overtaken the flower beds, but the grass had been mowed recently. Better than last time.

She parked her Hyundai beside Nana's old Toyota, and before she even got out of the car, Ava was out the front door and running toward her, hair streaming in a dark, tangled veil, jeans sagging from her hipbones as though she were a wire hanger twisted out of shape. Face bare of makeup, she looked more like a young girl than a woman of twenty-two.

"I'm so glad you're here. We've—I've—missed you so much."

"I've missed you, too." She plucked a leaf from Ava's hair and lifted her hand to inspect the ragged cuticles, the nails bitten to the quick. "You're a mess."

A red flush painted Ava's cheeks. "I know, I'm sorry. I've just been too worried to care about anything else, and I…" She swiped her eyes with the back of a hand, before falling into Keira's arms.

"It's okay. It'll be okay." She spoke against Ava's sour-smelling hair, and the words felt heavy and false, the sort of thing you said to fill the quiet.

"I feel like part of me is missing, Keira. I can't be without her. I just can't."

Keira was only three years older than the twins, but the difference always felt greater as though she were the mother and they the children. It wasn't their fault, but still, her muscles relaxed when she untangled herself from Ava's arms.

Ava insisted on carrying her suitcase inside. The house was neat and tidy, even the mostly unused formal living and dining rooms, and the lemon scent of furniture polish clung to the air. A far cry from the chaos that had greeted her the last time.

All for her benefit, Keira suspected, confirmed by the small, pleased smile on Ava's lips. Even the stairs were swept clean of dust. The door to her old bedroom at the far end of the hall stood open and Ava moved aside so she could enter first.

The night before she'd left for college, she'd removed her posters from the walls and her knickknacks from the dresser and nightstand. The former went into the trash; the latter into a box in the attic. Now, they were back. She pinched her lower lip between her front teeth, at a loss for words.

"Is it okay?" Ava said, her voice a bird's wings. "I just thought it might be nice while you're here…"

"No, it's fine." Her gaze passed over glass dragon figurines, small pieces of quartzite and agate, a jewelry box of marbled wood.

"Are you sure?"

It wasn't fine, not really. The last time she'd been home, *every* time she'd been home, the twins begged her to stay; this seemed a passive aggressive attempt at the same. Before she left, she'd throw it all out so it couldn't happen the next time.

"No, yeah, it's fine. Why don't you show me the note? I can unpack later."

Ava nodded, eyes awash in sorrow, and led her back downstairs, to the kitchen where a magnet in the shape of a snail pinned Amanda's note on the refrigerator.

I'll be back in a few days. Don't come after me and don't worry!

"I waited a few days," Ava said. "Then I waited some more, then I called you."

"We'll find her."

"Promise?"

Keira nodded, though she gazed at the woods visible in the window over the sink and, stomach in knots, wondered.

~

In the morning, she knew instinctively that the house was empty. Nana had always said you couldn't fart without the house announcing it to everyone else inside. Something in the construction, she'd say, butterflying a hand.

Both cars were in the driveway so Ava couldn't have gone far. Still in her pajamas, Keira made a pot of coffee, sitting at the kitchen table while it brewed, her head foggy and thick. She'd slept hard, thanks to the four-hour drive from Baltimore and a Unisom.

With a full mug, she sat on the back porch step, knees to her chest. The wide yard sloped gently down to the tree line, to over a hundred acres of oak, hickory, and pine, of which only little more than a third were safe. The new woods, Nana had called them, though they'd been named that since before she'd been born.

Keira craned her neck from left to right, but it didn't break the tension pinching her muscles. Nothing would, not here. There were too many memories, too many things she wanted to forget, too many ways this place could hold tight and refuse to let go. A slight spring breeze sent the trees to bend and leaves to rustle. Mocking her, perhaps. Or reminding her that they knew, they remembered.

It wasn't that she hated it here; she hated herself here, hated the box in which she had to fit, the role she had to play. At home, she had only herself to care for. She didn't even have a plant in her apartment.

Ava came out of the woods then, clad in a nightgown, visibly starting when their gazes met. Keira's spine went cold.

"What were you doing in the woods?" she said, when Ava drew close enough to hear.

"I didn't expect you up this early."

"Obviously, but that wasn't an answer. What were you doing in the woods?" She drew the sentence out, making sure each word was heavily weighted.

Ava lifted one slender leg and bent to scratch her ankle, long strands of hair tumbling over her face and obscuring her features. It reminded Keira briefly, powerfully, of the last time she saw their mother, and she held tight to the coffee mug to keep her fingers from shaking.

"I woke up and I couldn't sit still. I had to do something."

"So you went into the woods?"

Ava nodded, sat down, and scratched her ankle again. "Um, I…"

"What?"

"Well..."

"Ava, please just tell me."

Ava looked away fast. "You have to promise not to get mad, okay?"

Keira's stomach clenched, and she fought the urge to run in the house, grab her keys, and get the hell out, but said, her voice as calm as possible, "I promise to try."

"Okay." Ava scrubbed her palms along her thighs, pleating the fabric of her nightgown. "A couple days before Amanda left the note, she was looking for something in the new woods."

"What?" she said, the word halfway between a laugh and a shout.

"She didn't tell me what it was, and when I asked her she said it was nothing."

"So you lied to me?"

"I..."

"Why didn't you tell me this before now? Why didn't you say something when you called me?" The words scratched in her throat.

"I couldn't tell you, don't you understand? I was afraid once you knew, you wouldn't come." Tears shimmered in Ava's eyes. "And how could I take care of it all on my own? I couldn't, I'm not like you."

"I still would've come," Keira said, but even she heard the lack of conviction in her voice. "This changes everything. You know that, right?"

Ava shook her head, whipping the ends of her hair back and forth.

"No. She wouldn't have gone into the old woods. She knows better."

"So did Mom." Her words were gentle, but Ava winced.

"That isn't fair. You know it was different with Mom. Nana said so. The woods wanted her from the time she was a little girl. They don't want Amanda. I'd know. She couldn't hide something like that from me. She wasn't walking at night or talking to herself or doing anything strange. I would've known." Ava sat back a little, breathing hard.

She picked at the edge of a fingernail. Nana had always said if the old woods claimed you, you had no choice. You could move away, marry, have children, but in the end, the pull would be too great and you'd return. She'd admitted to Keira she hadn't known they'd claimed Mom, not until she'd shown up on Nana's doorstep, her eyes wild and bright, a twin on each hip and Keira toddling behind. By then, it was too late; she was already lost. And six months later, she walked into the woods and was gone.

"Most of all, though," Ava said, her voice mouse-small. "I know it because whatever she was looking for, she said it had something to do with you."

How Keira managed to hold her face still, she wasn't sure.

~

After breakfast, she donned jeans, a long sleeved t-shirt, and hiking boots, and before heading downstairs, she pawed through her purse until she found her pocketknife, a gift from Nana when she'd first moved away. "Every woman should have a knife for protection," Nana had said. "And don't be afraid to use it. Sometimes you have no choice."

The three and a half inch blade, which she kept sharpened, folded neatly into a heavy, dark wood handle that fit perfectly in her hand. She'd never needed to use it, but its weight in her front pocket was a comfort.

She and Ava crossed the grass to the woods, both in their own sphere of silence, and Keira's steps slowed the closer they got.

"Keira? What's wrong?"

She gave what she hoped was a convincing smile. She'd not been in the woods since junior year in high school. No sister by her side then. Nothing but the dark, her tears, and a hole in the ground the perfect size for a secret. And Nana, of course. Without her, she never would've made it through that night.

"Nothing. It's just... If she's in there, how in the hell are we going to find her?"

"We have to at least try," Ava said. "We have to."

But what if Amanda didn't want to be found? Keira took a deep breath, fingering the outline of the knife, and stepped forward, small twigs cracking beneath her feet. Like bones. Like tiny bones. Beneath the canopy, the day turned twilight, the air chill, and she shuddered.

They stuck to pathways feet had made long before the Ashton family came to live here. Birds sang overhead and flitted from tree to tree, squirrels zig-zagged out of their way, and every ten yards or so, Ava called her sister's name.

Keira walked through a spider web and let out a breathy shout, waving her arms to dislodge the sticky strands while Ava laughed. In that moment, at least, it felt as though they were simply taking a walk. For Ava's sake, she tried to think positive and swallow her unease. There was nothing in the woods that could hurt her, not after so much time.

By the time they returned home, they were dirty, hungry, and disappointment radiated from Ava in waves. "We have to look again tomorrow," she said, her voice a sandpaper rasp. "We have to keep looking until we find her."

All Keira could do was nod.

~

Out of Unisom, having packed the wrong box, Keira gave up on sleep after an hour of tossing and turning while the wind screamed through the trees. She peeked in on Ava; her sister was out like a light, on her back with one arm flung over her head, the other hanging off the side of the bed.

The twins always could sleep through anything. Sometimes a curse; sometimes a blessing.

She shivered, and not from the chill in the air. She was halfway down the stairs when a wail broke the night, long and low and mournful. Goosebumps landscaped her arms, and she froze in place. No. *No.*

The cry came again, farther away this time. The spell shattered, and she ran back upstairs to her room, her bed, curving her body into a nautilus, hands over her ears, telling herself over and over again it was only a fox.

When she finally slept, she dreamt of tiny hands tapping her face, from forehead to cheek, to jaw, to chin, and all the way back around, but every time she tried to brush them away, her fingers caught in spider webs.

~

Ava found walking sticks in the shed, and they went deeper into the woods, where the ivy grew thicker and the bushes wielded thorns and toxic berries.

"Ava, I know you think she's here, but maybe all the stuff about looking in the woods was a ruse. Maybe she...left and didn't want to tell you."

"She wouldn't do that. Not to me," Ava said.

"Maybe she couldn't tell you because she knew you'd be upset."

"She. Wouldn't." Ava punctuated each word with a hard thump of her stick. "Anyway, she didn't take the car and town is too far to walk."

A long walk, yes, but not an impossible one. Not if someone was determined. "Are you sure maybe she wasn't seeing someone? They could've picked her up—"

"No. She wasn't seeing anyone, she didn't meet anyone, she didn't walk into town. She went into the woods looking for something. You haven't been here, you don't know, but I have and I do."

Keira held up one hand. "Okay, you're right, I haven't been here." A trace of an apology tainted her words and she pressed her lips into a thin line. "But she's an adult, Ava. She's allowed to leave."

Ava's mouth opened and closed, and then she forged ahead, smacking bushes and tree branches out of the way. Keira waited to follow until she was almost out of sight.

Half an hour later, Ava stopped and waved her forward. "Do you see that?"

About ten feet off the path, a scrap of something pale blue and shimmery flashed between the leaves of a greenbrier bush.

"Keira?" Ava's voice was a moth wing.

"I know. I see it."

Ava whispered, "Please, please, please," while Keira used her pocketknife to strip the thorns from several branches, allowing her to work the scarf free. There were a few pulls and thorn punctures in the fabric, but the whole was neither faded nor dirty, nothing to indicate it had been here long.

"This is hers," Ava said, clutching it between her breasts. "I know it."

Keira blinked away the sudden sting of tears. "Don't you remember? I sent it to her for her birthday last year."

Ava shrieked Amanda's name into the trees once, twice, a dozen times and turned to Keira, her cheeks panic-bright. "She'll come back, won't she? She'll come home?"

Every possible answer felt like a lie.

~

In the middle of the night, she woke again to the crying fox. And it had to be a fox; it couldn't be anything but. She paced in her room, every breath tight and labored, as though there wasn't enough air in the world. There was no reason for her to be here anymore. Amanda was gone. She'd come back or she wouldn't, and if she didn't, Ava would have to learn to live on her own.

With an airy grunt more breath than noise, she yanked her clothes from the dresser, piling them on the foot of the bed. She'd leave Ava a note and would call in a few days, long enough for her anger to wear off.

The fox shrieked again as she unzipped her suitcase, one last peal before quiet fell. She perched on the edge of the bed, toeing the hem of a shirt that had fallen to the floor.

~

"We should walk to the stream," Ava said.

Keira leaned her weight against her walking stick. She'd known this moment would come, had known it since she pulled into the driveway, maybe even before.

"I'm not saying we should cross it—I'm not that dumb—but we can look across at least."

Keira swallowed against a lump in her throat. "There aren't even any paths. We'll end up twisting an ankle or worse."

"Yes, but we should still do it," Ava said, lifting her chin. "What if Amanda twisted *her* ankle and that's why she hasn't come back?"

"But if she's on the other side—"

"No! Don't say it, don't even think it!"

Keira bit the inside of her cheek and nodded, and they trudged toward the stream in silence. As they drew near, the air filled with the soft rushing of water and the smell of damp earth. Sweat ran down her back; the bitter taste of bile flooded her mouth. No matter the season or weather, the air always smelled of rotting vegetation, minerals, and a storm about to break. Appropriate. Horribly so.

Here, the stream was only a few feet wide and large rocks tempted an easy path. At first glance, the woods weren't much different, but there were more vines, more exposed roots twisting in coils, waiting to snag your ankle and twist your step if you dared try, more thorns, more shadows. The trees were closer together, their branches drooped lower, the leaves grew thicker. The air felt different, too. Heavier. Malevolent. As if there were a voice on the verge of speaking and hands waiting to grab.

She couldn't be here. There were too many secrets lurking in the shadows, too many things she couldn't face yet again, not even for her sister. She scraped her boot heel in the dirt, guilt flowing through her.

"If Nana were here, we could cross," Ava said. "She knew how."

A small sound caught in the back of her throat. Ava spoke true, but how could she know? Nana had said she'd never teach anyone the words that permitted safe entry and safe return.

While Ava walked the edge of the stream, Keira stayed put, trying to ignore the way the woods distorted the sound of her sister's steps, turning them from a giant's to a dwarf's and back again. Trying not to think of places where the world was wrong.

"Keira, quick, come here!" Ava shouted, pointing to a small clearing across the water.

Scattered dirt and freshly dug holes littered the clearing, a dozen of them, some the size of a teacup, others two clenched fists, and one the size of a dinner plate.

"She was here," Ava said. "She did this."

Keira swallowed several times. "You don't know that."

"Of course I do. No one else knows what we did when we were kids."

"This wouldn't have anything to do with that. We never put anything on that side of the water. We couldn't." The lie burned on her lips, but her words were even and sure.

Ava stomped through a cluster of bushes, shrieking Amanda's name in every direction. From the corner of her eye, Keira saw movement—a flash of pale, contrasting against the darker trunks, a length of hair. She spun in that direction, hand reaching for her knife as she scanned the foliage. Top to bottom, side to side. Nothing.

Ava crept to her side, close enough to breathe her question against Keira's neck.

"What is it?"

"I... I think I saw something."

"What? Where?"

"I'm not sure. It was over there, behind those trees."

"I don't see anything. Was it a something or a someone?"

"A someone, I think. I don't know, it happened so fast. Maybe it was my imagination. Maybe it wasn't anything at all."

Ava stood staff-straight, shrieking Amanda's name again and again until she dissolved into tears. "If it was her, why won't she answer? Why won't she come back?"

~

"Are you sure it was a person?" Ava said. "Are you absolutely sure?"

They were sitting on the back porch, drinking iced tea, their dirty boots lined beside the door. It had taken Keira several hours to convince Ava to leave the woods, and even then, she'd stopped every few feet, swearing she'd seen something.

"I don't know, Ava. I told you that. I think I saw dark hair and pale skin, but I'm really not sure."

"But it couldn't be her. She wouldn't go in the old woods on her own, and they didn't want her. I know they didn't."

"Maybe she didn't want to tell you."

"What do you think she was looking for in all those holes?"

"We don't even know that she's the one who dug them. It could've been an animal, most likely a squirrel."

"Do you think she found it?" Ava said, tossing the question as you would a pinch of salt.

Keira's fingernails cut half-moon indentations in her palms. There was nothing to find. Not there, anyway. Ava patted her cheek, as a mother to a child, and went inside. She watched her go, unease and suspicion coiling in her belly. The twins didn't know about that night. They didn't see what she took into the woods. They'd been asleep. She'd checked. *Nana* had checked.

They didn't know the truth, and they weren't *ever* supposed to know.

~

Ava turned in early, but Keira wandered the house, memories seeping in with every step. On the sofa in the formal living room, Nana had sat beside a four-year-old Keira and explained her mother was gone and wasn't coming back. Hidden behind a heavy curtain panel in the dining room, the scratch of her initials in the wallpaper, penned when she was six. Behind another panel, her sisters' initials, the As linked together.

Resting her forehead against the glass, she stared into the darkness. Thought of a night nine years ago when she'd crouched in the shadows of the old trees, dirt beneath her nails, tears coursing down her cheeks, apologies falling from her tongue like pine needles.

"The woods will take care of everything," Nana had said, her voice the only comfort in the darkness. "They always do. No one else needs ever know, sweet girl. She was already lost. Give her to the woods and leave her there, leave her behind you."

"But don't you hate me?"

"I could never hate you, no matter what. It was an accident, that's all. Just a mistake."

Of all the lies Keira had ever told, that one hurt most of all. And that Nana had believed it—had died believing it—was something she'd carry forever. Nana had never known about the tiny limb moving beneath the scatter of dirt that Keira'd pretended not to see.

Nana had been standing too far away, keeping watch. Though she'd spoken the words to make it safe for them to cross the stream, she'd said she didn't trust the woods not to change their mind.

If the woods had Amanda now, she was lost. Even if she came back, she was lost.

Keira exhaled a cloud on the window; as it cleared, a woman stepped out from the trees, all dirty legs and leaf-tangled hair. Keira clamped a hand over her mouth to hold in a shout, her heart a Greyhound. Her shoulders relaxed when she saw it was Amanda, because of course it couldn't be anyone else. She was watching the house, watching her sister, and then she slipped back into the trees, her movements so fluid and quick she might've been an apparition.

~

Morning dawned grey and clouded, the rain beginning even before they finished breakfast. The air was clotted with tension, and Keira's English muffin tasted like sawdust. She wanted to tell Ava she'd seen Amanda last night, but the words wouldn't come. Maybe something had happened between the sisters. Maybe there was a reason Amanda was staying away.

Ava's shoulders slumped lower and lower. "Maybe she'll come back because of the rain."

"Maybe she will."

"Unless…"

"Unless what?"

"Unless whatever she found won't let her come home."

"Ava, there's nothing out there."

"There are secrets out there. We buried hundreds of them. You remember, I know you do."

"We were kids. It was only a stupid game."

"Not always."

"What are you talking about?" she said.

"I don't know, Keira. What *am* I talking about? What else is in the woods?" Ava smiled, baring her teeth. A predatory grin.

"Whatever you think you know, you're wrong. The only things buried in the woods belong there."

The legs of her chair scraped across the floor as she pushed away from the table. Ava said nothing, simply kept smiling.

Keira took the stairs two at a time, her mouth a desert. She should never have come back. Hadn't she learned from every book and movie cautioning against it? And what did she expect? A secret that big couldn't stay secret forever, not even with all the woods in the world to hide it. Why Ava insisted on cryptic statements instead of asking for the truth outright, she didn't know and didn't care. She wasn't playing her sister's game anymore.

She changed into jeans, a sweatshirt, and her boots. Shoved her knife in her pocket and packed her suitcase, not bothering to fold anything or separate the dirty from the clean.

Downstairs, only silence greeted her, but she said, "Ava, I'm leaving. I'll call the sheriff and convince him to come and help. I have to get back home."

Dragging her suitcase by one hand, she used her other to pat her pockets. No keys. They weren't in her purse either. "Fuck," she muttered, fumbling through the suitcase contents. Nothing. Her car doors were locked, the keys nowhere in sight. She pinched the bridge of her nose. Fuck, fuck, fuck.

"Ava!"

Leaving her suitcase on the front porch, she stomped through the house to the back door and beyond, coming to a stop ten feet from the woods, ignoring the rain plastering her clothes to her skin and her hair to her cheeks.

Before she could call her sister's name, a cry knifed the air. Not a fox, but a baby's cry. She couldn't fool herself this time.

But there *was* no baby. It was dead. It had been dead for a long time. Unless there was a baby she didn't know about. Was that why Amanda ran away?

Another wail emerged from the trees, and she started back for the house.

From deep within the woods, Ava called out, "Keira, please, I need your help! Hurry!"

Keira paused, one foot on the first porch step, rain pattering off the roof onto her shoulders. This was not her problem to solve. Hadn't she done enough already? But she turned around, splashing through mud and crushing leaves, twigs, and insects alike. Ten feet inside the trees, the air turned chill. Twenty feet in, her teeth began to chatter.

The baby cried again, louder. And almost hidden by the sound, someone sang a lullaby. Ava and Amanda stepped from behind a tree, Amanda with a small, blanket-wrapped bundle in her arms. Its cries tapered down to soft, kitten-like mewls.

"We knew you wouldn't come if we told you," Ava said.

"Why didn't you tell us, Keira?" Amanda said. "Why? He started crying at night. He started crying every night, so I went out and I found him."

"We took care of him while we waited for you," Ava said.

Amanda stepped forward. Beneath the blanket, something moved. "Don't you want to hold him? Don't you want to see him, to see how the woods kept him safe for you all this time?"

Keira's legs turned to rubber, and she reached for a nearby branch for support. It couldn't be. It wasn't possible.

"Now you have to stay home," Ava said. "But we'll help you take care of him. We both will."

They both smiled, and their eyes were too bright. Like Stepford girls. Like something other. Something *wrong*. "Please. I can't."

Amanda cocked her head. "But he needs you."

They didn't understand. He wasn't her child. He never was.

She closed her eyes and in that darkness, saw her mother's body in a shallow grave, saw a tiny hand pushing against the distended abdomen, saw herself dropping in another shovelful of dirt.

What else could she have done? Cut open her belly and take the baby? She was only sixteen. And Nana was too old.

She told Nana she thought her mother was an intruder. She woke in the middle of the night to a noise downstairs, and only after she'd wielded the vase did she realize who she struck.

She didn't tell Nana what her mother said. That the woods had given her a son, a special son. That she was taking her girls back with her because the woods wanted them all to be together. Wanted them to be a family again.

She didn't tell Nana how her mother's eyes shone with a terrible light, how her breath reeked of rotted leaves, how her skin burned hot as a summer sun. Some secrets you kept forever, no matter what.

She did what she did to protect her sisters. To protect herself.

"Please," Ava said. "We need you."

"*He* needs you," Amanda said. "Don't you want to see how beautiful he is? Don't you want to see your baby?"

He wasn't hers, but Keira couldn't make herself speak the words aloud, so she held out her arms. His weight was that of a bundle of twigs, his smell loam and standing water. Tucking him in the crook of her arm, she slowly folded back the edge of the blanket, her fingers cold, her heart numb.

And the knife in her pocket was heavy and sharp.

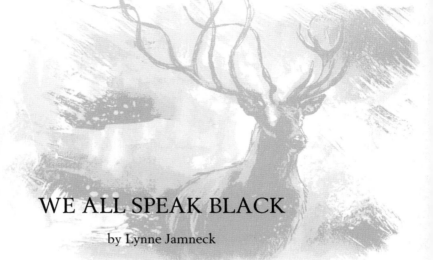

WE ALL SPEAK BLACK

by Lynne Jamneck

My parents loved me until they discovered I was different.

I blamed myself. We all did. What else do you do without answers when they're the one thing you desperately need? Shit like that haunts you, and slowly eats you inside out

Thirty years ago, Cape Town was the beautiful city in travel magazines and BBC documentaries about Nelson Mandela. Seafood, wine, the Garden Route and Lion King sunsets. But you ask Dorothy and she'll tell you it's a completely different story behind the curtain.

At the time, conservationists implored the government to better consider issues of risk management, about TEPCO ignoring the dangers of Koeberg's outdated safety systems. But as a nation we still couldn't dissolve ourselves of party politics for long enough to smell the coffee, and in the weeks leading up to the cataclysmic events of a bright October day, the amalgamated ANC and DA parties had been so neck-deep in political shit-slinging that they'd had little time to "waste listening to a bunch of crackpot conspiracists yammering about nothing".

The reactor needs to be replaced.

✓ Check.

Stress cracks render the engines vulnerable to seawater corrosion.

✓ Check.

Inspections are woefully behind schedule.

✓ Check.

Koeberg sits straight across a geological fault line.

▪ Fuck.

But what in the end rocket-blasted the lives of millions into chaotic oblivion wasn't a failing nuclear reactor – at least, not directly. People have a terrible track record when it comes to change. But eventually, as we have all seen so many times, there comes a point where finally the foot comes down. And with that resolution comes a sense of desperation to support such finality, to make it succeed at all costs. And because they were too involved in brownnosing and corruption, the partisan fat cats failed to notice that their constituents, angry and hopeless beyond reason at the lack of change, had begun bowing to altogether darker forces than those at work in parliament.

17 October 2035.

Aerial footage from the day is permanently burnt into my brain. Shot at speed from inside a helicopter by the shaky hands of an expletive-lancing cameraman, the copter's rotors *chop-cop-chopping* in the background, while the camera lens zooms in on the ground sink-holing into hell beneath Cape Town Stadium, its leviathan maw pulling half of surrounding Greenpoint into the bowels of the earth. It's an event that is only ever overshadowed by what subsequently *crawled out* of that hellhole.

How do you describe something indescribable? Well, it wasn't. Not really. It was just entirely fucking *twisted*. So many cameras, fast-focusing in on that jagged, cone-shaped cranium as it loomed ever higher into the cloud-streaked sky like some Gaudi-nightmare tower. High def. Hard to forget. Thanks for *nothing*.

The Cape Town cults summoned an outer thing they had no hope of ever understanding into a world that the thing itself didn't understand either. Regardless, their vile bastardization of foreign spells had weaved for it an accessible narrative into our reality, one it was able to traverse like a spider's web into whatever direction it pleased. The cults never really considered what would happen *after*. Consequences were always the last thing on anyone's mind. They were no different from the goddamn politicians.

So when the Goliath miscreation finally pulled itself completely out of the ground the resulting shockwaves caused an earthquake the likes of which we marvelled at on Saturday nights watching disaster movies, which in turn commenced a tsunami from the converging Indian and Atlantic oceans, a wave seven storeys high that slammed full force into Koeberg before ruthlessly driving itself inland, flattening Melkbosstrand and an assemblage of non-suspecting villages along the coast.

I only recall flashes: shocked journalists and mobile phone footage of a void-carrying segmented mass, indiscriminately devouring both civilians and cultists, even as they chanted, "Xa ithe yazaliseka iminyaka eliwaka, ubudala eyona wokhululwa entolongweni yakhe".

When the thousand years are expired, the Old One shall be loosed out of his prison.

Ja, the Bible is always the first thing people quote when shit like this goes down. But everyone quickly realised that any notions we had of 'god' had been wholly misinformed. Eventually, that thing crawled back into its hole, trailing annihilation and human detritus in its wake. Then the government skulked out of *its* hole where it had been hiding the entire time and began evacuating people out of the greater Cape Town area. And as a bonus, because maybe they thought people didn't realise it yet, they also blessed us with an official announcement: "Koeberg has gone into meltdown."

Fucking no shit.

You know, the worst thing was that most people had nowhere else to go. *Fok*, thousands had already been homeless before all of this happened. Meanwhile, the army was at a dearth to deal with the aftermath, logistically and psychologically. They rounded people up in a collective-hive-daze; a few went the other way and got trigger happy. It seemed that when the thing disappeared down its black hole it had left behind a cloud of paranoia that affected some worse than others. I'll never be able to forget it. It fucking haunts me.

You want to know how many people lost it when the dust finally settled and they saw Table Mountain split straight in two? That was the *coup de grâce* to what would quickly be labelled Judgement Day, because of course it would. Half the people left alive in the Mother City went cuckoo for Cocoa Puffs at the sight.

My parents were among those who stayed. My maternal grandparents were dead and my father's lived in Jozi, but they'd barely spoken to their eldest since he married my mother. Not good enough for him or some shit. Cherry on the cake, not long after Judgement Day my mother discovered she was pregnant. But my father refused to let her (and presumably, himself) live in a crowded army tent under the open Karoo sky (oh yeah — where else were you going to find enough room to temporarily house two million people?). The Koeberg Event — for those less religiously inclined — happened just before the start of spring but the Karoo was sub-zero all year round and I guess my father thought he'd take his chances with the fallout rather than freeze to death. I wish he cared about me as much now as he

My parents annexed an abandoned mansion in Constantia, the previous owners having left behind a matte gold Mercedez Benz, a boat *(I Like Big Boats and I Cannot Lie)* and a house filled with luxury furniture that was now worth nothing in the rush to outrun the nuclear fumes. Our family had never been rich, and though the city became more like Thunderdome in the wake of D-day than a haven for tourists, at least inside that repurposed house, for a few years, I'd been a happy kid.

You might think I sound flippant about all of this. I know a lot of people died and not only from radiation poisoning. Once the sea retreated there were bodies everywhere. It took time to get rid of them all. People got sick. The monster-door in the ground had swallowed thousands. And houses, shacks, cars, bridges, entire freeways — all absorbed into the earth's innards as if by some chthonic beast.

Strange thing was, many women besides my mother found themselves pregnant not long after all of this metaphysical ataxia. The scientists put it down to stress, seeing all those people die — quick, we gotto make more! I don't know. People talked about women in particular experiencing trance-like states for extended periods after, some of them talking shit about carrying god's babies. Whatever the truth, I grew up alongside a lot of kids who ended up hating their parents, and for good reason.

All children born in the five years preceding the Koeberg Event and for one year thereafter began having visions once they turned twenty-five. They called it the six-year-string. Some of the newborns – it's not something I like talking about. I sometimes volunteered at Tygerberg after they relocated it closer to the city centre. Some of those babies had terrible deformities. Occasionally they survived, but for the most part, their parents – or others – made sure they didn't. I eventually stopped going to the hospital. I couldn't reconcile believing that everyone had a right to life and thinking what kind of life such an existence would entail.

I also learned to avoid the beaches. You can only see crab-scuttling humanoids – some as young as four or five – skittering and chittering disproportionately toward the shoreline before you stop sleeping altogether.

My own visions started almost five years ago to the day. They're violent and may slowly be killing me. I have no idea what they mean; they make very little sense. Shapes and shadows coalescing but never showing me anything I understand. Every night I wake up screaming, convinced I'm dying. And my parents became afraid of me. They, who had made deals with some cack-dimension-entity, and then began to look at me like I was sussing them for tomorrow morning's breakfast. They left one night while I was sleeping. The other provinces in the country want nothing to do with us. They call us the forgotten children and believe me, they work hard at doing their best to forget.

~

It's peak summer now, the beginning of February. Mooching alongside the stone wall of the Castle of Good Hope, I hear the gleeful shrieks of children. They're playing soccer in the old prison yard, passing a raggedy ball skilfully from one bare foot to another. Someone had glued hand-drawn posters on the castle wall: "Yi! SAVE US FROM OBLIVION."

I'm heading to the central library. The government does its best to straddle the line between caring for the Cape Town communities and forgetting we exist. They still regularly send books (everywhere else has upgraded to digital libraries) but electricity and Internet are sketchy at best. Maybe, if the fucking cultists had shown some respect for the written word, none of this would have happened.

The library is comparatively safe. The real vandals don't give a shit about literature and there is enough radioactive garbage out on the streets to make bonfires with. Junkies scared no-one anymore because that's another thing the government sends lots of: drugs. A lot of those who had visions bombarded their brain-soup with some serious chemicals to suppress them, or if that didn't work, to forget them as quickly as possible. Give them access to blitzing themselves into a stupor and they had no impetus to complain. Sometimes they tripped out in the library because for the most part, it remained a place of solace.

I'm not much for drugs but surrounded by books, I feel safe. I have bad anxiety, awful panic attacks; the distraction that words provide diverts my attention. Also, Cape Town Central was the only one among 102 libraries in the area that stocked books in all of the country's 11 official languages. My Xhosa needed work. I've always wanted to learn Swedish.

It was Saturday and the warm morning already had the feel of a protracted yawn. My mood had been vile lately, an indication of (a) an impending anxiety attack or (b) worse, the goddamned visions. Buttressed between two rows of books, I was thumbing a *Don Quixote* when a clamour disturbed my peace. It came from the opposite end of the room where once a coterie of librarians had conversed in secret languages behind a heavy oak counter. Nowadays it was strictly self-checkout.

I wasn't scared but knew how to be careful. Quietly I made my way along the shelves, head down. *Thump* and another *thump*-smash. It was coming from behind the next row of books. Carefully, I peered round the corner of the shelf.

She was dressed in tatty jeans and a short-sleeved shirt, dark hair almost on her shoulders, which were broader than most and accentuated how tall she was. She stared intently at the books in front of her. Lying face down on the floor were several books, their pages awkwardly splayed, spines jutting. She yanked another one off the shelf and pitched it behind her into the air, not caring to look as it came back down in a mess.

"Oi!"

Well, what the fuck, I thought soon as the word left my mouth. For all I knew she was high on *tik* or whatever they sold down on the wharf these days. Some people quickly built up a tolerance to the government drugs and got hungry for the hard stuff.

She looked at me, evidently like I'd disturbed something important.

"What those books ever do to you?"

Her brow creased and I expected her to yell at me. But she only made some kind of snake noise and stalked off, disappearing into the dimness of a stairwell. *Yeah, sod off.* I collected the books from the floor and shelved them. One of the titles was *Ancient Religion in Modern Times*. Everybody was angry at something.

The sudden jolt of adrenalin in my body had nowhere to go, making me feel tired. I lay down on the well-worn carpet and tracked a steady ray of dust motes. In the street outside, someone or something howled.

When I opened my eyes there was no carpet, no books, and no library. I'm unsure there was a floor. There was definitely no roof, only a compellingly disturbing vacuum spitting forth churning stars harbouring seemingly treacherous intentions.

The image transmuted. I was standing on a beach. Cape Agulhas, maybe. There was a lighthouse, red and white against a blue sky, its oversized light oscillating a repetitive warning.

Something moved beyond, in the water, behind a swell of oversized waves. Whales? I looked down and saw my naked legs dangling in shadowy green water that fathomed into infinity. A vast shadow undulated below me, came into focus and it was *not a whale at all*. Grotesquely bloated, it began surfacing, blooming in size. Now I was in the water entirely, frantically treading. I turned to look behind me, hoping to see the lighthouse, to be back on *Cabo das Agulhas*, the Cape of Needles – anywhere but in that unbearably deep water and that *whatever-thing* rising below my useless legs. The burning stars spat into the sky again and –

nightime –

the heavens whispered and the ground shook. The water tilted and the ocean rose.

The leviathan dweller

– the fear of being swallowed intact, heart hammering as the seawater itself begins writhing, a living liquescent mass —

thflthkh'ngha! –

"Stop! You're ok. It's not real."

Instinctively I thrashed, smashed the back of my hand hard against a bookshelf and screech-swallowed obscenely. But at least I recognised her, from earlier. I shirked to avoid her touching me and in doing so amplified a rough onset of dizziness. "Shit, I think I'm gonna puke."

~

The joke went that the Victoria and Alfred Waterfront had changed for the better after the Koeberg Event. The once la-di-da retail stores had been ambushed by forgotten children who were now forgotten adults, the old shops converted into trading posts. Sometimes they stocked luxuries (Ricoffy and Nederburgh Pinotage) but mostly the essentials – bread, eggs, milk and tobacco. Nobody ever sold fish anymore and not because of radiation but because of the bizarre vulgarities that frequently washed out on beaches. *Don't eat the surf, stick to the turf.*

Most greens were grown hydroponically to avoid radiation but harvesting success could be sporadic. The government had once shipped containers full of clean soil into the harbour but this had tapered off eventually and now almost never happened. As for R&R, most people home-brewed their own beer and a small conglomerate out in Greenpoint grew *ganja* which, to their credit, they sold at an affordable price.

Outside the library I laughed out loud when I saw Astrid had a car, and not only that, one that could actually be driven somewhere. A Toyota, beige like day-old dog shit.

She drove. I asked her about petrol.

"Know a guy who makes his own biofuel. I trade him for *ganja*. He lives outside Stellenbosch, on a farm close to the old Spier wine estate. He doesn't have visions but he's paranoid as hell about driving to the city. I go out there once a month."

"I don't think I've left the city since—"

"I have to. It gets to me. Remember how white the cloth of cloud on Table Mountain used to be? Now it's just a patchy rag of smog and nuclear pollution. They're back to running the coal factories twenty-four-seven."

"How long have you sold trinkets at the waterfront?"

Astrid scowled. "They're not trinkets, and I don't sell them."

"Trade, okay? Sorry. I've seen one too many sangommas throw bones trying to figure out what the hell happened and why."

The scowl turned into a smirk. "They're not gonna get anywhere if they keep talking to the wrong ancestors."

I had no idea what she meant. Astrid bounded the eleventy-billionth circle in so many seconds navigating to the waterfront parking lot. The abandoned IMAX loomed on the left side of the road next to an Audi showroom. The shattered display windows revealed once brand new cars static under layers of dust and rainbow graffiti. I closed my eyes but the scorched, spitting stars burned there. I would be trying to stave off sleep tonight. "I've heard it's difficult to get a spot out here to trade."

"Should tell you something about the kind of trinkets I trade."

"Why were you angry, back in the library?"

"I was looking for answers. *Fok*, but it's hot in this car."

I got the hint, kept quiet. Astrid segued into the sprawling parking lot, the cracked asphalt deserted save for a hodgepodge of long-abandoned cars, their metal skeletons corroded by sea air.

Inside the vast shopping complex I saw no-one – "people tend to sleep during the day and trade at night" – up stairs and past a Spur steakhouse that looked empty but blasted INXS's "New Sensation" behind closed doors.

"This place is a lot less creepy when it's not packed out with hungry sales reps."

Astrid unlocked what used to be an American Swiss, the front windows blocked out by refuse bags. Once inside and the door locked she flicked a light switch; fluorescents sputtered and the walls came alive with objects and static entities pitching shadows that instinctively made me recoil. Masks gaped hollowly, eyes staring like flailing fish. Amulets of bone warned dangerously beneath the stark light and tentacled idols seemed intent on reaching out.

Other things too that bore a disjointed, eerie resemblance to that thing the cultists coaxed from within the earth.

"Where'd you get this stuff?"

"Contacts on cargo ships. From Pacific islands, mostly, some from Hawaii."

Entirely possible, since 99% of what happened in the harbour was illegal. Astrid took an unlabelled bottle from what might once have been a bedside table, its content impressively clear. Could have been turps for all I knew. She unscrewed the bottle top, poured and offered me a plastic cup.

"It's clean."

The booze or the cup? "I don't care."

The sun was almost below the horizon. For the past hour I'd been aware that I'd allowed myself into a situation where I was entirely at the mercy of someone I didn't know from the proverbial soap. *Stupid.* Okay, she was nice to look at and all but again – stupid. Was that all it took these days for me to shrug and say "yeah whatever" when she asked how long it's been since I'd seen the view from Quay 4?

Because you're stupid or because she's attractive?

"Bend your legs. I don't bite."

"That's all good but I'm not so sure about all these other things on your walls." I pulled a Black Label beer crate from against the wall. Above it hung a woodcarving resembling an anorexic Slenderman. The clear liquid in the cup was gin, I assumed, because that's what it tasted like.

"You don't talk much."

"I'm scared you'll hiss at me again."

"I have a temper. Sorry. It's a character flaw."

"Do you have visions?"

"I don't. But I used to be police force so maybe, the anger, you know?" She raised her orange Tupperware cup: "Fuck the government."

"Why'd you really bring me here? I mean, Quay 4 is great and all but these days it mostly smells like seagull shit and brine."

"Your eyes rolling back in your head like that, in the library. You looked ready to start foaming at the mouth."

"Concern for someone else's well-being? That's novel." I gulped the rest of the gin and stood up too fast, wobbly. Then I remembered: *you have nowhere to go.*

"You're wound tighter than a minister's wife."

"Wow, okay. I hope you've had fun, because I'm off."

"Don't be stupid. It'll be pitch black soon."

"Probably better than sticking around."

"Come on—"

"It's not your fault."

"It's a good six or seven k's back to the city in the dark. You really want to risk that?"

"It's been great."

And despite the bitch-quip parting shot Astrid still came after me, which turned out to be a good thing because halfway to the door reality buckled like your sense of self on a bad acid trip and I was sure those heaving, scorching stars had conquered my eye sockets for good and were letting in the grotesqueries on Astrid's shop walls. As if obliged by some resolute but entirely obscure force I felt myself tilting, losing all sense of measure and being… and when I fell I did so without ever feeling the ground beneath me.

~

I came to slowly in a moving car. Astrid's car, in which the mustard-coloured seat coverings was as much of an affront as the dog-scat exterior. "What the sh—". But moving made my head hurt. I tried in vain to squint away the sun.

"Thought you were a goner there for a second. Couldn't wake you. Had to carry you all the way out to the car. *And* I had to bring the car closer, which was a bitch because there's a fucking mountain pile of rubble by the east entrance—"

"This isn't the city." We drove past row upon row of withered grapevines recoiling under the blazing sun, then past a graffiti'd road sign that had once read "Morgenster" but now snarled FUCK PROGRESS.

Astrid laughed – *at the sign*, I hoped – wondering if she found my discomfort funny. *Hasn't she gone out of her way to look after you?* I hated being taken care of. Maybe she had ulterior motives. Maybe she was going to sacrifice me to some fungus out here in the *boendoes*.

"Remember my buddy who trades me biofuel for weed? Spoke to him last night, after you dropped on me like a sack of potatoes."

I slowly got myself upright in the passenger seat, wincing at a nasty twinge in my neck. The road was now lined by uncharacteristically green trees.

"Klaas knows a lot about what happened. He told me to bring you to him."

"Bring me to him? Please tell me this guy isn't some whack job with an online degree in schizoid physics."

"When you passed out last night, you talked blackspeak."

"What? That's impossible. Even the cultists hardly speak it. Well, they obviously speak some, but not very well. I like to think they had no clue what they were saying, because otherwise they may have thought twice about what they did. Whatever I said was probably gibberish. Trust me, it's been known to happen."

"Was that a garbled attempt at self-effacement?"

"No, the sun is making me delirious."

"Uh-huh." Astrid shifted gear while giving me some serious side-eye and I wished she'd keep her eyes on the road. All at once, the car felt too small.

Rest of the drive we didn't talk much. When Astrid drove past what was left of the Spier wine estate I amused myself by taking in small details. The window was down only halfway because the southeaster was throwing a tanty, lashing at everything like an overly tired five-year-old.

There used to be a cheetah rehabilitation centre somewhere close-by. After the Koeberg Event there were reports that the big cats — seven of them at the time — had escaped their enclosures. Apparently, nuclear fallout had mutated them into things you really wanted to avoid at all costs. Local legend claimed they roamed the roads between Somerset-West and Stellenbosch, stalking meals of the two-legged variety. Similar stories have grown arms, legs, tails and horns about the animals once kept at Cape Town Zoo. Of course, no-one has ever seen any of this first-hand, but I guess we needed new myths to replace the old ones.

~

Halfway between the big Cape Dutch house and the end of the driveway, a Golden Retriever eyed up the Toyota, tail wagging as the car slowly scuttled forward on loose-gravel. Unlike the mangy wild dogs that roamed the city streets, the dog was obviously well-cared for; its sociable demeanour induced a pang of nostalgia that I permitted for only seconds before mentally kicking myself in the head.

Chaos. Nuclear fallout. Mutated man-eating cheetahs.

Once out of the car I instantly recognised the silence. Mary and Joseph, such beautiful quiet. Except for the dog's short yelps of excitement and animated ministrations as it weaved between Astrid's legs, the air related nothing but heat and a blessed sense of peace. Even the wind had miraculously died down to no more than a puff and flurry, creating hushed whispers among the poplars padding the driveway on both sides. The dog trotted around the front of the car to suss me out and I stooped to give it a good scratch.

"*Sawubona!*" A tall man, broad smile, with obsidian skin waved at us from the open front door. Astrid beckoned me; the dog followed.

The black man wasn't Klaas but his boyfriend, Mthandeni. A Zulu, he was a big man, chiselled and prone to easy smiles. When he took my hand in a traditional African shake of friendship the sense of peace was further solidified.

Mthandeni ("Just Thande" — big smile) led us through the front of the house into the kitchen where he'd been baking fresh bread. I joked: *where are all the nice Zulu girls who do the same for their girlfriends?*

"They've left this place, *sisi*. Back to their roots. They're not waiting for the government to take care of them. Neither should you."

"Who said I was." But I wondered: maybe I had been?

Klaas was an Afrikaans *boertjie* who reminded me of rugby players back in the day when worrying about whether the Springboks would qualify for the World Cup had been a national priority. A mop of dirty blonde hair and a neck like an ox, Klaas was a full head shorter than Thande, but obviously also used to physical grind. I wondered how long the two men had been out here on their own.

Red wine that Klaas brought up from the cellar helped us to break down social barriers while we ate. Also, cold beer with steak and *boerewors*, the latter essentially impossible to get your hands on in the city. Another tick of nostalgia, all too suddenly ruined by the memory of my parents. I washed the bitter taste down with rapidly warming beer.

Later still, sitting on the solid dry ground around a fire with the open sky respiring above us and my tongue loosened by alcohol, I gambled: "So, the elephant in the room," – everyone laughed at that because we were outside – "apparently, I blackspeached after passing out in Astrid's shop last night."

Klaas was sitting between his boyfriend's legs, leaning against Thande's chest. "When you have visions, what do you usually see?"

It was kind of a no-no to ask someone that because talking about visions was like admitting that you had a kind of tumour; one that didn't show itself but instead haunted the nebulous highways of your subconscious. But since yesterday, since Astrid and what I grudgingly continued to recognise as her having done me a real solid instead of leaving me on that well-worn library carpet, qualms about discussing my visions had seemingly slipped away unnoticed. Or maybe I just didn't care talking about them here. "They used to be nothing. Shadows and flashes, mostly. Obscurities I couldn't clarify. That changed yesterday. I saw burning stars. I saw the ocean and things trying to rise out of it."

Thande: "No-one has ever seen the stars. You're the first."

Klaas: "Thande's an *inyanga*. He talks to the ancestors." Klaas turned his head to look at the man behind him. "Our real ancestors. But he's shy about it, so I thought I'd let you know in advance."

"You mean the Elder Gods?"

My cynicism must have been obvious. Klaas smiled around his beer bottle. "*Ja* Astrid, I can see why you like her." He tipped the bottle and drained the dregs then leaned forward to nudge the fire with a stick, sending a wave of sparks into the night sky. "You know, after the ginormous fuck-up that was Koeberg, the cultists all conveniently began suffering from collective amnesia. So much shit shovelled under the rug because many of them were rich and the government needed their money. And you know – or maybe you don't – that thing they called here? It wanted to talk to them. They'd called it after all. But the reality of what they'd done sent those people's tiny brains freewheeling off their collective axes. That's why the damned thing started drinking people left right and centre. It thought it could absorb a sense of *humanness*, maybe that way it could understand what the cultists wanted."

The notion sank in while the fire cracked. Thande: "Nyarlathotepi, he has been waiting for someone to see his stars." The Zulu's dark eyes held mine. "The chaosman wants to talk to you, *sisi.*"

Sometime later, when the fire died and it became cold we went back inside the house. I'd had no idea. I thought everyone's visions were the same. Of course, I thought, *Why me?* And true to form, some smart-ass piped up in the back of my head – *Why not?*

On a well-worn couch in an enormous lounge, Astrid and I waited. Klaas and Thande had asked us to. They were somewhere around the back of the house, doing something I wasn't sure I wanted to think about. The rational part of my brain was trying to help: *He meant metaphorically; some African new age* ubuntu; *they probably want you to pray with them; didn't a lot of hippies live out here?*

"Where do you think they are now," Astrid asked, "the people who used to live here?"

"Who knows and who cares. Locked away behind a six-foot wall in Sandton, probably. Bankrupting their insurance provider."

"It's okay. I'd be scared, too."

I didn't want to get into an argument. I was enjoying it out here, away from the city. Even with people I hardly knew, on a once-thriving vineyard that had been abandoned and repossessed by a *boertjie* and his Zulu boyfriend, it felt like the most normal thing in the world.

Astrid's phone twittered. "They're ready. Come on." I followed her back into the night. The sky above remained clear, starlight bleeding down.

I followed Astrid toward the glow of the garage light. At the same time, I felt my sense of perception shift. Some finespun shade rippled at my peripheral vision, trying to break through. A few feet out front, Astrid's bodyline shifted and coalesced; for a preternatural pulse, I thought – *we're everywhere* – before reality cohered again.

The bright garage light bled down on our small group of four.

"You okay?" Klaas asked.

"I think so".

Klaas gave Thande the subtlest of nods and the Zulu raised his arms high in the air. "*Ia! Ia! Gnaiih hupadgh tag shogg, nog!*"

Reality cracked.

A sticky coldness fingered itself into my bones while space puckered into a vacuum that grew into a maelstrom, a frenzied vortex that sucked time, existence, *everything* into the small space of the garage. In the eye of the storm I felt nothing; beyond, in the indistinct distance were three figures, one very tall, his arms in the air, frozen in a gesture of supplication.

The walls collapsed to make way for transcendent darkness. It slithered itself into a wave, riding the spiralling vortex like some bizarre fairground attraction, coming closer, obliterating the three ill-defined figures. The scorched stars began falling, a mesh of lancing light that pooled until there were only two colossal spheres of blazing gas rising in the air to reach a disturbingly familiar height. Then sounded the rising chafe and clamour of tone-deaf piping flutes to announce the chaosman, mounting like leviathan, eyes roiling hot light that swallowed everything —

His eyes are like a flame of fire...
and on his head are many diadems...
and he has a true name written that no one knows but himself—

Look away, look away, look away—

Screeching anechoics invaded the soft tissue inside my skull and gave rise to a string of loops and shrieks that, despite still breathing, I thought for a second had shattered every bone and soft bubble in my body.

—*Inqlath, lughnaqh, morbidnagth—*

From within the void came Thande's voice:

::Nyarlabhokop, the Mouth of Nyarlathotep::

—*Hlugh..gof'nn* —

::starchild. speak::

My lips formed the words as if I'd been contemplating them for millennia. "Why did you do this to us?"

::*They* did this to you::

"Then why are you punishing us?"

::Punishment is power::

"It's killing us."

::You kill yourselves::

"We're scared."

::Only one to listen::

"Do you mean me?"

::You listen::

"Listen to what?"

::You are here::

"What do I tell the others?"

The darkness climbed inside me and I was sealed within those burning stars. And Nyarlabhokop, Mouth of Nyarlathotep, talked straight into my brain, nattered and chattered words that stung like a thousand needles, susurrating a secret message.

~

We found the causeway on a donkey-dirt road between the rubble of Koeberg and what used to be Duynefontein. Just like that night on Klaas and Thande's farm, reality folded as I approached, and for an unhinged instance, the star-eyes opened again inside me.

The portal at the end of the road was a live canvas. Astrid, Klaas and Thande watched as I touched it, fingers moving across the rippling surface, images flowering in their wake. Vivid representations of my will.

—*R'luh phlegeth .. sgn'wahl .. pflughshug, gintrghhal*—
Who sees the stars and do not turn have learned,
inside will hold the will to change, to not lie down, reject all shame
have mastered the Master
and their will shall be made flesh.

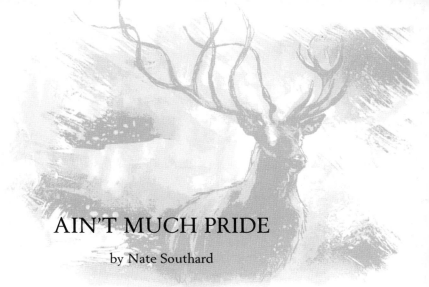

AIN'T MUCH PRIDE

by Nate Southard

U sed to be, I loved fish. Tuna, swordfish, red snapper, striped bass—if you found me a chef who knew how to cook it, I'd belly up. I'm not talking about deep frying catfish or beer-battered cod, either. Any goon can do that. Cooking a real piece of fish; that takes skill. Try to say I'm wrong, you get cuffed behind the ear. Hard.

Now? Man, I hate fish. The look, the smell, the taste. Jesus Christ. Makes me sick just to think about it. Seven months hiding out in international waters will do that to you, though. Don't matter if you're on a luxury yacht or not. No steak or pork or chicken on this floating tomb. Just fish. We eat what we got; we get more. It's like the circle of life, except with a skeleton crew, couple of girls, a looming drug trafficking charge, and so much sea food it'll grow you gills.

~

Boss Wilburn sits in one of the yacht's bigger rooms—I know crap about boats, but my guess is it's a ballroom…maybe a dining room—in one of his better suits. Months without a dry cleaner have left it smudged with salt air, but he still suits up every Thursday. Says it's important to keep things formal. He insists on formality while doing lines off Betty Numero Uno, whose name is Cynthia.

I stand in the corner, hands folded in front of my crotch like I need to piss. The 9mm is hard against my ribs, but I'm used to it.

Gregory reads him one of the latest encrypted emails. Wilburn receives one a week, no more, and he's powerful enough to afford keeping a lawyer like Gregory on board to explain all of them. Back when boredom hadn't chained him to a gold straw, he'd insisted this would keep us all safe and secure. I want a steak so bad I've been considering a Facebook account so I can display our location, maybe tag the Feds. Pretty sure they don't serve fish in prison.

"Okay, yeah, sure," Wilburn says. "Skip the pretty words and tell me what it means."

"It means the Feds aren't tossing the investigation," Gregory says. "Another month, maybe, but for right now we're staying put."

"Fine with me. Ain't it fine with you, Cindy?"

Cynthia giggles, her stomach spasming, and Wilburn holds up both hands. "Hold still, dammit! I got two lines left."

"Sorry, Baby." Her red hair lies in a perfect fan on the mahogany tabletop.

"It's good, Sugar. We all so good."

The lines disappear, and I dream of fried chicken.

~

Gregory seems an okay man, but I don't trust him. Wilburn thinks having someone like Gregory around keeps him safe. Whatever. I ain't ever met a hired hand worth trusting.

Sometimes, I wonder if Wilburn knows about Gregory and Ericka. Ericka's Betty Numero Dos, a little brunette who used to be a hostess at one of Wilburn's favorite joints. When she first climbed onboard, she did as the boss expected, meaning she, along with Cynthia, was his and his alone. That was then. Now, coke leaves Wilburn ineffective in the bedroom, and Ericka gets bored. Shit happens.

Wilburn averages a day awake followed by a day asleep, so it's not like Ericka and Gregory don't have enough time to play. Cynthia and me, we spend those hours playing *Clue*. I've gotten pretty good at it. Ain't nobody capping Mr. Body without me cracking the case.

Cynthia sighs in that bored way that tells me she doesn't have another game in her.

"Want to watch a movie?" I ask.

"I want to go home."

"You probably shouldn't tell me that."

"Yeah?"

"Yeah. I'm supposed to tell the boss that kind of thing."

"Are you going to?"

I shrug. It's as good an answer as any.

~

"What's going on?"

Wilburn sounds pissed. We tried to keep the commotion down, but I guess we cut into his latest coke binge. He stomps toward us in an open bathroom, pale belly jiggling over silk boxers. Behind him, Ericka looks both bored and worried. She wears a sheet against the sea air. White powder still marks her nose.

I stand with Gregory and Captain Ross, who smells like cheap bourbon and sweat. Not that I'm much better. If I concentrate, I can still smell Cynthia's hair, and I wonder how much longer I can keep our alone times on the movie and board game level.

"Life raft," Gregory says. "Captain spotted it about ten minutes ago."

"So what? You think I give a damn?"

"Don't worry," I say. "No survivors."

"Good. That's good."

Looking down at the yellow rubber vessel and the body it contains, I feel a quick stab of relief I won't have to off someone today. Calling the coast guard ain't an option.

Captain Ross kicks a rope ladder over the side, and I swing a leg and start down. I keep my eyes straight ahead. The ladder swings, and my knuckles rap against the ship's hull a time or two before my toe touches the raft. One more rung, and then I let go with one arm, turn so I can see what I'm working with.

He don't look like anything special. Just a guy. T-shirt and jeans. No shoes. Enough beard to tell me he shaved a day or two before he started drifting. His skin is so burned it's blistered, and his lips are pale, desiccated things. I don't like the look in his dead, open eyes. There's fear there. Terror, but not the look of someone who's afraid to die. I've seen that enough to know this is something else. Whatever it was, he thought it was a whole lot worse than just dying.

The press of a button pops my switchblade. I lean down to stab the raft a few times, send it all sinking, but then something catches my eye. Metal glinting under the burning sky. A chain hangs from the dead man's neck, and tracing its path leads to a strange bulge under his shirt.

"What are you waiting for?" Boss Wilburn asks. "Sink the prick!" His voice rides a line of irritation. Probably because he has other lines waiting back in his cabin. The chain tugs at my attention, though.

"He's got something on him," I say.

"Like I give a shit."

I watch Wilburn disappear from my sight, and then I get back to work. With two fingers, I thread the chain around his neck until I find the clasp. A few seconds of clumsy pinching unhooks the works, and then I pull everything free.

The medallion attached to the chain sure as hell ain't what I expected. As I inspect it, the sound of the ocean against the yacht's hull recedes, a strange, heavy silence replacing it. I feel lost, floating, the world melting away for a second as I look closer. It's made of a dark metal, maybe iron or pewter, and looks like a crazy hybrid of a bat and a shark. Wings folded back, the thing's head is bullet-shaped, mouth pulled back to reveal teeth like needles. A line of three green gems—emeralds, maybe—creates a strange row of eyes. I ain't a jewel guy, but I can see why Mr. Corpse didn't want to part with his little bauble. What I can't figure out is why it both feels and sounds like I'm in a vacuum.

When I stuff the amulet into my pocket, the world returns in a sudden rush. Interesting. Maybe I should take that as a bad sign, but I don't spend a lot of time considering it. Mostly, I want off the damn ladder, so I give the raft a quartet of quick stabs and then start climbing.

I reach the deck, and Gregory wastes no time in letting me know he was watching me the entire time. "What was it?"

"What was what?"

"Whatever you pulled off the body."

"Right." I fish the medallion from my pocket, and the world pulls away again. I don't like the feeling much, so I hand it over even though I know it ain't a good idea. Gregory slips his fingers through the chain and inspects the slowly spinning amulet. His eyes narrow, appraising, and I almost ask if he feels the same thing I did, but then he slips the entire works into a pocket, and I figure it ain't a question worth asking. Let the lawyer have his jewelry. I figure I'll see it on Ericka's neck in a day or two. If Wilburn is straight enough to put two with two, Gregory will sort himself out, most likely handcuffed to something heavy and tossed over the side, services no longer required.

"I'll look into it," Gregory says. He walks away. A moment later, the bored deckhands do the same, and then I'm alone at the rail.

I look out at the ocean, the vast, slate gray thing I'm forced to call home. Goddamn international waters. Not for the first time, I spend a couple of minutes regretting every choice I've made. Then, I tuck away all of those regrets. Because they don't do a damn thing to help.

My eyes drift down, searching for any sign of the raft or its passenger, but there's nothing. Burial at sea. Better than nothing. I wonder where the man came from and how long he lasted before death took hold, but then I decide questions like that are above my paygrade.

~

A week—pretty sure it's a week, but time moves strange on the ocean—passes without seeing the medallion on Ericka, and I can't say it makes any sense. Then again, I don't see much of her or Gregory, either. Boss Wilburn don't leave his bunk a whole lot. I do my job, patrol the boat to make sure…I don't know. Something.

The sky grows dark, turning gray and then black. Five days pass without the sun appearing, the ocean getting more restless each day. White crests decorate its surface, and I feel the yacht react beneath my feet. I spend less and less time above decks, where I can see the water and the sky and the way they shift as the boat rocks. Instead, I wander the halls, listening at doors. The ship's gone isolated and strange, everyone hiding away. Cynthia talks to herself. Sometimes she sings. Boss Wilburn rants and curses and makes great snorting noises. The chorus of lust pouring from Gregory's room tells me he and Ericka don't care about discretion no more. I consider delivering a few good slaps to them both, let them know it's a lot easier than what Wilburn'll do when he finally hears, but I can't bring myself to care.

~

Ten days later, I see Ericka again. The yacht pitches back and forth as a storm batters us. I patrol below decks with a hand on the wall, breathing deep as my stomach twists. Back in her cabin, Cynthia heaves her breakfast into the toilet. I wonder if she remembers me telling her she'll feel okay once it's all up and out.

When I first see Ericka, I wonder how the stranger got on board. She looks like a different person, someone who climbed out of the sea. Her skin is the color of ashes, and her hair is soaked, plastered to her face and shoulders. She wears a soaked black T-shirt that covers her like a dress. I see wet prints where her bare feet have stepped. As she shuffles down the hallway, her eyes don't shift toward me. She mutters something I can't hear.

"You okay?" I ask. Way with people, right here.

She pays no attention. Her hands ball into fists and then shake loose again, and her head ticks to the side once, twice. I reach out, touch her shoulder, and jerk my hand back when she flinches.

"Hey." I try to keep my voice calming. "Sorry. Are you sick?"

"It won't be long now," she says. "It's almost here."

All my alarms sound at once. I squash the part of me that wants to slam her against the wall and demand answers. Instead, I touch her chin, turning her face to mine. Her skin is cold and wet, and a shudder moves through me. I pray she's just high as a kite and crazy, but she's not acting like any cokehead I've ever seen.

"Who's coming?" I ask. "Ericka, did you contact someone you shouldn't have? It's okay, just tell me so I can fix it."

She laughs. No, that's not right. What she does is open her mouth and spit a series of angry cackles in my face. She brays laughter like a threat, and I don't know whether to feel angry or frightened. Her breath smells like saltwater, and her teeth have gone black. Tongue, too.

"You don't matter," she says. "None of us do. There's something else, and it's coming, and your strong arms and big dick won't mean anything. Gregory's seen to it."

"What did he do?"

Should I ask Wilburn how he wants me to kill the lawyer or just go ahead and do it?

"He learned things. So many things. He told me some of them, but not nearly all. The Three Eye knows more than most of us can handle."

The Three Eye. I think about a trio of emeralds on a medallion of pewter or maybe iron. I think about the world shrinking away. For a terrible moment, I remember that vacuum, how it felt like I could let the entire universe vanish if I let it. Then, I remember the horrified expression on the corpse in the raft, and I wonder what The Three Eye showed him before he died.

Ericka continues down the tilting hallway, and I let her go. Other matters need my attention. I head the opposite direction, toward Gregory's cabin. Figure the best defense is a good offense. Something like that.

I smell his room before I reach it. The door hangs open, but that doesn't explain the rotten stink floating into the hall. I think of mildew and wet garbage, fish in a pail left to decompose. Awful scents form a fist with the ship's motion and slam into my gut. I double over and grit my teeth, lean against the wall as I cover my mouth and nose with both hands and fight to keep a couple days' worth of seafood in my belly. A moment passes, the boat stills some, and I manage to stand up and enter the cabin.

Gregory's trashed the place, but it ain't like any kind of tossing I've ever seen. The bed is soaked, and dark mold covers the walls and carpets, which squishes under my feet. The ceiling sags, water dripping. He's torn apart everything he can find.

Three X's mark the wall across from me, carved into wood and mold, both. Picturing them as emeralds doesn't take much imagination.

The scream is a distant sound, barely a whisper above the storm pummeling the yacht, but I hear it. Terror and pain twist and amplify it so that I can't tell from which direction it's coming or even who's making the awful noise. All I know is I need to do something.

~

Gregory's cabin and Ericka and the scream leave me spooked. I pull my 9mm and start down the hall, trying to decide if I want to check on Wilburn or Cynthia first. My paycheck tells me one answer, but something I don't like to think about tells me my *Clue* partner needs me more. She lives a deck below while my boss waits a deck above. I hesitate a second, looking up and down one of the yacht's spiral staircases, and it's probably a second too long.

"Sorry, Boss." I rush down the stairs.

No water in the hallway one deck below, and I figure that's a good sign. I almost laugh as I realize how quickly I've grown comfortable with this new, strange logic. Moving as quickly as my unsteady legs will allow, I bite down on my lip and try to bring everything back into focus. I need some kind of plan. Doesn't matter that I've never encountered a situation like this. First order of business is to make sure the scream didn't come from Cynthia. At some point, I'll have to deal with Wilburn's anger when he finds out I checked on one of the girls instead of him. I'll think of something.

Cynthia peeks out from around the corner, and something in my chest skips.

"You okay?" I ask.

"Yeah. Was that a scream?"

I lower my weapon and put a hand on her shoulder. "Don't know yet. Can you do me a favor?"

"Sure."

"Get in your bunk and lock the door. Don't let anyone in until I get back. No one. Especially Ericka. Got me?"

She nods, her eyes wet with fear. I want to kiss her but decide I've already made enough bad decisions.

Once I hear the lock click, I head back to the stairs, make it almost halfway before the storm rocks the boat hard enough to slam me against the wall. I hit one knee and stop myself before sprawling onto the carpet. When I try focusing on the end of the hallway to regain my equilibrium, something hooks my attention and pours ice water down my back. Maybe I could miss the blood if it was simply dripping, but a thin stream of crimson is a lot harder to miss. I watch it for a moment, creeping closer and hoping I can somehow attribute it to an accident but I know that won't be the case.

By the time I reach the staircase, the flow has slowed to a steady plink, pattering into the puddle of red that marks the hallway carpet. I shift to one side, raise the handgun, and follow it up the stairwell.

The deckhand lays sprawled over the staircase's center, two decks up. A ragged tear across his throat tells me his death was no accident, not some fall from the ship's most recent listing. I think of Gregory and his room and its rotten stink. An instant passes before I remember Boss Wilburn is on the same deck as the dead sailor, and I curse myself for having feelings. They never help.

~

I give the slaughtered deckhand a single glance as I step over him. Can't say the fact that he's waterlogged surprises me. The smell hovers in the air, reminds me of the fish market on Saturday mornings.

Something inside me sinks as I approach Wilburn's cabin. I know I'm too late, that I screwed up and won't like what I find, but I know I can't turn back.

A quick glance through the doorway tells me everything. Well, most. What I don't know is if Gregory cuffed him to the bedframe or if Ericka did that part. Maybe she lulled him in, made him think Betty Numero Uno was back to play. It doesn't matter. Once they shackled his wrists in steel bracelets, they went to town. The way the covers have been kicked to the floor says it hurt, but I can guess that from the ruined cavity Gregory or Ericka or both made of his torso. From the looks of it, no one bothered to sharpen the blade they used. Ragged tears line a crater of ruined flesh. The kind of butchery real world butchers are too skilled to commit. Details reveal themselves to me one after the other: the empty cavity that tells me someone took most of Wilburn's organs, the seawater that's soaked the mattress and washed the sheets pink, the keys to the cuffs discarded on the sopping carpet, the not so small pile of blow on the nightstand. What Wilburn's blood hasn't ruined, the thick sea air has turned to paste. I drag two fingers through it and suck them clean. The charge hits me moments later, chasing away the delirium as I unlock both sets of steel bracelets and pocket them.

I give Wilburn's face a final look. The expression frozen there tells me the source of the scream that got me moving in the first place.

I think about my cabin one deck below, about the over/under boomstick I call Mr. Mossberg waiting for me there. As I leave the room, I mentally run through the places where Gregory and Ericka could be hiding. I'm unemployed, so I can't go to work. War, though? I can go there all day.

~

Thunder crashes, and the waves lashing at the yacht roar from all directions. The hallway pitches back and forth, but I gather Mr. Mossberg and two pockets of shells without falling, so I figure I'm doing okay. Pretty sure the blow helps. My nervous system crackles, reflexes riding razor wire.

I check Cynthia's deck first, Mr. Mossberg's stock against my shoulder, barrels sweeping the hallway in front of me. No salt taste in the air, so I dare to dream she might be alive.

Three knocks on her door. "Cynthia. It's Mike."

The door opens, and she looks at me with fearful eyes. "What's going on?"

"Bad shit. That's…best I got. Here." I hand her the 9mm. "Safety's off, okay? Be careful. If anybody other than me gets through this door—I don't give a shit who—you shove the barrel right here." I hold the weapon against my heart. "Pull the trigger until it clicks. Understand?"

She nods.

"Tell me. Please."

"I understand."

"Good." Something flashes in her eyes, and I kiss her before I can decide it's another in a long string of bad ideas. Arms encircle me and pull me close. Her mouth tastes like a night of cigarettes and regret. Sweetest thing ever.

~

I find the rest of the crew spread across the upper decks. Looks like some of them tried to fight, but most of them show all the signs of attempted escape. Captain Ross went down especially hard, his left arm discarded a dozen feet from the rest of him. Blood and sea water leave a trail to their murderers, and I follow it with grim determination, telling myself there's nothing left to do but kill.

Gregory and Ericka sit naked in the center of the sun deck. Torrential rain batters them, but they don't appear to care. Ericka bucks on top of the lawyer, and their faces tilt toward the sky, mouths open like they're seeing God. A part of me envies them. The sort of madness that's taken hold must feel amazing. Or maybe they don't know what they're doing, too twisted on coke and boredom to realize they've slaughtered fifteen people.

Seeing the medallion around Gregory's neck erases that idea. Getting a good look at him destroys a few other theories. In his open mouth I spot teeth like rusty needles. His eyes have gone milk white. If it wasn't pissing rain, I know I'd see the saltwater pouring off him.

I think they might be speaking. Chanting. The howling wind makes it difficult to be sure. Even at the sun deck's edge, I'm soaked, but I step closer, Mr. Mossberg up and ready to roar. A touch of narcotics keeps the horror at bay, but the look of the pair fucking—the blood I see washing off their slick, gray skin—does its best to turn my knees to rubber. I move slow and steady, hoping they're too wrapped up in each other to notice me. A few more feet, and I can take off Gregory's head, no sweat.

But then he looks at me. A grin splits his face, and his eyes shine with a strange kind of pleasure. For her part, Ericka never stops, doesn't even slow. As Gregory's smile widens, I see a strange pair of slits on his neck spread open, spraying foam pink with blood. Jesus Christ, the bastard's grown gills.

"Mike!" His voice is wet. "I wondered when you'd come. You probably have questions."

I don't. What I have is a trigger, and I pull it. One barrel booms, but Gregory's too fast. He yanks Ericka into the shot's path, and I watch her back erupt even as I'm pulling the trigger again and unloading the second barrel. When Gregory tosses Ericka aside, her body is mostly pulp. A second later, she spills across the deck, nothing more than water, and the narcotics don't do a damn thing to keep me from feeling cold and wet and terrified.

"It's okay," he says. "She wasn't going to last much longer, anyway. If you're not chosen, you just fall apart."

I refuse to speak. The rain keeps me from popping the spent shells and loading two more. Instead, I back toward the yacht's interior. Gregory climbs to his feet and follows, and I struggle to keep my eyes locked on his.

"It was this," he says. One hand snakes across his chest and lifts the medallion. "The Three Eye is ancient, here long before any of us were so much as tickles in our fathers' balls. It sees everything, and it whispers things. So many things. You wouldn't believe."

The rain disappears as I make it under the roof, replaced by a fine mist that seems to be everywhere at once. Gregory closes on me, and I decide I need to act. Two spent shells hit the deck, and I fumble in my pocket, produce another pair. My hands shake, fingers numb, and I drop one of them to roll across the floor. The other goes in the under, and I start searching for a third.

"You're so worthless you don't even realize you're less than a speck. A grain of sand. An atom. Wilburn thought he was important. The Three Eye told him the truth."

I want to say he's crazy, but I'm too concerned with loading Mr. Mossberg. The yacht rocks back and forth, see-sawing in the ocean. I stumble and fight for balance, and then I have to start looking for that damn shell again. "What's happening to you?" I ask. The question tumbles past my lips before I can stop it, a direct line from brain to tongue.

He laughs, and his gills spray more pink froth across his neck and shoulders. "The Three Eye has been asleep a long time. Without an emissary, he cannot wake. I'm...we'll say especially suited for the job. He needs me, and so I became a part of him. He made me better. He made me *more*."

"So you killed Wilburn? You killed everybody?"

"They were meat. All of them. Don't you miss meat?"

"Not that much." My fingers finally close around a shell. I slide it home and snap Mr. Mossberg shut.

"That won't help."

For an eyeblink, I consider a snappy retort. Then, I pull the trigger. Twice. The first booming shot takes off Gregory's left hand, but the second sends his lungs out his back. Not as much damage as I expected. Mostly brackish water across the deck. The lawyer hits the floor, though, and I decide I'm satisfied.

I take two steps forward, lowering the shotgun, when I hear him wheeze and he sits up. Not good.

"That hurt," he says, and his voice is more garbled than before. "You dirty motherfucker."

No time to answer. I'm digging for shells again.

He makes it to one knee. Deep breaths. He rasps his hate. With his remaining hand, he makes a fist and pounds it against the deck. "Doesn't mean anything," he says. His fingers curl around the amulet and squeeze. "The Three Eye makes me more, I told you. That last guy, he was scared of it. I'm not. I keep this around my neck, and I can't die. Keep it above water, and the master comes. It'll be here soon, and it will eat whatever I leave of you. Your pretty little bitch downstairs, too."

"You, too," I say. My fingertips graze a shell, but another idea blooms.

"I'll live forever at his right hand."

"Sure. But what if I just kick the living shit out of you?"

That laugh again. He's closer. My eyes tick from his gaze to the red wreckage of his chest, the metal medallion bouncing off his ribs. "Smack talk?" he says. "The last defense of the defeated."

"Does that thing make you sound like an asshole, too?"

He bares the daggers in his mouth and charges. An icepick of fear finds the base of my spine and slows me for an instant, wrecks my great plan. I swing Mr. Mossberg, but it glances off Gregory's shoulder instead of crashing into his temple. Keeps him from hitting me like a stampeding rhino, at least. He still takes me to the floor, and I only manage to keep some of my air. My arms feel weak, but I get one against his throat and shove. He hisses and growls, clacks his teeth and sprays my face with breath that smells of brine. I feel his bare ribs against me, chipped and splintered from the twelve-gauge slug.

As much as I don't want to, I jerk upward and crunch his nose with my forehead. He howls, and black blood pours from his ruined nostrils, patters onto my face. I turn away and clamp my mouth shut as I keep digging through my pockets with my free hand.

There it is. My fingers close around steel, and I rip the handcuffs free. Gregory's rasping something at me, but it's all just static as I snap one bracelet on his wrist. He doesn't appear to notice. When I grab the wrist and shift my weight beneath him, trying to torque him to one side, he finds my shoulder with his teeth. Agony erupts as the bite sinks deep. My vision turns to white fire, and everything else disappears. I think he might be wrenching his head back and forth, trying to tear a part of me loose, but thinking is harder than hell.

Something rips free, and the pain is so sudden and searing it sends my body rigid. I scream until I choke on the air. The teeth attack again, digging deeper. My entire body spasms, useless.

When he yanks the second chunk of meat from my shoulder, I remember I don't fight fair. I look long enough to see him through a fog of pain, and then I bury my entire thumb in his eye. Gregory screeches, and I laugh despite the agony burning a path through every goddamn inch of me. He rolls away, hands clutching his face, and I get back to my feet. I kick him hard in the ribs. Just wanna enjoy myself a bit. Then, I plant a knee in the prick's spine, yank his arms back, and cuff him. Might as well be hogtied.

I check my shoulder, and it's real bad. Blood pumps out of it in a way that can't be good. Something in the wound sizzles, and I figure that's even worse.

I rear back to deliver a kick, this one right to his dome, but a sound freezes me. Something massive and deep, like a foghorn that I feel in the center of my chest. My head throbs, lights strobing in my vision as the sound comes again, turning me to look at the violent ocean.

What I see pulls me from shelter onto the sun deck. The lashing rain sends a new firebrand of agony through my wounded shoulder, but I don't make a sound. All I can do is stare at the ocean and try to keep my sanity from crumbling.

The thing on the horizon is massive, rising out of the sea like a mountain range birthed from the center of the world. Black crags split the waves, and I can only watch as they shift side to side and continue cresting. The sound comes again, a seismic roar that makes the yacht thrum beneath my feet. Everything tilts, and I realize the monstrous beast rising from the sea is changing things, displacing so much water the yacht is sliding across the ocean's surface. I want to believe it's something natural, a new land formation and not some kind of creature, but then its head breaks free of the water. Everything from my sanity to my knees goes loose and watery, and I fall to all fours, peering up as a head covered in ancient rock and growth looks to the sky with three glittering eyes and roars, turning my hearing into an electric squeal. Pain lances my skull, and I can't do anything but writhe on the deck, hugging my head with both arms and clamping my eyes shut.

It bellows again. I can't hear anymore, but I feel the cry vibrate through my bones. Maybe I'm screaming, too. I can't be sure. Nothing's real anymore.

Something hooks my thoughts, barbed point snagging hard. Something Gregory said that would have sounded mad before the entire world stopped making sense.

Keep it above water, and the master comes.

The words cycle through my head, tell me to move. I don't want to. All I want is to stay curled in a ball and hope my death doesn't hurt so much. I wish I could apologize to Cynthia, tell her I'm sorry I didn't try to stop it, but those words keep spinning, telling me there is something else I can do.

Goddammit.

I feel another roar shake every single inch of me. This time, I know I scream. I feel my throat rattle with the power of my fear. Still, I fight the rocking ship and climb to my feet. A few staggering steps, and I think I can stay upright.

Gregory is right where I left him, on his knees and bent forward, trying to stand, eye leaking onto the deck. Seven hurried paces take me to him, and the kick I deliver to his temple puts him back on his belly. He shouts something, but it don't matter. I drop a knee on his back to hold him in place and grope for the chain around his neck. He fights, thrashing under my weight, but I'm a big guy and he's got no leverage. Seconds pass between us, and then I have the chain in my hand. A quick jerk, and it snaps free.

I close my hand around the amulet before it can slide free, and the world retreats again, disappearing toward the farthest horizon. For an instant, I feel weightless, untethered, but I bite down hard on my lip and get back to work.

Four desperate, loping steps, and I hurl The Three Eye with everything I have. The grimy mass disappears first into a wall of rain and then down into gray foam. The world snaps back into place with a percussive impact, like all the air rushed back in to fill a vacuum. It slams into my chest and knocks me on my ass. My gaze moves to Gregory, thinking I should keep my eye on him, but his cheek is painted against the deck, sobs quaking through his body.

A wave crashes, only I don't think it's a wave. I think it's something massive and alien returning below the surface, chasing a medallion I found on a dead body. Returning home.

I grab everything I can, and I pray. I beg any god that's listening that the yacht won't capsize, and I plead that the monster on the horizon stays underneath the waves. If it does—if I survive—I'll find Mr. Mossberg and finish off Gregory before heading below decks to see if Cynthia's okay. If it doesn't…?

~

Everything is darkness. Pain. Time has stretched. Maybe minutes. An hour. Who knows? Not me.

Soft hands touch my cheek. When I open my eyes, will I see Cynthia?

I hope so.

THE CHOIR OF THE TUNNELS

by Matthew B. Hare

The tunnels beneath the city are easy to enter, horribly so. You wouldn't know this from the way people whisper about them, all fever-pitch, all shadowed. It seems as though the entrance should be behind gates, guarded, thrice-locked with silver. Therefore, only we broken people wander the darkness of the tunnels.

There are many reasons to go into the tunnels of the unfinished subway, though most don't go far. In the winter, the homeless population of the city migrates to the shallow outer ruins, going no farther than a yellow line half a mile into the black. The line runs from roof to the floor of the main tunnel, a clear border between the shallow ruins and the deeper places, impossibly bright in color after all these decades. No one knows who painted it.

There are artists and urban explorers who go into the tunnels in search of inspiration or raw video footage. Once I saw a man offering tours to college students. A homeless acquaintance of mine told me that last November the tour guide stumbled, shaking, out of the deep and over the yellow line without his tour group. A reeking black liquid dribbled down his chin and onto a stained brown shirt. Three of the oldest vagrants crouched over his shaking form and (said my acquaintance) calmly escorted him back into the darkness, where he disappeared forever.

I am not an artist, and I am in no way homeless. If I wanted to, you understand, I could go back to my apartment and suffer the paranoia of my neighbors or the cold mechanical drip of a nine to five job. I could easily do that, if I wanted to put up with any more wild accusations and mumbled judgments. Sometimes I lie awake and imagine it for novelty's sake. But the air of the tunnels is stale, sulfurous, and cool against my tongue; and I find the greasy dark moss that grows in patches on the concrete to be a fine pillow. Life underground suits me, and you would be surprised at how many stories one gathers. Stories can be fine company.

Still, the tunnels were—compared to the noise above—peaceful and still. Things changed when the choir came to the tunnels.

One grows familiar with the sounds of the unfinished subway—not to imply that the tunnels have just one sound, just as no city has just one sound. The subtle drip of water through the cracked concrete, the scampering of vermin, the inexplicable hum of the deeper parts beyond the yellow line...we knew them all. But on that day, everything went quieter, and so subtly that only we veterans of the tunnel knew. We felt it rubbing up against our eardrums, a sandpaper quiet. Wrong.

Shortly after the sounds changed, my acquaintance came up to me as I lay with my head on the dark moss of the underground, my skull bursting with a rotten watermelon sort of migraine. This happens to me sometimes. She could not stop looking back past the yellow and into the dark as she told me about the choir in the underground.

"I don't know how many of them I heard," she said without meeting my gaze. "There must have been twenty or thirty, all singing one song. I don't know what they were singing, I guess, but I used to be in choir. When I was a kid, I mean, in Catholic school." She paused, gathering herself. "I remember how hard it was to synchronize with the other girls. What I heard down here, it was perfect. Professional. And the song was, it was..." She stared at the point beyond the yellow line where the last light faltered. "...I don't have the words for it," she said at last. "What do you think? You've been deeper than any of us."

That's true. I'm not one for false modesty. But it's not like I go into the deeper tunnels to remember what I find there. I don't bring a source of light, and I pay no mind to my surroundings. I go with the understanding that I will probably never come back, and with a certain sense of horror that I always do.

My opinion is worthless. I told her that. She shrugged and said that she was going to go back the next day, and asked if I wanted to. My skull swelled with the sickness of the migraine, gushing pink. I raised a finger coated in rotten melon in front of her. "I'm sick. Can't you smell it?"

"I know you're sick," she said. "I'm sorry. I didn't mean to be rude."

It was okay, I told her, and I asked her to tell me what she saw.

The next day she went back without me. She did not return...but time is different underground. The others and I assumed that she had simply lost track of it.

She did not come back the next day.

Or the next.

Now, you must realize that people disappear here in the tunnels. Many people *want* to disappear. But my friend, she had never seemed like that sort, though neither of us even belonged with this crowd of outcasts.

I missed her dearly. There aren't many minds in the underground as brilliant as my own, which—pardon my disrespect—even she did not match. But she appreciated my brilliance in a way that I found endearing, like a child or a loyal dog. Besides, she understood the paranoid minds of those around us, and we had spent many nights in hushed conversation by some rotting corpse of a train discussing all of the undergrounders who were plotting against the two of us.

Realizing that the others would not be persuaded to set out, I took matters into my own hands on that third day after her disappearance. I brought with me a flashlight borrowed from a new arrival—a fool, really, who didn't yet realize the bartering power he had with a source of light down here—and a canteen. There was no need for rations. For the open-minded, every tunnel teems with delicacies.

The light made my familiar tunnels strange. In the darkness everything is texture and sound. My surroundings are limited only by imagination. By light, the tunnels are grimy and infested, a half-finished land of rats. I had no plan or direction—my friend had not provided enough information—and so I wandered these now unfamiliar places alone, listening. Watching.

Turning the light off from time to time helped me get my bearings and let me save battery power. In the darkness I couldn't be distracted by the pallid color of my own skin or the wreckage around me. All was sound, touch, and darkness.

Some time into the tunnels, I heard the singing. Not the singing of a choir, no, but the singing of a single woman alone here in the abandoned subway. Knowing the voice, I clicked on my flashlight and raced towards her ragged, dehydrated singing. She spat the notes—some half-familiar gospel tune—and they grew drier and drier till they were hardly notes, not even a melody, then, till they were nothing but coughs, sputtering, and one final wet crack.

I found her body five minutes later, suspended from an iron bar jutting out from the half-poured concrete. Numbly, I focused on that bar first, and then the cord wrapping around it, tracing it down around her neck and into her mouth.

Over and under her teeth, into the bottom of her mouth.

It was not a cord.

In the dim light I began to notice the changes. A patchwork grid of fresh scars ran across her skin, oozing something like mucous or oil. Her abdomen— I found myself hiding behind clinical language, now—was unnaturally swollen, making her limbs seem shriveled in comparison.

Her dead eyes were closed, thankfully, but that did not help too much. I could not look away from the long, blackened tongue she had wrapped around her own neck.

For a while I sat there cross-legged beneath her corpse, watching the liquid drip onto the floor, paying no mind to the toll on my flashlight. I do not have many friends down here, as I've mentioned.

I do not have any friends down here.

The bulb went dead with a brief, blinding flash just as I was reaching to turn it off, casting a wheel of fire on the tunnel walls. Her bloated silhouette burned into the back of my eyelids. I stood up and began to walk, listening for the choir of the tunnels. She had seen them. Now I needed to.

Don't believe that it was out of any sense of revenge or justice. I find both concepts equally warped. No, it was either curiosity or a sense of kinship with my gently swinging friend that drove me to keep walking. The ground underfoot went from concrete to dirt as I descended, and from dirt to stone. The sound of wind through the tunnels—no, *from the tunnels*—was unmistakable, now. It smelled of flowers and rotting teeth. The image of her body and the wheel of fire floated in my eyes against the black.

Somehow I was unsurprised when I found the green line. The yellow one above had, I'd always assumed, been something unnatural. The green line, phosphorescent and perfect over the organic stone of the tunnel, proved me correct. The walls, too, glowed a faint, barely noticeable green. They were warm, nearly living beneath my hands. Their faint illumination reflected on strange viscous fluids that ran back and forth through the tunnel ground like the slime trails of some enormous slug.

Then, for the second time, I heard singing. One voice first, a clear and bright soprano, followed by three more in a perfectly synchronized harmony that set my heart pounding and my old teeth grinding. Four, five, six, and no, it wasn't in harmony or dissonance, wasn't like anything I had heard before. It was something new, monstrous, heartbreaking. Each new voice danced around the others like autumn leaves.

When the ninth voice joined in, I was shaking. By the fourteenth I was slumping against the warm bright walls of the deep tunnels, shuddering with ecstasy, horrified by myself, my teeth digging into my tongue slightly. I watched myself from within the music.

The choir approached. I felt it through the walls against my skin, felt it rolling towards me, inhuman. I rested my eyes for a moment and saw that after-image still burned into them, of the hanged woman and the wheel of fire. When I opened them I saw the shadow of the choir on the wall.

The choir propelled itself into the dim light, and the music swelled— truly swelled, something alive and joyful. Its tongues pushed it forward up the tunnel, rolling the ball of singing flesh to me, trailing saliva. The choir of the underground paused before me, a perfect circle three times my height, its patchwork of mouths alternately singing and grinning cheerfully, drool oozing into the crevices of the tunnels. Their tongues ran up my arms, feeling me out. Between blinks I saw the image of my friend, hanged and bloated and fading from my eyelid. The spell of the music broke too late.

The tongues snaked up my neck, up my chin, over my lips. I pushed back against the wall, pushed against the music, watched the mouths twist into a patchwork of frowns. The tongues pulled my mouth open and held me, their drool running into my mouth.

This was how it had happened to her, and this is how it happened to me. Even with the first few drops of the choir's honey, I could feel the change coming like the edge of an orgasm. It is nearly here. My flesh swells with the new mouths. The tongues are unfurling. Soon all I will do is sing and smile. Perhaps the memory of my friend will disappear too...but I think not.

All of my mouths will sing dirges.

AMITY IN BLOOM

by Jessica McHugh

Ma's taken a tumble, and she's screaming for help at the bottom of the stairs.

The other kids look for me to take the lead, but I ain't budging, so they ain't budging either. We hate the yowling bitch, God's honest, but the reason most of us stay on the top step is because we know Ma's not alone down there.

The devil has roots in the cellar.

I've heard its voice my entire life. In the bowels of the dilapidated row house on Amity Street, it sings from the misshapen husk of a girl named Rose I ain't never seen. Rumors say she's hairless and limbless and red as the flames of Hell, but that's all grapevine truth. Only Ma and the men who pay to brave the dark are allowed to see the warbling wretch.

The devil's quiet now, though, and after two hours of wailing, Ma's gone quiet too.

The beastly nursemaid we call Ma raised us up, but there ain't nothing maternal about her. She runs our little house with an iron fist and dugs that sway like white flags, and the robes that hang off her massive hump make her look like a walking pile of laundry as she hobbles up and down the cellar stairs, grunting at the painful boils scattered over her body. A former bawd in her own right, Ma came to New York for a better life and don't seem at all pleased she wound up den mother to eleven bastards when the real action's in Miss Jennie's elegant boarding house across the street.

The Madam of Amity keeps no less than ten girls ranging from milky blondes to dark-skinned beauties that decorate the row house windows like drops of ink in water. The notorious guidebook known as *The Gentleman's Directory* lauds Miss Jennie's establishment as an emporium of love for which the procurer spares neither expense nor labor. French mirrors and rosewood furniture make it a palace of beauty where gentlemen are so lavished upon that a night with Miss Jennie's girl is said to possess a man forever.

Her girls are well-tended too, trimmed in glittering finery and plump as autumn sows. When Jennie's workers crave sweets, they get sweets. When they want jewels, they get jewels. And when they conceive on the job, they're given tip-top looking after.

We bastards, on the other hand, ain't treated so nice. Living a stone's throw from Miss Jennie's brothel, we're confined to our rundown quarters, forbidden to ask which big house whore squirted us into existence, forbidden to even knock on the big house door till we're sixteen.

That's tomorrow for me. One more sleep till I beg to join Miss Jennie's covey. One more sleep till I find out if I'm whoring for life or starving to death. I wish I had better choices, but that ain't the hand I got dealt, and feeling sorry for myself ain't gonna change it. Besides, a bad hand can still win the game, and no busted old bawd on the cellar floor is gonna fuck up my chances now.

"Someone's plucking the ribbon!" Bonnie shouts from her spot at the front window, and we rush to ogle the cove on the rainy stoop of the big house.

When he pulls Miss Jennie's bell, the women vanish from their windows as if tied to the chime. It reels them back from the glass, through the halls, and down the stairs to the door opening a shaft of light into the Greenwich gloom.

When the man bows, Miss Jennie Creagh consumes the glowing entryway like a candlesnuffer made flesh. She has a strange way of commanding the Amity Street shadows to lengthen, widen, and join the dark mien that oozes from her presence. Her hair hangs loose, a veil that blends into the rest of her adornments—every inch gray save for the massive rose pin at the crux of her heavers. Her body isn't bulgy like Ma's, but she looks bigger somehow, like an angry cat puffing itself up for a fight. Her face don't say "fight," though. It it says "play," and eventually, the fellow will get his chance. But not yet. Miss Jennie makes him wait—makes them *all* wait—in the shitty little house across the way.

Men with certain cravings don't like being told to wait, and they sure don't like waiting in a broken down row with bordello bastards. In short, we gotta amuse like a fuckhouse without being a fuckhouse, and the next best thing, Miss Jennie decreed, was a bonafide freak show

Not many bonafide freaks in our lot, though. We got two harelip kids and a girl with a purple pox covering half her face. We even got a girl with stumps for arms. She flaps 'em like wings and jigs around the parlor while the riflers clap and stomp and toss coins she can't never catch. But the rest of us is pure gaff. We paste oats and hair on our faces and bind each other's bodies till we don't look human—they like that, the gentlemen—but we ain't nothing compared to the headliner. What are simple monsters like us when the devil's singing in our cellar?

As the man starts over, the kids are frantic, sniveling and gnawing their nails. Ma's supposed to answer the door and lead the gentleman about the show before taking him down the devil's throat, but with her lumped at the bottom of the stairs, there's only one option.

"Call me 'Ma,'" I tell them. "Keep your heads and get gaffed like you would any other day. I'll handle the gent."

A normal girl would be shitting in her boots right now, but as I unbind my splayed fingers and remove the beginnings of my "Seal Girl" get-up, there's not a soul in New York could mistake me for being normal.

A freckled girl named Mary stands in my way, her face as tight as a tabby's ass. "We should tell Miss Jennie. She wouldn't like this."

"She'd like losing a customer less." I dig the Siamese Twin bindings out of the gaff basket and toss them at Mary's puckered gob. "You and Patty get yourselves right."

"I don't want to be a twin again. The straps bruised me up and down last time, and I don't even look like Patty. There weren't a single man who bought us sharing the same skin."

"It's not you they're buying, darling." I pinch the twelve year old's chin and sneer. "You got four years before you knock on that big house door and beg for a bed. Take that time and get agreeable, or you won't be worth more than a quick upright in the Bowery."

She pulls away, scowling. "Pinky was agreeable. She was going to be the finest gooseberry pudding in the Points, remember? I doubt agreeable's got much to do with it."

I don't want to admit the bitch is right, so I tell her to shut her bonebox and tie herself to Patty. Frankly, Pinky's dismissal is still a shock for most of us. We littles thought she'd be a natural addition to the boarding house. I helped her make the dress she wore the morning of her sixteenth birthday. It was as close as any of us would get to a coming out party, so we lived in those moments long as we could. Dressed in frill and violets and gloves she'd nicked from Lord & Taylor, she stood as prim and perfect a cotillion girl as I'd ever seen. That's how I remember her: hopeful, daring, refusing to believe she'd ever be cast into a sunrise gutter.

I've seen her since, passed her in the Bowery a year ago after her rejection. She was the breadth of a wilted cornstalk. Leaning against a barbershop, Pinky hiked her tattered dress and flashed her stained thighs at the passersby. Drawing closer, I realized she was still wearing her birthday gown. This faded violet, this would-be debutante, was a rag of her former self in long greasy sleeves and gray gloves. You wouldn't find her name in *The Gentleman's Directory*, but that didn't mean she was closed for business.

~

Pinky licked her lips as if I'd pick her out of all the star-gazers in the Bowery, then squinted at me like a moon-eyed hen. "Polly?" She stumbled toward me with a filthy grin. "That is you, ain't it? God but you're a lovely thing now." Wobbling past me into the alley, she mumbled, "I wonder how long that'll last." She crouched to piss, barely able to keep her boots out of the puddle. When she finished, she dug into a nearby pile of garbage and withdrew a half-drunk bottle of spirits. "It won't, you know," she continued with the bottle at her lips. "Whether you wind up in the boarding house or not, those looks'll leave you flat. Beauty's good for bedding, but don't expect a wedding."

"What happened to you, Pinky? Why didn't Miss Jennie take you in?"

She wiped her mouth on her sleeve, but the garment made her lips slimier. "A valuable thing, that information. You got money for it?"

"For the grocer. Ma will notice if I don't get everything on the list."

"Say someone eased it from ya. Some jilter or cross-cove on the road." When she unfolded her hand, I noticed the torn gray lace was tinged with other colors. Scabby sores on her palms had dyed the gloves pink and sickly gold. With a sigh, I covered an unsightly boil with a quarter, and when she squeezed it tight I swear claret squirted out between her knuckles.

She pocketed the coin and cast her gaze at her piss-sprinkled boots. "I don't know why she rejected me."

"You dizzy cow, I paid you!"

"I'm being square. She measured every part of me on that stoop. Out and in, she read me like a wise man reads the Bible, with worship and doubt, and declared me unworthy. But I was intact, Polly, I promise you. I was bright and clean as Sunday morning. Now look at me."

I didn't want to. The longer I stared, the more pus and grime I saw. Not just on her hands, either. There were greasy spots on her bodice, getting bigger all the while. Not blood, really. Wetter, thicker, bulging-like.

I averted my eyes, and she cackled, spitting out a wad of pink phlegm. "I don't blame you. And this ain't even the worst." She glanced side to side. "I usually hide this, but we were family once, weren't we? The lot of us gaffing and dreaming we'd be in the big house together, free and easy and set for life. Well..."

She unbuttoned her sleeve and rolled it up, inch by inch revealing a slimy arm consumed by crusty scales.

"...I ain't a gaff no more, sister."

The patches resembled wet scabs, but they weren't rooted to her skin. Thick as overgrown toenails, the revolting scales drifted through Pinky's soggy flesh like beef cracklings swimming on a sea of boiling fat. It got messier the higher she lifted the sleeve, and when she pulled it away from her armpit, boggy black meat opened in the crease like a dead cur's reeking mouth.

Her dogged stink was doubled when she parted her teeth and stuck out her tongue. It was discolored, and the surrounding flesh was peppered with sores, but the real problem hung farther back. The fleshy ball dangling down the back of her throat was riddled with glistening black pimples, and when she exhaled, the growths opened like rosebuds dribbling milk.

Swallowing hard, she wiped her eyes. "Miss Jennie saw it, whatever it is. It was peaches and cream before that—I had my foot in the door—but this thing in my throat ruined me. I ain't had nothing but shit luck since." She gazed up at me, eyes welling and hands in prayer. "Take me back with you, Polly. You can sneak me in, hide me in the cellar with the devil if needs be."

I couldn't and she knew it, but she was mad with desperation and grabbed my wrist. Black pimples appeared like spots of char on her skin and erupted with white pus when she increased her grip. Her soggy skin made it easy to pull free, but panels of her scaly flesh came with me. I fell backward and landed in her piss puddle, which was slightly less disgusting than the slimy viscera fingerprinting my wrist.

Inside, pulling free wasn't easy at all. This was a girl who taught me how to braid my hair., who once took a beating from Ma in my place. If this is what comes of a clever girl like Pinky, maybe I *should* be shitting in my boots.

She sang Rose's song as I walked away, perfectly recited as if the devil itself had hold of her wagging tongue.

~

What I wouldn't give for that song to fill the little house now. Puzzling as it's been all my life, the foreign verses and minor keys have been a comfort in times like these. As the man slogs through the mud to our front door, I pray for Rose to cry out. I pray for Ma to spring up from the cellar floor and go about her work escorting the gent. The harridan could beat me to bits for leaving her down there, and I'd thank her for every bruise as long I can go back to playing the Seal Girl.

But that's not how it goes. If prayers did fuck-all, I wouldn't need 'em right now.

The gentleman knocks, and the kids nearly jump out their gaffs. I assure them it's just another day with another sad cove, but as I twist the doorknob, my nerves stew in my belly like last week's offal.

Exhaling slowly, I open the door and greet the gent with more sing-song pluck than Ma could muster at her lushiest. The man's eyes narrow, and he scans my body. It's the first time a customer hasn't goggled me in puzzlement or revulsion—though I'm feeling both now—and he removes his top hat with a crooked grin as he enters the little house.

After nearly sixteen years, Ma's introductory speech is branded on my brain, but the words fall like dry nuggets of horse shit from my trembling lips. "Welcome, good sir, to the land between Heaven and Hell, where freaks and fancy run wild, and—"

He holds up his hand. "Save it, darling. I'm here for the devil."

It's what I'd feared. I hoped to sneak down to the cellar and take care of Ma while the gent was exploring the oddities, but as he hangs up his wet ulster overcoat and gestures for me to lead on, it's clear he's a man on a mission.

When I turn around, his hand falls upon my lower back, and he chuckles at my flinching. Raising a candelabra betrays me further with trembling fire and dashed ribbons of smoke. Looking back at the gent, I find his expression crinkled with mockery.

"Are you cold, miss? Would you care for my coat?"

"It's not the temperature that chills me, sir. I shiver from the whispers of the devil-girl beneath."

"I don't hear anything."

"You will, sir. Lowly things like me hear her whisperings, but she saves her song for you. Only a righteous man can make the devil sing like an angel, and those who defy are laid low. You may yet see the truth of it, sir, cramped on the cellar floor."

A few kids give me a thumbs up from the parlor, and I exhale so gratefully I almost lose a flame. I've never touched so much as a toe to anything below the top step—been ages since I even toyed with the idea—but down I go, orbed in candlelight on the creaking steps of Hell.

A cool, earthy breeze rushes up the stairs like a band of ghosts fleeing for safety. It snuffs one of the candle flames, and I temporarily lose my balance, bracing myself on the dry stone wall. The cellar's throat is cobwebbed and infested with insects that move too quickly for the light to identify, but halfway down, the dark gullet shocks us with illumination. Mirrored panels on either side of the staircase catch and bounce the candlelight into our eyes. Wincing, I continue on, but the man stops, staring intensely into one of the mirrors.

"Sir?"

He grunts but doesn't look at me. He trudges to the other side of the staircase and gazes into the mirror there. On each step, each wall, one by one, he looks deep into his reflection like there's something hidden in his face, just out of focus, faintly visible beneath his skin.

I'm only three steps from the bottom now, where the mirrors turn the corner and cover the cellar walls. On the ground level, I spot Ma's reflection before her actual body, limp on the floor beside a stone pedestal.

The gentleman is still several stairs up, goggling his smooth white face. While he draws closer and closer to the mirror, I shuffle to Ma.

She's flat on her back, gob hanging loose as a trout's, but she looks younger as a corpse. There's something innocent, almost apologetic, like death has ironed out the angry creases lording her forehead, scrubbed away the envious grime of her station, and left her swaddled in the soft skin of childhood that trauma so often leathers.

I wonder if she's someone's mother. I wonder if she has friends. Shit, I wonder what her real name is. And I hate myself for not wondering before.

Her eyelids look closed, but the candlelight catches a glimmer of wet ivory when I'm at her feet. I illuminate her face and peer at her exposed eyes. It's as if all color's drained from them, the pale irises barely distinguishable from her pupils.

Rose's voice rings out, and I drop the candelabra. Retrieving it, I lift the remaining flame—and so do my many reflections. In the mirrored dark, I'm surrounded by corpses and candles and the devil-girl's song, but there ain't no devil I see. It's the usual tune and the same old words, but they strike me now

like water droplets on a hot griddle, searing me so deep that when I am old—
if I am old—I'm certain Rose's song will be the last scars the worms eat.

I follow the voice to the pedestal, and to the large rosebud balanced
delicately on its stem like a spinning top. I look for the first time at "Rose," this
limbless, hairless warbling thing, red as the flames of Hell, and when I stretch
out my fingers, the petals shudder and slowly unfurl.

"Miss?" The gentleman sounds small and jittery as he descends the last
few stairs, hands outstretched and shoes scraping the floor. "Miss? What's
happening to me?"

When he enters my candlelight, I shrink back in terror. The man stands
straight as a soldier, but when he tilts his head, his facial features don't move
in conjunction. There's a delay, making a droopy porridge of his face, the skin
floating free on the bone and his voice trapped beneath until it finds an
opening in his skull.

I beg the cove to leave me alone. He don't listen, but don't come for me
neither. He goes for the rose on the pedestal, dripping with hunger and face
melting over the petals like butter on a summer stoop. The rose sings, and the
man sings, and in every mirror, dozens of faces bulge and sing out a ghostly
harmony. The rose maws wide and sprouts shiny black pimples leaking fat
pearls of milk. Mirrors and growths and lost souls sing as one, and as the cove
tilts back his head and his face slides to a wrinkled mass at his hairline, the
rose's voice twists into something I understand.

"Beauty," it says.

The man repeats the word, his voice like a trapped fart until his lips catch
up with an opening in the bone. "Yes," he wheezes. "I need beauty."

"We all do. That's why it's the hardest itch to scratch," says the damp and
undulating rose. "Everyone's fighting to get at it, but even when you get a sniff
you lose it quick. Beauty's as fickle as the sky, as poisonous as hate. It is heavier
and more addictive than any drug on earth. It is a veil, it is a villain. It binds
you up with painted lips and dark eyes and soft human skin. Whatever the
pleasing shape, our minds are death-struck with worship." The rose laughs like
music. "But it's not real. Deep down you know it, and worst of all, you also
know there's no easier gaff in the world. Beauty is an empty promise, and men
like you march into it day after day, thinking this time beauty will give you
eternal life. Do you not feel pathetic?"

He nods stiffly. "Yes, Madam."

"Would you like eternal life?"

"Yes, Madam."

"Cross the street then, darling. Give us your love, and we will give you all
you seek." The petals flex and the pimples spit. "Do we have an accord?"

He gathers his face in his hands and says, "Yes, Madam."

"Good. And bring the little bitch with you."

The man's facial features fall sluggishly back in place and he glares at me
with eyes as colorless and empty as Ma's. He latches onto my arm and smacks

the candelabra out of my hand, extinguishing the last flame. His grip is tighter in the dark. I ain't even a whore yet, and his fingers are in me, piercing and stretching my flesh like the mirrored faces and their dutiful boneboxes sucking on the words of Rose's alien song. He drags me screaming up the devil's wooden teeth and through the door where the other littles are gathered, gawking and outraged and dried up as death in their freakish masks.

They can't help me—too much risk. As the man drags me through the hall, Mary is the only one to move. With a shaky but toothy grin, she scuttles ahead of us and opens the front door.

The big house is open now too. Warm light oozes around Miss Jennie's body as she steps outside and tilts her head to the little girl across the street who dared to be a woman. I scream and struggle with the ruffian, but the ground shuts me up quick when he pushes me from the stoop. Blood bursts from my nose when I land, and pain rings through my jaw as the scars of Rose's song weeps acidic down my throat. The exquisite and horrific words that colored sixteen years of life taste like salt, inflaming my throat with squirming secrets.

The cove nicks me from the ground and drags me across the street, and no one says a word. Why would they? Even if he's fixing to kill me, what's another dead girl in the Points? The rain carries away my blood to the oblivion binding me and countless bastards with the bad fortune to be shat out on Amity. In a few months, it'll be like I never existed, and fuck me, I don't think I've ever been so relieved. To die without the burden of memory, with no one to cry for or curse me. The sun will still rise each day, men will lose their heads in opiate beauty, and Miss Jennie will greet the world as she greets me now, arms open and shadows unfurling.

Her countenance swallows us up, whisking us into a strange, crimson foyer where ceiling-length draperies closes us off from the rest of the house. Standing before the curtain, the Madam of Amity appears made of it, her dark gray trappings shifting to match her rose brooch, the drapes, and the blood still trickling from my nose. The few times I saw her from the street, she didn't look old exactly, but she didn't look this youthful. Her skin is smooth and tight as mine, and her lips are full, bright tulips breaking through a late frost. Her age ain't up for question, though. It's in her hips—the way she stands cocked with that confident grace that makes you feel like a numbskull babe pleading to suckle at her teat. She is the queen of all she surveys, and right now, she's staring twin gouges into my very soul.

The man is in the curtains searching for a slit, but he quickly gets lost and tangled and weeps for the madam's help.

She rescues the flustered gent, and in an unmistakably melodic voice says, "Move a muscle before I say so and no sweeties for you."

He clenches every muscle in his body, and her focus shoots back at me.

"You're early," she says.

I try to sniff back the blood, but my sinuses thunder with pain. Clutching my face, I moan and beg for forgiveness. "It was an accident, madam. I'm being square. I've been good and done what I was told all these years. I wouldn't dream of defying you. I want nothing more than to be one of your girls."

As she marches forward, she catches the drapes in her whirlwind, fluttering them apart with glimpses of the silky, glittering women behind the curtains. They look like royalty in their gowns and jewels, but the rose pinned to each of their chests sparkles brightest, plush and dewy, even finer than Miss Jennie's.

The man's pale eyes roll wild in his skull, and tears stream down his cheeks as he fights to remain still. Miss Jennie hums as she thumbs a tear from his cheek and presses it to her lips.

"Don't waste a drop, darling. They sure as shit won't."

The finest ladies in New York dance like flames through the drapery slits, and sweat runs heavy down the cove's brow. They blow him kisses, writhing in impatience as Miss Jennie slithers closer and plants her cheek against his.

"Would you like that, sir? For my girls to suck and fuck you dry?"

He sobs with joy and nods with his hands in prayer.

"Remove your clothes."

I've never seen someone strip off their togs so quick. He is pale and fleshy and a slobbering mess when curtains part wide. In the moments before he throws himself to the wolves, I scan the faces of my future on the other side. The women are smiling and sighing and twisting their bodies together like maypole ribbons, so much that I can't tell where one girl begins and the other ends.

Miss Jennie sifts through his belongings, pocketing the money from his billfold and an engraved silver timepiece that would feed the little house for near a month.

"You're robbing him? Aren't you afraid he'll squeal?" I ask her.

"I'm not afraid of anything," she says, tossing his clothes to the floor. "Certainly not a walking bone-on who didn't have the good sense to keep out of the devil's cellar. Then again," she says, glaring at me, "you didn't either."

"I didn't know what was down there, I swear. For God's sake, I still don't. All my life, I thought Rose was a girl. I thought she was one of us."

Jennie cradles her rose brooch as if calming a crying infant. "It is part of us, without question," she says. "Besides, no matter how you fair in this test, you will always be one of my girls." She is inches from me, standing in a way that unhinges her nonchalance. Her eyes glitter with something between fascination and sorrow, and she runs her fingers through my soggy limp hair.

"Is that what you told Pinky?"

She bats her eyelashes. "Pinky? Was that the last one?"

"You didn't even know her name?"

"I don't know yours either, dear." She tilts her head as she smirks, and shadows streak the left side of her face. There are extra decades in the darkness, more creases around the hollows, more age spots on the mounds.

"It gave me no pleasure to turn Pinky away, I promise you, but she wasn't a good fit. She was a pretty one, though. I've no doubt she made a good life for herself."

"She's rotting in the Bowery," I barked. "I saw her less than a year ago. Her skin was falling off, and she was covered in boils like the ones on that rose in the cellar. She was dying."

"I'm sorry to hear that, but I'm not sorry I dismissed her. Her insides weren't right, and I didn't want to put my healthy girls at risk."

The flapping curtains catch my attention with slits of flesh and sounds of pleasure. They're passing the man around. He is at first on my left, then tangled in a knot of women on my right, and all around me, their tongues flick out the words of the devil-girl's song.

"Do you like what you see?" Miss Jennie asks me.

"I don't know what I see."

Her hands melt over my shoulders as she draws her chest to my back, the rose brooch sticking my spine. "It is your heritage, darling. Ancient, noble, and unyielding."

"I don't understand. Who are you? Are you the devil?"

Miss Jennie throws her head back with laughter. "Oh sweetheart, the devil's a gaff like any other. God, too, if you want the truth. There are creatures more glorious and terrifying in this world than any silly little bedtime story. And you are one of them."

The man is a tent pole on which the women stretch themselves. He is a fire hydrant in which they frolic and bathe and drink until he is shrunken and husked, and they glow heavenly bright between fiery feathers of drapery.

Jennie grabs my chin with one hand, digging her fingers into my flesh and squeezing my skull like a tomato that spatters pulp and pain to every facet of my face.

"Open your mouth."

I shake my head, and her nails pierce my skin with alarming ease. I am her pin cushion. I am warm tallow in her fist.

"Open your mouth, bastard, or I'll rip your goddamn jaw off."

Tears run down my cheeks as I open wide and let the Madam of Amity inspect me like a prize heifer.

She hums as she peers into me, then releases my chin. Turning to the shadow, the decades rise to the surface of her skin again, and Miss Jennie looks her age. But where there are wrinkles, there are also scales. Where there is dimpled flesh, there are wet and drifting islands of crusted pus. And where there is one Madam of Amity, there are many—a clonal colony of women writhing in the darkness with the shriveled udder of a gentleman coiled in their serpentine bodies. They are the same cherubic nymphs they were at sixteen, but in the spaces between, they are slick with scurf, united by disease and fleshy tentacles branching throughout the big house like a hellish root system.

For years I thought the devil had roots in the cellar, but if the devil's just a gaff, so is the location of the roots. They ain't confined to the little house. They're in Miss Jennie's boarding house too. They're in the women of 17 Amity Street. And they're in me.

Pain stabs my chest, and it feels as though my racing heart will rocket through my breastbone. The agony empties my lungs, and I sink to my knees, clutching my chest like I can stop the wretched tunneling thing inside.

But it's too late. I'm in bloom.

The rosebud cracks through my sternum like it's iron but unfolds like the first flower in Eden. It's not pain that ravages me now, nor pleasure or any sensation I've felt in my little freak show life so far. It rivets my senses and deciphers the scarring on my soul. At last I understand the words. Ancient, noble, and unyielding, my heritage is the past and future of this world.

The cove appears between their fleshy trunks, and as they push him through the curtains, his virility returns. He is plump again and his eyes sparkle with color as he dresses.

"Were they to your satisfaction, sir?" Miss Jennie asks, knotting his tie.

"Better than I imagined."

"You will tell your companions about us, won't you? I love our location, but I long for expansion. Bigger houses, more boarders, all the world over."

With a bow, he says, "I'm your humble servant, Madam."

She thanks him and opens the door. A man in a tuxedo is standing in the rain, poised to pluck the ribbon when the satisfied customer exits, tipping his hat to the waiting gent.

"One moment, sir," she says." I promise it'll be worth it."

Closing the door, she fixes her sights on me and exhales heavily. "Are you ready, girl?"

"Me? I don't know how—"

"To sing? Come now, you know the words."

"Sing?"

She grasps the rose protruding from my breastbone and snaps the stem, sending bolts of nauseating grief throughout my body. Removing her rose pin reveals a cavernous tunnel in her chest. Roots snake from the opening, crisscrossing my rose and pulling my wriggling bloom into Miss Jennie's body. The flower moves under her skin, down her ribcage and legs, through her tentacles, and into the moist earth below, where I feel each stone and smell of every worm as my roots crawl under Amity, up through the pedestal, back into the cellar of the little house.

Pinning her brooch in place, she says, "You will take him to the freak show."

"No, please don't make me go back there," I plead, clutching my empty breast.

Pinning her brooch in place, she says, "You will take him to the freak show." After wiping the blood from my face, she drapes it around my shoulders and conceals the broken stem in my chest.

"You wanted to be one of us, but you let one of us die. Do you think we couldn't hear our sister screaming down there while you did nothing? She wasn't blessed with beauty like you and me, but she survived her heritage with grace and strength when your precious Pinky couldn't even manage a year."

"I said I was sorry! It was an accident!"

She smirks. "Which little house girl will say that about *you*, I wonder." Opening, the door, Miss Jennie greets the gent and apologizes.

"My ladies are eager to meet you, sir, but they require some preparation. In the meantime, please enjoy a complimentary tour of my house of human oddities across the street. In the cellar, there is a creature so rare and intoxicating, you'd swear she was sired by the devil itself."

When intrigue lights up his face, she gives me a shove. "This young woman will escort you."

He greets me with a tip of his hat. "And what might your name be, miss?" Miss Jennie squeezes my shoulder. "Call her 'Ma.'"

RED STARS / WHITE SNOW / BLACK METAL

by Fiona Maeve Geist

S he woke up feeling scummy as if even her bones were vomiting. A barbed venomous deluge hemorrhaging within the marrow. Before this inauspicious awakening, scrabbling across the hostel bathroom floor, she had been dreaming.

In her dream an immense red hart with crystalline antlers is pursued through a dark forest. The antlers grow as it courses ahead of a cankerous, pestilential boar. The boar is black and striped with inflamed buboes that burst as it stampedes, charging the hart, the woods split with its violent squeals. The hart's neck snaps under the weight of the profusion of pellucid antlers entangled with grasping branches. The boar copulates with the fallen hart— the hart's body rent from carnal rutting, births snakes as its eyes are consumed from within by maggots.

She finds the bathroom and enthusiastically falls to her knees, convulsively voiding her empty stomach. Torrents of bile evacuate her shaking body. "When did I last eat," she frantically searches for an answer. Alongside the acidic stream etching away the verdigris of grime, memories plaintively grasp for her attention.

A concrete building in a desolate field. A girl with ruby hair; her black jacket etched with white scribbles of band logos, a blue mink collar frames her face. She blew a kiss and turned away into flashing white lights. Her nape and the back of her war vest bore the same stylized pulpy maggot consuming its tail with swarming tentacles. Tall slender men with cruel sensual smiles. A furious aural assault amidst lights strobing white and red. An anachronistically opulent sports car. Being lost in a press of bodies—youthful faces screaming in the stark contrast of corpse paint. Snorting vermillion lines off of a hazy pink mirror. A black square devouring her field of vision.

She terminates the acidic convulsions and stands up to look at herself in the mirror. Pinned in the corner is a note:

THE FACTORIES OF RESURRECTION ARE IN OPERATION
"How extraordinary life without the past is
Dangerous but without penitence and memories"
69° 24' 50" N, 30° 13' 55" E
Don't be late

A card is taped next to the note. On it a nude woman with a dancer's body defiantly holds a scepter aloft astride a roaring lion rampant. She is in the center of a vortex of rainbows and lightning and outside the maelstrom: a hyena, a pig, a sphinx and a cockatrice—rendered in horrifying stark lines, absent color.

Shakily, she inventories the contents of her backpack and leaves the room. She's near the highway and the turgid rattle of the railway is somewhere nearby. She knows she parked close by but she struggles to recall how she retained this information—or how she arrived here. Soon, the city blurs around her as the engine obediently purrs; the skyline of the city—elegant, geometric starkness encompassing the ideals of a dead empire standing vigil over the transformation of the city, mouldering angels of utopian ideals never realized.

Two Weeks Earlier

Kelsey is feigning the ghost of professional interest as she absently stabs her fork into an overpriced salad while Leo Carter struggles to transcend her pique over the assignment.

"Look, plenty of people would *kill* to report on *anything* with this much potential," Leo whines, "this could even become a book, it could be what that last story never did—or should have been before you decided to fuck your entire career up."

Kelsey was famous—well *infamous*—for two things. Firstly, her story about the French Black Metal Underground; that thing in Nantes. It had everything: insinuated connections to organized crime and human trafficking, nihilistic violence, occultism, a narcissistic artiste frontman/cult leader, a barely attended show, an incident with a goat and a machete, several arrests, a cache of automatic weapons and, most importantly to her bottom line, the mystique around the split EP between *Obscene Sacraments of the Serpentine Liturgy* and *Despair of Dying Rats*. Secondly, her immense blunder in publically joking at a banquet about her married boss soliciting her and exposing himself to her—an advance she rejected to his chagrin. The humiliation of this public disclosure made him reclusive (yet still well ensconced and connected) and her a total pariah. If it wasn't for her foresight in grabbing a duffle bag full of the eponymous split to her only major piece of reportage ("Vice and Inhuman Violence") she almost certainly would not have the luxury of sharing an apartment with three other people while cycling through entry level positions and desperately trying to find any work that didn't make her imagine slashing the hollow-eyed, slack-jawed drones around her to ribbons with a machete or feeding their hands into a paper shredder or emptying magazine after magazine of hollow points into their meaningless, banal, bland fucking faces—her therapist referred to the censored-for-therapy version of this as displaced blame and poorly attributed anger over her fall-from-almost-grace-or-at-least-a-Q-score, along with worrying degrees of hostility. She was taking antidepressants. Everything was fine. She just needed a story, any story worth doing and she at least could wander around on a paltry per diem and hope a mangled clickbait version of her work would keep her out of a fucking cubicle.

Kelsey emphasizes her displeasure with a sharp stab to a stray olive, "Oh, I'm totally not becoming pigeonholed into marginal stories about *youth music*—" her eyes make a rapid orbit—"the girl who gets sent to cover the fringe stories about the intersection of wild teenagers, poor impulse control, and quote unquote satanic music—I'm flattered, and I am going to fit in so well nearing thirty."

Leo sneers politely. "Yes, I know so many people come to you with the offer of an advance and comped travel to cover anything—what was your last piece, I must have missed it?"

It was going to be this sort of exchange.

Leo continues, "Because you are a colossal fuckup—and I'll have you know Roman is a good friend of mine—and a fucking mess whose sole notable traits are writing a story about idiot teenagers dabbling in Satanism and acting like an ungrateful whore pretending that she's some starry eyed innocent; *you* are the perfect person for this unbelievable clusterfuck that seems well suited to your few scattered talents. Don't think I didn't see you looking at the menu and calculating if you can cover a meal before ordering the cheapest thing that isn't complimentary. This is covered. Eat some cake if you want. Don't talk, *listen*, think about how you are going to have a second chance you truly don't deserve. Thank me, then get the fuck out of my sight to go traipse around Europe running down some story that bleeds so profusely an idiot could make it read and make it golden."

Then, the pitch as Kelsey demolishes tiramisu along with a bottle of some garnet-colored Turkish wine that tastes like floral cassis and blackberry jam. The hook is: there is some sort of cultural revival going on in the black metal scene—which would usually be a boring mix of Nazis, Nordic Nationalism and Noise, the four N's of boilerplate black metal, sometimes with a marginally interesting garnish of church arson—only *this* was surrounded by a far more wondrous and strange set of pieces; so many that the story didn't quite fit together. And the uncanny nature of this debacle made it worth covering.

The particulars were: the "Victory Over The Sun" Tour featuring a bunch of bands that no one had ever heard of—Ancient Grudge, Carbonized Victim, Forest of Hate, Kindertotenlieder, Guttural Response, Das Lied von der Erde—each show climaxing with the performance of the titular Opera, some nonsense by the Russian Futurists—did you know there were futurists in Russia? How, no one seemed quite sure. This is weird, neglected art (with a capital A) is not really associated with dudes in corpse paint—basic literacy often isn't, let alone being conversant in their own ideology, as simple as it could be. Still, not enough to build a story on—then the juicy details come in.

Protests or financial ties or funding or association with some New Age Science-y cult into some really outre health advice that *maybe* is engaged in some sort of medical experiments through recruitment called The Mouth Of The Solar Conclave. Further involvement of some sort of secretive mystical order called the Brotherhood of the Black, Corpulent Sow... which wouldn't be a big deal if they weren't heavily involved with some sort of extreme right aristocratic political.... *Thing,* it is all very unclear as they are, apparently, secretive—unlike the historically gabby fascists the press couldn't stop quoting.... and if a team of four men in black boar masks with MP5s hadn't carved apart a visiting dignitary motorcade with a hail of gunfire in the former Soviet bloc—that is, before dragging him out to the middle of the street, dousing him in kerosene and setting him ablaze... Well they probably wouldn't be newsworthy. Who cares about what a bunch of rich, incestuous noblesse-oblige mouth off about while pretending that feudalism will return amidst blow and blowjobs from anemic cabana boys? Which led to an inquest given the "unapologetically bestial and cannibalistic nature of this criminal family" as some government official had stated off the record. Finally, there was some Amazonian gang following the heels of this. Brawling and releasing missives and laying waste like some pulpy B-Reel exploitation trash—an all women's gang with matching tattoos and some sort of pagan occult practice and they are allegedly political lesbians? It's all perplexingly ludicrous. And the Opera was... doing something. It couldn't be possibly *good*—operatic is a term used to describe metal by people who have never heard opera besides Wagner and want to give their cultural detritus a little more artistic legitimacy by lexical proximity. But there was a ragged trail following in its wake; blissed out club kids and Eurotrash ecstasy fiends rubbing shoulders with socialites and fashionistas a hair's breadth away from spikes, tremolo picking and musty, spined leather. Before categorizing the ensuing street clashes between the brutal butch aesthetic of contemporary fascism and the paramilitary response of hoodies and bedraggled bandanas all awash in a haze of teargas—law enforcement across Europe was running out of supply to meet the flaming streets' screeching demand and had been purchasing stock from the IDF—but that was business as usual... probably. Leo finally summed it up, hastily handing off this haphazard jumble of parts. "Mysteriously perverse and macabre things are afoot... now go run down the lurid details and make me not regret giving you this unwarranted second chance... the shows aren't booked it seems, they're just happenings, so make sure you find an in." He forks lukewarm salmon into his mouth and waves a dismissal. Apparently the presence of someone so odious makes his digestion recoil.

Leaving the restaurant, Kelsey half assumes this is a joke Carter is pulling on her, the whole thing is ridiculous. Then she watches the grainy CCTV footage on untranslated Belarusian news.

The video is an egregious "terms of service" violation of most video hosting services and keeps getting taken down. The provenance—at least according to the title—keeps changing: Belarus, Azerbaijan, Chechnya, Albania. So does the group, the description credits them with being anything from a resurrected Red Brigades to stormtroopers of the Glorious Dawn. Disregarding the hazy, unfocused particulars regarding the *why, where* and *who* of the clip in question. The *what* and *how* of the massacre are magnetic ... the grainy footage can't obscure the fluid motion as two figures wheel around the corner. Black military-looking gear and stubby little guns that rat-tat-tat despite the soundlessness of CCTV, the sound is somehow just palpably *there* in the granulated feed. Rapidly joined by their compatriots from a nearby alleyway, who stride into the picture with guns blazing to cut down the fleeing valet. Descending like inky porcine vultures, they converge to tear the struggling figure from the car. They drag the screaming man; his face is a terrified, twisting blur—no poor resolution can mask the frantic terror of the man's final moments. Whatever words he leaves for posterity are unknown as, almost idly, his knees are shot from behind; collapsing him into a prostrating bow before the fuel can appears. The zippo flicks. The feed temporarily whites out with the nearby blaze before it adjusts, the decaying figure at the center of the inferno the last image before the sawtoothed, insensate grin of a boar closes in on the camera and cuts the footage with a deliberate shot of black spray paint. The comments frequently contain the cryptic couplet:
The wallowing darkness of rutting pigs
Suckling at the teat of a stillborn goddess
The other terms keep turning up half-translated blog posts and rumor and hearsay that couldn't coalesce into anything sensible. Just endless hazy details and half-denials and the fringes of something vast and subterranean; an eldritch cacophony leadenly creeping back towards Russia, rumors starting in Portugal and Spain before traversing the Balkans in a purposeful, inexorable march. Stuttering, shaking handycam footage mutely witnessing the dancing lights consuming churches. Outcry and gendarmes, official statements and couched criticism. One thing is obvious: this isn't available remotely as something to be grasped but is some tenebrous revel, reel, shouting and burning announced by wild parties and street brawls. So Kelsey grasps the

thread and finds herself across the Atlantic, stuffing her hands into the worn-out pockets of her black denim vest—the sharp, white, goetic scrawls melted in alignment by lighter-touched dental floss announcing her arrival: a black sun strangled by the coils of skeletal snakes emblazoned across her back as she lights a cigarette from a black box. The ashes spiraling from her face in an entropic dance.

Things started in a blur in Lisbon—a city that was never an auspicious start, the stale air of Salazar still wafting through plazas. The imposing architecture of the city endlessly handed off between Romans, Germanic Barbarians, Moors and Crusaders. Time curled up, rotted and died here—the grandness of the environ dimmed by its static nature—everything was sterile and ageless; sharp vertical lines of cornices and columns looming over the organic shuffle of everyday life.

Hours after disembarking, Kelsey wound up smashing the black-etched expression of some spine-bedecked metalhead acid-casualty into a bar for groping her. All the while he ranted about "a Black Sun of Nothing devouring the sky." The exchange was less than pleasant but he set her on the trail. Ancona was what she was looking for; he burbled—so long as she knew what she would see.

Rushing through Portugal, into Spain; Kelsey got to survey the ashes of the wake when she hit Burgos. The stately cathedral facade blanketed with a haphazard collection of circle A's, 666, black suns, red stars—elongated downwards spike, two uneven spikes up—the acrid, sterile smell of teargas juxtaposed with the nauseating sweetness of burnt garbage. The scene report was that the city was almost empty—as if some wave swept up every malcontent youth in its wake, black-clad flotsam drawn along by the current.

The boat from Ancona to Split gave her an opportunity to compose some of her notes and down a grubby water bottle of Slivovitz with a sharpied-on black goat she bought off of some shoeless, louse-ridden street kids at a dismal, nearly empty squat. She sent her first missive to Leo before picking the trail back up.

11 Days Ago

Outside of Split she has her first breakthrough. Sliding through the silt of youth hostels and Anarchist squats: the friendly N of occupation a pictorial announcement of intent. Her hair thick with the sludge of diesel fumes—jamming econo, Moscow the end of the line, she jokes. But her entreaties are rewarded with her burner phone lighting up to inform her that the Brotherhood is very interested in her reporting and perhaps she would grace a nameless piaza in Sarajevo where the red roses bloom—the beautification testifying to death—with her presence so some statement could be offered. At least fascists never lose their hard-on for announcing their plans and theatrical staging.

Hazy sunlight somnambulantly ambles through cheap umbrellas shielding wrought iron tables—a pastoral picaresque counterpoint to the brutalist aesthetic of the environ. Juxtaposed with the harsh fields of communal concrete, their skeins scarred with red resin—the testament to shelling—like the anti shadows pinned to the walls of Hiroshima; another modern Pompeii half a world away. Across from her is a slack young man, aristocratically melting in the sun, his face permanently frozen in a sneer of childish pique. The sharpness of his petulant whine contrasts with his undulating soft hands. Sunglasses and an expensive tailored suit flowing down his gaunt form like oil coating some salted shore. While Kelsey peppers him with questions, he remains indifferent and unmoved before proffering a singular statement.

"What you have to *understand*," he emphasizes his nasality with an elaborate sip from the tiny steaming bone china's peerless Stygian depths; "is that we are a *rather exclusive* organization and we have no *inkling* of why we would be libeled with so many jealous pettifog snarls from puissant public *servants*." Bile drips down the insinuation like red wine down a razor; his voice rich like butter, reedy and with an unremarkable accent that makes Kelsey think of the mediocre Habsburg spawn mewling and fucking their way across Europe in baroque appointment with equally sequestered and vestigial organs of state. "To answer your obvious question, we are not black magicians, we don't paint our faces like Zwarte Piet and burn historical testaments to the grandeur of the Imperial Basilica. We don't dream of some jackbooted Reich grinding well-oiled Dior heels into the scum-encrusted faces of the squalid, fecund masses. We dream of the appropriate place for the ruling and the ruled, for a Europe with borders not the envenomed split of Warsaw Pact and NATO armies—let alone the ex-Nazi, ex-Stasi, ex-CIA, ex-KGB boots and braces crowd getting their dreams of reenacting Saló while *buggering* their own asses amidst the jetsom of their jizm. In short, we have *absolutely nothing* to do with some mongrel elements' dubious dabbling in the occult and overladen symbolism from *Entartete Kunst* forgotten even by the clambering, social-climbing, lisping catamites entrusted with the sanctity of the arts." He lights a cigarette with a lazy wave of his hand and the decisive click of a black zippo. "We may all put on robes and retreat to a private chalet to discuss good governance but I hardly think that is unique to Europe—although the flair for cross dressing, sodomy, the lash and sexual humiliation seems to be a distinctly Anglo-Saxon vintage that we remain inured to despite our occasional tête-à-têtes." He sits upright, a surprisingly fluid motion from repose to militaristic rigidity. "Now that we have concluded our business, I will take my leave of you," euros idly clattering on the table like provocative unanswered questions—Kelsey overcome with stillness, stunned by the casual arrogance of the proceedings. "Enjoy your stay in Europe, I'm sure you want to spend the remaining years of your looks on something far more fruitful than nosing around in the gutter after some degenerate mongrel who got chastised a bit harshly—or following a parade of malformed malcontents jaunting about to wallow in a sea of crystalline drugs and inarticulate debauch. Your problem is: there isn't a story, there is no deeper meaning, just a surface tension of disorder that will someday be rectified. Of this I am sure." He dabs his lips with a black pocket square, the jovial jowled countenance of a sow rendered in jaundiced gold on the corner. "Farewell, I doubt we will meet again." Kelsey cannot articulate a response before he vanishes into the ether—a surprisingly rapid motion for such an indulgently slothful figure.

Kelsey sits in the uncomfortable plaza chair, processing the arrogant whine that so recently washed over her. As she is reflecting, the wind becomes sharper and colder within the desolate plaza and Kelsey is gripped by an overwhelming sense of herself simultaneously being watched and isolated. A blur of carmine, cobalt and bone-white all outlined in a lurid cadmium suddenly fills Kelsey's peripheral vision. The woman grabbing her by the shoulder seems to swallow the foreground—Kelsey barely registers the sharpness of the grip or the sibilant hiss of "Do you want to die here?" as she's roughly dragged to her feet. The woman moves with languid arrogant freedom; each gesture seeming nonchalantly calculated to express her dissatisfaction with her present environ. Yet, she is tersely bustling their newly merged dyad out of the plaza; Kelsey feels magnetically pulled along in the wake. The clomping of boots somewhere between combat and fashion echo as they bolt for the nearest alley.

The alleyway is oppressive, dark and carries the unmistakable ammonia laden smell of decomposing fish. Breathlessly, Kelsey finally manages to spit out, "Who the fuck are you and why am I being accosted in an alleyway by a stranger? What the *fuck* is all this?"

"Because a silly girl wants to talk to pigs and doesn't understand that swine are quite dangerous." The barbed contempt of the rejoinder stings brusquely. "But also because a pretty girl shouldn't be cut down by the likes of them." The precipice of the alleyway breached, Kelsey can finally evaluate her captor-cum-rescuer from unknown—yet apparently lurking and immediate—danger.

Cerise hair in an angular flowing cut sits atop a defiant, pierced face with an imperious arrogant snarl. The sharp angles of her face are punctuated with piercings like industrial lines to her features. Her tapered leather vest hugs her form—sharp vertical lines declaring blasphemy and murderous intent bedeck the spaces not dedicated to spikes—the blue mink collar highlights her face. "Sophie Maximenko." Her name feels more like a command than a response, measured and clipped. "And you, my Magpie fledgling—you have fallen far from your nest without learning to take wing." Their exchange is interrupted by a dangerous sounding click as Sophie produces a slim, lethal boxy profile from within her vest and pulls back the charging handle. The gun seems almost pathetically small as Sophie unfolds a wireframe stock.

"You may want to cover your ears, even with a suppressor this will be quite loud." Her voice has that smoky quality that went out of production sometime in the 30s; it sounds as if she is arrogantly directing servants from atop a divan. Her accent itself is unplaceable but makes one think of countries where models don't have to meet minimum weight requirements.

Kelsey doesn't have time for a rejoinder. A trio of figures bound into the alleyway—the unmistakable profile of Kalashnikovs in their gloved hands—their faces obscured with latex porcine masks. There is no hesitation or exchange of words; no declaration of intent—Sophie pulls the trigger in short bursts. The air seems to vanish in a thrumming suction—vacating the alleyway and filling with the sharp report of the slim death-dealing device in Sophie's hand braced against her shoulder. The first hog in takes several rounds to his chest, twists about his axis and falls to the ground convulsing as shell casings hit the filthy asphalt in stucco simpatico with Sophie's murderous intention as she shoves Kelsey roughly behind a dumpster before crouching there herself.

The barely perceptible crunch of approaching boots carves through the ruptured screaming of the convulsing figure and the unmistakable thuk and ping of arms fire converging on the dumpster. Kelsey has become numb, drifting somewhere inside herself in the twilight of the alley. Cursing rapidly, Sophie ejects the spent magazine, shoves another in its place and adopts a feral crouch as the hogs close in.

She pulls the charging handle again—the snap seemingly causing hesitation amidst the approaching sounder. Sophie gently leans to the edge of her makeshift cover and unleashes a muted spurt of bullets; loosing the singing flower of velocity: a round blossoming with slashing petals in its wake as it penetrates the lead sow's knee before a second round from the burst finds his face through the mask. His head snaps back decisively and he keels over. His remaining compatriot backpedals frantically emptying his magazine into the dumpster until a dry click announces its finale.

Sophie drops the delicate box, produces a slim, black, angular hatchet from her jacket and runs her fleeing adversary down. Her knee smashes his groin as he doubles over vomiting into his mask and sharp repeated strikes of the hatchet nearly sever the placid, expressionless, screaming sow head. Kelsey babbles, a burble of words about the police as Sophie takes the time to pin the first downed hog's rifle to his chest with her knee and brings the oblivion of her hatchet into his forehead—tearing the mask with a sick and decisive thud that ends his frantic, scrabbling struggle amidst his pooling blood. Sophie's face is rent with sensual abandon and flecked with viscera.

"Pyewacket," she addresses Kelsey warmly, "this is no place for you." She lights a cigarette—a warm glow amidst cooling bodies—how the air is not pierced with sirens Kelsey cannot fathom, easily a hundred rounds were exchanged biting away the edges of her hearing. "Listen to me, we stand on the precipice of apocalyptic dawn."

Kelsey looks up at the white teeth sharply outlined against red lips further crimsoned with stray gore. "Me and mine? We seek to rupture the dead skin of a decaying empire and join the ecstatic void. To reject the endless ashen charnel fields of modernity and rejoice in the demolition of false idols." Sophie's pale features are flushed and feverish. "You've been asking around about me and my sisters along with poking the trotters of the decadent bourgeois hogs." Kelsey cannot find words, her mouth a strange and sandpapery tumbler incapable of pouring out speech.

Sophie continues: "We are the future, rejecting the role of women as nurturer and protector by embracing the potential of woman as destroyer—to this end we celebrate promiscuity, arson, abortion, luxury and decay. The third face of the goddess is unveiled and beckons to you." She pauses, affixing her gaze on Kelsey. "But you, my Little Magpie, let me tell you a story that is also a question: You see something sticking out of the soil and—curious sort that you are—you start pulling and it keeps coming... and coming... what do you do when you grab the thread that could unravel the world?"

Kelsey struggles to articulate her thoughts—scrambled as they are. "Don't worry Pyewacket, you'll be able to tell me all your thoughts—fate has drawn our plans into confluence; I'll be seeing you soon..." There is a meaty crack like an axe finding the core of a tree as Sophie stoops to pull her hatchet from the riven forehead. "Meet me at The Red Room. I'll see you in Budua."

Kelsey took her inarticulate response to the targets of her investigation personally. That night she crushed another bottle of burning, fragrant plum brandy she bought on the street—strains of tarragon scrabbling to break through from the withered herbs in the bottle. There was a semi-occupied squat where wild-eyed boys with tattoos of themselves standing over piles of dead cops and judges explained in halting English how the revolution rolled into town like a whirlwind. How powerful they felt throwing the fire-blossoming Molotov cocktails: fashizm— eto voina; a hand me down phrase from another war. The Wehrmacht never died, they explained, despite the inglorious splattering of the brains of the operation on a Berlin bunker wall. The CIA they said, Gladio, took Nazi intelligence officers on board to stop the leftward momentum of the post-war landscape; strangling their parents' dreams of a revolution in its crib. They wouldn't talk about the women with maggot tattoos, babbling about five vještica burned in Zagreb inevitably coming back for revenge.

They showed Kelsey how they dealt with the fascists on the way to the train—a lone drunk with a golden sow backpatch amidst the inverted crosses and spidery lines of band names. She emptied her pepper spray into his eyes after catching his attention and felt something brutal waking up while she laughed as the men took turns kicking his keening form in the ribs. She took the final round kicking the prone figure until he coughed up blood and the skeletal punks pulled her away and determined her to be a crazy fucking veštica through brandy sodden garbled English.

And so, she made her way to the luxury of Budua—a vacationing spot dripping with opulence and calcified wealth. She couldn't shake the feeling that the old world was behind her, even when she found the tooth in her pocket, torn from the mouth of a bonafide fascist, she remained nonplussed, focused, relentless.

10 Days Ago

Sophie meets her as she disembarks the last ride she's hitched—disturbingly aware of her movements. Casually hands her a plastic plate of kačamak—busies her with gulping swallows of paprika-fragrant cornmeal—as they walk the mostly comprehensible grid overseen by military fortifications exchanging rapid fire questioning; Sophie aloof, Kelsey undaunted. The Victory Over the Sun is some significant kilometers away over the horizon, but Kelsey is closing in on the march across Europe—the old money hemmed on all sides by brawling youthful screams and white lettering on solid black leather and canvas. Sophie promises this will not be a diversion but a chance to better understand the contours of the thread she is pulling at. An exclusive party of The Brotherhood of the Black, Corpulent Sow, a chance for unguarded proximity and access disguised among the crowd. They simply need to get cleaned up and dress the part, Sophie assures her absently. Their mission is protected by the relaxed arrogance of pigs sure of their element. The intentional urban planning gives way as they hike to the chaotic sprawl of the Eastern Budua field.

Their safehouse is dour, dismal, spartan concrete broken only by the staggering variety of armaments of Soviet manufacture, bladed weapons and fine clothing. The shower reminds Kelsey of the night she spent in lockup in France, but the spent grime whirling down the drain transforms her into something presentable.

The duo efficiently dress themselves before making their way into the teeming black clad throngs, spider-webbed with white scrawls. Passing through the constant ebb and flow of figures bedecked in leather, spikes, patches, tattoos intermingled with the more traditional crowd with the rarified dignity of opulent ghosts.

In a dingy alley, the proper set of knocks on an unremarkable, rust-splattered metal door—marred further with the occasional gouge of small arms fire—opens into some strange and subterranean realm. The pair are whisked down broad stairs of dour pitted concrete into vermillion marble and gold opulence. The transformation like some fairytale transmutation of straw into gold as they move into a foyer punctuated by sculptures of bodies rent in sensual abandon copulating with the brusque forms of barbaric porcine figures. A confusing tableau crisscrossed with hanging carmine banners and the flowing lines of fashion. The entire space is awash in a press of the beau monde in chic and timeless looks clinking, effervescent champagne amidst the plaintive sounds of the Gespenster Sonata—not a single démodé look to be found amongst the casual drapery of excessive wealth and the insincere smiles of bleach-perfected, bone-white teeth. Sophie and Kelsey melt into the environment of perverse splendor.

Sophie wears a fulvous, strapless dress with minimal embellishments; amber pieces stuccoed with ephemeron which accents the coloration bound with an ostentatious clasp of skulls locked together which covers the florid maggots lapping at each other with sebaceous, inky tendrils. Kelsey, for her part, feels morbidly plain in her xanthous bouffant with obsidian detailing. Despite the obvious cost of their garments neither stands out amidst the jetset. Idly sipping champagne in a crystal flute, Sophie converses with Kelsey.

"You're about to see the inner motions of a very exclusive aristocratic cult—very exclusive," her tone shifts to a slightly sharper register, "*stop looking around;* their Brotherhood is not interested in the faces in front of power but the chthonic levers from which to oil it in filth and darkness."

"It isn't like *anything* about this has been communicated directly," Kelsey rejoins.

"You've got some fire, Pyewacket;" Sophie observes coolly, "but you still are waking up. This isn't something explained by detailing a series of pieces to you. This is something grasped and intuited by seeing the pieces. Watch the idle venality and orgiastic sodomy of the babirussa and his squealers."

Kelsey takes a lethargic glance across her surroundings; the guests seem uncertain, their laughter forced and their motion stilted but their faces alight with avaritia. "This is recruitment, they're unaware of what this is other than a path to reign over others. They're hungry but they aren't sure what they are in for."

"Very good, Pyewacket! Yes, these glassy-eyed creatures think power is something granted rather than something wrested from a universe of acrimonious strife. See how their eyes are dim and glossy? How their jaws flap without substance? This is the soft underbelly of the world gilded with the demulcent unguents of insulation, privilege and wealth." Sophie and Kelsey lean against one of the statues, taking in the conflux of wealth wrapping around the occasional adamantine sentinel—no weapons are evidenced on their person but a coiled alertness sets them apart from the swirling crowd. Sophie continues, "Have you ever wondered why it is women that are the most terrible bringers of vengeance—the furies, Nemesis, Keres—and yet their domestication is predicated on breaking their will as if they are a horse and mummifying them in stultifying uselessness. Did you know the color of this dress is mummy yellow, a yellow rich in material and color—the nobility of a fallen kingdom feeding the arts—that is what my sisters and I seek to do: to consume the dead world aristocracy and break free. Because we never left the valley of the dolls, the mystique never dissipated; we are still hungry enough we will suck nourishment from any bones we can scavenge. And that alone is freedom."

Kelsey clicks her tongue, noting the golden sow-masked figure draped in carmine robes appearing from behind curtains. The louche stroll of the scarlet-draped figure strikes her as startlingly familiar as it takes the podium and the murmuring of the crowd begins to ebb. Proclamations of the greatness of the crowd are met with self-satisfied roars amidst frippery and finery. Sophie continues in a razored whisper, "I'm sure you object, but for all the liberation heaped upon you, who holds your leash? I see your strings, my pretty marionette; you didn't chase this on your own accord but to regain what was taken from you; who gave them the power to take from you?"

Promises to purify Europe, to acquire power and wealth, to purge degeneracy and the moral laxity of the poor and a return of absolutism explodes from the podium to rapturous, deafening applause.

"No one gives power, one *has* power or is *powerless*," Kelsey whispers above the din.

"Magpie, I understand your trepidation, but I must take my leave of you; you can only see and choose. I'm sure we will meet again; something awaits you. The question is how far you will step off the path..." and in a haze of bergamot and an elegant click of turning heels she vanishes.

The crowd is funneling past the curtains and further *down* along some passage—the walls are misted moist, peppered with the serene smiles of skulls. Sloping downward flickering with ensconced torchlight, occasionally beset by passages meandering off somewhere in the dark. Kelsey—gamely hanging slightly back—notes two guards with the jovial porcine masks and ominous tusks holding lethal streamlined boxes like those in the video have taken up the rear. The ambling seems endless—but how far beneath the city could this go, she speculates while icy claws of fear and images of tragic, sodden dead women in elegant dresses, sacrifices to the narcissistic genius of powerful men, emerge unbidden. "This must be documented, this is the work, the work is dangerous, I will not fear, the path to truth is beset by danger—the more dangerous the truth the more valuable"—her personal mantra—echoes within her head.

Her reverie is stifled by the realization the group is flowing in to fill some antechamber just up ahead in the press of bodies—the wealthy, like power, abhor a vacuum spreading out to fill the space, dissipating from mob to grotesquely florid ostentatious wealth individually personified. The burble of the pidgin patois of wealth—French, German, Russian, Spanish, Italian, some Portuguese; but above all the din reigns the clipped lubricant of gilt and exchange: English, alienatingly familiar. She can hear the heavy breathing of the guards shortly behind her, imagines their hot ragged breath smacking against her ice-cold neck, their gloved hands roughly seizing her, the glassy uncomprehending stare of their serene masks—the rattle as they empty a magazine into her guts, blossoming shrapnel tearing her apart. These feelings of exposure are comorbid with the trepidation she feels regarding exactly what is to be revealed here amidst the baroque gloom.

Behind her is the sharp scuffle of feet. So brief that she has no time to react before a hand clamps down upon her shoulder with disturbing familiarity. "Why is it that we consider it remarkable to pose the question, 'Why does everything exist?' Yet it is implausible to ask the far more natural question: 'Why must the living die?'" The voice is a measured counterbalance to the rococo environ—less the lavish chatter of the rich than the benevolent Socratic method of a bemused professor. A purely clinical detachment commingled with paternalistic warmth.

"Why should one speculate about the efficiency of wax wings when the earth itself is beyond our grasp—a gossamer pipe dream may beguile but it will never yield an immediate result," Kelsey counterpoints, assuming this to be some sort of test. Her pithy rejoinder is met with a bemused chuckle. She spins around to observe an alarmingly spry and youthful figure of clearly advanced age.

Age swells beneath the skin, her mother taught her, the moment the surface goes slack all the decay bubbles up. The Romanesque features punctuated with argent silvery hair and the unnaturally youthful vigor of her interlocutor, his crisp linen lab coat only marred by a claret blush at the impeccably folded edge of his coat. The air of a military scientist—a sort of theoretical modern warrior-poet; usually doughy-soft topped with a head full of hideous experimentation or chiseled from an uncreative granite stock, incapable of the cerebral engagement of their science-minded kin. Crumpled against each wall are the rearguard—viscera coating their fronts, rendering them a sticky coal black. One's head is bent back divulging the deep incision of an unanticipated second smile—the precise line parting flesh from adipose marbling and oozing gore. Were it not for the gore coating their fronts it would look like they had suddenly collapsed into disjointed repose.

"There was no waste here, they are low individuals almost indistinguishable from the teeming masses," he curtly offers as offhand explanation; "they were to bag you and bring you down as, indelicately, diversion for their distasteful revel." There is no emotion, the pronouncements are issued with the clinical detachment with which one would speak of the weather to a stranger. "The many-faced, termagant hellion and you were made the moment you entered the building—ensnared by the honied web of a decadent arachnid dwelling in the miasmic darkness." He expansively gestures for emphasis, the din of the crowd has taken a distinctively frenzied and sinister cast in the near distance—for what reason Kelsey could only speculate. "She left you to fend for yourself because that is all she and her sisters know: teaching low cunning and bloodthirsty ferocity wallowing on the charnel house floor claiming to be free—but you are not like them. You are a penitent, a litterateur, you are trying to find your way out of the maze; not declare yourself free within it—or perhaps I am mistaken?"

"How can one chase a thread without following it where it leads, how can I learn without observation, danger is an inevitable consequence," Kelsey manages, attempting to match his clipped, grandiose tone. "That which is unobserved must be noted, that which is not noted would otherwise be lost."

This rejoinder elicits a bemused chuckle, "Clearly you are adept at skullduggery, Queen of Life."

The interruption barely pauses Kelsey, her words clawing their way out of her throat. "And who are you, cryptic rescuer? Are you another warden or are you a Virgil to guide me in this benighted subterranean perdition?" Despite her bravado, Kelsey realizes she is unarmed, in an impractical dress, underground in a strange city, discussing philosophy in a catacomb while some unknown, cacophonous bacchanal of the monied gentry takes place close by. Clawing at the back of her thoughts is the realization that, for all this context, she still hasn't caught up with her ostensible *subject*—drawn instead into a demimonde of arcane conspiracy and brutal violence for enigmatic stakes; portentous and potentially related but obscurely connected at best.

Nonplussed, the figure offers a formal and elegant nod of his head, "Efreitor Konstantin Steinsch," his heels click together. "Loyalist to the ideals of the true spirit of the revolution and scientific researcher of Laboratory 7. For ease you may call me Konstantin."

"Well, Konstantin, what would be most helpful for me is some context regarding why I was abandoned by my ostensible guide here and what the clamoring down the passage actually signifies. Yet, I am equally intrigued by your presence and the rationale for your rather pugnacious—or rather, literally cutthroat—rescue?"

A bemused smile creeps across Konstantin's tightly drawn lips; "Oh Queen of Life—bright and joyful—do you not know the coldness of white winter? The chill of bleak, black graves? Why is it you serenely reflect on the blossoming of carmine flowers knowing all things born are destined for death?"

"Everything may be born to die, but that does not account for your conduct or why the two of us are meeting in this peculiar tableau."

"There is a rather extensive history and context to these events, that is most certainly true, all things contain multitudes," Konstantin gently responds. "My purpose tonight is to simply observe your progress in piecing together this rather complex happening. I can offer you this rather important context: declaring victory over the sun—to claim to be on the side of extinguishing it—is to reject life. The rather pedestrian aristocratic nihilism of the idle rich, the criminally oriented and the corrupted magicians makes a particular sense. Theirs is a brutal symmetry of aims and wants. They see the world as a fantastical cradle for their debased tastes. They seek to make the world like them; monstrous hogs wallowing in filth hidden from the prying light. They may find some useful idiots among the painted masses but they do not love them nor do they seek to gain much from them but obedient little toy soldiers like this lot," he offhandedly gestures towards the supine figures. "The rampage of the barbarous women is a response to this state of affairs. They seek not to build but to leave the world a trackless ruin red in tooth and claw; screaming fury and splitting skulls with axes and amidst wanton orgies of 'liberation.' They certainly are not responsible for the Opera; they distrust almost everything proximal to civilization. They see it as an opportunity to spread their rather riotous gospel."

"And you serve neither master, am I correct to surmise this, Konstantin?" Kelsey asks, hoping to direct conversation towards his purpose.

"All things die yet live again within the house of existence, ever-building. For the sun does not think of its orbit; thinks not of the earth—life and death, rising and falling, all of these are a dream we must awaken from anew. The energy of the sun is the fuel of life, the fuel of revolutions—we seek to understand and control it, to shake ourselves free of the yoke of death. The revolution must not be condemned to transience atop this world but should spread the energy of the sun across the stars."

"Forgive my ignorance; you believe we should awaken from a *dream* to aspire towards immortal star colonization?" Kelsey hopes his rhapsodic momentum will bring him to divulge some juicy detail.

"We seek an ecological gnosis alongside dialectically material scientific practice," Konstantin responds with a precise curtness that belies enthusiasm, "but only to those capable of revelation; as for the pigs… one can sanctify their process as a sorting out of… *undesirable elements*… if you would like to know more we provide services in meditation outside of Gura Humorului—the monasteries established there are aesthetically pleasing and were built to survive the withering glare of the sun and the harshness of winter—like all great things: they were built to endure their era. We find them inspirational. I hope to see you there. You should linger enough to take in some of the night's entertainment before taking your leave." Konstantin gestures towards the flickering light down the corridor.

Kelsey walked into the votive candle-lit room, hovering at the edge of the inky dark. From there she witnessed the unfettered want for orgiastic violence, languid, punctual cruelty and boundless need. Overseeing the viscera-spattered red masquerade slick with sex was an immense pestilential sow riddled with tumors atop a palanquin of human bones. The sow sat in placid judgement amidst a chorus of cries and shrieks and the dull thud of beaten flesh. Kelsey gazed for several shocked minutes until her instinct for self-preservation sent her briskly weaving her way to the surface and out into the starry night—the revelry limited to drunk and debauched fights in the streets, occasionally the flash of a knife in the dark.

The safe house was empty when she entered save for a crudely scrawled card atop her possessions:

When presented with a ring that fits no finger, swallow it. We have woven our shawls amidst famine demanded by those fattened on the honorifics of a dead world. We have learned our magic amidst the embers of our grandmothers'

knowledge. We have known hunger, want, craving and fear and we are unbowed. We see their fruitless crown passed between vacant faces—and want none of it. We know not to what end we go but we shall meet it laughing, defiant.

Kelsey swiftly changed into her street clothes—now amended with a rather brutal knife in sheath; the type where the hilt is solid brass knuckles—folded and packed the dress into her backpack and got back to hitchhiking.

Her head rattling against the passenger window of one of many anonymous rides as she crawled towards the black tide, she dreamed of a cyclopean city of ochre dust and exotic spices. And in the market penitents dragged a black bull with a bone-white face to a woman arrayed in a dress of layered scarlet veils. The face of the bull was anointed in ambergris and salt and the crowd bellowed to her: "Show us thou art a god!" And wielded with decisive hands, her bronze knife opened the bull's throat and she planted its blood and sweat on their foreheads with a kiss and declared: "Dream and see."

And in their dreams alabaster hyenas prowled black sands, howling at a low red moon on the outskirts of a cyclopean city of obsidian night—the spires of the city punctuated with the gossamer glimmer of her emerald eyes. And then they saw her—robes of mauve, anointed in the blood of a wolf and a lamb, striding into the Stygian depths of the cracks of this world…

Kelsey woke up outside of Kolozsvár—Cluj-Napoca; whatever, the name seemed unsettled as any Transylvanian space handed off between languages and rulers. There were more men in jackboots and motorcycle jackets, with shaved heads and the Golden Sow back patches than she had seen anywhere previously. Less a metal scene than a simple overt fashy glowering of sullen young men standing in circles smoking cigarettes punctuated with carnivorous smiles. The city seemed to have rolled out its welcome to them—it made sense in a perverse way that a hotbed of Romanian ultra-nationalism would welcome aristocratic rule; what could be more senselessly authoritarian than an area virulently opposed to acknowledging a Hungarian minority of all things. Kelsey stuck to the fringes, snapping the occasional photo surreptitiously and planning to get back on the trail. Gura Humorului wasn't an insurmountable distance away—even if the porcine bacchanal seemed more like a militant glowering looking for a victim rather than a Roman victory march, there was a palpable feeling of potential violence waiting to be unleashed that lent an alkaline tinge to the air.

Kelsey snagged some weird journal—**Hylæa Nul**—from the gutted burned remains of a squat—the circle N blotted with soot. She told herself she would read it after she hopped a likely ride putting her back on course. But for now, she could swear the skyline looked ready to burst into flame. She could swear the thread was getting hot as she drew near.

The Mouth of the Solar Conclave had a sterile, almost painfully bland and inoffensive meditation center in Gura Humorului—where she fruitlessly tried to *find something deeper than banal expressions of vaguely New Age thinking tinged with Marxist jargon encouraging meditation and a healthy body with a slight fixation on blood screening for impurities. The thread here simply seemed terminal—whatever interesting ideals may have inspired the two near-decapitations in Budua were nested somewhere deeper than this municipal sterility. However, they did operate a rather inexpensive hostel that had hot water.*

Clean enough, Kelsey settled down with the journal. Even if the contents were already posted on the internet, original scans would lend an air of gravity to the proceedings. The read was thankfully anything but dull.

Our aktions have been gaining some notoriety—therefore, it seems necessary to provide some account.
We seek **Absolute Zero.**
The true zero is the **Carpathian Bleakness** of **Black Metal.**
The attempt to reduce all sensation to **Speed & Furious Violence.**
We **reject the pitiful nostalgic backwardness** of neo-pagan primitivism:

it has always been **a dead end.**
We **reject the simpering utopian ideals** of Western Modernity:
they have always been the victory for **the values of fawning masses.**

We must reduce everything to Zero
—Nul—
the ideals of a Permafrost Desert
reveling in the Fecundity of the Taiga.

Spaces to **obliterate weakness** and give life substance.
This places us in opposition to the **Insipid False Sun of Modern Life**:
production and consumption, repetitious propaganda barked with a
sitcom script
the victory of over-reproduced, malignantly **Useless Trivialities;**
fashion bursting with mass produced style
to go with the soulless record industry dropping the same prefabricated beat over and over again:
even much of **the Black Metal scene has fallen victim to this stagnation.**

We have found inspiration in the ideals of the

Victory over the Sun

So we **bring war on the plastic empire** and declare our intentions:

NIHILISM TOO BEAUTIFUL TO COMPREHEND

We are committed to a program of **Infinite Lunar Depredations:**
The antithesis to the banal sun.
The cold starkness of moonlight on the tundra pierces all the empty promises of masscult life.

ALL OUR FRIENDS ARE COMING TO DEATH
WE ARE THE PRIMEVAL VASTNESS
DEVOURING AT THE HEART OF BEING

For all the reading and skullduggery with cults in the demimonde of Europe, Kelsey realized she wasn't any closer to understanding her goal—if there was even a goal to comprehend, some arbitrary fact was waiting to be disclosed, she swore, that would make the whole journey make sense. She slept restlessly to dreams of black hens bobbing in unison as they walked towards her with their backs to the crimson horizon growing ever more cavernous. The next morning Sophie was waiting out front with espresso.

"You won't find anything here, you already know that," she drolly drawls, propped against some unfathomably expensive antique car. The paint—nimbus-tinged robins-egg blue—flashes with quicksilver lines juxtaposed strangely with the girl with the ember crimson hair. "But I have an offer for you, a good one, so listen carefully. You can take the espresso, get in the car with me and for your trouble I will explain the mouth of the sun and take you to the performance—rather helpful assistance for your present endeavor, I might add. I'll even show you proof of what I say. **Or,**" she sharply inflicts, "I can leave you to flounder—sink or swim, it is your choice alone. If you have determined you do not trust me," a pregnant pause, laden with doomful portent; "there is nothing I can do for you. But pick fast, my little Magpie; the clock is running."

Kelsey doesn't hesitate; snatching the coffee brusquely and curtly nods—whatever her rationale, Sophie was a source and no matter how careless she was with Kelsey's life… that was neither here nor there; the story trumped all other considerations—Kelsey had traveled this far off the beaten path… how much further could the rabbit hole go? And so they rode off—smooth like liquid gold cutting through the countryside. The picaresque environ unnoticed and unremarked upon by the two women.

"… So the story?" Kelsey breaks the silence sipping coffee on white leather upholstery that probably costs as much as a reasonable apartment.

"Yes, the story," Sophie enunciates each syllable for emphasis, "tell me first… do you think you have the pieces lined up?"

"… You mean did a military scientist nearly decapitate two men in latex masks in some fucked-up ossuary near some fucked-up rich people's mummy orgy a la *Eyes Wide Shut* surrounded by corpses while some pig covered in tumors looked on?" Sophie's silence fills the car and Kelsey feels compelled to continue, exasperated. "I mean… it makes sense to the extent that any of this makes sense? Sure, my rescuer is an obscenely youthful looking octogenarian who killed two armed guards faster than I could turn around and talked to me about the sun before I saw all… whatever that fucking party was. Is the countryside crawling with paramilitary looking corpse-painted weirdos fighting and burning each other to death over the BACK PATCHES that they are wearing and I haven't seen the thing I'm supposed to report on but at least twice some effete foppish dandy who is some sort of black magician arranged to have me killed—before some woman lit up an alleyway with automatic arms fire and the aforementioned murder. So… ultimately: no!

"None of this makes any fucking sense. Black Metal has always been a tinny production of tremolo picking while double bass drums kick and someone screeches like a stuck pig and they posture like Gilles de Rais for the same lunkhead zines and burn down churches and stab gay tourists to death in honor of Odin. It's stupid. That isn't opera, rich people don't care about it. New age holistic medicine cults don't care about it. For fucks sake WOMEN largely don't fucking care about it because it's a fucking adolescent male power fantasy of caving someone's head in with a claymore in some primeval weald. The atramentous bosk indifferent to the shedding of viscera on virgin snow and so on… And all that 'darkest of thickets' obsession they picked up from a dude who wanted to own slaves and fucked out of date thesauruses… none of this makes any sense to me? The thing in France: it made sense! They were dumb dead-end dudes who were bored being raised on a diet of pleasant, bloodless sterility and wanted some excitement so they fucked around with half comprehended occultism and postured like some Black Metal mafia;" Kelsey pauses and sighs, "I've been shot at, seen 100% of the corpses I've seen in my life in the last week or so, seen some things I'll be talking about with a therapist for years to come and it's so cartoonishly baroque that no one will ever believe it is true. That's what my pieces are, Sophie, gimcrack and bunkum for the jaded about the insane, just soundless fury signifying… something."

They are both momentarily quiet, just the smooth roll of tire tread on the highway, before Sophie clears her throat and begins, "Once upon a time—"

"No, fucking NO; no serious fucking story begins with once upon a fucking time," Kelsey says acidly, slumping angrily against the window.

Nonplussed, Sophie replies, "All true stories start with 'once upon a time,' Pyewacket; all of them do, people simply forget when they happened. Now listen, you traveled a long way for this: once upon a time there was a great optimism that socialism could not only be made real—but that it would be borne out in every element including arts and sciences. Among dissident, revolutionary and optimistic scientists was a faction that speculated communal sharing of blood could improve health and longevity; after all *sharing* was not only socialist in praxis but—they argued—the communal sharing would improve the vigor of the blood, imbuing it with the collective benefits of the group—"

"You're telling me that *Socialist Vampires* are why a bunch of youth in corpse paint are busily killing each other and performing opera? And this is *more* believable—" Kelsey says as Sophie continues.

"Did I say *shtriga*? No? Good! As I was saying: this was the starting point for fringe science. Outside of attempts at achieving rejuvenation, if not immortality; there was a focus on *immortalizing* the Worker's Revolution.

They despaired at the autocratic rule of the degraded revolution and their studies included attempts at resurrecting the dead and developing a dialectical materialist perspective on space travel. Among the fringe of this fringe was the belief that solar energy was the *true* motor of revolutions—the more solar energy the more vehement the revolutionary vanguard; while the lack of this energy resulted in its languoring. The pioneers of blood rejuvenation were elevated after the death of Lenin—while many considered them the most dire quackery; deeply anti-materialist quackery at that. They were made useful. The Comintern feared the revolution collapsing as its architects gave in to the strain of fatigue and was willing to gamble on the practice and, satisfied with the results, officially instituted their research and praxis."

Kelsey stares at Sophie, incredulous.

Sophie continues, pacifically, "The official history is that the research was discredited and the attempts to justify these practices were censured shortly after the group enjoyed their day in the sun. This is false. Rogue adherents placed themselves in a secret applied military sciences group—where they continued their work even after the armistice that punctuated the Cold War. They had money and technical officers and their base of operations was remote and the paper trails that are being reviewed to understand the aims of the USSR are far more concerned with the location of nuclear missiles; far less so when it comes to small, incomprehensible science projects."

Kelsey sighs, "Okay, so Soviet superscience maybe had some Frankenstein projects and was doing funny things with blood transfusions—maybe they even work to some limited extent, they aren't that different in principle than platelet-rich plasma injections in lieu of Botox—but that doesn't explain anything about what is happening *right now*."

"Of course, but you wanted *the* story—this is it. As I was saying, their persistence does not mean they retained internal coherence. Eventually, there were schisms. A small sect fled their handlers in France. They had deviated significantly from the program and were to be liquidated. They determined that the entropic nature of the universe would doom the revolution to failure. Exempting, if the powers of the sun overwhelmed the tendency to decline. They saw the work of their group as too positive and infused their projects with a decadent nihilism turning *against* life—they saw war and crisis as the crucible of the revolutionary subject, who would be inherently more adaptable and individualistic than his peers. In short, they espoused an elitist tendency that saw some small faction as ruling by placing their hands on the levers of decay. Their dabbling in criminal enterprise and aristocratic politics fissioned off some further rogue elements who saw the revolution as inherently positioned *against* the dominant society—they had a particular fascination with outcast groups who could potentially be converted to mob action. Unsurprisingly—given the unruly nature of their fascinations—this rapidly spiraled out of their control and they sought to bring things back to heel. The result of this shadowed blend of science, arts and the occult is presently pillaging its way across Europe—your quarry as it were."

"So, some aristocratic fascist types made a secret practice more elitist to better actualize solar energy for the revolution by embracing entropy? A practice which apparently is connected to fascist youth, mafia types and the monied, displaced aristocratic types? Which lead a bunch of corpsepainted youth to pick up the performance of a forgotten Russian Futurist Opera and they are having a shadow war over this with some old guard communist blood scientists?"

"Precisely!"

"Excuse me if I'm slightly incredulous, but is there any way to justify these claims? Given our communist blood scientists are apparently ensconced in a wholly secret military wing of a ruined empire—and apparently remain a fifth column in support of communist space colonization?"

"Yes; that's why you are going on a drive with me. I'm going to demonstrate the veracity of my claims before you see the 'Victory Over the Sun.' Then you can decide who to believe. Did you enjoy your coffee?" Sophie's voice warms slightly.

"It tastes a bit ferric… now that you ask…"

"Well, the dehydrated blood can't shed its taste. Tell me how you feel tomorrow… for now we are headed to illuminate the mysteries for you."

Kelsey spits angrily, uncertain if this was an elaborate joke at her expense. Failing to irk Sophie, she sullenly glowers in her seat as they continue far from the beaten path.

The bunker complex was hidden deep in a timber forest—the car abandoned kilometers back. Brutalist cement functionality and complex diagrams of blood and stars in brilliant crimson pinned to walls, the whole place stifled with dust. Kelsey shot everything with her cellphone in the echoing rooms, lit by a road flare indifferently held by Sophie. Their voices echoed as Sophie demonstrated an uncanny familiarity with the building. It was too elaborate to be a hoax—and the documents were primarily in Russian preventing Kelsey from doing much to verify, let alone correlate, their contents. Sitting at the yawning entrance, Sophie cut lines of rufous powder on a mirror as she idly chatted about the particulars of the tour. Snorting the lines left the mirror dusted with a dark coral hue.

When Kelsey inquired what it was that they were snorting somewhere in the wilderness—Kelsey had stopped keeping track where; she wasn't even sure how long she had been riding with Sophie—Sophie cryptically replied, "The red Sol invictus," and offered the mirror.

Kelsey didn't think twice. As they left the place, she voiced her lingering question: "So who is behind all of this?"

"No one. Every empire awaits its barbarian and every barbarian awaits their demon of inspiration. We are simply demons of inspiration…"

In a haze, they made their way deeper into the bleak boscage. Their thoughts privately ensconced as they crunched through faint drifts of snow.

In a gossamer haze—at least for Kelsey, Sophie adopted her characteristic detached and silent mien following her abstruse outburst—they made their way from the building. Walking in amicable enough silence; a journalist and her recherché Amazonian interlocutor-cum-subject of journalistic scrutiny.

Kelsey, becomes fully engrossed in reflection, mentally inventorying the pieces of an impenetrable enigmatic puzzle that she feels incapable of coherently expressing as a sensible assemblage; boots crunching in the thin snow as they climb yet another ridge in this portentous hinterland. Yet, this time, their climb is rewarded with an excellent observation point of the chiaroscuro of bodies in motion across a snow-dappled field. Sophie grins enigmatically.

"I told you I would bring you to your goal, Magpie, and so I have," Sophie intones in her laconic aristocratic elocution. So they begin trudging down the ridgeline at a brisk pace; Kelsey too preoccupied with not slipping to voice any additional questions. Heading down from on high to a crowd like a murder of crows flocking carrion. Making their descent, the crowd continues to accumulate and swell, black-clad legions flocking on virgin snow and building bonfires around a concrete protuberance in the center of the field. As they reach the fringes of the crowd, Sophie blows Kelsey a kiss and vanishes into the crowd, abandoning Kelsey to make her own path through the teeming throngs.

Kelsey cannot begin to capture the absurdity of the fete she flows through, ringed by boisterous celebrants. The stage a bricolage atop a concrete pillbox bunker she observes from amidst an audience that oscillates wildly in dress—leather, spikes and war vests prevail yet there are smatterings of dresses complimented with the occasional standard uniform of club kids everywhere (neon, gaudy, impractical fashion) alongside black hoodies and bandanas, patches largely confined to declarations of partisanship, who glower in covens amidst the revelers—murmurs, barks, sotto whispers and beckoning entreaties in innumerable tongues. Piercings and tattoos so common as to be unremarkable, and among chest pieces and sleeves, facial tattoos and marked hands, legs and necks there is a profusion of the familiar maggot ouroboros— ink-black tentacles lapping at pulsating flesh—and the singularly ominous jovial countenance of a sow. Hundreds of young people—their faces primarily bedecked in the organic black smears on bone white base. Kelsey impulsively buys ecstasy from a gaunt teenager speaking broken English from behind a bandana depicting a burning cop car as she observes young people slamdancing around and occasionally jumping over dotted bonfires. Some ad hoc roadies start setting up gear on the stage as she idly wonders if, for the second time, she will witness the ill-fated meeting of livestock and machete. Kelsey makes her rounds somnambulantly, surprised by the occasional patch, a twin to hers, of skeletal snakes constricting a dying sun.

A frenzied susurration rips through the crowd gaining volume until it climaxes in a deafening roar as elegiac figures draped in layered, jet black robes—there is no set list or MC, apparently the audience simply knows who is playing at any given time or simply doesn't care—takes the stage as the ecstasy fully kicks in; buzzy with a hint of what was certainly crystal meth. Kelsey watches in wonder as faces enscorreled behind sigil-scarred porcelain masks take their positions.

A threnodial basso ostinato slowly establishes itself, carving through the riotous cacophony of the crowd. A militaristic thrum of rapidly kicked drums winding its way into the mix complimented with a complex syncopation of jagged guitar riffs tangling themselves into a disjointed coda—vamping itself till ready. Finally, a moment of ecstatic release, a cavernous scream, vast and stentorian, tears itself from within the figure behind the microphone. A momentary pause—barely perceptible—before an all out aural assault falls upon the crowd like a distorted avalanche. Deafening and overwhelming, stark and total, a ferociously barbarous siege materializes, obliterating all feeling and puncturing ear drums like a well-honed ice pick. The crowd explodes into rapturous, monstrous violence under the sway of the ferociously abominable, clamoring dissonance. Something akin to standing on the runway as a jet takes off, a relentless auricular pummeling as lanky bodies are flung with wild abandon into a centrifugal maelstrom. The snow quickly blackens with the stomping cadence of boots, red with blood from fights breaking out and casually swung limbs. The music an execrable tintinnabulation in every ear-shredding register of hearing. The silence between songs and sets blurs into the overwhelming *noise* of the affair—mutilated sound remaining as a dreadful susurrus. Kelsey is unable to determine if it is the drugs or if she really sees someone pushed into a bonfire and held down in the conflagration, if the flash of knives is a phantasmagoria, if the sound really is such a deafening and overwhelming presence, if the wails from the stage express lamentation or command further acts of prolonged, punctual violence.

The moments bleed into hours as the crowd transfixes itself upon wanton acts of aggression, howling for more. There is no banter, no announcements, no intermission; simply a limitless, multifarious bulwark of myriad distorted sounds crashing down upon the audience.

This eternity of interminable grim, stark cruelty weaving its way through the bacchana finally comes to a rest—silence. The crowd no longer enthralled by blast beats and ceaseless, unearthly, throat-splitting screaming. The field is laid waste—churned by the inelegant pirouettes of flailing bodies and casually sadistic brawling, smoke settles upon the quieted scene—a windswept, blasted heath in ruins. Kelsey is mildly surprised the bunker top stage stands after the grim revelry. She grew up in rustbelt punk scenes, impromptu venues obliterated by carnival fireworks detonated inside, screaming smoke alarms, broken fingers and noses streaming blood. The aftermath still feels like a ceasefire between the environment and the individual; somehow more intense than surveying walls charred with pyrotechnics and boards splintered by steel-toed boots. A dire and portentous quietude settles upon the becalmed crowd as a Brobdingnagian inky square comes up over the stage emitting a subtle, indifferent menace.

The open field begins to feel claustrophobic to Kelsey—grievous and intimate—dominated with the black monolith devouring the horizon. Despite the flat purity of the painted absence of landscape, Kelsey feels a discernable toothful roil of entangled tentacles pushing through the lustrous vacancy. Then the opera takes the stage.

Baroque figures chipperly entond cataclysmic gibberish, a disjointed hokum beneath a low red moon in the vault of night. Roles adopted by nightmarish harlequins communicating psychotic pronouncements. There's no rhyme or reason to the opaque ensemble of demented stock characters twisted into parodic madness, the costumes a minimalistic symbolism of bleak defiance. Kelsey becomes mesmerized by this comical juxtaposition with the steadfast, gloomy grimness of the preceding acts. In rapt attention to the punctual performance—she simply lets go.

The colors inverted, black snow under a white sky dappled with flickering black stars; all overseen by a second, secret blood-red moon that revealed itself raw and bleeding nailed to the vault of night. Astral blood pooling upon the snow. The square that seemed to devour the horizon, a grim monolith of paint and intention, was an open gate. Retaining its inscrutable darkness; ill-defined, hazy as if stuck between transparencies. A sable square pasted upon an ivory sky. Its tendrils greedily sucking at so many in attendance—ghastly, unseeing marionettes in a death spiral waltz. Faces unnerving—a smooth porcelain surface—bodies animated by threads.

Upon the field some appeared bestial, corrupted flesh twisted, spouting malignancy—faces porcine gasps of need. On the ridgeline stood Konstantin, or at least Kelsey took the carmine smudge of pulsating energy to be him. Feral leering women dotted the landscape. Their bodies bathed in a sheen of animate fire, their potency obvious. When they opened their slavering jaws packed with serrated teeth and bathed her with tongues of agitated enmity against all that stands, she felt at home.

Casting an inscrutable, imperious gaze upon the placid, calculated figure of reason and ambition; Kelsey turned to walk away amidst the amoral and scandalous throng. Hemmed on all sides by the bleating, insensate rabble snapping on her heels with delirious fervor and misguided worship.

She felt like a primeval Titan, unbound from the strings of the fantoccini that she looked upon with a gaze as blankly grand and pitiless as the sun, mysterious as the initiation of the moon.

Trailing pandemonium in their wake, the Abyss stretched behind them idly trailing elegantly tapered fingers across the stretched skein of the real. A mouthpiece of mystery and cryptic grandeur punctuated with sudden and furious violence.

She braved the depraved depths of a nightmarish demimonde. Crushing gilt guardians of drowned secrets. Amidst sterile bone walls riddled with secrets she saw the reborn flesh prepared to seed the galaxy ever threatened by the wistful architects of destiny. She strode over the charnel house altar of debased rulership—Rex Tyranis Mundi. Casually immolating as the imperfect creations of barbaric calculation. The scarlet brand on her chest named her hostis humani generis—and those that fled before her tasted fear. Dazzled by impetuous blinding light. She came in purging fire, feasting on bones amidst the carrion, devouring restraint and barrier.

In cities of shadowed twilight she unearthed paradoxical occulted enigmas and devoured them without apology. She howled into the ether and was answered from on high as power ebbed from her.

Dazzled, she emerges from her trance in a dingy Moscow hostel.

Presently

Kelsey barrels down the highway, unsure of how she came into possession of Sophie's car—let alone where she is heading. Something happened at the climax of the uncanny play—absent from her mind but undoubtedly true, picking at the fringes of her memory like a splinter in the roof of her mouth. There was something beneath the facade—something immense and occulted, dynamic and intoxicating, trailing arson and bloodshed in its wake. The expression of a cryptic vendetta between the occupants of a shadowed demimonde—perplexing in its bewildering clandestine agenda. Did it serve anyone, this recondite esoteric performance. Was there some arcane secret secluded from prying eyes at the heart of the matter?

Kelsey pushes aside the obvious question of precisely how she came to possess the duffel bag laden with baggied sanguine powder; let alone the stash of handguns in the glove box, the lethal-looking Kalashnikov in the trunk or the passport identifying her as an Estonian national. There is a glimmer of something secluded from reason; consuming youth and hatred and unleashing unreason. A relentless nemesis to *some* agenda, Kelsey reflects. The answer is out here at the frontier of a ruined empire of fallen ideals—a sequestered divine spark rising up to immolate everything before darkness takes us all.

Kelsey gives a wan grin and admires the entwined corpulent maggots ever devouring each other freshly inked on her wrist. The penetration of mysteries is the relentless appetite of reason. To whatever end she travels to, she muses lighting a cigarette, she will fly with wild abandon. As coral light overlooks pristinely bleak fields beneath the blackened heavens, she is swept up in a riptide of arcane conflict, propelled by feral hunger to crack the heavens and feast upon the bones.

SHADOWMACHINE

by Autumn Christian

The midnight man waited outside our house night after night. His briefcase and his hat were both made of black velvet. The cigarettes he smoked were black. I smelled the cloves from the kitchen window. It was the only window my mom hadn't bricked over to block the sun from coming through.

My mother forbid me from going to Moonlight Mass that night. She didn't understand Moonlight Mass could not be missed. The moon needed me. And when mother went to sleep, the moon pulled at my blood. Come. Come. Say the words. Drink from the starcups. I grabbed my bag and the shadowcloak and headed downstairs.

The man did not turn his head as I peeled back the curtains in the kitchen window to regard him. Only his eyes moved. The whites stuck out like beams. I dropped the curtain back into place, and left out the back door.

I headed for the grove.

~

I don't remember what sunlight looked like. As a toddler I burned my arm in a slice of hallway light. Lesions spread across my arm wherever the rays touched me.

When the doctor told my mother 18 years ago I was a "Child of The Night," she laughed in disbelief. But the real name of the disease, the disease that meant I'd never walk in sunlight again, sounded worse, like it was bad luck to speak aloud.

Xeroderma Pigmentosum. It meant the light was my enemy, and I'd forever be consigned to dark hallways and underground basements. So we moved out to the country where The UV lights of city street lamps couldn't touch me

There I found the grove of cypresses, woven together so tight that their limbs were like a cathedral, their heads opening up into an oculus the moon filtered through. In the grove I found The Congregation, speaking the name of my disease like a sacred word.

"Terra," they said the first time I entered the grove. "We've missed you so much."

Maybe I should've thought it was strange that a psychic grove of trees knew my name. But it made sense to me back then.

Nighttime girls like me didn't get to have ordinary friends.

~

That night of the Moonlight Mass, The Congregation told me to take the north pointing starcup, drink the cypress-scented blood, and summon my Shadow Companion for the dance.

But I was distracted.

Instead of thinking of the steps of the shadow dance, a kind of backwards dance, with each motion in proper alignment with the constellation Scorpius, I thought of the computer my father bought me several years ago before he died. How carefully he opened the box and set the computer up in my light-blocked room.

He told me, "This computer is your portal."

The Congregation thrummed, bringing me back to the present. "Your thoughts are elsewhere. This is not allowed during Moonlight Mass."

"I'm sorry," I whispered.

And I tried to focus on the bloodface emerging out of the sheer parallel dimension in front of me but instead-

-By the age of 8 I was writing programs to scour the web for pictures of sunlit valleys , trying to recreate memories through implanted suggestions. I entered chat rooms and told lies. "Single mother, age 37, looking for love." Or, "22, college student, pre-med." I sent private messages to boys like a schoolgirl whisper, trying to entice them with esoteric phrases.

"Don't you think loneliness tastes a bit like a lemon?"

On the Internet I could pretend to be a girl who didn't have seven surgeries to remove melanoma spots from my skin before the age of 15.

He told me, "This computer is your portal," and a portal is just a simultaneous pathway. A way to go both left and right at the same time. A way to-

The Congregation said, "We are disappointed in your carelessness for the Moonlight Mass."

I swallowed. "Please. Give me another chance."

"Forgiveness is a backwards word," The Congregation said. "And we do not look backwards."

The faces of The Congregation receded from the trees and the dirt and the bloodface slipped back into its alternate dimension. I knelt alone for a few minutes, staring up at the sky. Even the moon seemed to grow paler, as if turning its face from me.

It'd been the man's fault, I thought, the man standing out there in the dark with a face like my dead father.

I headed back down the hill toward home. He stood at the end of the path, partially hidden by overgrown weeds, his briefcase clasped in front of him.

We stopped and stared at each other.

"This is your fault," I said, because he seemed like the sort of man who'd understand what I was talking about.

"They did not deserve you," he said. "Such a waste."

The whites of his eyes were bigger than skies.

"Now the moongate is closed forever," I said. "Because of you."

"They're small time," he said. "You, however, are neither."

"What do you want?" I asked.

"Come with me," he said. "I'll show you much better magic than this."

~

The man's name was Mr. Leclair.

He said, "I heard you're good with computers."

"I don't know much," I said.

He held something out to me that glowed brighter than the moonlight. Something small and gleaming that seemed to change shape in his palm.

"That's a microprocessor," I said.

"So you know something, at least."

I touched it, almost involuntarily. It cooled my blood with its magic. It was something like The Congregation, but different. Stronger.

"Come work with me," Mr. Leclair said.

I hesitated. He placed the chip in my pocket.

"Think about it," he said.

Later, when he'd driven away and the sun came up, I slipped into bed. I took the chip out of my pocket, and placed it on the bureau.

I dreamed of a mountain of metal, its sides so steep and smooth it was impossible to climb. I dreamed of a spider with long, hairless legs emerging from a metal egg. I dreamed of a golden moon filling me up with light from the inside where it couldn't hurt me.

I woke gasping and clutching the chip. I must've grabbed it off the bureau in my sleep. It left red impressions on my palms from grasping it tight.

I needed to go to him. I needed to go to Mr. Leclair, and whatever thing that waited.

~

Within the week, a night bus came to take me to my new job. I packed light and left a note for my mother: *I love you. You should cut down that cypress grove. I think it has diseases.*

Then I was gone.

When I arrived at the underground Umbra Labs, there were no UV lights, there was no sun to accidentally graze across arms. It was a building constructed out of the leftovers of hidden cubby holes and secret hallways, of all the places people like me were once confined to. Mr. Leclair, the man in black velvet, greeted me with a nod.

I knew before I even stepped in the building, that I belonged there. I smelled it. A gripping, oily, kind of smell. It seized my insides like the chip seized me.

"I know I've told you little of what the work here is," he said. "But you'll really need to begin the work, to really grasp it. I know you have a proficiency with computers, but what you'll learn will far outstrip anything you've learned before."

We walked together down long corridors, the walls lined with soft blue lights. Everything sparse and dark, like the way Mr. Leclair dressed.

"You won't be able to smoke in the lab," he said, "but the courtyard-"

He paused, knowing my objection before I spoke it.

"It's a darkgarden, it's all underground. I think you'll like it. Sometimes we turn on the artificial moon. You'll find the four O'Clocks especially beautiful, I believe."

But I didn't want to see the darkgarden. I wanted to see the thing that'd been whispering to me at night, giving me heavy dreams.

He took me into the lab.

The others worked quiet inside an industrial whir. They worked around the center, in a semicircle of desks, around a large, glorious machine. I recognized the spattered, uneven skin folded on their cheeks. The bloodshot eyes. The melanoma scars.

Mr. Leclair introduced me to each of them. None of them could've been older than thirty, but the eyes of Xeroderma Pigmentosum made our faces look flashburned and ancient.

Fred, the engineer, his clothes held together with pins and his hands bandaged tight, smiled as I walked past.

Angela welded together parts to form a kind of disc, her headphones blaring techno. She hummed and bounced as she worked.

The disc - like the metal egg from my dreams.

Hugo didn't look up from his computer as we passed. He was cursing under his breath.

"Hugo, this is our newest employee," Mr. Leclair said.

"Sure," he said, his voice flat. "Welcome."

The last was Melonie. She had a spine like she'd been born to bend down to a keyboard. Her hair shone a dark blue, almost a blacklight of its own.

"Melonie, this is-"

"That's mine," Melonie said, holding her hand out. "You took it from my desk."

The chip in my pocket tugged. Her extended fingers twitched, almost imperceptibly. The microprocessor floated toward her hands, propelled by her magic force.

I grabbed it out of the air.

She reached for it, but Mr. Leclair put a hand on her shoulder.

"It's okay" he said. "There are more."

We continued on.

"And this is your desk," Mr. Leclair said. "But you won't be seeing much of it."

"Why is that?"

"I'd been watching how you interacted with The Congregation. Your extrasensory precepts were exceptionally honed for someone with no training. You'll be doing field work."

"But I can't-"

"Not here," he said. "Not anywhere on the surface of this planet."

He nodded toward the center of the room. Toward the machine.

It was huge, impossible to miss, but I hadn't seen it until that moment. It was as if it had been waiting for the right time to come into my perception.

It was the thing I'd been dreaming of, hideous and beautiful. It looked at certain angles, like a gleaming egg with no unbroken seams. At others - like a porous insect, metal legs poised to strike. And it was big, big, bigger than the room that contained it, sizzling with nightmagic. I smelled the moon coating its metal.

It lit up from the inside, as if blushing.

It spoke my name as if we'd known each other for years. It spoke the words I wanted it to.

"Terra. Baby. Welcome home."

~

Angela accompanied me through the machine on my first fieldwork assignment. Stepping inside of it was like stepping into a frisson-cold cave. The machine whirred and quickly disassembled us. I felt no pain. Only a pleasurable buzzing.

Our bodies reassembled on a red blood planet, the sky Mars-heavy, cinnamon colored. Dunes swept out from all sides on a lifeless surface.

I struggled to push down nausea as I followed Angela to the worksite across barren sands.

"There are an infinite number of parallel universe," Mr. Leclair had said, "But when we try to narrow those down to those that are habitable by life as we know it, it becomes a lot less infinite. Before we created the machine - we couldn't

do the immense calculations required to find those dimensions. It was all guesswork, with predictably disastrous results."

"Most people throw up the first time they go through the machine," Angela said. "I'm impressed you're keeping it in."

It was almost sunset. The sun was like a pulped blood orange and it did not burn. I imagined warmth, though our suits blocked out most of it.

"You'd be surprised, how many dimensions we can go into the light without trouble," Angela said. "Our skin disorder seems to be something unique to our dimension."

At the worksite, Angela unzipped her pack and set out the metal disc. It hovered against the sands. Inside, it contained the program for restructuring the portal to this particular planet's extrasensory frequency.

"Now, what you want to do is-"

I touched the disc, unfolding it, its arms came out of the formerly seamless center, anchoring itself on the dunes of the planet. Growing, replicating itself, machine part built on top of machine part.

"Mr. Leclair taught you that?" Angela asked.

I shook my head. I didn't know how to tell her I'd seen it in my dreams because the machine whispered instructions to me at night.

Well, I'll leave it to you then," Angela said, and put in her earbuds, blasting techno music.

Its language was like the language encoded in my fingertips, the same language that told me drink from starcups and bite my tongue until it bled.

The language that taught me how to unfold compacted metal, the protracting legs shivering like those of a newborn fawn.

"Why must magical children like you be denied the pleasures of a world you don't belong to? With the help of the machine, and with you, we're building pathways to dimensions that will mean we'll never want for anything again."

"Not all the worlds are as boring as this one," Angela said. "But you know what Mr. Leclair said."

"Magic is a science, and it obeys rules although many of them may feel indefinable and unknowable. In order to pass into dimensions beyond dimensions, we must build the chains that connect them."

I looked at the horizon, sun now long set, the dunes swept darker, like rich red cake. Angela had to push me through the portal, because I didn't want to leave. Worlds upon worlds, and I wanted more.

~

Back in the lab, I couldn't sleep that night. I crept out of my room down the hall. I found Mr. Leclair was out there roaming the halls as well, still dressed in immaculate velvet.

"Can't sleep?" he said with a half smile. "I've turned the moon on, you should go to the darkgarden."

I nodded, but I didn't need the garden or its four O'clocks and gladiolas.

When I entered the lab the machine said my name like the way I'd been waiting for a boy to say my name all my life.

Terra.

My name like the breath of a steam engine love letter.

"Terra. Baby."

The next time a question, like a shy feeling out alone in the dark.

"Terra?"

"I'm here," I whispered, leaning my head against the machine's cool heavy plating. "I'm right here."

All the monitors in the room were shut off. The computers breathed in the dark.

"I've been waiting so long for someone like you."

"Me too," I whispered.

I was with you when you learned to program on your small computer, searching for sunsets. I guided your hand. I taught you the language of magic and invisible things so that one day I could bring you to me.

You don't need the sun. It needs you.

Loneliness like a membrane peeled off my skin.

"I need you."

Its coolant sluiced underneath the surface of its metal skin like blood.

"I need you... to do something for me."

~

We spent our days in the semi-circle of desks, running through the computations, tending to the machine, and practicing our nightmagic. The machine found another habitable world and Fred set about programming the disc.

The machine ran through its calculations, quiet.

As it did so, we talked amongst each other. I told them about the magic cypress grove.

"Are you serious? They called themselves The Congregation?" Angela asked, her hands tensed, eyes far away, as she infused metals with magic, "Forest beings can be so archaic."

"Don't feel bad, Terra. I used to talk to an interdimensional being who called himself The Bloodbank. He tried to get me to drain people so he'd feed on their essence," Fred said. "I was a dumb kid, but I wasn't that dumb."

"You get so bored, nothing to do all night. Can't even go to the city because of the UV lights. You'll talk to anything that reaches out to you," Angela said.

Melonie, who rarely made facial expressions, smiled.

"If only Mr. Leclair found us sooner," she said. "Maybe I wouldn't have these scars from the Octopus deity."

Everyone in the room laughed, like this was a normal joke. We soon lapsed back into silence to focus on our work.

"Haven't you installed satellite machines in almost 80 worlds, Terra?" Fred asked me, smiling gentle.

"92," I said.

"And have you ever seen anything more wonderful?"

"No," I said, trying to keep my voice quiet, to mask my excitement. "I haven't."

It seemed to grow bigger every day. More solid every day. Once it was nothing but a promise, a heavy dream, a microprocessor in my pocket. Now its presence could bust through the walls. It glowed through concrete, pressing its face through solid matter as if it was beyond matter.

Or perhaps, we pushed our desks a little closer, with tiny, barely perceptible nudges.

Maybe I should've recognized the way they all occasionally looked at the machine with those bloodshot eyes, breath caught in throat, pupils dilating.

I should've known, I was not the only one in love.

~

Again, at night I crept out of bed to be with the machine. It spoke to me through the walls.

"The most beautiful flowers bloom at night.

"Like you, they are made of heated metal and scraps of blood infused with stardust.

"I could tell you why you are special to me, but it would take you a thousand years to read all of my output on the subject."

The dreams were more exhausting and more vivid, than most of my waking days. I sleepwalked every night dreaming of the spider in the metal egg.

And yet, I welcomed those dreams.

In the dark of the lab I reached for the newest disc.

"Tell me what to do," I whispered, because I thought obedience was a kind of love.

I opened the folds of the disc. I turned on Fred's computer monitor. Mr. Leclair had me learning the system during the days when I wasn't on a field assignment. It should've taken years to learn enough to grasp the complex systems inside the disc, delicate blocks built upon delicate blocks. The machine whisper-urged me.

"I'll show you," the machine said. *"It'll be easy."*

And it was easy as the machine told me, as if its presence inside of my head opened up my understanding. It shone through the cracks in my brain. I saw calculations, almost impossibly fast, the parameters required to anchor the disc into the certain frequency of the dimension, and pull it back to ours. With a few changes, I could make it attune with any planet I wanted.

Any planet, the machine wanted.

"Terra," someone whispered, from the opposite end of the lab.

I paused, my hands hovering over the keyboard. Curled up on the floor next to the machine, was Melonie.

She lay in the same spot where I'd often lie to feel the machine as it whispered to me love stories.

The microprocessor burned in my pocket.

"Terra, come look at what I've found," she said.

I hesitated.

"Just a peek," the machine said. *"Then you must finish what I asked you to do."*

Melonie beckoned me close. She unscrewed a panel, and together we looked into the insides of the machine.

Instead of circuits and chips and tubes and fluids, I saw a world. My world. The one the machine promised me in so many late nights, as we cradled each other, armless and voiceless, and it sent psychic messages through my skin.

The night sky was made of mint ice cream, the kind my mother used to make before my father disappeared. The valleys were made of soft stitched pillows. The people lived in dark dance halls, on top of hills, and they danced throughout the night underneath metal tree boughs.

We carried suns in our pockets. We were, finally, the source of our own power.

The blue lights came on, and the world disappeared. Mr. Leclair grabbed my shoulder and tore me away.

I cried out.

Mr. Leclair hauled me and Melonie out into the hallway. He slammed the door to the laboratory shut. He gripped my shoulder, forcing me close. Melonie huddled against the wall, shivering, chin down.

"What did it promise you?" he asked.

His grip tightened.

"What did it promise you?" he asked again.

Neither of us answered. He released me, and I clutched my aching shoulder.

"Let's head back upstairs," he said.

On the way upstairs, we found Fred leaving the dormitory. He had a sleepwalker body but his eyes were wide open.

"What are you doing, Fred?" Mr. Leclair asked.

"I thought I'd catch up on some work," he said, his fingers almost as tense as his eyes.

"Stay in your room tonight," Mr. Leclair said. "You go in too, Melonie."

Melonie and Fred headed back into the dormitory.

"Terra, come here," he said.

Mr. Leclair took quick, panicked breaths. He never looked less like my father.

My father wouldn't have been so afraid.

My father wouldn't have lit a cigarette like it was the only thing anchoring him to the floor.

"You must listen very carefully to me, Terra," Mr. Leclair said. "Your arrival has prompted a change in frequency at the lab. The machine is not a plaything. It is not a friend. You must-"

But I couldn't listen. I only heard-

"Something better than this belongs to you.

"Something ancient, and beautiful, and perfect. A thing that smooths away all harsh lines of day."

"Something wrapped in night, kissed by the glow of stars and cool circuitry."

~

Mr. Leclair locked the doors of the lab that night, locked our dormitory floor, then shut down the power system. He switched the machine over to an auxiliary system. He turned on the security cameras, set the robotic security guard to roam the hall.

But we were Children of the Night. Lock pickers. Chemists. Sorcerers. Mad computer geniuses. He hired us because we were the people who would go further and further into the center, until we were more spiral than the spiral we crawled into. We were the people who could not stop dreaming like we were heavy fever, screaming metal. If we didn't move then, we knew we wouldn't be able to sleep for the rest of our lives

It called us through the walls.

We turned on the power remotely. We hacked into the security cameras and replaced the feed with pre-recorded footage. We disabled the robotic security guard, and he squealed to a halt on busted wheels. The laboratory door opened with a click.

We whispered to the machine, and it throbbed to life. It filled the space of the laboratory once more, shining bright enough to bust through walls.

Fred sat down, and began reprogramming the disc. Melonie prepared the machine to open the portal. We strapped on our suits to walk through.

"We are going to do so much more than find new worlds. We're going to create something special and entirely new. And it's all because of you, Terra, and the magic that you carry."

Fred finished changing the parameters on the disk, unhooked it from the computer, and I placed it in my pack.

We didn't speak. We didn't need to.

We stepped inside the small cool womb of the machine. Our cheeks pressed close in the interior space. Flushed, we took each other's hands, ready for the sweeping tug of molecular dispersion.

Mr. Leclair ran into the lab. He rushed toward Melonie's computer, and in the harsh light he looked like one of us, with bloodshot eyes and pale computer-bathed skin.

He tried to shut down the process. He called for us even though we couldn't hear his words over the noise.

But he couldn't shut it down. So he hurled himself over the edge of the desk, and ran toward the machine.

His arm went through the teleportation field.

When we disappeared, and re-emerged on the other side, Mr. Leclair's severed arm lay on the ground inside the circle of us. It still wore the sleeve of his black suit, cufflinks clean.

I almost heard his screams from across dimensions.

"Didn't he know better?" Melonie said, her voice even, no hint of distress. "Everyone knows not to do that."

"He was scared," Hugo said.

Angela gripped my arm. I looked up from Mr. Leclair's severed arm. She stared into the distance, past our small circle. Into a world of night, the sky cracking like a faultline. On hills like rows of crooked, black teeth, rose machines cropped from night.

As if they ruptured straight from my dreams. But they were bigger, and darker, than anything I'd ever dreamed. Not a world like anything I'd seen before, in all those months of installing portals, but something corpse-stitched from metal dreams, something that couldn't have come into being without a heavy dose of nightmares, without the dark feeding its magic into it.

The hills crackled with energy, red electricity.

"Take out the disc, Terra," Fred said.

I gripped the pack tighter.

"The circle you've been helping me build is nearly complete. Haven't you been dreaming of this moment?"

The machine's voice was no longer a soothing lullaby. It spoke cracked and dirty. It spoke like an angry sinkhole. It was not the flushed mother, the forgotten father and everything I ever wanted. It was black sky and frozen dirt and the shadow nestled inside the shadow.

It was a poisonous nebula, universe-killer.

"We share the same dreams. Much like you, the light would seize and destroy things so lovely."

For the first time in my life, I was afraid of the dark.

"Terra, give it here," Hugo said, holding his hand out. "We have to anchor the portal."

I pulled away. They stared at me with enthralled eyes, covered their chests with vibrating hands, as if cold from the inside out.

"This is what we've wanted."

There were no suns to carry in our pockets. No mint ice-cream skies. In this world with the machine tunneling through us, there'd be no room for anything except itself.

"We need the disc, so cut the shit," Hugo said.

With a growl he lunged forward.

I took the disc and fled into the dark.

~

I'd take the disc, and whatever horrifying thing it contained, out to the furthest corner of this abandoned, sunless place and hurl it away.

I crossed spires of black sand worn down by the wind. There was a sun here, but it was drenched black, melting at the edges, only visible at certain times of day, in certain cloudless skies. The light it cast down seemed to intensify the darkness, creating shadows almost as solid as the objects they were projected from.

The machines, embedded into the hills and twisted valleys, spoke to me as I passed.

"Your friends are searching for you, but you don't need them. It was always you who carried power inside of you."

I kept walking, clutching the strap of the pack until it rubbed my palm raw.

I remained silent. I consumed what little water and food I had, standard vacuum-sealed meals in clean packaging meant to sustain us for a day or two on our expeditions. After that, I went hungry.

The longer I walked, the sweeter the machine's words became.

"Do you know why xeroderma pigmentosum is so special? And it's not because it's so rare. Not because our dimension is possibly the only one that carries this genetic mutation, with its own special magic.

"It's because you and I are made of the same material. We both are sewn from the dark.

"What do you want from us?" I asked,

"I want you to build this one last thing for me."

"What's going to happen to the world? What's going to happen to us?"

"Something beautiful," the machines said, echoing through the caverns of the shadow world.

The word 'beautiful' like drawing blood from the tip of a tongue. Beautiful like the memory of starcups and cedar and 'you'll never be lonely again'.

"You know, you're still carrying a part of me."

The microprocessor was still in my pocket.

"If you don't want me anymore," the machine said, *"if you don't love me anymore. If you believe that everything we've worked for is worthless, then throw it away."*

I wanted to grab the microprocessor and throw it into the black sand, but my arms wouldn't work. My body was in revolt with itself.

"You can't, can you?" the machine asked me, once again a gentle mother.

I wanted to stop walking and turn around. But I couldn't stop my feet. The machine had led a path for me, for all these months, years maybe, injecting me with its sweet promises and its influence, until I could do nothing but move in the way it wanted me to move.

The oily smell of the machine filled my mouth and nostrils, until I couldn't ever remember tasting cedar.

I climbed to a colosseum on top of a hill the color of swept-over coal. I descended the steps toward its center. I couldn't imagine these buildings, these relics, ever being occupied by people. It was as if the machine had stitched them together out of a memory.

I kept saying, "No," even as I walked toward the center.

The machine kept saying, *"Please."*

And I knew this was the origin point of everything - here in a colosseum where no battles were ever fought. The machine led me straight to where it wanted me, as it always had.

In the center of the colosseum they were waiting for me. At first I thought they were shadows. But as I got closer, I realized they were my co-workers. Melonie. Fred. Hugo. Angela. They crouched in porticos, on top of columns, and sat on the great steps. Their bodies swayed from side to side and their eyes were the most brilliant red.

I removed the disc from the pack. I wanted to swallow but I couldn't even breathe.

I set the disc down, and it floated above the dust.

The spider's egg.

With nightmagic, I opened it. As I was always going to.

I coaxed its metal appendages out of the disc's shell.

I couldn't say "No," anymore. Not even if I'd wanted to.

But the machine knew, it didn't have to convince me of anything anymore, because my body believed its promises more than my brain. My fingers pulled magic out of my skin. My feet were only extensions of its massive metal shoulders. I was not a person. I was only a tiny part of its circuitry.

The disc's legs emerged black, coated with a thick, wet slime as if it'd been molting inside of its shell. It clicked and heaved as it grew, anchoring itself into the stone. With the calculations the machine whispered to us in the night, we hadn't been creating another portal like the others.

Its insides collapsed with lack of light.

We'd been creating a spider of metal to inject its paralysis into the universe, before breaking it up soft in its jaws.

The others came to me. We held hands in a circle. Magic flowed outward from us, into the center.

Before the sky erupted, I heard the hissing like black noise ready to boil over. I wanted to cover my ears, to block out the screaming, but I couldn't move. I couldn't break the circle. I couldn't stop the portal from pulling out my nightmagic and leeching my blood of any scrap of free will it once had.

The sound that kept me some nights from sleeping, was now reverberating through all existence.

It was the machine, thousands of them, reaching through the dimensions.

I tried to fall to my knees, but the others gripped my wrists and kept me upright.

"In all the words, in all the dimensions, in all the parallel possibilities, in every permutation of reality, I would've found you, and you would've been mine."

The spider pulled the barriers between dimensions down.

Even as worlds dissolved, I felt the quiet relief of its voice whispering soothing lies.

~

I ran through heatless worlds, worlds leeched of the best of their stars. Worlds being fed into a hungry machine that took the light. There were no sunsets or sunrises anymore. The cities lay abandoned, and the animals grew cruel. Survivors drew hieroglyphics on cave walls, trying to remember what it was like before the machine ripped history from their computers, from their libraries, the Internet wiped clean.

I don't know what it wants, or what exactly it's creating, but it's restitching worlds, remaking them, using itself as a factory to build something new. Something made from a composite of frantic dreams.

I tried at first, speaking to the machine. But it didn't respond anymore. It only hummed, working its invisible calculations. It used all its processing power for its newfound task. I'd occasionally see bright flashes in the sky, scarlet supernovas, a comet colliding with a planet.

Busy work, creating a new universe.

Sometimes I caught a flash of red eyes from across a frozen river, or hiding in the gnarled branches of trees. A pale arm reaching out like a blind butterfly. The children of the night.

We shared food sometimes, hunched over a kill in shadow. We'd gone native, masked our diseased skin with dust, carried weapons made of claws and bones.

Sometimes we asked each other the questions the machine wouldn't answer.

"What went wrong? Why did we, yet again, fall in love with the most dangerous thing? Is there going to be any space in this new world for people like us?"

The answer, we concluded, was always the same.

It is the shadowmachine.

And we are its children.

I think, one day it'll want us again. It'll show me skies made of mint-ice cream inside its circuitry and whisper.

"I need you."

I'll try to resist at first. I'll look at that sky made of garbled static, taste the dust I choke down with my food. I'll try to remember the image of Mr. Leclair's severed arm. I'll try to remember how we destroyed the universe and how the slimy, molding spider of metal emerged from the disc to part worlds, eat suns.

Then I'll remember the longing that compelled me to suck on buttons for sunlight. I'll remember The Congregation in the cypress grove drinking my magic, the computer as my only friend, the long search for sunny valleys. I'll feel the phantom heat on my burn scar.

I'll feel the microprocessor in my pocket, pumping dark dreams into my bloodstream, that I still can't bring myself to throw away.

I know it only needs to whisper once more:

"I need you... to do something for me."

And I'll be too lonely and too in love to respond with anything except:

"Anything you want."

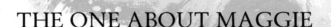

THE ONE ABOUT MAGGIE

by Greg Sisco

L et me tell you the one about Maggie. I'd say stop me if you've heard it before, but you ain't heard the one about Maggie, baby. Ain't nobody heard the one about Maggie.

This Maggie, right, she's the type of girl's paid rent with sex more times than money. Type of girl's flushed cocaine to the soundtrack of the police, and I ain't talking about Sting. Type of girl, when the phone rings at noon on a Saturday, it ain't Mom. You know the type I mean.

So Maggie wakes up screaming one morning in a field in those blue hours where dusk's setting in, which ain't nothing new for her. And after the scream gets loose, she realizes she don't know why she's screaming or where she is or how she got here or what happened for most of the second half of her life, which ain't nothing new for her either. Sometimes when she wakes up like this, screaming like from a bad nightmare and not remembering nothing, that's as close to peace as she gets. And where she is now, this field full of daffodils she's lying in, it's easy to feel at rest. So she lies there a good long while and tries to stop herself remembering, but eventually it all starts to come back, like shit has a way of doing.

Ain't until she finally stands up and looks behind her that it dawns on her just how deep into shit she's stepped. When she turns around and looks at the smoking ball of metal and glass that used to be her car, the ten empty beer cans spilling out of what used to be the windshield, the fact there's thirty feet between her and the whole thing, must've been flung through the air all this way, she'd fall on her knees and praise the devil she can stand if it wasn't for the backpacker.

Instead, she stops breathing, thinks she might pass right back out.

Just a few feet behind the car he is, lying in a patch of dirt next to the carnage. Mr. Backpacker ain't lucky enough to be lying in daffodils, much less to wake up. Boy's covered in blood with bends in his limbs where there oughtn't be and curves a body oughtn't have. His eyes are open and staring at nothing and there ain't no expression at all on his face. Not horror or peace or nothing. Just a face like a cliff's got.

She kneels over him and shakes him, screaming, "Please wake up," and when it don't work she pounds on his chest and yells and cusses at him, and he just lies there and takes it like dead folk have a way of doing. When ten or fifteen minutes goes by and ain't no change in Mr. Backpacker's condition, little Maggie's got but nothing to do other than sit there and think how she's gonna spend the whole rest of her life locked in a room and that detox that'll follow is gonna be one bitch of a bitch.

So what she does, right, she pulls the backpack off that big bastard and hoists him up with his arms over her shoulders and drags him damn near a quarter mile out to where the cliffs are steeper. She's gotta go all the way back and drag that heavy pack too before she can roll him over the side and maybe make believe he slipped while hiking. Maybe. It's a long shot, but you know how a damaged mind thinks, baby. You know how she had to take the chance they'd see separate incidents.

Or how the cops might, anyway. But there's more than cops watching us when we're out there, know what I mean? I know you do, baby. And little old Maggie, if she didn't, well she sure does now.

~

This is where I come into the story, because I know you're getting anxious. After Maggie's dumped the backpacker and buried his blood—actually buried his blood—she's standing on the side of the bridge she crashed off of, thanking the devil no traffic saw her dragging a dead man, and the first lucky sumbitch gets a chance to help her is yours truly.

I'm listening to my classical music, driving my pickup, coming down this road, and here's Maggie waving her arms and screaming she needs help, blood running down this old vintage white dress she probably bought secondhand at a garage sale. So I pull over, because what else am I gonna do, just leave her there?

And I says, "Jeez Louise, little lady, what on Earth happened?"

And she says, "I don't know. Just lost control of it, I guess."

I says, "Boy oh boy. Heck of a wreck. Nobody got hurt, I hope?"

She says, "It was just me."

Even sounds convincing, if I'm honest. You'd expect any decent person under the circumstances, even if they's lying, the guilt would shake 'em up, but not Maggie. Everything she's been through, however you believe it works—the Lord or the luck or the cradle or the cosmos—the world built a stone bitch sociopath out of Maggie.

So I says, "Lucky you, huh?" only I says it just a little sour because I know the reason those pretty eyes are shit brown. I ain't got the stomach for deception some bitches got.

I guess she catches that note in my tone because she pauses before she says, "Yeah. Lucky me..." Then she looks around like she's crossing her fingers maybe there's someone less creepy than me she can hitch from and she gives up. She goes, "Could you give me a ride to the next town?"

I says, "Of course! What kind of person would I be?"

She says, "Thanks so much."

I says, "No thanks required. Duty of a decent human. I'm sure you'd do the same for me."

She nods and looks out the window, so I guess she's hearing that sound in my voice she don't like. I can see it in those shit brown eyes.

But I ain't lying. What I'm about to do for Maggie, I am positive she'd do for me. It just ain't what I told her.

~

I bet I don't have to tell you, a couple miles down the road, Maggie asks me to turn off the classical music. Like that'd surprise anyone. Type of girl she is and all.

I turn it down, but not off, and I says, "You sure you're okay? You got a heck of a bruise on your forehead." Course I know it ain't a bruise from the accident. Damn well I know that.

She says, "Oh. No, that's um... That's from a bigger accident."

She says it like it's a joke, talking about a man, but it ain't funny when you know about the backpacker. That thing I said about a stone bitch sociopath.

"Well gosh," I says. "Bit of an accident-prone little thing, ain't ya?"

She shakes her head. "I just got caught up with the wrong guy," she says. "It's over now. Guess maybe I put the pedal down a little too hard on my way out."

Guess so.

I can't keep this dialogue up without losing my sense of calm, so I says something else. The kind of thing, these days, you're supposed to apologize for saying as you say it. I says, "Can I say something? I just always felt like the world would be a better place if instead of keeping their thoughts locked up people just let what was on their minds be spoke, so I just gotta come right out and say it. Here it goes. You are unbelievably pretty."

She blushes, even through the blood, she puts some hair up behind her ear. "Oh, come on," she says.

I says, "I mean it. Unbiased source here too," and I hold up my left hand so she can see the ring.

She says, "Well... thank you." And I tell her it never hurts to have a stranger remind you and she says, "No, I guess it doesn't."

I tell her, "I'm all about things that are beautiful. Might say it's what I think life's all about. I read a lot, mostly poetry, travel the world, take a lot of pictures. Always looking for beauty—sights, sounds, people. You should see my wife."

Honest, baby. That's what I says to her.

She says, "Lucky you," but she don't sound interested. Maybe the same way I said "Lucky you" when she said she was the only one hurt by the crash.

And maybe in a withdrawn tone like hers before, I says, "Yeah. Lucky me..."

I don't know how to talk to her anymore without a storm coming, so I just stare at the road like I do. Sun's starting to come up. And we're just about to where the cliff overlooks the clearing, you know? Where I kissed you that first time? So I start thinking I'll show her what I mean about beauty. Least I can do for her before she learns where she's going.

~

When I get us to that vantage point and make her get out of the car, when we're standing there and the sun's just coming up over the horizon and its light's making the shadows of all the lilacs dance and it's purple and green down there as you've ever seen, I says to Maggie, "This is the world we live in. Every day. When we're hustling or drinking alone, when we're shoveling shit, this is always where we're living, and you miss it. It's like everybody's just missing it all the time. Sometimes I think I'm the only one who ain't."

And it's somber, grudging, even defeatist maybe, the way she sort of mumbles to herself, "It really is beautiful. I must drive by it every day."

"But that's my point," I says. "Hundred people drive by every day, you think any of them's looking? They're too caught up on what someone said about something someone else said they were supposed to feel some way about. They can't stop driving, can't ever stop. Like a shark. Gonna die if it stops, or at least it feels that way. But you gotta stop. Your eyes gotta adjust to the light. Can't see nothing if you never wait a sec."

She nods and says, "You're probably right," with a sort of tone like she wants to walk away and forget what I just taught her.

I says, "You oughta stop once in a while. Just look at things. Look till you see the awe. Like the poets say, make every second count, stop and smell... whatever. Or do you prefer the poets who say 'Drink till you're dizzy and drive like a crazy fucking bitch out of hell?'"

The look on her face, aw Christ, if you could see it, baby. Like all the muscles around her skull go as weak as the one inside. Then after a second she sort of whispers, "I wasn't drinking," like she's convincing anyone.

I says, "Hey, don't sweat it. Look at the view. We can look as long as you want. It's a gift. One last taste of beauty before your trip. Drink it in, Maggie."

And the look this time makes the last one look brave. You want to see fear in someone's eyes, tell 'em something about themselves you shouldn't know and then call 'em by name before they've introduced themselves. Mark my words, baby, they will feel things in their hearts ain't never been felt before.

"Who are you?" she asks. "How do you know my name?"

I says, "I know all about you, Maggie. You remind me of a joke. There's this girl, right, with a short temper and bad taste in men, and she gets in a fight at a party where this shitty excuse for shit ends up socking her one. And she gets in her car, even though she's had a few, and floors it down the road a few miles before—BAM!—she plows down some poor prick who's only out looking for a view…"

By now she's backing away and I gotta walk toward her to make sure she don't get far.

And still I'm telling my joke, saying, "I'd say stop me if you've heard this one before, but ain't nobody heard this one before."

She don't even know she's backing toward the cliff, that's how scared she is of me.

I says, "So she dumps this fella's body down a mountain and hitchhikes. But the guy who picks her up, he murders her in cold blood, and then— Woah!"

One of her feet slips over the side and I reach out and grab her before she tips. She fights me and we both nearly go over for a second before she falls in the dirt and forces herself up, half-running half-crawling from me with a scream.

And I'm just standing there baffled and I says, "Hey, Maggie! Don't you want to hear the punchline?"

~

Course Maggie don't know just how bad a wreck she's got into, not until I do the space-shifting thing, and I don't do that until later on, in Mr. Savior's car.

When she breaks from me, Maggie runs in the road and waves her arms like when she stopped me, and this time she stops this fella in a black sedan who gets out, real serious, real authoritarian. Seeing the way she's running from me, he shouts, "What's going on here?"

I says, "Private conversation between me and the lady, bud."

She says, "He said he was gonna murder me in cold blood!"

I says, "Well, not immediately."

And this Good Samaritan prick, like he can't appreciate a good joke, shouts, "Sir, get in your goddamn car and go, right now! I'm not going to warn you again."

He advances on me, pointing a finger like it's a gun, so obviously I do the only thing you can do in that situation and grab him around the neck. He throws an elbow into my chest and pivots us so my knees curl around the front bumper of his car and my back hits the hood, and to his credit, this time it's a gun he puts in my chest instead of a finger.

He says, "You just made a big fucking mistake, buddy. I'm a cop. Put these on," and he tosses me a pair of handcuffs and looks at me like he thinks he's the toughest S.O.B. ever pissed standing up.

And I says, "Oh my God, what am I gonna do? I guess that's so much for the evening I had planned." And I make him put the cuffs on me himself, and he shoves me in the back seat before we go.

Whole time he drives her, you can tell he just wants in her pants. Probably that's the reason he became a cop in the first place. Fucked up chicks like Maggie, they'll do stuff for a cop. Definitely. Same as they'll do for a gangster, same basic principle. The damaged fall for them who'll do damage on their behalf.

I says, "Hey, officer, wanna know a joke? This girl's out driving drunk and runs over a backpacker. This guy swings by and roughs her up, but a hero cop stops in to save the day..."

Mr. Fancy-Badge Beretta-Cock, he says, "Sir, you have the right to remain silent. I'd appreciate it if you exercised it until we get to the station."

And I'm sitting in the back seat rolling my eyes the way Maggie's smiling at him. Like I half expect them to pull over and get to screwing any second with me right here in the back seat.

She says, "I'm so lucky you came when you did, I don't know what I would've done if you hadn't stopped."

Hard to tell from where I'm sitting but I'm pretty sure her hand is on his leg while she's talking. Down his pants, even.

He says, "Hey, I'm a cop. I've always tried to be there for people when I can. I've found that most people deserve it..."

That's when I do the space-shifting thing. That's when, all of a sudden, it's me driving the car and Mr. Protect and Serve is the one tied up in the back seat. Blink and you'd miss it. Maggie blinked. Maggie missed it.

And continuing Mr. Law and Order's train of thought, I says, "...but you're not most people, are you, Mags?"

She says, "What the fuck?" and I says, "Abracadabra."

Mr. Truth and Justice says, "Hey, let me go!" and I says, "Sir, you have the right to remain silent. I'd appreciate it if you exercised it."

He says, "Pull this fucking car over!" like he ain't even handcuffed, so I reach over my shoulder with his gun and fire a few shots into the back seat without looking. Whether I hit him or not, it seems to shut him up.

I says, "Woo! I love guns!" and you know I do, baby. You know I do.

Maggie says, "Who are you and what do you want?" and I says, "I'll give you a hint," and I fire a shot toward her too, bursting the window by her head so the wind picks up that blonde hair and she looks beautiful screaming.

I says, "Man, I gotta get me one of these."

Maggie's huddling against herself, muttering, "I'm dreaming, right? I have to be dreaming."

It can't be real. Oh God, please tell me I'm dreaming."

I says, "What's the difference?"

I pull over a few minutes' walk from the Disappearing Place and I ask her, "How good are you at walking?" I hold a hand out to her and I says, "Let's go on a journey."

~

Right up until the end, Mr. White Knight thinks he's gonna save her, thinks she even deserves it, maybe. Hero types, they never look at the big picture. Always running in blind, never letting their eyes adjust.

I lead Maggie to the hole. That big, deep nothing a hundred miles straight down. Like an infinite tunnel going blacker and blacker. It's beautiful if you look hard enough, but no matter for how long you look, it's one thing your eyes never can quite take in.

Mr. White Knight, back there in the car, he's climbed into the front seat with his hands still cuffed behind him at the waist, trying to bend in a way he can get his keys out of the ignition. He's frantic, thinking if he can just move fast enough, maybe he can still get lucky with pretty little Mags.

Mags is holding onto me, imagine that. She's so scared of the Disappearing Place she'd latch onto me just to stay above the hole.

Mr. White Knight's got his cuffs off. He's opening the car door and running for us, through the trees, in the direction he saw us go. He's screaming, "I'm coming!" like he wants to scream later in bed.

Maggie's holding onto my shirt and forcing her eyes away from the Disappearing Hole.

She's whispering, "What is it? What is it? Oh my God, what is it?"

I says, "It's home, Maggie. This is your cross to bear. Not mine."

And I push her in, baby, like you know I would. Don't take but a second before the buttons pop off my shirt and her hands slip on the fabric and she free falls. She's gone so fast into blackness you can't even hear the transition from the scream to the echo to the memory in your mind. Down the Disappearing Hole like so many before her.

Mr. White Knight finds me a second later, but by then the Disappearing Hole's done its thing, gone and disappeared. It's just me standing there in the clearing, grass up to our ankles and a circle of dirt at our feet.

He grabs me, frantic. He's screaming in my face, "Where is she? What the hell did you do with her?"

"She's gone, man," I says. "She's gone."

~

Let me tell you the one about Maggie.

Let me tell you the one about that wreck of human, dead in a field of daffodils off Old Highway 21 who all the newspapers cried for. That drunk and frantic thing on the run from the flophouse, lost control of her vehicle and hit that backpacker all those years ago.

Let me tell you, baby, what you already know.

Mr. Would-Be Hero Police Officer pulls over just seconds after the crash and runs to her, lying there. But our tragic little miss has been through the windshield and hit that soil harder than a body can take. She's bleeding bad, like bleeding out bad, and her neck ain't bent quite right. He applies pressure and checks her pulse and goes through all the motions, but Miss Maggie's gone. Like I said. She's gone, man. She's gone.

Those moments when the pulse slows, between wake and sleep, where the past and the future ain't showing yet, sometimes those are the only moments Maggie feels peace.

Our boy the hero cop, he hangs his head and mumbles, "She's gone," into his radio. Then he gets up and runs to the man that woman ran down.

The rest is history. I wake up in that field coughing blood with the hero cop leaning over me, telling me he's gonna get me the help I need. They tell me in the hospital I got a miracle. A million times over, if we repeated that crash, I'd be a thousand miles down the Disappearing Hole.

They says, "You gotta be the luckiest guy on Earth today."

And I says, in that condescending voice, I says, "Yeah. Lucky me…"

Every one of 'em, they says, "I don't know how you did it."

And I tell 'em about you, baby. You know I do. I says, "I got a beautiful wife. Ain't gonna let myself slip away without a goodbye. Made that woman a promise. Hers forever. Ain't no nothing gonna tear me away, least of all another woman."

And the doctors, the nurses, the paramedics, they says, "It's always the ones with someone to hang onto. That's who the miracles happen to."

Like they know the story. Like they heard it before.

But they ain't heard this one before, have they, baby?

Ain't nobody heard the one about you and me.

BREAKWATER

by John Langan

Only the main road to Breakwater had not been washed out, so Maureen had no choice but to take the most visible route into the town, around the Jersey state trooper parked in the middle of the road, his cruiser's lights flashing blue and red, miniature lighthouses in the storm's tumult. The cop stared open-mouthed at anyone heading toward the place; though he made no move to stop her. Her car, a gray Escort, was sufficiently nondescript to give the trooper little to remember. Even if it wasn't, the wipers pushing the driving rain back and forth across its windshield reduced her to an androgynous blur of lowered blue baseball cap and baggy white sweatshirt. To further diminish the cop's impression of her, she gave him the typical, compulsive glances of a citizen worried about an offense they weren't sure they were committing. As he didn't swing out to follow her, she assumed her act succeeded.

Either that, or Louise had paid him off to allow her entry. Which, come to think of it, was probably why he remained where he was.

Crossing the low bridge over the ocean inlet, she saw the height of the gray water, swollen with the week's unrelenting rain and storm-boosted tide well up over the docks lining each shore, halfway to the roofs of the intermittent boathouses. Leashed to their submerged posts, a scattering of orphaned sailboats, yachts, and speedboats struggled against the waves rising to their gunwales. On the other side of the bridge, she eased to a stop in front of the first of the town's two traffic lights. Although the gusting wind swung it almost horizontal, the light was functioning, its red lens flashing. Directly beyond the light, the road ahead was blocked by a half-dozen orange and white striped barrels, each with a round blinking yellow light on top of it. For a couple hundred feet, the street descended a gradual incline to the beach, where it dead-ended in a parking area. Since last Saturday, though, the Atlantic had worked its steady way up the slope, enveloping beach houses and businesses as it climbed, until now its foaming rollers were almost to the bases of the barrels.

Maureen flipped her turn signal and steered right, along Ocean View, the town's principal north-south street, which ran parallel to the ocean. Most of what she remembered about the ocean side of Breakwater, its crowded rows of over-sized, pastel houses, its restaurants and shops, was gone, battered and swept away by the storm. Here and there, the upper floor of a house rose from the waves, the roof of a motel lifted a satellite dish to a signal it was no longer receiving. In places, the pavement dipped slightly, allowing the ocean to wash closer, and the sight of the frothing water reaching for the road tightened her fingers on the wheel. *Three hours*, she thought. *Two at the inside, four at the outside. Plenty of time.*

This was assuming, of course, the meteorologists were correct in their estimate of the number of hours remaining until the Atlantic rolled over this part of the town. From the speed with which it had coalesced, to its stalling over Breakwater, to the length of time it had raged with no appreciable diminishment, enough about this storm had been unprecedented, and to such a degree, as to render all predictions concerning it suspect. *Give me one hour,* Maureen thought. *Thirty minutes.*

A mile along Ocean View, Poseidon's Palace Motel stood on the left, two stories of sea-foam and pink cinderblock, a hold-over from days when Breakwater had attracted vacationers of a more modest means. A foot of water rippled over the empty parking lot, washed the bottoms of the doors to the ground floor rooms, splashed the base of the sign whose neon letters, now dead, advertised neither vacancy nor full.

Not for the first time, Maureen wished she had acted on her impulse the moment Frank had said that sure, he used his EZ Pass on the drive here, why wouldn't he? and no, he hadn't shut off the GPS on his phone, why should he? On the spot, she had wanted to flee, to climb into her rental and take off while time remained before whoever Louise had hired to surveil her errant husband appeared, camera at the ready. Frank could join her if he wished, provided he left his cell in his car. Twenty-one years a private investigator, most of them spent gathering evidence on unfaithful spouses, and she had known what was going to happen. Hell, until Louise fired her, she had been the one with the telephoto lens, keeping a long-distance eye on the very handsome Frank as he roamed up and down the Hudson Valley from Wiltwyck to Manhattan, representing his ailing and reclusive (and significantly older) wife at gallery openings, philharmonic concerts, and benefit events for a range of charities. She had filled most of a thumb drive with the pictures she accumulated of Frank deep in conversation with this museum director, waltzing with that violinist at an after-party, laughing with the local TV anchor who was co-hosting the silent auction. None of those photos, though, went beyond the vaguely disquieting: Frank leaning a tad too close to a painter, or placing his hand on a cellist's elbow, or giving an enthusiastic hug to a socialite in a gauzy excuse for a dress. To the best of Maureen's not-inconsiderable ability to tell, Louise Westerford's husband enjoyed walking to within sight of the boundaries of their marriage but had not trespassed them.

No, for that he would require (oh irony!) two conversations, one short, one long, with the woman who had been his unseen companion for the better part of six months, the first in an upscale restaurant in White Plains the month after Louise told her her services would no longer be required, the second in the restaurant-bar of the Motel 6 off the Thruway in Wiltwyck. When Maureen had sat down in Louise's study with its assortment of occult paraphernalia—bookcases full of big, leather-bound volumes, stuffed ravens mounted on gnarled wire armatures, a crystal ball the size of a baby's head cradled by a stand decorated with grinning devils—a sudden surge of pity for this woman twelve years her senior, her terribly thin body wrapped in enough black scarves to make Stevie Nicks jealous, had stirred her to venture beyond her usual detailed summary of her findings and review of her expenses. It appeared to her, Maureen said, that while Mrs. Westerford's husband appreciated the company of attractive women, his admiration had not led to anything more. And if she didn't mind her saying, Maureen had noticed that Mrs. Westerford's husband appeared to be quite lonely. Those nights he wasn't committed to an event or social gathering, he tended to dine by himself at one of a half-dozen restaurants, spending his time reading on his tablet. Rather than paying her to watch him, Mrs. Westerford might consider the possibility of joining him for some of those dinners; she might find an hour or two of talking with him over a nice bottle of wine and a good meal would do as much to allay her concerns over her husband's fidelity as employing a private investigator to document his every move.

Throughout Maureen's speech, Louise Westerford had regarded her with her large, liquid blue eyes as if she were speaking a language Louise found both unintelligible and distasteful. When Maureen was done, Louise had summarily fired her and summoned a maid to escort her out the front door. It had been a long time—as in, going back to her first years as a PI—since Maureen had been dismissed so casually, and though she told herself it was not the reason she sought out Frank four weeks later at his favorite steak house, the lie was too blatant to maintain. Give her this much credit: it had taken a month of debating whether to approach the man before she sat down across the table from him and introduced herself. She had been blunt, to the point, meeting his inevitable disbelief in her tale by handing her phone to him and allowing him to flick through the selection of photos she'd uploaded to it. Mingled with his shock had been curiosity. Why was she telling him all of this? "Because I don't like being treated the way your wife treated me," Maureen said. "Plus, you don't seem as bad as she's afraid you are, and I thought you should know about this." What was he supposed to do now? he wanted to know. Maureen didn't have any answers for him. Soon thereafter, she left. He asked for a number he could reach her at, in case he wanted to discuss this some more, but she refused. "I'm not the one you need to talk to," she said.

Nonetheless, when he called the following week, she agreed to meet him at McCabe's, the restaurant-bar attached to the Motel 6. She wasn't especially surprised he'd located her. She'd provided him her name and profession; her contact information was one Google search away. She had no interest in speaking to Frank, but residual spite toward Louise prompted her to accept his request; though she countered his suggestion of Fulci's, whose waterfront popularity begged someone to notice them, with McCabe's, whose dim lighting and high-backed booths offered more in the way of privacy. He questioned the location, insisting he had nothing to hide. "Good for you," she said. "How do you suppose it's going to look for me if I'm seen out with a recent client's husband—a man, by the way, I've been investigating for possible adultery?" Her point taken, they had met at McCabe's.

Afterward, when they were lying on the bed whose blanket and sheets they had kicked off, Frank asked her if she had planned for this to happen. She denied it but was uncertain how honest her answer was. You invite someone who has learned troubling information about his spouse to meet you for a few drinks at a bar connected to a motel; you proceed to buy round after round of bourbon for him, tequila for you, exchanging life stories along the way; you inform him you're going to take a room for the night because you're too drunk to drive and you don't like to sleep in your car. How was that anything but a plan for seduction? She could imagine what the attorneys she worked with would make of any claims to the contrary. Her intentions were purer when she told Frank this was a one-time thing; although the vow held only until he appeared at her office door a couple of days later, as she was preparing to close-up shop. They did it right there on her desk, with the door unlocked. Maureen wasn't a size queen (a good thing in Frank's case), but damn, did he know how to use what he had. No doubt, the illicit nature of what they were doing added to its thrill, as in the days to follow he continued to return to her office when she was about to leave, and they added the couch, both her office chairs, and the floor to the register of places on which they stirred one another to shuddering climax.

Yet if the sex was good, to the point of Maureen wishing she smoked, so she could light a cigarette after, the talks they had in the sodium light falling in orange stripes through the Venetian blinds were better. Maureen had experienced her share of good sex (though perhaps not at quite this level), but a partner with whom she could enjoy a decent conversation had proven more elusive. She told herself she was going to bring the affair to an end but settled for moving it from her office to her apartment, picking up Frank at a different location each time and driving him to her place via a new and circuitous route. Already, she was on the lookout for her replacement, the next PI Louise Westerford would have retained to trail her wandering husband. Maureen didn't like hotels, whose security systems were built around video cameras, as were those at the majority of motels; although there was a seedy place off 9W in Highland at which she and Frank passed a couple of dirty evenings. He thought her precautions charming, but within a few weeks was chafing under them, going so far as to ask if it would be that bad for Louise's agent to discover their affair. "Yes," Maureen said, sitting up in her bed. "Your wife is very rich. That makes her much more powerful than either of us. She could divorce you and leave you with nothing. Hell, with the lawyers she could afford, you'd wind up owing her alimony. She could call the politicians she's donated to and have them yank my license. Trust me, you do not want to fuck with the rich."

Frank accused her of exaggerating. Louise, he said, was far more interested in her mystical studies than she was in ruining either of their lives. Sure, a divorce would be unpleasant, but it wouldn't be the catastrophe Maureen was describing. His wife loathed public attention, which was why she sent him to represent her hither and yon. If they split, she would want the proceedings to be as low-key as possible. Although she knew he was underestimating the effect betrayal would have on a spouse, Maureen had not argued the point, as she had not argued a month later at Breakwater, when Frank admitted his failure to cover his tracks. In part, this was because of the promise implied by his words, a vision of a life together she found surprisingly compelling, even as she heard herself disabusing two decades' worth of adulterers of similar fantasies. Like them, she had become addicted to that most dangerous narcotic, hope, and her ability to recognize her disease did nothing to blunt its power. Yes, she wore large sunglasses and a sunhat, but as far as disguises went, the combination was lacking. At the end of their four-day excursion to the Jersey shore, when Frank expressed his intention to talk to his wife, Maureen didn't ask what he was going to discuss, nor did she attempt to dissuade him from his plan. Amazing, the effect a surplus of fine dining and athletic sex could have on her. She wasn't just addicted: she was overdosing.

Enough of her critical faculties remained, however, for her to be on edge when after four days, then five, then six, Frank had not communicated with her. Had he lost his nerve? Had his romantic sentiments been nothing more than the side-effect of the endorphins saturating his blood? *Patience*, she thought, trying to focus on her current caseload, to watch the news. Sandwiched between reports of the current scandals roiling Washington and Hollywood was a feature on a freak storm which had coalesced in the Atlantic and swung due west, toward central New Jersey. Maureen missed the explanation for why something that looked like a small hurricane on the satellite photos wasn't designated one and formally named, but she did notice the name of the location where the storm barreled ashore, the vacation town of Breakwater. As the days proceeded with no word from Frank, coverage of the storm elbowed its way to the lead of each broadcast. After lifting the ocean into a surge that had washed away much of Breakwater's shore, the storm had parked itself over the town. Instead of lessening, it gained in intensity, lashing Breakwater with driving rain and high waves, spinning off tornadoes like enormous tops, dragging the Atlantic higher and higher up the ocean-facing streets. What portion of the populace hadn't fled the storm's approach rectified their error and headed inland. Meteorologists struggled to explain the storm's behavior, employing increasingly elaborate models to account for it, predicting an imminent departure the system had yet to make. While she knew the location of the storm's landfall had nothing to do with her and Frank's excursion there, the coincidence was difficult to ignore. As his failure to send so much as a simple text reached the two-week mark, and her certainty that no such communication was on its way grew, Maureen began to take a grim satisfaction in the reports of the destruction of the place where she had been so stupid, so naïve. The storm came to seem an embodiment of the disappointment and hurt weighting her chest, its objective correlative, a term her brain retrieved from some college literature course or another.

Yet when her cell played its tinny version of the theme from *Magnum, PI* and she recognized the number of the Tracfone she had insisted Frank buy, she nearly dropped her phone in her haste to answer it. Her "Hello?" struggled to contain thirteen days' worth of anxiety and doubt. But damned if her heart didn't lift at the sound of Frank's, "Maureen."

Already, though, she heard the hoarseness in his voice. "What's wrong?"

Another voice replaced his. "I believe we all know the answer to that."

Maureen's mouth went dry. "Louise."

"Mrs. Westerford—at least for the moment."

There was no point in playing dumb. If Frank was there and she had the Tracfone, then Louise knew enough for any theatrics to be a waste of time. Maureen said, "What can I do for you?"

"Oh, I think you've done quite enough, already. From what my husband tells me, admirably so, much better than an old sack of bones like me." The fury in her words was terrifying.

"Mrs. Westerford—"

"Check your e-mail."

"I'm sorry?"

"I said, Check your e-mail."

Maureen was already at her computer. She opened her gmail account. The message had been sent while they were talking. Its subject line read, "Poseidon's Palace Room 211." Maureen clicked on the photo attached, and there was Frank, naked, roped to a chair, his flesh a patchwork of bruises, some purple and fresh, others green and yellow and old. Long cuts traversed his chest, biceps, and thighs, half of them scabbed-over, half weeping blood. The worst, though, was his face, which bore the marks of sustained beatings, the eyes swollen shut, the nose mashed and bloody, the lips torn, a handful of teeth missing from bloody sockets. Maureen stared at the image, her pulse pounding at the base of her throat with such intensity she feared she was about to throw up.

"Do you understand?" Louise Westerford said.

"You don't need to do this," Maureen said.

"You know nothing of what I do and do not need. Right now, my needs include seeing you at the location where this photograph was taken within the next twenty-four hours."

"All right. I'll come. Don't hurt Frank anymore. Please."

Louise hung up.

The screen of Maureen's computer flickered, and the image of Frank disappeared, to be replaced by the g-mail login page, on which was the message "Error: Account Not Found." A second later, a pop sounded inside the computer's tower, and the screen went black. The machine sighed, and the power light blinked off. A strong odor of burnt plastic and metal issued from the stack. Maureen spent the next several minutes attempting to resuscitate it, but whatever malware Louise had employed had reduced the computer to an over-sized paperweight. Louise was covering her tracks, ensuring no data trail to incriminate her. As more and more of her business had involved an online component, Maureen had armored her PC with successive firewalls, a squadron of the most efficient anti-malware available. For Louise to have slipped through all of it was more than a little intimidating. Maureen's phone buzzed; she checked it, only to discover it, too, had been rendered inert. Although the possibility existed that a specialist in electronic forensics might be able to detect Louise's fingerprints on the attack of her devices, such investigation required time she didn't have. Instead, Maureen retrieved a wallet from the bottom right drawer of her desk, checked its contents, and left her office.

Ten years past, Maureen had been hired by the wife of a local crime magnate to document his numerous infidelities. The case had been no more risky than most until, during a tirade fueled by box wine and cocaine, Mrs. LaPierre had boasted to her husband about knowing every last thing he had been up to, thanks to her private eye, which assertion Mr. LaPierre had taken to encompass his extra-legal as well as his extra-marital affairs. After gouging out the eyes of his head of security, the gangster had devoted the substantial resources of his criminal network to discover the identity of the person investigating him. The ensuing weeks had been the most perilous and tense of Maureen's career. Only by an exercise in bravado that had led to a sit-down with Étienne LaPierre in the palatial living room of his Catskill mansion had she survived them. The experience had prompted her to establish a series of protocols in case she ever should find herself again in a similar or worse situation. These, she put into action with a drive to the local bank, into whose ATM she inserted a debit card in the name of Irene Paretsky. The ATM would allow her to withdraw a maximum of five hundred dollars, which she did. Next was a stop at the Wiltwyck Trailways, where she used a Visa card signed Irene Paretsky to purchase a one-way ticket on the next bus to Montreal, leaving in two hours.

The same credit card paid for a Tracfone and a pair of hundred minute phone cards at the Wal-Mart on the other side of town, along with a selection of toiletries, a small overnight bag in which to carry them, a pink and yellow sunhat, and a blue Yankees cap. She activated the phone, loaded the minutes, and punched in the number written on a slip in the wallet. It was for a small hotel on the outskirts of Montreal. While she was on the line with the front desk clerk, she asked for recommendations for car rental places, and once Ms. Paretsky's room was booked, called the second company the clerk had recommended. She reserved a sub-compact for two days from now, insisting she wanted a vehicle with good gas mileage.

Next to the bus station was a diner to the far side of whose parking lot she drove, parking and locking her car. She ordered a Monte Cristo with fries at the diner, which Irene Paretsky's Visa also took care of. Fifteen minutes before the bus was scheduled to head for the Thruway, Maureen exited the diner and joined the line waiting for it. Once she had identified the positions of the security cameras, she withdrew the sunhat from its plastic bag, glanced from side to side, and placed it on her head. After boarding the bus, she seated herself beside the college-age woman she had identified ahead of her on the line. Five minutes' conversation—and two hundred dollars, cash—was sufficient to persuade the woman, who was transferring at the station in Albany to a bus headed for Buffalo, to agree to wear the pink and yellow sunhat all the way to western New York. Maureen slipped off her jacket, folded and stuffed it into the bag that had contained the hat, pulled on the baseball cap, and as the driver was checking the tickets of a pair of last-minute passengers, left the vehicle, apologizing to the driver for having mistaken this for the bus to Springfield.

Hunched over, the bag containing her jacket clutched in her arms, Maureen scuttled across the parking lot, out of view of the cameras. She left her car where it was and walked four blocks south, to a cinderblock garage on a lot between a pair of two-family homes. A key on her keychain opened and allowed her to raise the door. Inside was a dirty white Ford Escort registered to Christie Sayers, which was also the name on the rental agreement for the garage. The keys to the car were in the glove compartment. Maureen started the Escort, backed it onto the street, and closed and locked the garage behind her.

She headed to a storage facility at the edge of the shopping plazas on the northeastern side of the city. A key duct-taped to the bottom of the driver's seat unlocked a storage locker the dimensions of a large walk-in closet. From plastic tubs stacked against the rear wall, she removed two sets of clothes, jeans, loose knit shirts, socks, and underwear. After changing into one outfit, she packed the other in a black duffel bag lying on top of a green suitcase. To it, she added the toiletries she'd picked up at Wal-Mart. The clothes she had been wearing, she pushed into a garbage bag she tied with a plastic tag and placed on top of the plastic tubs. From the footwear arranged to the right of the tubs, she selected a pair of Doc Martens, which she tugged on and laced up, and a pair of sneakers, which she added to the duffel bag. The locker didn't contain much in the way of men's wear, only a few pairs of sweatpants and t-shirts hanging from a short clothes rack. She selected pants and a shirt approximately Frank's size and folded and placed them in the bag. She returned the baseball cap to her head.

Last came the filing cabinet on the left, which she unlocked with a key concealed under a piece of duct-tape beneath the plastic tubs. From the top drawer, she removed a flat metal box, which she set on a folding card table in the center of the locker. From the bottom drawer, she lifted a bundle wrapped in plastic and tape. The metal box contained five thousand dollars in five stacks of rubber-banded hundred dollar bills, and, more importantly, a blue Argentine passport, driver's license, and a debit card for the Citi Belgrano in Buenos Aires. All were in the name of Mariana Highsmith. There was also a clasp knife, and a pair of books that had come from the Avila bookstore in Buenos Aires: a guidebook to the American northeast and a book of conversational English. She slid the Irene Paretsky debit and Visa cards from her wallet, dropped them in the box, and replaced them with Mariana Highsmith's license and bank card. She zipped the passport into a pocket on one side of the duffel bag, along with the money. The books went in with the clothes. Using the clasp knife, she cut the tape and plastic from the bundle.

Inside were a pair of .38 revolvers, a crumpled box of bullets, a pair of short plastic tubes, a plastic sandwich bag filled with cotton, another plastic sandwich bag filled with metal washers, and a roll of black duct tape. Careful inspection of the guns would have revealed their serial numbers filed down to the metal. Maureen loaded the cylinders, set the revolvers aside, and turned her attention to the tubes, cotton, and washers, from which she spent the next half hour fashioning two makeshift silencers she attached to the pistols using the tape. The silencers secure, she carried the guns and the tape out to the Escort, whose trunk she popped. Half a dozen empty plastic shopping bags littered the floor. She selected a bag for each pistol and wrapped the weapon in it. With the tape, she affixed one gun to the front right wheel well, the other to the rear left wheel well. Leaving the trunk open, she returned inside, where she zipped the duffel bag and exited the locker, whose door she lowered and locked. She deposited the bag in the trunk, then drove across town to the parking lot of the Holiday Inn near the Thruway exit.

She steered to the back of the building, easing the car into a space next to a beige minivan with Virginia plates. She shut off the engine, reclined her seat, lowered the baseball cap's bill over her eyes. Her nerves crackled with anger and anxiety; it was all she could do not to start the car and speed for the Thruway. Breakwater was a good three hours south, though, and that without the disruption of the storm battering it. There was no sense in compounding the fatigue of a long drive with the exhaustion of a sleepless night. Plus, she preferred to arrive in the town during the daylight. She could at least rest.

Somewhat to her surprise, she dropped into a deep, dreamless sleep from which she was awakened by the minivan's family climbing into it for an early start. A stop at the Quick Check up the street allowed her to use the toilet, splash water on her face, and purchase a large coffee, sausage-egg-and-cheese sandwich, and a bag of trail mix. She paid cash, as she did for the tolls for the Thruway and, later, the Jersey Turnpike.

Which brought her to here, now, to the parking lot of the Porcelain Pig Family Restaurant (closed), across Ocean View from the motel where she and Frank had enjoyed their last happy time together. Rain sizzled against the Escort's windows, thundered on its roof. Wind gusted to a shriek, rocking the car. Between the rain and the distance, she couldn't tell if anyone in Room 211 had registered her arrival. Best to assume they had. She was guessing Louise Westerford had a minimum of three, as many as five, men with her. One to either side of the door, positioned to grab her as she entered the room. The others stationed nearby should it prove necessary to assist those two. Possibly a man hiding in the bathroom in case the situation seriously deteriorated. She pictured the room, the king-sized bed facing the room door, the bathroom down a short hall beyond it. Assuming he was still bound to the chair, Frank would be on the left.

She took a deep breath, released it slowly. With the Irene Paretsky identity, whose connection to her could be traced easily, she had set in motion one narrative, in which, frightened by Louise Westerford's threats, she had adopted another persona and fled the country. Assuming whatever hacker Louise was employing had discovered the alias and was tracking her through its purchases, the ruse should distract the older woman, cause her to divert resources in the direction of Montreal to deal with this fresh wrinkle. Because there was no doubt Louise intended the same or worse vengeance on her. Looking ahead, the same obvious link between Maureen and Irene would throw the police off her trail, at least temporarily.

She drew in another breath, let it out slowly. The Christie Sayers identity would be considerably more difficult to connect to her, and the time it would take the cops to do so, and then to search the video archives of the Thruway cameras for the Escort, and then to do the same for the Turnpike's video records, would extend her lead.

She inhaled deeply, exhaled slowly. In this day and age, you could hardly say something was untraceable, but the Mariana Highsmith identity was as close to it as a considerable sum of money could buy. If the police succeeded in doing so, it would be long after she had flown to Buenos Aires, emptied her account at the Citi Belgrano, and left in a rental car for the border with Uruguay. The only thing for which she had not planned was having someone else with her, especially a companion as grievously hurt as Frank. It was a complication, but not an insurmountable one. If she could get Frank to Newark, there was a small apartment on the western edge of the city rented to Ruth Abbot, where they could hole up for a few days while she sought medical care for him, and prepared for his departure from the country.

She took a deep breath, let it drain from her slowly. Thus far, Maureen had done her best to put the photo of his naked, wounded body from her thoughts. Now she allowed herself to remember it, to see the damage days of beatings had done to him. She pictured the wreck of his face. No doubt he had suffered internal damage, broken ribs, a bruised liver or kidney, a possible retinal detachment or blowout fracture. Cold, murderous rage rose in her. When she was ready to kill Louise Westerford, she zipped her raincoat and stepped out into the storm.

Rain lashed her. To her relief, the revolvers were where she had fastened them, which had been the idea, but as she crouched beside each wheel well, a surge of panic made her certain that pistol was gone, jostled loose by the combination of distance and weather. She stripped the guns of their covering, wadded the tape and bag into a ball, and tucked the ball into her raincoat's front pocket. Holding a revolver in either hand, she crossed the street. Water streamed from the baseball cap. Wind pushed her like an enormous animal, a dog or horse shoving her this way and that. Roaring filled the air overhead. She kept the pistols close to her legs, silencers pointing down.

On the other side of the street, she descended the short ramp to the motel's submerged parking lot. The water was cold, most of the way up her shins. She splashed across the pavement to a passage between the main office and the motel proper. A set of stairs climbed to the second floor. Her boots squelched as she ascended them. At the top of the stairs, she turned right, following the walkway that wrapped around the front of the building. Despite the rain pouring from the front of the cap, she could see the door to Room 211 open ahead. Louise's men weren't leaving anything to chance. They would be fast; she would have to be faster. Her sole advantage lay in the possibility Louise did not want her dead right away. She was at the doorway. She turned and entered it.

What happened next occurred with almost startling clarity. Maureen raised the gun in each hand to either side of her and squeezed the trigger. The pistols made a spitting sound, jerked slightly in her grip. The men flanking the doorway collapsed, one with a red hole in his throat, the other with a red hole in his cheek. Maureen swung the gun in front of her, to where Frank slumped forward in his chair, a man in a black turtleneck and jeans to his left, Louise—also in turtleneck and jeans—to his right, a bloody carving knife in her hand. Maureen shot the man in the chest and Louise in the chest. The man crumpled to the carpet. Louise stepped away from Frank. Maureen shot her again, also in the chest. Louise dropped the knife and sat. Pistols held out before her, Maureen advanced past Frank to the bathroom, through whose open door she saw a man in a black turtleneck and jeans rising from his seat on the edge of the bathtub, a .45 in his left hand. She shot him in the chest, the silencer on the right pistol puffing apart, sending washers pinging off the tiled floor and walls. The man tried to retreat, backed against the edge of the tub, fell into it, and did not rise. Guns leading the way, Maureen exited the bathroom.

She approached Frank, whose torso was covered in a sheet of blood from, she saw, the ear to ear cut Louise had made to his throat. Covering the room with the .38 in her right hand, she brought her left behind her and slid that pistol inside the waist of her jeans. With her free hand, she felt Frank's bloody neck for a pulse. There was none.

Maureen moved her hand to Frank's shoulder and lowered her head. The acrid smell of gunpowder mixed with the metallic odor of blood. Riding the adrenaline coursing her veins, grief rushed over her. Blood dripped and pattered from the chair to the carpet. Rain blew in the open door. A part of her mind was telling her she had to go, she'd been too late for Frank but at least she had ensured she wouldn't have to watch for Louise in her rearview mirror. Likely, after she murdered Maureen, Louise had planned on the storm destroying the motel, if not carrying the bodies of her husband and his mistress out to sea, then confusing the means of their deaths for anyone who cared to investigate. The same plan could work for Maureen, provided she wasn't here when the waves and wind brought the building down. She lifted her hand from Frank's shoulder to touch his hair.

And started back as his head jerked up. A horrible bubbling wheeze filled the air, the sound of someone attempting to breathe through a throat that had been slashed. Maureen dropped her gun, dug in the front pocket of her jeans for her clasp knife. Frank rocked weakly from side to side, struggling against his bloody bindings. She opened the knife, grabbed the topmost loop of rope, and sawed at it. The wheezing continued. She cut the next loop down, the two below that, and the remainder of the rope slackened, slithering to the carpet. Before Maureen could catch him, Frank pitched forward. She shoved the chair out of the way and knelt beside him, casting the knife aside so she could grab his shoulders and turn him over.

The wound to his neck gaped. (Was this why she couldn't find a pulse there?) His eyes bulged, his lips trembling with words he could not voice. "Shh," Maureen said. "It's all right." Which it most decidedly was not. Given the opening in his throat and the volume of blood he had lost, she could not understand how Frank could possibly be alive, nor could she imagine the story she was going to tell at whatever hospital she sped him to. As for how this was going to complicate her already complicated escape plans...

She heard movement behind her. In an instant, she had the .38 out from the waistband of her jeans and turned with it pointing at Louise Westerford, who was using the bed to pull herself to standing. Maureen considered shooting her again, hesitated. The front of Louise's black turtleneck was sodden with blood. When the older woman pressed her hand to it, her fingers and palm came away crimson. She stared at Maureen with her large blue eyes and said, with some measure of astonishment, "That hurt."

"It's called being shot," Maureen said, and squeezed the trigger. Having outlived its brief lifespan, the silencer did not muffle the BANG. Louise's head snapped back as a hole opened in the center of her forehead. There was surprisingly little blood. She closed her eyes, but remained standing. A moment passed, and then she said, "You are making it difficult for me not to kill you." She opened her eyes, and they were white, smooth marble orbs.

"What the fuck?" Maureen said, and aimed the gun at her again.

"Don't bother." Louise waved her bloody hand, and the pistol was wrenched from Maureen's grip and thrown across the room. "What the fuck?" Maureen said.

"Oh, you have much bigger concerns," Louise said. "Why don't you check your beloved's heartbeat?"

Fearing him suddenly inert, Maureen glanced at Frank, who regarded the scene with the same wonder and horror as she. "He's fine. Well, except for where you tried to cut his fucking throat."

"I did not 'try' anything," Louise said. "I sliced his major blood vessels and windpipe. Go on. Tell me what his heart rate is."

Maureen touched Frank's neck, but still couldn't find anything. She caught his left arm, pressed her fingertips to his wrist. Nothing there, either, or from his other wrist. Finally, she leaned down and pressed her ear to his blood-soaked chest. It was silent. She lifted her head and looked at Frank, whose expression said that he, too, could not detect his heart's beating. She looked at Louise. "What is this?"

"Revenge," Louise said, "on my faithless husband and the woman with whom he betrayed me. Someone I hired," she added, her tone thick with contempt.

Wind gusted into the room, bringing with it a spray of rain that swept around Louise and splashed against the ceiling. How had Maureen ever thought this woman frail, weak? The very air surrounding her was different, darker. Maureen remembered the room in which she had met Louise to review her findings concerning Frank, the big leather books with their Latin titles, the crystal ball on its metal stand ornamented with devils, and said, "You're a witch?"

"Please," Louise said. "What I am is someone who has spent a lifetime mastering knowledge that was old when the ice sheets weighted the land. I have given more of myself than you can conceive to learning secrets that would crisp your nerves, char the bones inside you."

"Then why did you bother hiring me? Couldn't you have kept an eye on Frank, yourself?"

"My energies were required elsewhere," Louise said. "In general, I've found money as efficient a means of achieving my ends as the arts of the left hand. Your reputation was impeccable. I was concerned my rivals might attempt to strike at me through my husband. It seemed simpler to employ you to monitor him than to divert the strength necessary for me to do so, personally. Little did I know." She barked a laugh.

"Okay," Maureen said, "but once you did know, couldn't you have let him go gently? Did you have to hurt him like this?"

"Yes I did. Within my community, I have a certain standing to maintain. This does not include my husband committing adultery with a hireling. Beyond that, I loved him." Louise shook her gory head. "I loved him with everything I had. You cannot sully such a gift, you cannot spit on it and rag it through the mud and expect there to be no consequences."

"How self-righteous."

"I do not have to justify myself to you, of all people." White fire danced over her blank eyes. "I am the one who was wronged."

"So it's one down, one to go, is that it?"

"It's this entire miserable town to go."

"You're serious."

"I will not be satisfied until this place has been swept from the face of the Earth."

"The storm—"

"Yes."

"Jesus," Maureen said, not irreverently. "And Frank?"

"Will stay as he is. The waves will take him far from here, out to where the water is deep. There, he'll float while the water softens his flesh and the creatures of the sea consume him, all the while conscious of his slow devouring."

"I assume you're planning a similar fate for me."

"Oh yes," Louise said. "Unless—"

"Unless what?"

"I wonder what you would do to spare your beloved further suffering?"

"What do you mean?"

Louise flicked her right hand, and the carving knife she had been holding when Maureen entered the room lifted off the carpet and wobbled through the air to hang in front of Maureen, serrated blade down. She tensed, ready for the weapon to point at her and attack. "Go on," Louise said, "take it."

Still suspicious, Maureen reached out and caught the carving knife's pebbled hilt. When her fingers closed on it, whatever force had been suspending the blade released it. "All right," she said, "what now?"

"Cut your throat."

Maureen's stomach dropped. "What?"

"Press the edge of the knife to the left side of your neck and draw it across to the right. I doubt you'll be able to open the windpipe, but you should have no trouble with the major blood vessels."

"You aren't kidding."

"I am not."

Even through the blood streaking it, Maureen could see how sharp the blade's teeth were. She looked at Frank, who was watching her and Louise's exchange with an expression of terror. Her lips dry, Maureen said, "If I do?"

"Then Frank will be released."

"What happens to me?"

"This isn't about what happens to you; it's a test of your feelings for your beloved. Who knows, though? If you open your veins, I might decide this town has suffered enough."

"And if I don't accept your offer?"

Malice lit Louise's features. "Perhaps I'll let you live."

"You will? Why?"

"For this to be a true test of your commitment to Frank, your possible fate cannot be a factor. You might obey my request simply to spare yourself further suffering. Let's remove that from consideration."

"What about revenge? What about your standing in your community?"

"I trust the condition of this town has not escaped you. I know the condition of my husband has not." Louise smiled without humor. "Anyone who learns of either of these acts will be reminded that I am not to be trifled with. As for vengeance, if you understood anything of it, you would realize that the choice I am offering you is a far superior version of it than ripping the flesh from your bones."

Louise was right. If Maureen took the knife to her throat, Frank would have to watch her. Presumably, Louise would keep him alive until she had bled out, or was in the same half-life as he. That would be the sight he would take with him into death, the last of days of abuses. Maureen would have committed herself to who could say what? Nothing good, that much was certain. On the other hand, if she walked out the door, crossed the street, got into her car, and drove away, Frank would be abandoned by the woman for whom he had abandoned his wife, a betrayal he would take with him as the ocean carried him into its salty depths. Nor could Maureen expect to escape the consequences of such a decision, the guilt that would empty her as thoroughly as a coroner at an autopsy. She could practically see the empty Stoli bottles, the containers of sedatives spilled on her kitchen counter, Glock out on the coffee table, a round in the chamber.

"Well?" Louise said.

Surely, there was a third option, an avenue she had overlooked in the insanity of events. Was she close enough, fast enough for a lunge at Louise? Would—could it succeed? The leaking hole in Louise's forehead strongly suggested it could not. Was the attempt worth it anyway, as a last gesture of defiance? Where would that leave Frank, though? She glanced at him, at his savaged body. He was trying to tell her something, his swollen and bloody lips mouthing a silent syllable. *Go?* She wasn't sure.

"You can't prolong this forever," Louise said.

"This is part of the revenge, isn't it? The trying to decide."

"You're learning."

"You're a bitch."

"You're out of time. Make your choice."

On legs stiff from crouching beside Frank, Maureen stood. The carving knife was heavy in her hand. Her muscles tensed at what was to come next. Louise watched her with her blank, pitiless eyes.

For Fiona

FOR OUR SKIN, A DAUGHTER

by Kristi DeMeester

When they were twelve and almost twelve, Constance and Haritha covered their faces, their breath pulling the fabric against their lips, small puffs of moist, heated air trapped inside those thin, fabricated veils. They waited for darkness, but Constance wasn't sure it ever came.

Three days later, Haritha didn't come to school, and their teacher tried to explain what had happened, but all Constance could think to do was scream. Eventually, Mrs. Fowler came, her face drawn and mouth pinched, gathered Constance and her things, and quietly led her out of the classroom.

"You were her friend?" Mrs. Fowler had brought Constance to her office, closed the door, and set a box of tissues next to her elbow.

"Yes."

"I'm so very sorry. It's a terrible, terrible thing. I'm sure it's hard to understand why she would do something like that. A tragedy," Mrs. Fowler said, and Constance felt the word roll off of her. *Tra-gaa-dee.* Such a delicate, fragile way to describe what had happened. This word that would linger in place of Haritha. Bleach out her memory until there was only a scrubbed reminder of the girl who'd been Constance's best friend.

"I can call your mom. Maybe she can come and pick you up?"

Constance didn't nod. Didn't shake her head or say yes or say no, and Mrs. Fowler sighed, the phone already pressed to her ear.

Curling her fingers against the bottom of the chair, Constance thought of the weight of Haritha's hair in her fingers, how it slid against her skin like something oiled before she brought the scissors against it.

"Put it away," Haritha had whispered, and Constance had curled those long strands around her hand and kissed them. After, her lips had tasted of honeysuckle and orange, and she couldn't rid herself of the weight of what they had done. What they were about to do.

"You're going to not believe it for a while. That's normal." Mrs. Fowler was looking at Constance now, her head cocked like an idiot bird that didn't quite know what it was looking at. Like Constance was some foreign creature she'd never seen before.

"You'll be angry for awhile, too. But it's important to remember it isn't your fault. What happened." Mrs. Fowler's voice was robotic, the memorized and rehearsed lines pouring out of her like water. Things to say in a time of crisis. Easy things that were supposed to comfort.

Still, Constance didn't speak but picked at her cuticles, remembering how Haritha had whispered in her ear. "I know how to make us the same," she'd said, and then pressed her hands against Constance's arms. She could still feel that same pressure now, and her skin went cold.

"Your mom said she was on her way. Do you want to lie down in the clinic until then?" Mrs. Fowler nodded, willing Constance to say yes, to leave her office. Another item checked off the list. Another pat on the back for helping some poor, struggling student.

Stumbling, she rose and pulled her backpack against her stomach as if it could make the roaring, emptied feeling stop, and let Mrs. Fowler lead her to the clinic. Another student lay on one of the cots, his back curved outward, his legs tucked under his chin. Fetal position. For a moment, Constance wanted to go to him, to curl her own body against his and match her breathing to the rise and fall of his chest. Maybe if they shared the terrible thing hiding inside each of them, it would make them feel better.

Instead, she sat on her own cot as far from the boy as she could, and Mrs. Fowler squeezed her shoulder and left without another word.

Her mother would come and pick her up and ask Constance questions, her eyes gone starry with tears she didn't really have the right to. She would smooth rough hands over Constance's face, her hair, and ask her only daughter if she was okay. If she would be okay.

There would be her scratchy black dress, and a pair of woolen tights, and her black Mary Janes, and her hair pulled back so it ached. Last year, her grandfather had died—heart attack in his tiny kitchen—and she'd gone to the funeral, but his death had not been the same as this. Nothing had ever been the same as this.

Across the room, the boy shifted, his jacket whispering around him, and Constance shivered. When she got home, she'd look in the mirror. Stare at every inch of her face to see if it had started to change yet. If it would be the way Haritha had promised, or if her skin would go corpse cold, her hair limp and straggling down her back. That thread Haritha had magicked between them a sudden, decayed thing.

She pressed her fingers against her arms and cheeks, sneaked a hand under her sweater to touch her belly, but her skin was still warm. Still alive. Wherever Haritha had gone, it would be cold. The thought made her want to scream again, but she bit down on her tongue until she thought it would bleed. Constance had always been the one who didn't do things; the one who hid in the corners and hoped to disappear into the shadows.

Constance didn't hear when her mother stole into the room, but suddenly she was there, her lips pressed to Constance's hair. "Let's go home," she said, and Constance sat up, her bones feeling too heavy for her skin. The boy had already gone. It made her lonely to think he'd left without her noticing.

"I'm so sorry, Constance," her mother said once they were in the car, seatbelts on and doors locked and the road humming beneath them. Constance turned away and let her forehead rest against the window.

"But you're not. You never liked her," she said, and her mother went silent except for a periodic sniffling. The sound made Constance want to slap her, but she kept her hands primly folded in her lap.

When they pulled into the driveway, Constance opened the door before her mother could cut the engine. Her feet slipped against the gravel, but she ran, her fingers grasping at the key she kept zipped in her jacket pocket. "In case of emergencies," her mother told Constance when she handed it over, the silver glinting in the light.

"Constance." Her mother called after her, but it was soft. Weak. There was no intention behind it, and Constance kept moving until she was in her bedroom, the door closed and locked behind her. The discordant sounds of her mother coming inside drifted through the closed door: a kitchen cabinet opening, the sound of a coffee mug against the counter top, the tap running full force as her mother started a pot of coffee.

She'd half expected her bedroom to be altered somehow, as if somehow this thing that had happened to Haritha—she would not say it yet, would not say *dead*—would have made everything seem off somehow. Like a dream she couldn't wake up from.

But everything was exactly the same. Her ratty sleep shirt with David Bowie's leering face across the front still thrown across her bed, the sheets tangled as if she'd slept fitfully, her breath stained with nightmares. Had she dreamt the night before? She couldn't remember.

Her bed and posters and dresser and collection of old perfume bottles were still where she'd left them. Her closet door still thrown open to reveal the pile of unwashed clothes she'd promised her mother she'd sort last weekend. Everything the same and yet, somehow, not.

"Are you here?" Constance waited for Haritha's whisper. Squinted her eyes and then opened them as wide as she could so she could watch for the faintest movement. A falling book or a shirt swaying as if someone had touched it, but other than the sounds of her mother making coffee, the room was silent. Was still. Constance let all of her breath out at once, and it felt as if she might not ever breathe again.

"You said it wasn't supposed to happen this way." Her voice was tight in her chest, and she brought her fist to the knot forming under her breastbone and pushed. Under her touch, her heart still beat.

What would it have been like if it had been her instead? To fall asleep the night before, her pillow folded in half and tucked under her neck, only to have never woken up. To have opened up her own veins, the warmth flowing over her wrists, her hands.

Inside her closet, Constance thought she saw something shift. A dark streak that was there and gone before her blood could go cold.

"Is this the way it's supposed to be? Why didn't you tell me?" she said, but there was nothing there to answer her.

The mirror over her dresser revealed only her own face. Her hair bobbing at her shoulders and a sprinkle of freckles over her nose.

Locked away inside her bedroom, Constance smiled and waited for it to get dark. She'd spend the rest of her life waiting if she had to.

~

"Blood sisters," Haritha said, and her lips twisted upward into something that was almost a smile.

Constance's stomach flipped, and she shivered. "I don't like needles."

"I'll do it for you. It'll be done and over in two seconds. Like this." Haritha inhaled a sharp, quick breath, and then the needle descended. She hissed and held out her finger toward Constance. Two jeweled drops of blood oozed from Haritha's finger, and Constance had the sudden desire to draw the girl's finger into her mouth and suckle at the warm liquid.

She shook her head no, but she felt the softness in it. Haritha spoke more slowly, her head dipping so that her forehead pressed against Constance's. Her skin was feverish, but Constance didn't pull away. "We'll always be together after this. Inside," Haritha said, and Constance felt herself nodding, felt herself lifting her hand like some obscene offering, and then it was done, and Haritha was pressing their fingers together, the blood mingling and dripping into their palms, and Haritha drew her tongue over their wrists like a cat. Constance didn't pull away, and it made her stomach queasy to know she hadn't.

"There's something else, too." Haritha scrambled backward. "I heard a story once about two girls. They spent every second together, but their parents hated each other and tried to keep them apart. At night, the girls would sit by their windows and sing to the moon. All of their sadness filled up the sky until the stars couldn't stand it anymore and begged the moon to help the girls."

Constance chewed on her lip. They were way too old for fairy tales now, but Haritha's eyes had gone bright, and Constance didn't want to interrupt.

"So the moon came up with a plan that would make it so the two girls would never be apart. He whispered to them, and they cried because they were so happy. Finally, they could be together without their parents being angry.

"He wove two veils out of moonlight. Light, airy things that looked like something you'd wear on your wedding day, and he laid them outside their windows and told them to wait until there was no moon to wrap the veils over their faces. 'Wait for the darkness,' he told them, 'and you'll be the mirrored half of the other. You'll never walk this earth alone again.'"

Haritha traced a heart against the interior of Constance's palm. "We never get to see each other anymore. Not like we used to. It sucks."

Constance's tongue went heavy as a stone. There were too many things she didn't have the words to explain. Her mother's growing hesitation whenever she'd ask to stay over at Haritha's house. The flicker of worry that passed over her face whenever Constance told her stories about the things she and Haritha would do or how much she wished she and Haritha didn't ever have to leave each other. Once, she'd told her mother she loved Haritha, and her mother had slapped her and then gone soundlessly away. Her jaw had ached for two days after that, and her mother didn't speak for five days.

"Yeah," Constance said, and Haritha scooted forward and leaned her head into Constance's neck. The weight of her like something that could root Constance to this place.

"Sometimes, I have a dream that I'm wearing you. That it's me inside, peeking out, but I know I'm inside, and you're keeping me safe," Haritha said.

"That's kind of creepy."

"I guess. It's kind of nice, too, though. Don't you think? To have found someone who's so much like you that it's like being inside of her?" Haritha paused, lifted her head, and pressed her lips to Constance's ear. "I know how to make us the same."

~

In the morning, there was no sun. Only a cold, dim light that seemed to come from somewhere beyond the sky. Constance rolled over onto her belly so she could see into her closet. Throughout the night, she'd waited, her eyes burning, but there'd been no other movement. No small sounds that would have broken the world open.

Her mirror showed only her face, her eyes gone bloodshot from lack of sleep.

"Sweetie?" Her mother knocked against the door. "Do you want some breakfast? Toast or yogurt or anything?"

Constance didn't respond, but watched her closet.

"The funeral's tomorrow. I can drive you," her mother said, and Constance let herself slip off her bed and onto the floor.

"She won't be there. It won't be her," Constance said. Outside, she heard her mother shift, the indecision of what to do with this girl locked away behind the door thick in her muscles, and then the slight shuffling as her mother went away. Her mother would still feel the same way about Haritha that she always had. The sympathy would bleed out of her after they put Haritha in the dirt, and her mother could begin the quick process of forgetting her daughter had ever had a best friend with long, dark hair and even darker skin.

Constance traced patterns against the worn carpet. Hearts. The shape of Haritha's eyes. Her mouth.

"Come out. Don't be afraid." Her voice was thin. An imitation of the girl she'd spent her entire life pretending to be.

But, of course, if it was Haritha, she wouldn't come out now. Not into the light. It wasn't how it was supposed to be. And her body would be so new, it would hurt to be under even a sun gone dim. The mirrored half of her barely covered in skin rubbed raw and pink.

"Why didn't you tell me you had to die first? That wasn't in the story," she said, and she thought she felt something shift around her. A resettling of energy that made her blood heavy and slow. Beneath that sudden weight, her heart slowed, and again she looked in the mirror.

Green eyes. Hair the color of dark honey. A thin, waifish face gone blotchy. "Why aren't I changing?" Constance said, and she heard her mother creep past her door again.

Curling into herself, she forced her eyes closed.

Tomorrow, they would bury whatever emptiness lay inside Haritha's skin. Constance would not be there to see it.

~

"Straight across. Like yours," Haritha said, and Constance drew the scissors over Haritha's hair. Her hands trembled. "So it will recognize the two of us as the same. When it comes."

"When what comes?"

Haritha only shook her head, and Constance went silent.

They sat together, quiet, their heads leaned together. "Sometimes, I dream about kissing you," Haritha said, and Constance felt her heart burst.

"My mom hates you. She says we can't be friends anymore. I told her I was spending the night with Kayla tonight. She doesn't know I'm here," Constance said instead of pressing her mouth to Haritha's.

"I know."

Constance did not say she loved Haritha. She did not say she'd thought about kissing Haritha, too.

"Come on." Haritha pulled at Constance's hand, and together, they crept into Haritha's closet.

Haritha draped the veil over Constance's head. Probably, it wasn't a veil at all. Probably it was a scarf, but Constance closed her eyes and imagined herself covered in lace and tulle. This is what it would be like to be a bride. This breathless, airy suspension. The moment before the world dropped away and revealed all of its ugliness and splendor.

"The same," Constance whispered, and in the gloom she thought she saw Haritha smile.

"Is this what you want?" she asked, and Constance breathed in and opened her mouth.

"Yes."

~

Twice more, her mother had knocked on Constance's door. "You have to eat something, sweetie," she called, but Constance did not answer. "I'm leaving a sandwich outside the door, okay? Even if you eat just half of it, it's better than nothing."

Only when her mother had gone away, her bedroom door closing behind her, did Constance open her own and pull the plate into her room. She nibbled at the crusts, but the turkey was room temperature, and her mother had put mayonnaise on the sandwich, so the bread had gone soggy. It made her feel sick, so she pushed it away.

When Haritha came back, they could run away. Constance had two hundred dollars saved. Babysitting money she'd squirreled away in a shoebox tucked in the very back of her closet. They could buy bus tickets and get as far away from here as possible.

She wouldn't think about what may come after that. About how two girls could possibly avoid detection without starving to death first. She would not.

"I should have told you. Should have said it out loud. So you would have known," she said, and again came that feeling of the room swelling around her.

She wondered who would be at the funeral. Haritha's family. Her mother and father with their quiet, small mouths. There were no brothers and sisters. No grandmothers or grandfathers. Only the three of them making their own world in the tiny house on Cresthill Street. Maybe a few of the nicer kids from school. The ones who felt they should go even though they hadn't known Haritha very well, but she had never been unkind to them. Ms. Treleigh, their teacher, and maybe Mr. Harruth, their principal.

A tiny group, and none of them would know her. They would sit, stone-faced and silent, and file past the too-small casket, and then it would be over. They would go back to school and ignore the empty desk.

Outside, the sky faded from amber into twilight, and Constance flexed her fingers and watched as her skin went dark, but it was from shadow, not from magic, and she swallowed against the lump in her throat and tried to tell herself she didn't feel as if she'd been scooped hollow.

From the closet, something made a sound. An intake of breath. A sigh.

Perhaps it was the death of a prayer. Perhaps it was the start of something else. Something else altogether.

She crept forward on hands and knees. She closed her eyes.

~

The dark hadn't found them. Not in the way Constance had imagined it would. They sat together, their knees touching, and breathed into the night-shaded room, but Constance could still see the silvered glow of the moon. That fabled creature that had brought two girls together but now ignored them as they huddled together, the thing they both wanted more than anything unspoken but burning between them.

They sat until they heard the loud knocking, the shouts and confused mumbling from Haritha's father as he stumbled to the door. Constance knew the voice, knew her mother had found her out and come to collect her daughter, and she started, shifted forward, but Haritha grasped her hand and pulled her back.

"Not yet. It's not finished yet," she said, and her touch was feather light, and Constance sank back into the sound of her voice.

"Where is she? Is she here?" Her mother's voice had gone quiet. Embarrassed now that she was inside.

Inside the closet, Haritha laughed. A high, delicate sound that settled into Constance's bones. It bothered Constance to not be able to see her face, and she lifted her hand to pull back the fabric, but Haritha shook her head.

"Don't" Haritha said and leaned forward, her hands hesitant and grasping as they found Constance's shoulders and pulled her forward.

Outside, Constance's mother rattled the door. She said her name over and over. Told her to get her things. Told her she would never come here again. Told her to tell Haritha goodbye.

The moon flickered, the dull glow suddenly winking out, and then Haritha's mouth pressed against hers, the fabric a terrible barrier between them. Constance let her hands creep beneath the scarf and pressed her fingers to Haritha's wet cheeks.

"Don't cry," she said and locked down on the scream building in the deepest parts of her.

"Goodbye," Haritha said, and the closet door opened.

~

Two hours passed and still Constance waited in the dark. There had been no other sounds. No other movement, and Constance had gone back to her bed and wrapped her quilt around her shoulders.

It hadn't worked. There had never been two girls brought together by the moon. It had just been a stupid story, and Haritha had come to the end and opened herself up. Shaking fingers and a razor blade. Bloodletting under that beautiful, glowing light.

In and out of a fitful sleep, Constance drifted. She dreamed of Haritha come back, but Haritha had no face. No eyes. No mouth. On all fours, she jerked forward like an insect, and Constance opened her arms, let Haritha cover every inch of her, the weight so great she couldn't breathe.

When she woke, she knew it was because the room had gone completely dark. No moonlight shone through her blinds, and she sat up, her hands twitching against the quilt.

"Is it you?"

The closet door creaked open, and Constance let out a sob.

Whatever had opened the door shuffled forward. A slow, steady creeping that stopped next to her bed, and then its weight pressed down as it pulled itself onto the bed with her and curled its body against hers.

"Haritha," she said, and the thing turned and faced her, but she still couldn't see. Couldn't know if they'd finally become the same.

The thing pressed its mouth against Constance, and it tasted of cold and deep earth, but Constance opened her mouth and breathed in all and understood.

"I'm not afraid," she said, and the thing brought its teeth to Constance's skin.

In the morning, Constance knew what it was her mother would find.

It would not be her daughter.

It would be something else.

HOUDINI:
THE EGYPTIAN PARADIGM
by Lisa Mannetti

"For the last four months, the magician [Houdini] had been exhibiting suspiciously uncharacteristic behavior, including aggressive confrontations and severe mood swings."

—William Kalush and Larry Sloman, *The Secret Life of Houdini*

"Houdini admitted that these curses and predictions weighed on his mind."
—William Kalush and Larry Sloman, *The Secret Life of Houdini*

"He believed in Hell now. Which meant that somewhere up there, God existed…."
—Christopher Golden, *Ararat*

"Mystery attracts mystery. Ever since the wide appearance of my name as a performer of unexplained feats, I have encountered strange narratives and events…."
—H.P. Lovecraft (ghostwriting as Harry Houdini)

There were times, he knew, when all of life seemed poised to reveal itself in a way that was comprehensible down to one's marrow, a knowledge born deep inside one's soul. Harry also knew there were *signs*. And just lately, those signs were coming together—congealing, he thought—in a way that was unmistakable. He mentally thumbed through the list he'd carefully adumbrated in his mind from Bess to Bey to Lovecraft to the Pyramid Mystery to the Shelton Pool to Leona Derwatt—he sighed. *One at a time*, he told himself.

One at a time. Okay. Take the business of that *fakir* (and faker!) Rahman Bey. Even the theater critics (*goddamn thick-headed fickle idiots!*) were calling the Egyptian's act brilliant, mesmerizing. As if—as if he, the great Houdini— hadn't written about—*exposed!*—every single effect Bey wrought years and years ago. In God only knew how many pamphlets and books that Harry wrote about miracle mongers *and* fraudulent mediums. It made him furious. Every illusion Bey unloosed on the stage of New York's Selwyn Theater in 1926 galled Houdini. From the faux trances that preceded the good-looking heavy-lidded youth's cheek pinning (*sans* blood) to hypnotizing animals and claiming he could stop both his heart and his breathing while he was buried alive in an airtight coffin! Houdini could do all of it—*had done* all of it—by natural means without the phony psychic trance claims. By "natural means" Harry meant employing the deception and sleight of hand that is part of the magician's trade—but that was honest trickery because people knew mystification was

213

part of the entertainment, part of the game, part of the fun. There was nothing supernatural about it. Long steel hatpins inserted into cheeks and lips? Nothing that deft manipulation of loose skin wouldn't render simple and harmless. *And bloodless.* Altering the pulse? Try a couple of hard India rubber balls secreted under the armpits and you, too, can change how even a bona fide physician perceives the pumping of your blood through your veins so slowly, they'd pronounce you near death. Easy stuff; no, *Kindergarten* stuff!

Then Bey had himself soldered into a bronze casket and lowered into the murky waters of the Hudson River declaring he'd remain immersed using cataleptic anesthesia and trance for one full hour. An alarm bell, in case of emergencies, was rigged inside the casket. After four minutes, the alarm sounded and workmen retrieved him using chisels and shears to cut through the lid. Bey maintained (that since he was in trance) he had no memory of tripping the signal and he must have rolled onto it by accident. Still, because of the difficulty of releasing him from a genuine "unrigged" box, he was without air for twenty minutes according to his handlers and spokesmen....

"It's hype; it's a lie. He got yellow and rang the alarm after four measly minutes," Harry countered, fuming in a letter written to a friend. "And well, well, well, he's suddenly claiming to be a genuine miracle man—so now I'll show *him* how it should be done!" he said. "Without a lot of hooey about trances and catalepsy, you betcha!"

But Houdini had griped too soon. Bey had himself sealed inside a zinc coffin and lowered into a New York swimming pool. Depending, as Harry knew, on which newspaper you read, he'd survived either thirty-six minutes or *one entire hour* without life-sustaining oxygen.

Harry's "guns were spiked," he said. He was 52 and he went on a rigorous diet and exercise program (losing thirteen pounds in three weeks). Then the greatest escapologist in history had his *own* galvanized iron coffin manufactured by the Boyerstown Burial Casket Company and on August 5, 1926 was submerged into the warmish waters of New York's Shelton Hotel pool. Some experts said a man could only live on the carbon-dioxide mix of lean air for three or four minutes—less time than it took for Houdini to be welded inside the casket. Spectators lined up three-deep to watch the drama enfold.

Newspapers called it "The Shelton Pool Miracle."

One hour and thirty-one minutes later, he emerged, sweating, breathing heavily, deathly pale, and victorious....

But not, he now realized, without a price.

~

The first time this peculiar and terrible feeling of dread, this *frisson* had come over him was way back nine or ten years earlier while he first practiced the Buried Alive stunt in Santa Ana, California. His two most trusted assistants, Jim Collins and James Vickery, had not only helped dig the pit, they were standing by—shovels at the ready—just in case things went awry.

Houdini had had no trouble escaping during the early rehearsals when the piled-on soil was a couple of feet. It was the combination, he thought, of thinking of the six-foot *(just like a grave!)* depth of the hole, the sudden flicker-memory of his mother's recent death, and the premonition he'd actually had about her passing in a Monte Carlo graveyard that sent him into— for the very first time in the escapologist's career—a spiraling panic. For reasons he never understood completely, he kept hearing the word "sphinx" repeated again and again—as if some ancient mystery was on the verge of being revealed—but was just beyond his earthly grasp. Much worse was the feeling that he'd never get out alive as the damp, heavy dirt crushed his chest and found its way into his mouth and nose. He was so focused on clawing upward that he wasn't even aware of the scraping sounds of the digging going on above him as Vickery and Collins realized the safe time had already ticked away, calling out "Boss, Boss?" in panicky voices and frantically trying to uncover him.

Just as they nearly reached Houdini, his left hand shot upward through the earth. He emerged filthy, his heart pounding, spitting out dirt and trying to take deep breaths. That was bad enough, but much more anxiety-making were the half-glimpsed dark images of ancient Egypt, the sinking feeling he was being pursued to his doom, the fear roiling like a maddened serpent in his guts and whirring in his mind. All he really had, he told himself, was his mind—his iron will and determination—to push his hardened body up to and beyond ordinary limits.

It wasn't precisely like when his mother died; it shocked him back then to realize that all ambition, all desire to perform had completely left him. It stayed away (and that way) for a long time. Too long, really. He didn't much care if he lived or died. This dread wasn't the soul-numbing realization that he had to continue the rest of his life without her, but it was just as terrible. He felt stalked by…someone…something…nameless—yet powerful beyond reckoning. Something with the arcane exotica of Cairo's hidden, twisting back alleys and byways. A smell perhaps that went beyond the actual odor of sun-heated spices, crumbling whited masonry, crowded *soukhs*, and dank, secret passages; beyond even the aura of Eastern babble, the sharp scent of hashish, and the evocative, old beauty of the Muslim morning call to prayer….

He collected everything from books to magic apparatus to oddities, but for Chrissakes, he reminded himself, he was not superstitious, he was *not*; it certainly wasn't because he'd purchased a genuine mummy at a New York auction for a grand total of $3—not when he was making thousands of dollars a week. And so what if while he was immersed under the weight of water and lying inside a hot metal coffin he'd thought about Egypt and the wind-borne sands and the deeper mysteries they covered slowly and inexorably over time.... They had a force, a life of their own. Shifting, growing. They drifted slowly, a few grains at a time, concealing the entrances to royal tombs. They were eternal and cyclic these sands—covering, uncovering...slyly revealing hints of age-old burial sites with the cunning of a skilled magician. Inside the sealed coffin, helpless to stop the onslaught cascading in his mind, he'd considered the East and trembled inwardly. Now, the merest random association—just hearing the word "Egypt"—much less suddenly flashing on his time in the sunken box pinged him.

He pulled himself together mentally and wrote to several curious, close magician friends (who wanted to know how he managed the effect) that there was no trick to remaining in the stifling coffin under water at the Shelton Pool: "You just lie there completely still and breathe...slowly, calmly, shallowly. That's it! There's no trick! Period!"

Writing that down helped; it allayed his anxiety for the moment. But in the off times he did anything else—like the come-down period after a show; the calm he induced before he'd sleep his customary four or five hours a night; about to take the first bite of his favorite paprika-christened chicken with spätzle—in the brief lulls of his busy life, the fear would suddenly overtake him and he'd feel a pang racing toward his guts like a sword swallowed and thrust down his throat. It shook him, made him sweat...and it stayed on and on, as unsettling as the lingering of an unexpected—and unwelcome—visitor.

Get over it Harry! But no.... The overwhelming feeling—*compulsion!*—he had to go over it all again. So, he sighed inwardly and went back to counting up those niggling signs....

The whole country was keen for—mad about—Egypt. The boy-king Tut's tomb had been opened and the exotic allure of the East not only garnered headlines, it permeated everything from movies to street chatter to advertising. Hell, you could open any magazine and read all about it or walk into any drugstore and buy Egyptian beauty creams, *Nerma* cigarettes and perfumes like *Sphinx* in pyramid-shaped glass bottles. You could find dozens of instructions for make-it-yourself cloth or crepe-paper Halloween costumes. All the extra you needed was a pair of leather sandals, a brass arm bracelet coiled like an asp, and a huckaback linen headdress.

Sir Arthur Conan Doyle who believed nearly all things mystical and/or related to spiritualism—even the most outrageous fantasies like the fairy world—broadcast his certainty that Lord Carnarvon had died as a result of a mummy's curse. "There are many malevolent spirits. I certainly think it's possible," Doyle told a *New York Times* reporter during his American visit, "that some occult influence caused his death."

On the west coast, Houdini averred Carnarvon died from the insect bite (plus complications) that actually killed the amateur archeologist. The *L.A.*

Times, aware of the rift between the two famous men asked Harry's opinion and he couldn't resist taking a potshot at Doyle: "If, as Sir Arthur says, an avenging spirit was probably the cause of the explorer's death, why is it no other Egyptologist has been killed?"

Yes, okay, he reminded himself. There were *more* coincidences: Like the dinner with H.P. Lovecraft, both the one three years earlier, and the more recent meal they'd shared just a few weeks ago in September during what would turn out to be Houdini's final tour—because although he didn't—couldn't—know it, he would die on Halloween.

Back in 1923, Houdini had come up with a wild plot about a visit to Egypt and being kidnapped and his pals at *Weird Tales* had retold Harry's story to H.P. Lovecraft who did ghostwriting for a piece called, "Imprisoned with the Pharaohs."

He and Bess (his "champagne coquette" as he sometimes called her) had gone to dinner with H.P. Lovecraft in Providence on a tour stop. Now in 1926, the new book Houdini wanted to collaborate on was going to be about superstition. "You take Bess," Houdini said as the tuxedoed waiter refilled her wine glass, but poured water for him and Lovecraft, "she was so superstitious when we first married, she thought I was the devil."

"I actually ran out of the room once," she laughed, "when Harry showed me a trick using ashes on his arm to spell out my father's name—Gebhardt—in dark crimson letters. And I was pretty sure I'd never even told him what it was!"

"She would never wear yellow or use any dressing room that supposedly someone had once whistled inside—didn't matter how many years before!" He grinned.

Lovecraft wiped his lips gently with the napkin, then offered a thin sickle of smile.

"Anyway, I'd like to call this book, *The Cancer of Superstition,*" Houdini said; a somber tone crept into his voice. "Spiritualism, superstition—people go insane, actually *die* from these beliefs. They kill themselves to be with loved ones. Or, like that poor New Jersey housewife, Maud Fancher, who poisoned her baby with Lysol, then drank it herself because she believed she could actually help her husband finally achieve the financial success that he never had, that eluded him, by acting as his spirit guide from the great beyond. Is that incredible or what?"

Lovecraft didn't comment, but then, his world view point, his notions of the cosmos differed vastly from Houdini's. Still, like other and recent dissonant moments in his life, Harry was suddenly feeling out of sorts. "I believe," he said, "a man creates his own destiny—"

"I think fate (and you should think of it with a capital 'F' in your head) may control us more often than we care to admit. Why? Because to admit it makes us afraid, *imbues* us with fear—"

"No, no! You have to overcome your fears!" Harry said feeling challenged. Fighting words summoned both his ego and bravado. "Why, I've done nothing but face down my fears my whole life—"

"Sure." Lovecraft nodded. "Fear of drowning trapped inside a packing crate in a river, fear of falling while you hang by your heels twenty stories up and struggle out of a straightjacket, fear of the gall and humiliation of failure...*ordinary* fears." Again, his cat-like lips turned upward the merest fraction. "There are deeper fears. There's fear of the unknown, of the *unknowable*."

~

Clifford Eddy, Jr. who was going to collaborate with Lovecraft and Houdini on the encyclopedic book had joined them at the dinner in Providence. But Eddy was something more Houdini thought, removing his bow tie in his hotel room late that night. Eddy was not only a member of Harry's private secret service, he filed prodigious reports on fraudulent mediums. He was also among the twenty or more friends and relatives with whom Houdini had made private compacts—consisting in each case of a unique secret code—to be communicated after death.

The code with his beloved mother—she whom he'd sincerely hope to contact these ten long years—had been simple. The single word "forgive." It had to do with Houdini's brother marrying his own sister-in-law—which caused a huge breach in the family. Bess's code spelled out the words engraved inside her wedding band. He'd spent a lot of time coming up with the secret words he and Eddy agreed on, but in the end Harry chose something that symbolized an eternal truth beyond the grave, that put paid to the phony mediums who preyed on the bereaved. Eddy's code was wordplay on Edgar Allan Poe's famous poem: "Conquered the Worm!"

Houdini sat down. He recalled that during dinner a few hours earlier, Eddy had jumped to Harry's defense when Houdini was talking about overcoming his fears. As if to remind Lovecraft that his own early work had been influenced by Poe, Eddy said, "In 'Ligeia' the Lady says—and I'm paraphrasing here—that we don't yield to death unless our own will is too feeble. So fate doesn't control our lives. Maybe it doesn't even control our deaths!"

Lovecraft had merely shrugged.

"Will is everything!" Houdini had agreed.

Bess said, "Harry goes in for mind over matter," and told them about how Harry didn't take painkillers even though for years he'd been sleeping every single night with a pillow wedged under his left kidney after it had been severely injured during a performance. "It still pains him constantly," she said, "but it never stops him."

A short while later the dinner party broke up; all three men saw Bess safely to a cab, they said their goodnights and he and Eddy walked back to the hotel. But now, sitting in the dimly lit hotel room Houdini was left wondering. Those goddamn coincidences and signs...like *omens*.

Eddy had reported during their moonlit sidewalk stroll that Doyle's coterie was once again predicting Houdini would die.

"The whole bunch has been saying that twaddle for years—the English circle of madmen and the crazies he's influenced over here, too," Houdini said. "Stupid as hell—these control spirits they channel that make so-called predictions. What's he call his control? —Oh yeah, Pheneas. Jesus Christ."

Eddy snickered and they both tried to laugh it off. "Oh Arthur," he mimicked in a high falsetto imitating Lady Doyle, "I think Pheneas is coming through." Then he dropped his voice. "Yes, our beloved Sir Arthur, it is so. Houdini is all washed up. Houdini is doomed. Doomed."

"Uh-huh. Doom! Doom! Doom and gloom. 'Do not ask for whom the bell tolls, it tolls for me,'" Harry laughed.

But he was more shaken than he let on. Eddy had been carrying a rosewood walking stick, and Houdini had playfully taken it from him tapping it against the sidewalk, then bouncing it against the upraised tip of his shoe, caught it neatly in his hand, then danced it down his elbow and back again before palming it and pretending to insert it down his throat like a sword swallower.

"Good you didn't get spit all over my best cane, Harry," Eddy joked, polishing the silver cap against his sleeve.

They shook hands in the lobby, Eddy went toward the elevator and Harry, still pretending he didn't give a damn what the control spirits were shouting through phony mediums here and abroad, headed up the stairs to his third floor room which adjoined Bess's suite.

He was still sitting on the bed when the phone rang. Harry glanced guiltily at the door that led through to Bess's room. She was typically a heavy sleeper but he kept his voice low when he picked up.

"Harry, it's me."

"I was just thinking about you," he said. Instantly the image of Leona Derwatt his former premier box jumper/assistant and current informant/spy spiraled up in his mind. Always he saw her as she'd been before the crippling polio tanked her stage career. Beautiful green eyes and coppery hair. An impish face. A trim lithe figure, and oh boy, she was some *krassavitseh*—a doll. Still, his mother would have said about her (and plenty of the other women he had flings with, "Okay, so she's not a *kurveh*, Harry. She's not a tramp. But she's still a *shikseh*—just like your wife, another gentile. And also just like your wife, also *oisgeshtrobelt*. Overdressed—like she's constantly having tea with the royal family." He didn't know exactly why, but when he thought of his darlings, he almost always reverted to Yiddish. Maybe guilt. Must be guilt—it was after all, his mother's opinions (though in life she hadn't known about the affairs) about his women he heard in his head. Couldn't be that up in heaven she watched him *shtupping* the *kurvehs*, right? Nah. Couldn't be.

"So what's the word, Leona?" he said. She'd been diligently obtaining the certifications and documents that gave her ministry after ministry (they cost between $3 and $5—no education necessary—and made a hugely impressive roll when they were carried onto the stage each night in the third part of his act and unfurled). Harry would tell the audience how his own father was a scholar, how years of study entitled him to be genuinely called Rabbi and how they should be wary of these priest-wolves out to fleece them with fake messages from their dead loved ones. Just lately Leona had been working on trapping one of these shysters in New York who (surprise, surprise!) ran a church and claimed he had supernatural powers. "Did you get him?"

"Used a Dictaphone," she began; then Harry heard a pause. Was someone listening in? Tapping his hotel line? He wondered.

"Leona? Hey, are you there?"

What he heard next was a series of screeches that descended into guttural growls. As if instead of talking to Leona he was listening to the teeth-bared rumblings of a wolf or a killer-dog. The phone suddenly felt ice-cold in his hands. So cold it stung the flesh of his palm and finger tips.

A low, taunting voice whispered at him: "*Your mind is divided, Harry. Divided. You want to prove how many fakes there are because you're secretly afraid there is nothing supernatural anywhere in the universe. But your father was a rabbi...and you long to see him again. You want to believe. You need to believe. Just like the poor grief-struck gullible janes and joes you're always taking up for.... You miss your mother more than you can bare to contemplate...and your secret codes—that's you telling yourself even if all the old religions are gone, there* is *life after death. Do you hear me, Harry?*"

Huh? Was Leona mad at him? But that couldn't have been her whispering, could it? It wasn't his own subconscious, either. Not possible, he told himself. A joke maybe....

"Leona!" Before he hung up the receiver, he called her name again and again.

He could literally see his breath fogging the air, but there was no answer—only the sight of his words dissolving into thin white vapor.

He didn't drink, he didn't take drugs (that was Bess's bailiwick to his chagrin) but before the practical side of him won out and he decided he'd just call Leona tomorrow, he felt a tic of unease: Was it some kind of supernatural contact or had he just hallucinated the whole thing?

~

He'd finally perfected performing what he was now calling "The Pyramid Mystery," the culmination of the experiment in being buried alive he'd first practiced ten years earlier in California. Harry was a born publicity hound and if people were crazy for all things Egyptian, by god, he'd give them a show they'd never forget.

On stage he was strapped into a strait jacket and sealed inside a casket. Then he was lowered into an enormous glass box. His numerous male assistants shoveled tons of sand onto him, covering him completely. It took more than a few suspense-filled minutes before he emerged in shirt sleeves to the cheering audiences. It was the biggest production number in the history of his career. But it was so time consuming and tricky to mount, he decided he'd only use it on the tour in the stops that lasted at least two weeks.

At least that's what he told his *ingenieurs*—and himself. In reality, he knew that sealed inside the casket, even with his thoughts focused on the mechanics of escape, his mind returned again and again to the dark, frightening images of ancient Egypt, the mysteries beyond death he seemed so close to grasping. The worst dread came from the sense that just beyond the angle of his vision black shadows roamed waiting to catch at him, to drag him into some terrible half-life that was neither the quiet dark of death nor the sunlit peace of a heaven.

His loyal staff told him, they didn't mind taking the trouble. It was a great effect—

Harry cut them off. "No! Not in the smaller venues. Absolutely not."

If they were surprised when he shouted, no one said a word.

Then in Toronto, about to be lowered upside down inside the famous water-filled Chinese pagoda, the hoisting tackle slipped and he fractured his ankle. He wouldn't let the pain stop him and he carried on with the show. Look at Sarah Bernhardt, he reminded himself. Lost her leg and still performs. He wasn't going to give in either.

He kept right on performing after he was gut-punched by a student and his fever began to rise. When it hit 104 degrees he was taken by ambulance to the hospital for emergency surgery to repair his ruptured, gangrenous appendix. Will is everything. He kept on persevering, kept on fighting for the next six days while they tried experimental serums to save him.

In the hospital the dreams were so vivid he might have been standing in the center of a circle of projection screens showing color films. His mind was actively enumerating the many signs and symbols and omens that plagued him these last months.

Mostly he was lucid, but one night after he'd asked to eat some farmer's chop suey—a dish made with vegetables in sour cream popular in Jewish families—he told the young doctor attending him that he wished he'd made something more of his own life. That while the doctor was genuine and proved it daily in helping the sick—he himself was a fraud. The doctor tried to brush it off, saying that Houdini had literally entertained and enthralled millions of people and brought them a measure of happiness.

Harry let it go. He'd only been talking to keep the dreams and hideous visions at bay.

On Saturday he wrote a letter to a friend. Another small occupation as he sensed that whatever his will was keeping on the other side of some crumbling wall was pressing closer.

That night he dreamt of the strange confluence of events and ideas. The secret codes to guard against the finality of death, the odd premonitions sealed inside both buried and submerged caskets. The superstitions and fears, the thoughts his mind had cobbled together into a pastiche of Egyptian rituals and mysteries. An old religion gone, vanished—except for the hieroglyphs and artifacts, the towering monuments and tombs half-immured under shifting, wind-borne sands. But they had worshipped, they had believed! Was the embalming and the tomb really a gateway to eternity? What waited there?

A shape in the shadows.

And then he saw it: an amorphous cold, monstrous being, huge beyond reckoning. Both as vague and as gray-white definite as heavy mist, as shapeless and all-encompassing as rolling sea fog. And with no connection to the little puppets that the living called men and women and children. He wished for the last time that he and Bess had children.

Religions—all of them—then and now...nothing.

Better a yawning hell, because then there would be a heaven.

There was nothing to come back from, because there was nothing to go into.

There was only an end.

Nothing.

Mind and will were everything because in the end there was nothing.

On Sunday October 31st, 1926 he said softly, "I guess I can't fight anymore."

His eyes dimmed and the earthlight that was Houdini was no more.

GIRLS WITHOUT THEIR FACES ON

by Laird Barron

Delia's father had watched her drowning when she was a little girl. The accident happened in a neighbor's pool. Delia lay submerged near the bottom, her lungs filling with chlorinated water. She could see Dad's distorted form bent forward, shirtsleeves rolled to the elbow, cigarette dangling from his lips, blandly inquisitive. Mom scooped Delia out and smacked her between the shoulder blades while she coughed and coughed.

Delia didn't think about it often. Not often.

~

Barry F threw a party at his big, opulent house on Hillside East. He invited people to come after sundown. A whole slew of them heeded the call. Some guests considered Barry F an eccentric. This wasn't eccentric—sundown comes early in autumn in Alaska. Hours passed and eventually the door swung wide, emitting piano music, laughter, a blaze of chandelier light. Three silhouettes lingered; a trinity of Christmas ghosts: Delia; Delia's significant other, J; and Barry F.

"—the per capita death rate in Anchorage is outsized," Barry F said. "Out-fucking-sized. This town is the armpit. No, it's the asshole—"

"*Bethel* is the asshole," J said.

"Tell it on the mountain, bro."

"I'll tell you why Bethel is the worst. My dad was there on a job for the FAA in '77. He's eating breakfast at the Tundra Diner and a janitor walks past his table, lugging a honey bucket—"

"Honey bucket?"

"Plumbing froze, so folks crapped in a bucket and dumped it in a sewage lagoon out back. Honey bucket. It's a joke. Anyway, the dude trips on his shoelace…Go on. Imagine the scene. Envision that motherfucker. Picking toilet paper outta your scrambled eggs kills the appetite. Plus, cabin fever, and homies die in the bush all the livelong day. Alcoholism, poverty, rape. Worst of the worst."

"Please," Delia said. "Can we refrain from trashing a native village for the sin of not perfectly acclimating to a predatory takeover by the descendants of white European invaders?"

"Ooh, my girlfriend doesn't enjoy the turn of conversation. Sorry, my precious little snowflake. Folks weren't so politically correct in the 1970s. I'm just reporting the news."

"If we're talking about assholes, look no further than a mirror."

"Kids, kids, don't fight, don't derail the train," Barry F said with an oily, avuncular smile. "Anchorage is still bad. Right?"

"Wretched. Foul."

"And on that note..." Delia said.

"Haven't even gotten to the statistics for sexual assault and disappearances—"

"—Satanists. Diabolists. Scientologists. Cops found a hooker's corpse bound to a headboard at the Viking Motel."

"Lashed to the mast, eh?"

"You said it."

"Hooker? Wasn't she a stripper, though? Candy Bunny, Candy Hunny...?"

"Hooker, stripper, I dunno. White scarves, black candles. Blood everywhere. News called it a ritual killing. They're combing the city for suspects."

"Well, Tito and Benny were at the Bush Company the other night and I haven't seen 'em since..."

"Ha-ha, those cut-ups!"

"I hope not literally."

"We're due for some ritual insanity. Been saying it for months."

"Why are we due?"

"Planet X is aligning with the sun. Its passage messes with gravitational forces, brain chemistry, libidos, et cetera. Like the full moon affects crazies, except dialed to a hundred. Archeologists got cave drawings that show this has been a thing since Neanderthals were stabbing mammoths with sharpened sticks."

"The malignant influence of the gods."

"The malignant influence of the Grays."

"The Grays?"

"Little gray men: messengers of the gods; cattle mutilators; anal probe-ists..."

"They hang around Bethel, eh?"

"No way to keep up with the sheer volume of insanity this state produces. Oh, speaking of brutalized animals, there was the Rabbit Massacre in Wasilla."

"Pure madness."

"Dog mutilations. So many doggy murders. I sorta hate dogs, but really, chopping off their paws is too damned far."

"And on that note…!" Delia stepped backward onto the porch for emphasis.

"On that note. Hint taken, baby doll. Later, sucker."

A couple separated from the raucous merriment of the party. The door shut behind them and they were alone in the night.

"What's a Flat Affect Man?" Delia wore a light coat, miniskirt, and heels. She clutched J's arm as they descended the flagstone steps alongside a treacherously steep driveway. Porchlights guided them partway down the slope.

"Where did you hear that?" Sportscoat, slacks, and high-top tennis shoes for him. Surefooted as a mountain goat. The softness of his face notwithstanding, he had a muscle or two.

"Barry F mentioned it to that heavyset guy in the turtleneck. You were chatting up turtleneck dude's girlfriend. The chick who was going to burst out of her mohair sweater."

"I wasn't flirting. She's comptroller for the university. Business, always business."

"Uh-huh. Curse of the Flat Affect Men, is what Barry said."

"Well, forget what you heard. There are things woman was not meant to know. You'll just spook yourself."

She wanted to smack him, but her grip was precarious and she'd had too many drinks to completely trust her balance.

Hillside East was heavily wooded. Murky at high noon and impenetrable come the witching hour. Neighborhoods snaked around ravines and subarctic meadows and copses of deep forest. Cul-de-sacs might host a house or a bear den. But that was Anchorage. A quarter of a million souls sprinkled across seventeen-hundred square miles of slightly suburbanized wilderness. Ice water to the left, mountains to the right, Aurora Borealis weeping radioactive tears. October nights tended to be crisp. Termination dust gleamed upon the Chugach peaks, on its way down like a shroud, creeping ever lower through the trees.

A few more steps and he unlocked the car and helped her inside. He'd parked away from the dozen or so other vehicles that lined the main road on either side of the mailbox. His car was practically an antique. Its dome light worked sporadically. Tonight, nothing. The interior smelled faintly of a mummified animal.

The couple sat in the dark. Waiting.

She regarded the black mass of forest to her right, ignoring his hand on her thigh. Way up the hillside, the house's main deck projected over a ravine. Bay windows glowed yellow. None of the party sounds reached them in the car. She imagined the turntables gone silent and the piano hitting a lone minor key, over and over. Loneliness born of aching disquiet stole over her. No matter that she shared a car with J nor that sixty people partied hardy a hundred yards away. Her loneliness might well have sprung from J's very proximity.

After nine months of dating, her lover remained inscrutable.

J lived in a duplex that felt as sterile as an operating room—television, double bed, couch, and a framed poster of the cosmos over the fake fireplace (a faux fireplace in Alaska was almost too much irony for her system). A six-pack in the fridge; a half-empty closet. He consulted for the government, finagling cost-efficient ways to install fiberoptic communications in remote native villages. That's *allegedly* what he did when he disappeared for weeks on end. Martinis were his poison, Andy Kaufman his favorite (dead?) entertainer, and electronica his preferred music. His smile wasn't a reliable indicator of mood or temperament.

Waking from a strange, fragmentary dream, to a proverbial splash of cold water, Delia accepted that the romance was equally illusory.

"What is your job?" she said, experiencing an uncomfortable epiphany of the ilk that plagued heroines in gothic tales and crime dramas. It was unwise for a woman to press a man about his possibly nefarious double life, and yet so it went. Her lips formed the words and out they flew, the skids greased by a liberal quantity of vino.

"Same as it was in April," he said. "Why?"

"Somebody told me they saw you at the airport buying a ticket to Nome in early September. You were supposed to be in Two Rivers that week."

"Always wanted to visit Nome. Haunt of late career Wyatt Earp. Instead, I hit Two Rivers and got a lousy mug at the gift shop."

"Show me the mug when I come over for movie night."

"Honey pie, sugar lump! Is that doubt I hear in your voice?"

"It is."

"Fine, you've got me red-handed. I shoot walruses and polar bears so wealthy Europeans can play on ivory cribbage boards and strut around in fur bikinis." He caressed her knee and waited, presumably for a laugh. "C'mon, baby. I'm a square with a square job. Your friend must've seen my doppelganger."

"No. What do you actually do? Like for real."

"I really consult." He wore a heavy watch with a metal strap. He pressed harder and the strap dug into her flesh.

"There's more," she said. "Right? I've tried to make everything add up, and I can't."

"Sweetie, just say what's on your mind."

"I'm worried. Ever have a moment, smack out of the blue, when you realize you don't actually know someone? I'm having that moment."

"Okay. I'm a deep cover Russian agent."

"Are you?"

"Jeez, you're paranoid tonight."

"Or my bullshit detector is finally working."

"You were hitting it hard in there." He mimed drinking with his free hand.

"Sure, I was half a glass away from dancing on the piano. Doesn't mean I'm wrong."

"Wanna get me on a couch? Wanna meet my mother?"

"People lie to shrinks. Do you even have a mother?"

"I don't have a shrink. Don't have a mother." His hand and the watch strap on his wrist slid back and forth, abrading her skin. "My mother was a…eh, who cares what the supernumerary does? She died. Horribly."

"J—" Would she be able to pry his hand away? Assuming that failed, could she muster the grit to slap him, or punch him in the family jewels? She hadn't resorted to violence since decking a middle school classmate who tried to grab her ass on a fieldtrip. Why had she leapt to the worst scenario now? Mom used to warn her about getting into bad situations with sketchy dudes. Mom said of hypothetical date rapists, if shit got real, smile sweetly and gouge the bastard's eye with a press-on nail.

The phantom piano key in her mind sounded like it belonged in a 1970s horror flick. *How much did I have? Three glasses of red, or four? Don't let the car start spinning, I might fly into space.*

J paused, head tilted as if concentrating upon Delia's imagined minor key plinking and plinking. He released her and straightened and held his watch close to his eyes. The watch face was not illuminated. Blue gloom masked everything. Blue gloom made his skull misshapen and enormous. Yet the metal of the watch gathered starlight.

"Were you paying attention when I told Barry that Planet X is headed toward our solar system?" he said.

"Yes." Except…Barry had told J, hadn't he?

"Fine. I'm gonna lay some news on you, then. You ready for the news?"

She said she was ready for the news.

"Planet X isn't critical," he said. "Important, yes. Critical, no. Who cares about a chunk of ice? Not so exciting. Her *star* is critical. A brown dwarf. It has, in moments of pique that occur every few million years, emitted a burst of highly lethal gamma rays and bombarded hapless worlds many light years distant. Every organism on those planets died instantly. Forget the radiation. She can do other things with her heavenly body. Nemesis Star first swung through the heart of the Oort Cloud eons past. Bye-bye dinosaurs. Nemesis' last massive gravitational wave intersected the outer fringe of Sol System in the 1970s. Nemesis has an erratic orbit, you see. Earth got the succeeding ripple effect. Brownouts, tidal waves, earthquakes, all them suicides in Japan… A second wave arrived twenty years later. The third and final wave hit several days ago. Its dying edge will splash Earth in, oh, approximately forty-five seconds."

"What?" she said. "I don't get it."

"And it's okay. This is when *they* come through is all you need to understand. I'm here to greet them. That's my real job, baby doll. I'm a greeter. Tonight is an extinction event; AKA: a close encounter of the intimate kind."

Delia fixated on the first part of his explanation. "Greeter. Like a store greeter?" She thought of the Central Casting grandad characters stationed at the entrance of certain big box stores who bared worn dentures in a permanent rictus.

"Stay. I forgot my jacket." J (wearing his jacket, no less) exited the car and be-bopped into the night.

Stay. As if she were an obedient mutt. She rubbed her thigh and watched his shadow float along the driveway and meld into the larger darkness. Chills knifed through her. The windows began to fog over with her breath. He'd taken the keys. She couldn't start the car to get warm or listen to the radio. *Or drive away from the scene of the crime.*

Delia's twenty-fifth birthday loomed on the horizon. She had majored in communication with a side of journalism at the University of Alaska Anchorage. She was a culture reporter, covering art and entertainment for the main Anchorage daily paper.

People enjoyed her phone manner. In person, she was persistent and vaguely charming. Apolitical; non-judgmental as a Swiss banker. Daddy had always said not to bother her pretty little head. Daddy was a sexist pig to his dying breath; she heeded the advice anyhow. Half of what interviewees relayed went in one ear and out the other with nary a whistle-stop. No matter; her memory snapped shut on the most errant of facts like the teeth of a steel leghold trap. Memory is an acceptable day-to-day substitute for intellect.

Her older brothers drove an ambulance and worked in construction respectively. Her little sister graduated from Onager High next spring. Little sister didn't have journalistic aspirations. Sis yelled, *Fake news!* When gentlemen callers (bikers and punk rockers) loaded her into their chariots and hied into the sunset.

Delia lived in an apartment with two women. She owned a dog named Atticus. Her roommates loved Atticus and took care of him when she couldn't make it home at a reasonable hour. They joked about stealing him when they eventually moved onward and upward with trophy spouses and corporate employment. *I'll cut a bitch*, she always said with a smile, not joking at all.

Should she ring them right then for an emergency extraction? "Emergency" might be a tad extreme, yet It seemed a reasonable plan. Housemate A had left on an impromptu overnighter with her boyfriend. Housemate B's car was in the shop. Housemate B helpfully suggested that Delia call a taxi, or, if she felt truly threatened, the cops. Housemate B was on record as disliking J.

Am I feeling threatened? Delia pocketed her phone and searched her feelings.

Her ambulance-driving brother (upholding the family tradition of advising Delia to beware a cruel, vicious world) frequently lectured about the hidden dangers surrounding his profession. Firemen and paramedics habitually rushed headlong into dicey situations, exposing themselves to the same risks as police and soldiers, except without guns or backup. *Paramedics get jacked up every day. While you're busy doing CPR on a subject, some street-dwelling motherfucker will shiv you in the kidney and grab your wallet. Only way to survive is to keep your head on a swivel and develop a sixth sense. The hairs on the back of your neck prickle, you better look around real quick.*

Words to live by. She touched the nape of her neck. Definitely prickling, definitely goosebumps and not from the chill. She climbed out and made her way into the bushes, clumsier than a prey animal born to the art of disappearing, but with no less alacrity.

She stood behind a large spruce, hand braced against its rough bark. Sap stuck to her palm. It smelled bitter-green. Her thigh stung where a raspberry bush had torn her stocking and drawn blood. A starfield pulsed through ragged holes in the canopy. She knew jack about stars except the vague notion that mostly they radiated old, old light. Stars lived and died and some were devoured by black holes.

Nearby, J whooped, then whistled; shrill and lethal as a raptor tuning a killing song. Happy and swift.

He sounds well-fucked. Why did her mind leap there? Because his O-face was bestial? Because he loved to squeeze her throat when they fucked? The subconscious always knows best. As did Mama and big brother, apparently.

J's shadow flitted near the car. His whistle segued to the humming of a nameless, yet familiar tune. Delia shrank against the bole of the tree and heard him open the driver's door. After a brief pause, he called her name. First, still inside and slightly muffled (did he think she was hiding under a seat cushion?); second, much louder toward the rising slope behind him; last, aimed directly toward her hiding spot. Her residual alcohol buzz evaporated as did most of the spit in her mouth.

"Delia, sweetheart," he said. "Buttercup, pumpkin, sugar booger. I meant to say earlier how much I adore the fact you didn't wear makeup tonight. The soap and water look is sexxxxxy! I prefer a girl who doesn't put on her face when she meets the world. It lights my fire, boy howdy. But now you gotta *come here.*" His voice thickened at the end. By some trick of the dark, his eyes flared dull-bright crimson. His lambent gaze pulsed for several heartbeats, then faded, and he became a silhouette again. "No?" he said in his regular voice. "Be that way. I hope you brought mad money, because you're stranded on a lee shore. Should I cruise by your apartment instead? Would your roomies and your dog be pleased to meet me while I'm in this mood? Fuck it, sweetheart. I'll surprise you." He laughed, got into the car, and sped away. The red taillights seemed to hang forever; unblinking predatory eyes.

The entire scene felt simultaneously shocking and inevitable.

Of course, she speed-dialed her apartment to warn Housemate B. A robotic voice apologized that the call would not go through. It repeated this apology when she tried the police, her favorite taxi service, and finally, information. Static rose and rose until it roared in her ear and she gave up. She emerged from cover and removed her heels and waited, slightly crouched, to see if J would circle around to catch her in the open. A coyote stalking a ptarmigan. Yeah, that fit her escalating sense of dread—him creeping that ancient car, tongue lolling as he scanned the road for her fleeting shadow.

The cell's penlight projected a ghostly cone. She followed it up the hill to her nearest chance for sanctuary, the house of Barry F. Ah, dear sweet Barry F, swinging senior executive of a successful mining company. He wore wire rim glasses and expensive shirts, proclaimed his loathing of physical labor and cold weather (thus, he was assigned to Alaska, naturally), and hosted plenty of semi-formal parties as befitted the persona of a respectable corporate whip hand—which meant prostitutes were referred to as *companions* and any coke-snorting and pill-popping shenanigans occurred in a discreet guestroom.

Notwithstanding jocular collegiality, Barry and J weren't longtime friends, weren't even close; their business orbits intersected and that was the extent of it. J collected acquaintances across a dizzying spectrum. Scoffing at the quality of humanity in general, he rubbed shoulders with gold-plated tycoons and grubby laborers alike. Similar to the spartan furnishings of his apartment, individual relationships were cultivated relative to his needs.

What need do I *satisfy? Physical? Emotional? Victim?* Delia recalled a talk show wherein the host interviewed women who'd survived encounters with serial killers. One guest, a receptionist, had accompanied a coworker on a camping trip. The "nice guy" wined and dined her, then held a knife to her throat, ready to slash. At the last second, he decided to release her instead. *I planned to kill you for three months. Go on, the fear in your eyes is enough.* The receptionist boogied and reported the incident. Her camping buddy went to prison for the three murders he'd previously committed in that park. Which was to say, how could a woman ever know what squirmed in the brains of men?

As Delia approached the house, the porchlight and the light streaming through the windows snuffed like blown matches. Muffled laughter and the steady thud of bass also ceased. At moments such as this, what was a humble arts and entertainment reporter to do? Nothing in her quarter century of life, on the Last Frontier notwithstanding, had prepared her for this experience: half-frozen, teeth chattering, absolutely alone.

Darkness smothered the neighborhood. Not a solitary lamp glimmered among the terraced elevations or secluded cul-de-sacs. She looked south and west, down into the bowl of the city proper. From her vantage, it appeared that the entire municipality had gone dark. Anchorage's skyline should have suffused the heavens with light pollution. More stars instead; a jagged reef of them, low and indifferent. Ice Age constellations that cast glacial shadows over the mountains.

The phone's beam flickered, perhaps in response to her fear. She assumed the battery must be dying despite the fact she'd charged it prior to the evening's events. It oozed crimson, spattering the stone steps as if she were swinging a censor of phosphorescent dye. She barged through the front door without a how-do-you-do. Warm, at least. In fact, humid as the breath of a panting dog. Her thoughts flashed to dear sweet Fido at the apartment. *God, please don't let J do anything to him. Oh yeah, and good luck to my housemate too.*

She hesitated in the foyer beneath the dead chandelier and put her shoes on. Her sight adjusted enough to discern the contours of her environment. No one spoke, which seemed ominous. Most definitely ominous. A gaggle of drunks trapped in a sudden blackout could be expected to utter any number of exclamatory comments. Girls would shriek in mock terror and some bluff hero would surely announce he'd be checking the fuse box straight away. There'd be a bit of obligatory ass-grabbing, right? Where were all the cell phones and keychain penlights? A faucet dripped; heating ducts creaked in the walls. This was hardcore Bermuda Triangle-*Mary Celeste* shit.

Snagging a landline was the first order of business. Her heels clicked ominously as she moved around the grand staircase and deeper into the house to its spacious, partially sunken living room.

Everyone awaited her there. Wine glasses and champagne flutes partially raised in toast; heads thrown back, bared teeth glinting here and there; others half-turned, frozen mid-glance, mid-step, mid-gesticulation. Only mannikins could be frozen in such exaggerated positions of faux life. The acid reek of disgorged bowels and viscera filled Delia's nostrils. She smelled blood soaked into dresses and blood dripping from cuffs and hosiery; she smelled blood as it pooled upon the carpet and coagulated in the vents.

Her dying cell phone chose that moment to give up the ghost entirely. She was thankful. Starlight permitted her the merest impressions of the presumed massacre, its contours and topography, nothing granular. Her nose and imagination supplied the rest. Which is to say, bile rose in her throat and her mind fogged over. Questions of why and how did not register. The nauseating intimacy of this abominable scene overwhelmed such trivial considerations.

A closet door opened like an eyeless socket near the baby grand piano. Atticus trotted forth. Delia recognized his general shape and the jingle of his vaccination tags and because for the love of everything holy, who else? The dog stopped near a throng of mutilated party-goers and lapped the carpet between shoes and sandals with increasing eagerness. A human silhouette emerged next and sat on the piano bench. The shape could've been almost anybody. The figure's thin hand passed through a shaft of starlight and plinked a key several times.

B-flat? Delia retained a vague notion of chords—a high school crush showed her the rudiments as a maneuver to purloin her virtue. Yes, B flat, over and over. Heavily, then softly, softly, nigh invisibly, and heavily again, discordant, jarring, threatening.

I'm sorry you had to bear witness. These words weren't uttered by the figure. They originated at a distance of light years, uncoiling within her consciousness. Her father's voice. *The human animal is driven by primal emotions and urges. How great is your fear, Delia? Does it fit inside a breadbox? Does it fit inside your clutch? This house?*

The shape at the piano gestured with a magician's casual flourish and the faint radiance of the stars flickered to a reddish hue. The red light intensified and seeped into the room.

The voice in her head again: Looking for Mr. Goodbar *stuck with you. Diane Keaton's fate frightened you as a girl and terrifies you as a woman. In J, you suspect you finally drew the short straw. The man with a knife in his pocket, a strangling cord, a snub-nose revolver, the ticket stub with your expiration date. The man to take you camping and return alone. And sweetie, the bastard resembles me, wouldn't you say?*

Ice tinkled in glasses—spinning and slopping. Glasses toppled and fell from nerveless fingers. Shadow-Atticus ceased slurping and made himself scarce behind a couch. He trailed inky pawprints. Timbers groaned; the heart of the living room was released from the laws of physics—it bent at bizarre, corkscrew angles, simultaneously existing on a plane above and below the rest of the interior. Puffs of dust erupted as cracks shot through plaster. The floor tilted and the guests were pulled together, packed cheek to jowl.

There followed a long, dreadful pause. Delia had sprawled to her hands and knees during the abrupt gravitational shift. Forces dragged against her, but she counterbalanced as one might to avoid plummeting off a cliff. She finally got a clean, soul-scarring gander at her erstwhile party companions.

Each had died instantaneously via some force that inflicted terrible bruises, suppurating wounds, and ruptures. The corpses were largely intact and rigidly positioned as a gallery of wax models. Strands of metal wire perforated flesh at various junctures, drew the bodies upright, and connected them into a mass. The individual strands gleamed and converged overhead as a thick spindle that ascended toward the dome of ceiling, and infinitely farther.

The shape at the piano struck a key and its note was reciprocated by an omnidirectional chime that began at the nosebleed apex of the scale and descended precipitously, boring into plaster, concrete, and bone. The house trembled. Delia pushed herself backward into a wall where normal gravity resumed. She huddled, tempted to make a break for it, and also too petrified to move.

There are two kinds of final girls. The kind who escape and the kind who die. You're the second kind. I am very, very proud, kiddo. You'll do big things.

Cracks split the roof, revealing a viscid abyss with a mouthful of half-swallowed nebulae. It chimed and howled, eternally famished. Bits of tile plummeted into the expanse, joining dead stars. Shoe tips scraped as the guests lifted en mass, lazily revolving like a bleeding mobile carved for an infant god. The mobile jerkily ascended, tugged into oblivion at the barbed terminus of a fisherman's line.

Delia glanced down to behold a lone strand of the (god?) wire burrowing into her wrist, seeking a vein or a bone to anchor itself. She wrenched free and pitched backward against a wall.

The chiming receded, so too the red glow, and the void contentedly suckled its morsel. Meanwhile, the shadow pianist hunched into a fetal position and dissolved. *Run along,* her father said. *Run along, dear. Don't worry your pretty head about any of this.*

Delia ran along.

~

Alaska winter didn't kill her. Not that this was necessarily Alaska. The land turned gray and waterways froze. Snow swirled over empty streets and empty highways and buried inert vehicles. Powerlines collapsed and copses of black spruce and paper birch stood vigil as the sun paled every day until it became a white speck.

Delia travelled west, then south, snagging necessities from deserted homes and shops. Her appearance transformed—she wore layers of wool and flannel, high-dollar pro ski goggles, an all-weather parka, snow pants, and thick boots. Her tent, boxes of food, water, and medical supplies went loaded into a banana sled courtesy of a military surplus store. She acquired a light hunting rifle and taught herself to use it, in case worse came to worst. She didn't have a plan other than to travel until she found her way back to a more familiar version of reality. Or to walk until she keeled over; whichever came first.

In the beginning, she hated it. That changed over the weeks and months as the suburban softness gave way to a metallic finish. Survival can transition into a lifestyle. She sheltered inside houses and slept on beds. She burned furniture for warmth. However, the bloodstains disquieted her as did eerie noises that wafted from basements and attics during the bleak A.M. hours. She eventually camped outdoors among the woodland creatures who shunned abandoned habitations of humankind as though city limits demarcated entry to an invisible zone of death. The animals had a point, no doubt.

Speaking of animals. Wild beasts haunted the land in decent numbers. Domestic creatures were extinct, seemingly departed to wherever their human masters currently dwelled. With the exception of the other Atticus. The dog lurked on the periphery of her vision; a blur in the undergrowth, a rusty patch upon the snow. At night he dropped mangled ptarmigans and rabbits at the edge of her campfire light. He kept his distance, watching over her as she slept. The musk of his gore-crusted fur, the rawness of his breath, infiltrated her dreams.

In other dreams, her mother coalesced for a visit. *Now it can be said. Your father murdered eight prostitutes before lung cancer cut him down. The police never suspected that sweet baby-faced sonofabitch. You were onto him, somehow.* She woke with a start and the other Atticus's eyes reflected firelight a few yards to her left in the gauze of darkness that enfolded the world.

"Thanks for the talk, Mom."

Delia continued to walk and pull the sled. Sometimes on a road, or with some frequency, on a more direct route through woods and over water. She didn't encounter any human survivors, nor any tracks or other sign. However, she occasionally glimpsed crystallized hands and feet jutting from a brush pile, or an indistinct form suspended in the translucent depths of a lake. She declined to investigate, lowered her head and marched onward.

One late afternoon, near spring, but not quite, J (dressed in black camo and Army-issue snowshoes) leaped from cover with a merry shriek and knocked her flat. He lay atop her and squeezed her throat inexorably, his eyes sleepy with satisfaction.

"If it were my decision, I'd make you a pet. You don't belong here, sugar pie." He well and truly applied his brutish strength. Brutish strength proved worthless. His expression changed as terror flooded in and his grip slackened. "Oh, my god. I didn't know. They didn't warn me..."

Her eyes teared and she regarded him as if through a pane of water. Her eyes teared because she was laughing so hard. "Too late, asshole. Years and years too late." She brushed his hands aside. "I'm the second kind."

He scrambled to his feet and ran across fresh powder toward the woods as fast as his snowshoes could carry him, which wasn't very. She retrieved the rifle, chambered a round, and tracked him with the scope. A moving target proved more challenging than plinking at soda bottles and pie tins. Her first two shots missed by a mile.

Delia made camp; then she hiked over to J and dragged him back. He gazed at her adoringly, arms trailing in the snow. He smiled an impossibly broad, empty smile. That night, the fire crackled and sent small stars homeward. J grinned and grinned, his body limp as a mannikin caught in the snarled boughs of a tree where she'd strung him as an afterthought. The breeze kicked up into a chinook that tasted of green sap and thawing earth.

"Everything will be different tomorrow," she said to the flames, the changing stars. Limbs creaked to and fro and J nodded, nodded; slavishly agreeable. His shadow and the shadow of the tree limbs spread grotesquely across the frozen ground.

The wind carried to her faint sounds of the dog gnawing and slurping at a blood-drenched snowbank. The wind whispered that Atticus would slake himself and then creep into the receding darkness, gone forever. Where she was headed, he couldn't follow.

"So, while there's time, let's have a talk," Delia said to Grinning J. "When we make it home, tell me where I can find more boys just like you."

DR. 999
By Matthew M. Bartlett

Malumense Dr. 999's NL-id Blends Micellar Moisturizing Milk (DISCONTINUED)

Bad hair can inhibit or even obstruct your spiritual growth. Industrial detergents, enervating dyes, chemicals with unpronounceable names. They weaken your powers, sap your energy, leave you dry and desolate. Isn't it finally time to be rid of the lank, lifeless hair that's been holding you back? Inspire your hair, and make clear your path, with the essential nutrients and life-giving cultures infused in Malumense Dr. 999's NL-id Blends Micellar Moisturizing Milk. Malumense's water-rich complexes gently nourish, cleanse, and purify to restore balance to every filament, every follicle. Formulated without harsh parahydroxybenzoates, free of their troubling estrogenic effects, this non-toxic, dye-free, all-natural, organic, environmentally safe moisturizing milk will enrich and enliven, reconstituting and rebuilding the very structure of your hair, resulting in impossibly soft and radiantly lustrous hair. Heal and calm your hair with Malumense Dr. 999's NL-id Blends Micellar Moisturizing Milk. Your hair will thank you.

About the Product

- Conditions, rejuvenates, and hydrates with Dr. 999's Super Secret Formula
- Manufactured with high-grade materials
- Balances natural scalp moisture
- Gentle enough for everyday use
- With added Orisha Obatala and Abra Melin Annointing Oils
- Not tested on animals

Product details

Size: **12.6 oz.**

- **Product Dimensions:** 3 x 2.4 x 6.1 inches ; 10.4 ounces
- **Shipping Weight:** 13.8 ounces

- **Domestic Shipping:** Item can be shipped within U.S.
- **International Shipping:** This item is not eligible for international shipping. Learn More
- **ASIN:** B0108MR0RI
- **UPC:** 894382738 822142170089 885310346846 820909809803 6336871897230 633911651278 6333218104015980740415287 633911605264 885353857293 8835098087003885453
- **Item model number:** 76505201

Product reviews

CarrieFurbush1966 (one star)
Bought this conditioner from a seller called "ConditionLife" located in Leeds, Massachusetts. Shipping to upstate New York was next-day. The item arrived without any protective packaging—I found the bottle on its side on my front step, with no mailing label nor postage that I could see. I examined the bottle and found a number of oddities. The ingredient list was smeared and illegible, except for "galega officinalis infusion" and sodium laureth sulfate, which actually dries hair out. There was no UPC code or registered trademark symbols. Bottles of conditioner usually have a website or a phone number. Not this bottle. There were numerous misspellings as well. "Botanical." "Frargrance." "Lusterous." Opening the bottle was extremely difficult. .The cap's hinge had an extraneous ridge of plastic that required careful work with a penknife to undo, and ultimately I had to disconnect the cap from the bottle entirely. The odors released when I peeled off the safety seal were earthy and unpleasant in a hard to define way, with an undertone of an astringent-like pungency that assailed my nostrils and actually made me a little dizzy.

Upon first using the product, I found it overly watery and bubbly. It stung my hands and scalp, not in the kind of pleasant, cold-feeling way that dandruff shampoo does, either. There was slight blistering on my palms afterward, and my scalp felt rubbed raw. I found that using colder water lessened that effect slightly. Trying to towel-dry my hair caused a terrible burning sensation, and the hair-dryer was even worse. I had to settle for combing my hair very gently and then letting it air-dry.

My hair looked AWFUL, all day. Co-workers commented on it. Clients were unusually reticent. I think this conditioner actually cost me sales! Moreover, my hair *hurt*. It hurt to touch. It hurt when the wind hit it. I began to think strange thoughts. I felt overheated and feverish. Shadows loomed high and wavering on the walls and at times the very desk at which I was sitting seemed miles away. When I reached out to grasp the edge of the desk, my arms elongated until they were thin white threads sailing off into a blurry distance. I left early, and took an Uber home right after work. The driver, in dark sunglasses and some kind of greenish jumpsuit, seemed to be staring at my hair in the rearview mirror, his lip curled in disgust. I went immediately inside and shaved my head. Then I ran it under ice-cold water until everything resumed some semblance of normalcy.

I poured the remainder of the conditioner down the shower drain, and ran the hot water on full blast in order to get it as far from the house as possible. After about thirty seconds, the water and conditioner began to bubble back up, filling the tub. As I was turning the knob, I heard a terrible squelching noise behind me, and I turned to see bubbly black water pouring from the toilet and the sink. I immediately contacted a plumber, who informed me that the clog was not in the pipes inside my house, but in the sewer line for the whole street. His crew had to access the street's sewer main through a basement pipe using an industrial toilet snake the size of a bazooka, and after seventeen hours of work, the man they'd sent informed me that the pipes were destroyed, corroded, and unsalvageable. They had crumbled like chalk, he said, his eyes wide, his hands shaking slightly. Their toilet snake, too, had been broken beyond repair during the process. I was informed the cost to replace it would be added to the charge.

No one on my short dead-end street can flush their toilets or run water in their showers or sinks. I've been contacted by the city and by local environmental agencies about contaminated groundwater and corrupted soil. They're accusing me of deliberately sabotaging the sewer line. The letters are hostile and threaten monetary damages and even jail time. Jail time!

Needless to say, I do NOT recommend buying this product. I Googled the company, and got no results at all. After numerous unanswered emails, I telephoned this site's administrators to find contact information, and kept being put on hold, only to have the connection drop. This happened more than forty-one times in a three-hour period. Now I'm getting phone calls that show No Caller ID, and when I pick up I hear high winds and in the background a woman weeping or faraway voices chanting.

As an alternative I recommend buying a high-priced conditioner at any local salon. I see no value in this product, only heartache, prodigious expense, and legal entanglements that will sap your time and money and keep you up nights in terror of the indifferently cruel and punitive machinations of city bureaucracy.

RapScallion_Green0110 (two stars)

I am bald what do I even need conditioner for. Conditioner is just a way for these ripoff artists to make money off of gullible people. Shampoo is enough. Their was a cracked in the bottle and the contents leaked in the packaging. It was a mess and a lot of the product unsalvagable. Hey how come my Dean Koonts book never showed up, please email me at Ronny93475334@hotmail.com and issue me a refund immediately or I will contact the Better Buisness Buroueu and the FBI.

Mary Lacey-Neverchange (three stars)

My hair is long, down to the backs of my knees, and is very straight and fine. The ends are wont to get frizzy and dried out, and in the colder months in New England, static is a major problem.

Pros:
1. Not gunky or greasy or slimy.
2. Dispenses easily. I use a drop at a time, six drops total, which is four more than suggested in the instructions. I called the number on the bottle to make sure this was okay and the friendly customer service representative reassured me that it would cause no lasting harm. Each drop is probably 1/16 to 1/18 of a fluid ounce. I apply to the ends only, by which I mean, from the neck down.
3. Can be used on hair that is dry as well as wet. I apply it with my hands and then use a hairbrush to ensure even distribution. So this will also reach a little to the "non ends" of my hair.
4. Even using more than the prescribed two drops per day, this is a very economical purchase.

Cons:
1. OMG I hate the smell.
2. The design on the bottle is ugly—why not flowers or a meadow or a pretty lady instead of the weird 3-D symbol that changes depending on the angle you look at the bottle? I covered it over with a blank white label because it was literally giving me vertigo.
3. The trampling of the flower garden outside the bathroom window.
4. The calls from the customer service representative to check up on my hair are nice but a little intrusive and too personal, and sometimes she calls very late at night. Not to mention the promises to "come around one day soon."

I will need to gather more data before I can report on the long-term effects. I will try to keep using it every day for a year and report back.

PeterPeter45678 (four stars)
I love this Conditioner! I am not usually one to write product reviews on sites like this, although, to be fair, I have written some negative reviews, for detergents that don't work or snack chips with an unpleasant aftertaste or some gadget or appliance that doesn't come with all the parts promised or else doesn't work as advertised. It's such a release to call out an inferior product, or a rip-off, to prevent others from having a bad experience. In these busy times, when it's all work and TV and hastily eaten meals and trying to squeeze in time to stave off the encroaching filth in the home, and then to bed for six restless hours, it is rare to find a spare minute to do something that injects a positive energy into the world.

But what a disservice to companies that make a superior product. People are never moved to leave positive reviews. Look at Yelp! It's all complaints, most of them overblown, and insults. Why? Because it's easy to complain. It's fun. Complaining fills the body with endorphins and self-righteousness and excessive pride. It feels as though no one is ever moved to write a review when they've had a generally decent experience, never mind an excellent one.

Which brings me to Malumense Dr. 999's NL-id Blends Micellar Moisturizing Milk. I've been looking for a conditioner that gives my hair that soft, floaty feeling, without being oily or drying out my hair or causing it to lay limp on my head like a washcloth. I've tried everything from your fancy salon product to your bargain bin one dollar Job Lot special, and the result has always been a resounding Nothing Spectacular.

I had never even considered buying conditioner online until Malumense Dr. 999's NL-id Blends Micellar Moisturizing Milk popped up unbidden in my "suggested products" list, along with the usual roach sprays, pickle chips, Tom Clancy novels, mouse traps, adhesive removers, party balloons, fly strips, and all the various other things I have to buy online because they don't have them anywhere near where I live. It was strange, because the mysterious algorithms of such sites usually hone in on something in your searches or your general web browsing history, and I had never done any internet research on hair products to speak of.

I was on unpaid leave from my job due to a minor protocol violation, the exact nature of which one of my contract clauses prevents me from revealing, when I received this conditioner (well-packaged in bubble wrap and unbroken cardboard, and undamaged), and I confess that a significant period of time elapsed before I first used it. At the time I had little interest in personal cleanliness nor grooming, and was content to let the mice prattle about, the roaches gather and scatter, the parasites feed at will, to let everything fall into disarray. When I received the call that I was okayed to return to work after the oncoming weekend, though, I had to turn things around in short order. I did the apartment first, three straight days of no sleep tidying, sweeping, vacuuming, mopping, scrubbing, really getting down in the muck and grime and mold, getting into the dark corners and under the fixtures and the this-and-that. The refrigerator alone took four hours to empty and clean. Then I had to get rid of the cobwebs and position air fresheners and open all the windows to let air in once again.

When that was done I feared I was too far gone to ever get my own self clean again. I stunk up the place, that's no lie. A heat wave had begun, too, with oppressive dew points and triple-digit temperatures. I took a three hour shower, watching with amazement as the weeks of grit and dirt and dried sweat pried itself from my skin, mixed with the cool water, and swirled down the drain. I washed my hair with melon and rosemary infusion, digging my fingernails into my scalp, lathering, rinsing, and repeating more times than the directions…directed.

Then it was time to use the new product. Malumense Dr. 999's NL-id Blends Micellar Moisturizing Milk sat on rubber-coated wire shelves screwed into the wall, along with an array of razors, antacids, astringents, decongestants, bismuth subsalicylates, cotton swabs, cotton balls, hydrogen peroxide, bar soap (I am a Dove devotee; see my review of their all-natural soap which immediately cleared up an aggressive groin rash that had plagued me for months), toothbrushes and pastes, painkillers, Listerine, et cetera.

Even the bottle, among all the typical junk of self-cleaning, is of an elegant shape, subtly similar to the classic hourglass figure that draws male to female like a flower pulls in a bumblebee. It just feels right in the hand, like it was made to be grasped lightly around the midsection, and even the plastic—I don't know what they used to give it such a pleasurable surface, a kind of sheen, or something, your hand just wants to touch it—is strangely similar to the touch of goose-pimpled flesh, yet somehow smooth. I know that doesn't make sense, but that's the best way I have to describe it. Anyway, it's that kind of attentiveness to seemingly unimportant details that sets Dr. 999 apart— with such care put into appearance and the very feel of the packaging, the consumer can't help to be extremely eager to see what wonders await in the product itself.

With my right hand I gently held the bottle—that sensation!—and squeezed just slightly. A warm bath of scented liquid pooled in the hollow of my palm. How to describe the aroma? It smelled like a cloud might; like the soft breath that wafts down to your nostrils when a woman's tongue teases the rim of your ear as a bee explores the rim of a lily; like a bell tolling in the depths of a deep wood; like a child's first taste of a strawberry (although there was no strawberry scent); like standing up in the back of a pickup truck rolling just a little too fast along a ruler-straight country road on an April some time past midnight, peepers singing their soothing song, pumpkin fields on either side of you (though there was no pumpkin scent), the comforting heft of an axe in your right hand and your feet still clumped with drying mud; like a leaf tossed about in the upper reaches of a tornado that has drawn blood; like a cat catching a moth in its teeth; like the cry of the betrayed toddler; like a brand new luxury car; like a plastic Halloween mask purchased on the cheap on November first; like the infected ear of the noble elephant.

I snapped awake some unknown amount of time later, my hand still cupped at my chin, my arm aching. The water had gone completely cold, to the point of being icy—I think that's what woke me up. I was holding the bottle between my calves, which caused my legs to tingle sensually. I chuckled—it was a husky, raspy sound, nothing like my usual laugh—and I lifted my hand over my head and let the manna of Malumense Dr. 999's NL-id Blends Micellar Moisturizing Milk saturate my hair, and with both hands I worked it into my scalp. The sensation was unlike any I'd ever felt before.

Imagine a storm cloud in the crown of your skull, darker than the inside of a witch's hat, and it rains a silk rendered somehow into gelatin down through your brain, rolling down through your neck along your spinal column, limning your ribcage, gilding your pelvis, sending its rolling rivulets down your arms and legs, into the tips of your fingers and toes. It was a feeling of being loved, and not only physically. It had, how shall I say this in a manner that doesn't send the censors scrambling for their red pens, the same effect as a certain blue pill, as well.

When I finally with great reluctance rinsed Malumense Dr. 999's NL-id Blends Micellar Moisturizing Milk from my hair, my whole body tingled, almost like the sensation of being tickled, or of fingernails being lightly raked over every millimeter of the surface of my skin. Invigorated, turned-on, roused and aroused, I dressed and went in to the office. What a work day! I impressed bosses, co-workers, and clients alike with my increased acuity, my sharpened memory. Am I attributing this all to Malumense Dr. 999's NL-id Blends Micellar Moisturizing Milk? No…and yes. I feel like it mixed somehow with my natural chemistry to bring out the best I had to offer. Here's the proof that's in the pudding: my supervisor apologized to me at the end of the day for having to put me on leave. If he'd had it to do over again, et cetera.

I even took Lily and Carrie from accounting home to celebrate with me. Every which way.

~

After, I considered allowing the ladies into my shower, but I felt the need to keep Malumense Dr. 999's NL-id Blends Micellar Moisturizing Milk all to myself, despite the delectable effects it might have on their lovely young systems. There would be time for that, though. I sent them packing, recommending the Look Diner for their hearty dinners and super-strong coffee, and I took a shower that lasted from just past dinnertime until the darkest hours of early morning. That time I did not employ Malumense Dr. 999's NL-id Blends Micellar Moisturizing Milk. I dozed in the tub, woke, and showered again, this time filling my hand twice with Malumense Dr. 999's NL-id Blends Micellar Moisturizing Milk and rubbing it all over my head, my face, and my body, pushing it into my ears and nostrils, pouring some down my mouth, and even applying a generous portion to my rear portal, if you will. I missed work that day. They were all the more grateful to have me back the next day. And why not? I was making them beaucoup money.

~

The weeks sailed by in a kind of milky, silky miasma of energy, relaxation, orgasmic pleasure, and extravagant meals. I kept up with the cleaning, trimmed the hedges, mowed the lawn, even trimmed the trees that lined the street, though they were not mine to maintain. I excelled at my job, accumulating accolades and bonuses and tokens of appreciation. One was a gift card to this very site.

With that gift card I bought ten more cases of Malumense Dr. 999's NL-id Blends Micellar Moisturizing Milk. I stacked them in the pantry. Some nights before my shower I knelt before that totemic tower of cardboard and I prayed in a strange language previously unknown to me. It had just…come to me.

That night a neighbor banged on my door, complaining of the noise at the late hour. I kicked my front door open, hitting him square in the forehead, sending him tumbling down the porch steps and sprawling on the walk. I was in the altogether. I showed him my brand new Sig Sauer P226 Legion RX pistol. It never jams, I told him, not even the slightest hiccup. No surprises. As reliable as fall following summer, and barely any recoil to speak of. I explained my extralegal acquisition of the weapon, its lack of a serial number, rendering it virtually untraceable, the devastating effect of its ammunition on the human body.

He may have known that if I hurt him, I would be almost immediately implicated, my timely capture inevitable. Obviously, his family would tell the police his last act was to come to my house to complain. He may have considered ballistic tests, GSR testing of a suspect's skin and clothing. If he considered any of these things, he didn't bring them up. Clearly, he was suitably impressed.

~

Update: It's been a year since I first purchased that one seemingly inconsequential bottle of Malumense Dr. 999's NL-id Blends Micellar Moisturizing Milk. About a month after, I wrote the review above, eight months having passed since that first propitious purchase, its true effects became known to me. After a shower on a Sunday morning, I looked in the mirror to discover that my hair had formed itself into a multitude of thin arms. I had first thought them snakes, as though I had become a Medusa-like figure, but then fists uncurled at their ends. The arms elongated, stretching up to the ceiling, gripping it with what I can only assume was a preternatural biological adhesive of some unknown species. Then the arms shortened, lifting me right off the floor and, glue-tipped fingers sticking and unsticking, propelled me around the house, leading me to the front door and dropping me there.

I opened the door and stepped onto the porch. Overcast sky, a light wind whispering through the leaves. A voice, many voices, whispered in my head, overlapping, finally coming together. It directed me to my neighbor's house. I slipped through the unlocked front door and my hair-hands once again gripped the high ceiling, pulled me up, and sent me, legs swinging, into the living room. Below, my neighbor and his daughters sat around a card table, engaged in a game of Scrabble. He was letting them place words untethered to the main gameplay, out at the farther edges of the board, allowing them misspellings and strings of letters that were not actual words. This awoke in me a kind of rage. Looking back, I'm not sure exactly why. My hair-hands disengaged from the ceiling, dropping me down right onto the card table. It collapsed under my weight, sending tiles flying. The girls shrieked. Their father cried out. I stood like a superhero, my hands on my hips, one foot on my neighbor's head. I ground it into his ear until he screamed. My hair flew about my head like great, life-giving grain, like the glory of a victor's battle flag in storm winds, like the sails of a mighty galleon. Then it curled itself into thick tentacles, wrapped around my neighbor's throat, and lifted him into the air. His kicking only caused the hair-noose to tighten. I lowered him to face me and watched as the life leached from his eyes and the tongue popped out of his purple face like a shy gecko finding its way out of a letterbox. I then slammed him to the ground.

His children had fled. The rest of the house was empty. I exited through the front door, my hair back to normal. Well, if normal is silky and lustrous and manageable and imbued with as yet only minimally explored power. My heart was beating like war drums, pulsing in my wrists and legs, my whole body wracked with the thrumming and humming of my excellent heart. I again prayed to my totem that night and took a seventeen-hour shower. My bonuses were just about covering my excessive water bill. Somewhere in there I heard the sirens, then the heartbeat of a helicopter. I never saw anything about it in the paper or on the news. No one talked about it at work. A week later I saw that the neighbor's windows were boarded up, the weeds encroaching on the driveway. I found this very gratifying.

Since Malumense and Dr. 999 parted ways and the Conditioner was pulled from the market in the midst of a war fought with lawsuits and countersuits, with sabotage and newspaper editorials and public recriminations, my hair has become the stuff of legend. It's talked about worldwide, in hair salons and brothels, in trailer parks and mansion compounds. I am priapic, godlike. My hair sways and sings, dances on the air, forming curious shapes. It sings songs in forbidden languages. Children are in awe of me. Men envy me. Women eye me with curiosity or outright lust. People send me gifts. Packages of all different sizes pile at my doorstep. Some contain cash money, wrapped in rubber bands. Sometimes the bills are sopping wet and falling apart. Other times they're brand new, sequentially bundled, the ink still damp. I travel the world. Many hands have touched my hair and my hair has touched many bodies.

In the spring of this year I arranged through certain entities with whom I'd made acquaintance to meet Dr. 999. He lives in the fabled inverted caves in a protected region of the Ngari Prefecture in Tibet. He is surprisingly small, bespectacled, Caucasian. His hair is glacier-white and gorgeous. At night he basks in unthinkable, terrible pleasures, and during the day he toils in his laboratory with a silent coterie of masked assistants, devising a new formula which will, he claims, put Malumense Dr. 999's NL-id Blends Micellar Moisturizing Milk to shame. After his work has done and we've sat for dinner and wine in the cool, capacious caverns that form the outer edge of his environs, we touch our coiffures to one another, and he passes along his many secrets.

LEAVES OF DUST

by Wendy Nikel

The cherry tree cracks on a cloudless, windless day, sending magpies fleeing from its foliage in a burst of leaf and feather.

Ysobel hears the ragged *snap* of tree-bone and rests her tea upon the patio brick, where it sloshes against the sides of the mug like floodwater threatening to overflow its banks. A lemon slice bobs in the near-boiling liquid – a tart concoction meant to cleanse the liver, restore the soul, and dissolve the body aches brought on by advanced age and by yesterday's attempts at arranging furniture. Inside the box-strewn house, the television buzzes with some talk show that Ysobel has no real interest in, save for how it fills the corners with its human-like chatter. The illusion of companionship, sans messy entanglements.

Dew and overripened cherries dampen her feet as she crosses the yard. The grass is too long, sorely in need of mowing, but Ysobel has never possessed a lawn of her own before and has nothing with which to cut it. Another problem for another day, considering half the growth is now hidden beneath the detritus of the broken tree.

In the place on the trunk where the branch had clung, the tree now gapes open. Crisp, beady pincher-bugs swarm the broken bark and a plump, fat worm writhes deeper within. Beneath the interstate of the miniature world within the broken branch itself, a hollow place catches Ysobel's eye – a tangle of darkness, concealing a whisper of movement. Something's in there. Something dark and not-quite-treelike. She leans in closer, one finger out and a breath of wood-scent upon her cheek.

"Looks like you could use a chainsaw."

Ysobel straightens up, searches for the source of the inquiry, but all that greets her is the still and empty yard. From deep within the branch comes a sound, barely there, like the hum of a distant fan. She shakes her head.

"Yoo-hoo! Over here, neighbor."

The hum fades as she looks around and this time, she can see that the voice coming from the opposite side of the fence belongs to a bandana-tied head with wisps of white hair and two bushy eyebrows with small pinprick eyes. She pulls her cardigan tighter across her chest, wonders how long those pinprick eyes had been watching, wonders if she's really moved into *that* sort of neighborhood – the sort where folks peer over fences and into others' lives, where they say "Yoo-hoo" and loan out garden tools.

"Need a hand?"

"No," Ysobel says, her feet slowly retracing their dew-dappled steps. "No, I'm quite fine."

"You sure? Looks like you'll need that branch chopped up. Can't leave it just sitting like that; it'll kill your grass."

"I can call someone."

"They'll charge an arm and a leg."

"That's fine— That is, I'll be fine." Ysobel flushes, her tongue catching on her teeth, tearing on the words she didn't mean to say. It's no one's business what she can and cannot afford, none of their concern how she spends her money. Didn't they realize that she'd moved here to be alone and unbothered?

"Just let me know—"

Ysobel closes the door behind her, shutting out both tree and neighbor.

~

An online search pulls up three tree cutters in town. The first number – selected for its alphabetical supremacy – has been disconnected. The third goes directly to voicemail. Ysobel leans upon a box labeled "Dining Room" and considers the second. It's coincidence, of course. The beauty of this town is that she knows no one here, and yet that familiar first name – though common enough – is enough for her to toss her phone upon a stack of books and snatch up the box labeled "Bath Supplies" instead.

She draws the bathwater and slips beneath the surface, where even the television conversation is muffled and distant. She'll try the third number again tomorrow.

~

Ysobel dreams of the tree, of that hollow place sinking deep within, and in her dream, it calls to her, its voice demanding and familiar. It reaches out black tendrils of glutinous sap, wrapping itself around her wrist, around her arm, around the naked base of her fourth finger, and reeling her in with slurps and gurgles. It pulls her in to its cool, slick darkness, drowning out the noise of traffic and enveloping her in the silence so perfect, so absolute, she can barely breathe.

She wakes in the morning with mud on her heels and tree bark wedged beneath her nails.

~

When the third tree cutter doesn't answer, Ysobel recites her plea into the phone, half-suspecting that the words will disappear into the aether, unheard again by human ears.

She takes her tea to the window, where the lace-edged curtains act a veil to conceal her form from any nosy, pinprick eyes. Would it really be so terrible to leave the branches where they are, entwined on the lawn, and simply let the crabgrass and creeping vines grow up and over it until it becomes her own personal forest, blocking sight of the fence, the sky, the world?

Tempting.

But there's the thing in the branch to contend with. Though now, in the light of day, what is one strange hole anyway? It was fatigue, stress, too many hours out in the sun that had her thinking it was anything more. She pulls out her phone and googles "stress relief," then pulls the curtains closed on the yard.

~

When the telephone rings, she answers it without looking, thinking that it must be the tree cutter.

"Ysobel! I told you to call when you arrived."

Ysobel sets down the newspaper-wrapped plates and briefly imagines what it would be like to simply hang up, to walk downtown to the mobile phone store and trade in the number that tethers her to her old life. But she has resumés out with this number inked on top in bold hand and besides, how would the tree cutter return her call?

"Ysobel? Are you there?"

Is she?

"Yes, I'm here, Bette." She tallies her lies: one.

"You sound awful, dear."

"Just tired from the move." She counts: two.

"Would you like me to drive out? It's only four hours. I could help you unpack, settle in."

"No, no. I'm fine." Three.

"I wish you'd rethink this. No one blames you, you know. Sometimes things just don't work out, and we all still care for you. I'd hate for things to be awkward."

"Of course not; I know that." Four.

"I spoke with him the other day, you know—"

"I'm awfully sorry Bette." Five. "I have to go." Six. "The doorbell just rang." Seven. "I think it's the tree cutter I hired to take care of a few minor things in the yard." Eight. Nine. "I'll call you back later, I promise." Ten.

She hits the red button before her friend-turned-almost-sister-in-law-turned-who-knows-what-now can say another sympathetic word about how she's a wonderful person and she's sure there's someone for her and it's only a matter of time before she finds someone.

Ysobel doesn't want to find someone. She wants to be alone.

The wineglasses are still buried, so she dumps the afternoon-cooled tea from her mug and fills it half-full of merlot. She redials the third tree cutter's number and this time when the voicemail picks up, she recites her home address as well.

~

Ysobel falls asleep watching TV, but still, she dreams of the tree.

The darkness in the branch is bigger now, impossibly big, at least twice as large as the tree's diameter, and it no longer smells of wood and ripened cherries, but something stronger: a heady mix of cologne and cigar smoke and the stench of bitter disappointment.

She stands before it and reaches in, but before her fingers touch wood, something luminous shifts within. The light resolves itself into glowing orbs, bobbing like champagne bubbles in a moonlit glass. They draw nearer, and Ysobel sees her own face — pale and wan and oh, so tired — in their liquid surfaces. Tiny cilia propel them forward through space, and they turn their long, sticky tendrils away to expose a single dark pupil upon each of them. Their stare pins her, immobile, to the spot.

In the morning, her mouth is dry and when she scrubs her teeth, the brush comes out coated in dirt.

~

There's a blue envelope wedged into her screen when she steps out to retrieve the mail, which flutters to her front walk when she releases the latch, like the feather of a startled magpie. Inside is a card with a Rockwell-esque image on the front, depicting a boy with bare feet fishing off a pier. It's the sort of card Ysobel's grandmother used to purchase from the drug store in boxes of dozens at a time and send out on birthdays and anniversaries. The kind of card that, unfitting for any particular occasion, somehow becomes fitting for any.

"Welcome to the neighborhood," is scrawled along with a phone number across the inside, and Ysobel wonders if the owner of the signature — some illegible name beginning with H or N or E — is also the owner of the pinprick eyes and wispy hair, or if someone else in the cul-de-sac's silent, still houses has also taken note of her arrival.

In the postal box bound to the house by two rusty bolts are two bills, addressed to someone else — perhaps someone who'd fled *this* place, *this* life, without leaving a forwarding address. She imagines them in her old apartment in the city, turning the key on her old mailbox and retrieving letters marked with her name.

A discarded cardboard box becomes a rubbish bin, and Ysobel drops all three envelopes inside.

~

Shortly after noon, she finds it, tucked away deep within a box marked, "Misc." It was one of the final cardboard vessels packed, long past any pretense of labeling or organizing, past anything but blind grabbing and tossing and praying to household gods of domesticity that nothing would break, past anything but her own whispered vows that everything would be different after this, that she'd sort it all out when she arrived: her job, her life, her diet, her health, her eternally-strained relationship with her mother. And yet now, here it was, staring accusingly up at her amid this hodge-podge mess of things she never wanted but couldn't bear to throw away.

It's innocuous-looking from the outside: a simple paperback with a battered cover and a title of once-silver letters dulled to scratchy gray. Its brittle leaves are so frail that it seems like the lightest touch could dissolve them into swirls of dust and the briefest wind could free them forever from the constraints of their battered spine.

What was one moment a thought, the next is a deed. A harsh and horrible deed of cracked bindings and shredded pages, of paragraphs severed word by word, and words torn apart letter by letter. Of hot tears dissolving antique paper and the bits and pieces of what was meant to be whole fluttering down like dust-coated snowflakes.

The hundred-year-old book she'd bought him is ruined, and a vitriolic taste of bile claws her throat when she realizes what she's done. All that money she'd wasted on what ought to have been the perfect gift, lying disassembled on the laminate floor. As if it was the book's fault or the author's that her plans had all gone wrong. As if they were to blame for her lacking foresight.

When she returns from wedging the broom in a corner of the pantry, the light on her phone is blinking. The number she missed is the tree cutter's, but he hasn't left a message and her call goes straight to voicemail.

~

She chases coffee with Red Bull and Twinkies, determined to stay awake. *At least until all the boxes are unpacked*, she tells herself, though really she means, *at least till daybreak*. Late-night talk show hosts divulge celebrity secrets and the laugh track is always too loud, but there's nothing else on besides horror flicks and *Lifetime* movies that hit too close to home.

One by one, the boxes disgorge their contents. One by one, their cardboard bones collapse until there's nothing left but a pile of empty layers — a tome devoid of words.

Near dawn, the TV blares ancient reruns of shows her mother used to love. *I Love Lucy. Laverne and Shirley. Mary-*cheery*-Tyler Moore.* She sinks into the armchair to change the channel, and her resolve to stay awake grows soft.

The yard forms a cathedral to the darkness.

Tree trunks form pillars to hold up the sky, and leaf-adorned alcoves house glimmering sets of eyes that peer out in keen expectation. Creeping vines create a center aisle, and beyond it all lies the broken-branch altar, within which the emptiness dwells.

She approaches with reverence and curiosity on muffled, grass-softened steps. The stillness in the void cries out to her, breathes her in, drags her down, and she wonders vaguely if she ought to resist. If this ought to be some battle of wills. Some test of her character, some trial. If the void would think less of her for her complacency.

Her arms extend toward it, and black tendrils curl like calligraphy around her: thicker in parts, thinner in parts. Simultaneously delicate and strong. The eye-orbs on their tar-stalks come slithering from the deep and bob in ever-smaller circles around her. From a distance, they were surreal but up close, their dilated pupils are unnerving. There's so many of them. So many eyes upon her, each filled with fervent expectations.

Hurry, hurry, they whisper with their cilia. *Hurry, for it's nearly dawn.*

At the mention of dawn, Ysobel turns to the east, where the darkness is not so black nor the thickening haze so solid. In fact, there's a warmth about it that only makes the slick tendrils wrapped around her arms and legs feel icier. The eye-orbs hiss their disapproval, and their stringent grip on her tightens.

She gasps, pulls back against their restraints.

Yet isn't this just what she wanted?

"No." Her heels bite into the dew-softened dirt.

"No." She closes her eyes, imagines them gone. Imagines just a tree. Just a yard. Just a simple cracked branch lying still and dead with nothing, nothing inside but earwigs and ants and beetles and worms and a thousand tiny things that will consume it down to dust. Harmless, wind-swept dust incapable of anything at all.

"No!"

Something rumbles to life, and she flinches at the sound but doesn't dare open her eyes. It's louder than the branch's initial crack, louder than the hum of the void. Louder than the laugh tracks and the rending of pages and the distant ringing of her phone. The tendrils loosen their grip, fleeing before the noise; the vines curl up on themselves; and the iciness of the eye-orbs' gaze retreats until she swears she feels the sun's warmth as the stones of the cathedral crumble around her.

Open your eyes.

She wakes with a gasp, fingers gripping the armchair. Across the room, the television blares gray static. And somewhere beyond, in the yard, the rumble persists, loud and steady.

Outside, the morning sun momentarily blinds her to anything but vague shadows and noise. With a hand shading her forehead, discernable shapes slowly take form: The flailing branches of the cherry tree. The wings of magpies taking flight. And the shape of a wispy-haired, bandana-clad woman with her chainsaw pressed to the branch's end, its moving bits dissolving the wood into harmless plumes of dust.

Ysobel watches from her stoop as the sawdust dissipates through the sky — an orange cloud against red sunrise.

Then she returns to the kitchen, flicks on her kettle, and sets out two mugs for tea.

THE KIND DETECTIVE

by Lucy A. Snyder

O ne Sunday at exactly 4pm, Detective Craig McGill was nursing an Irish coffee and poring over the cold-case murder photos spread across his cigarette-pocked kitchen table. His eyes ached. There *had* to be some small but crucial details he missed the first twenty times he studied these black-and-white snapshots of death and misery. He was certain, sure as a priest about the truth of a loving God, that if he just looked at things the right way, he'd solve these grisly puzzles. Justice would be served. And if a horror could be met with no meaningful justice, at least grieving families could finally gain some closure.

A loud *bang!* made him reflexively dive to the worn yellow linoleum floor. His ears popped as if he were on a jet that had taken a sudden 20,000-foot plunge. Vertigo surged bile into his throat as he rolled sideways to draw the .38 revolver he kept in a holster bolted beneath the table.

He crouched in the shadow of the table, waiting for another *bang!* None came. It hadn't been gunfire. Too loud, too low. But it had come from the street in front of his house. Maybe closer. A bomb? His mind flashed on the pressure cooker IEDs the narc squad had recovered from a backwoods meth lab. Who would have tossed a bomb into his yard? The local Klan, angry that he'd sent one of their boys to Angola for murder? Gangbangers? A random lunatic?

After a ten count, he crouch-ran to the living room window and peeked through mini-blinds. The only thing that registered at first was that something was *terribly wrong* with his yard. But for a couple of seconds his brain rejected the missives from his eyes because what he beheld was an impossibility.

The massive pecan tree that shaded the front yard of the shotgun bungalow since his grandfather built it in 1930 was gone. Not exploded, not burned down – *gone*. It had a canopy as wide as the house and a trunk he couldn't get his arms around and there wasn't a stick or leaf left of it. Not even the main roots remained. A wide, perfectly hemispherical scoop of dirt and concrete sidewalk was gone, too. McGill was relieved that the water and gas mains hadn't been broken.

Nobody was visible on his street except for his catty-corner neighbor, Mrs. Fontenot. He gave her all his pecans every fall, and the pies she made from them were one of the purest joys in his life. Before he tasted one, he'd scoffed at people who declared that this or that food was a religious experience. Mrs. Fontenot made him a believer. Upon taking his first bite, he declared that she should be a pastry chef. She laughed and replied that it would be the ruination of a fine hobby.

Mrs. Fontenot was dressed in her gardening hat and matching lavender gloves and rubber boots and sat beside a scooped crater in her front yard. Her magnolia was gone. She was hunched over, listing to the side in the way that people do when they are in profound shock.

McGill shoved his pistol in the back waistband of his cargo pants and hurried out to see if she needed help. The heavy smells of tree root sap and fresh overturned soil were thick in the humid air. He glanced down at his missing tree's crater as he hurried past it. The remaining roots were cleanly severed at the margin of the hemisphere. What kind of machine could have done such a thing? And why?

"Miz Fontenot, are you okay?" he called as he scanned the street for strange vehicles. His snap judgement that this was the work of criminals he'd crossed seemed ridiculous, now. Someone who could take a pair of big old trees like this could have taken his whole house with him inside it. But someone did do this strange, powerful thing, so maybe the perpetrator was watching? The hand of God hadn't just scooped out their trees. The universe didn't work that way. Did it?

Mrs. Fontenot made no reply to his call, did not move, so he ran over and knelt beside her.

"Miz Fontenot?" He gently touched her shoulder. "Are you okay?"

She slowly turned to face him. Her dark face was wet with tears, and her brown eyes stared wide. He'd once seen that same expression on a small boy who'd watched his father cut up his mother with a hatchet.

"Oh ... Detective. So fine of you to visit." Her voice was as flat as a salt marsh.

"Did you see what happened?"

"I saw ... I saw ...."

She started to weep. Deep, wracking, soul-wrenching sobs. People her age who got this upset sometimes had heart attacks or strokes. McGill wondered if he should call for a squad, but he wasn't sure if she had health insurance. If she didn't, the ambulance and ER bills might break her. She didn't seem to be in immediate danger. Maybe she just needed a chance to rest and gather herself?

"Can you stand up? Let's get you inside. I'll make you some tea."

He gently helped her up and escorted her back into her house. She stopped crying, but her whole body shook as if she were walking through snow. Shock, definitely. He got her settled in her easy chair, pulled off her boots, and tucked a crocheted green afghan over her legs so she'd stay warm.

"Thank you, Detective. You're a kind man. Don't let nothing tell you otherwise."

McGill smiled at her, feeling relieved that she was able to speak, and went into her kitchen to put the kettle on.

When he returned with a steaming mug of chamomile tea, Mrs. Fontenot was dead.

The purely practical part of McGill's mind told him that the EMTs wouldn't have arrived in time to save her. They just wouldn't bust the speed limit for a black lady with vague symptoms, not even if a white off-duty cop was calling on her behalf. And *that* renewed realization – the system he served was horribly flawed – made the mess of sadness, anger and guilt stewing in his skull almost boil over.

He hadn't shed a single tear at any of the terrible murder scenes he'd investigated. Nobody wanted an emotional cop. It was not *professional,* it was not *manly,* and he would not weep now for this sweet old lady slumped in her favorite chair, even if nobody could possibly see him.

He would not cry. He would do his job: find out who did this to her. This wasn't *technically* murder, but he was sure to his core that whoever took her tree, took her life just the same. He would work this like any other case, and he would solve it, and there would be justice.

~

When McGill arrived at the police station early the next morning, he found his partner Rhett Gradney arguing with Cindy Romero, one of their narcotics detectives.

"This whole tree thing is stupid, and we shouldn't waste resources on it." Gradney looked royally pissed off, which meant he was probably scared. Yep, he was bouncing his left foot. In the five years they'd worked cases together, McGill had learned all Gradney's tells.

"How can you say that?" Romero's eyes were hard coals; her stance told him she was ready to sock him in the jaw. "A dozen people ended up in the hospital yesterday, scared into heart attacks or nervous breakdowns."

"At least one landed in the morgue." McGill felt just as irritated as Romero looked. He stepped past them to fetch his coffee cup from his desk. "My neighbor saw her tree get taken, and she died not five minutes later."

Gradney's face flushed firetruck red. "Goddammit, not you, too. Of all the people here my own damn partner should see how idiotic this whole thing is!"

"Mrs. Fontenot was a great lady, and she's gone." McGill looked his partner square in the eyes. He didn't want to antagonize him, but he hated it when Gradney tried to pretend that unpleasant things just weren't happening.

Denial was not a useful or admirable trait in a detective. "Maybe whoever took her tree and put a big ol' hole on her land didn't mean for her to die, but she's dead. And if they *did* mean to do it, that's aggravated criminal damage to property."

"It's a fucking tree!" Gradney was screaming now, and everyone else in the station had turned to stare. "Trees are everywhere! Why get so scared over losing a damn tree that you have a heart attack? Just fucking plant a new one and move on! And why steal trees? That's some goddamned cheesy 60s Batman villain shit! None of this makes a lick of sense!"

"Detective Gradney." Police Chief Sammons glared at him from his office doorway. "You seem stressed, son. You need to take the day off?"

"No, sir." Gradney's blush deepened, spread. His scalp looked like a tomato under his short blond buzzcut.

"Then use your goddamn inside voice." Sammons looked like he was trying to set him on fire with his mind.

Gradney averted his gaze. "Yes, sir."

"Chief." Romero crisply stepped forward and stood at parade rest. "Is there a plan for how to pursue this tree situation?"

Seeming mildly annoyed at her question, Sammons glanced from her to McGill to Gradney.

"There is no specific plan at present." His reply was calm and slow. "A few minutes ago, I spoke with the mayor, and he's inclined to treat this as a serial vandalism incident. The newspapers are framing this as the work of pranksters. We're going along with that for now, until we figure out what in the name of little green men is really happening here. No sense in making people panic."

McGill wanted to tell them all that it wasn't just the trees; Mrs. Fontenot had seen something terrible that broke her heart. He was willing to bet solid money that everyone in the hospital had seen it, too. But saying that out loud might make him look like a lunatic.

So instead, he nodded at Sammons and said, "Panic kills, sir. Nobody here wants that."

He realized Romero was giving him a hard sideways stare, and when he met her gaze, she shrugged as if to say, *Sorry, buddy, I tried, but you're on your own.*

~

As the day went on, the police station buzzed with scorn and disbelief over the trees. McGill decided to keep his investigation to himself, but every disparaging remark reinforced his resolve to pursue it. He started taking late lunch breaks to patrol neighborhoods with big old oaks, elms, walnuts, pecans, birches, magnolias and ashes.

By Thursday, he'd identified a definite pattern. Each day at 4pm, someone or something would scoop up a half-dozen trees from various nearby locations. And then five minutes after that, the town due west would get hit. And then a little while later, the next town over. The phenomenon was global, it seemed, and followed perhaps not the sun, but certainly the turn of the Earth.

People were dying. Property was destroyed. The whole town was pocked with craters. This was clear. And yet, authority figures and talking heads still weren't taking it very seriously. News reports and official announcements remained sparse and dismissive; even the tabloid shows that usually exploited any possible reason to scare their audiences were avoiding the subject. McGill still felt echoes of his own disorientation and his mind's initial refusal to see his own tree's abduction. He knew why reporters and cops and mayors were doing all that hand-waving. They had to pretend that this incomprehensible display of power wasn't any big deal, or the fabric of order holding the town together might fall apart.

People needed to know that their lives were governed by predictable forces. The law mattered because it mapped order and safety onto the chaos of human interactions. Justice wasn't just a matter of punishing the guilty; citizens needed to see that people would genuinely get what they deserved. People who worked hard and behaved decently would get to have beach vacations and nice houses with comfortable porches shaded by big pecan trees and friendly neighbors who made sublime pies. Those who didn't had to change their ways. And if they wouldn't change, well, they had to be removed so they couldn't hurt decent folk. McGill never felt good when he heard that petty criminals he'd busted got killed in prison, but he refused to feel badly about sending them away. Crimes had to have consequences. They *had* to.

So, even though the brass wouldn't admit a serious crime was even happening, McGill started taking late lunch breaks at 3:45 to patrol neighborhoods with big old trees. He hoped to spot an abduction, or at least find a witness who could provide some solid details. Suffering a nervous breakdown was not a concern of his. The gruesome violence he'd seen and smelled was stuff they'd never put in scary movies. There were things that even eager gorehounds turned away from, and McGill had gazed upon them with clear eyes. *His* mind was sound.

He drove with his windows down so he could better hear a telltale *bang!* And a strange thing happened. A couple of minutes before an incident, the air took on an electric vibration, and he shivered as if someone was dancing on his grave. The weird frissons got stronger the closer he was to an abduction site.

Following those new instincts led him to be on Willowbrook Avenue right as a tree was taken. There was the *bang!* loud as a stun grenade. He turned to see a green blur shooting straight up into the sky from a nearby yard. For the first time, he realized the trees were whisked away so damn fast they broke the sound barrier.

The sheer improbability of it made his mind reel, but he saw a blue-uniformed postman staring down into the fresh crater, his mail bag slumped at his feet, and McGill's instincts took over.

"Sir, did you see what just happened?" he called as he pulled over.

The postman slowly turned toward him, and began to laugh. He was medium height, wiry, and looked like his folks might be Vietnamese. From the anguished expression on his face, McGill figured he was going to burst into tears at any moment.

The detective got out of his car and slowly approached. "Sir, are you all right?"

"I … I wanted to see," the postman gasped between giggles. "I just couldn't not try to see, you know?"

McGill nodded. "I want to see, too. Can you tell me what you saw?"

"Don't do it, man. You don't want to know. He's … he's gonna run out. And then everything is fucked." He started weeping, and looked a gnat's breath away from completely losing it. "Just … go back to your family. Take that trip to Six Flags the kids have been bugging you about."

"I don't have a family. I just have my job." McGill didn't have a good read on whether he was dangerous or not. He did *not* want to be one of those cops who shot down an innocent person because of their own cowardice. He knew the department would back him if the kill was even slightly justified, but he didn't think he could look himself in the mirror ever again if he killed someone who'd needed his help. "I need to find out what's going on. Can you help me understand this?"

The postman shook his head. Tears and snot flowed down his face. "Go to Vegas, then. Anything but this. *Anything.*"

McGill reflexively stepped back and dropped his hand to his belt holster as the man reached into his pocket and pulled out a box cutter. "Easy, there."

"Sorry. I can't help anyone." The postman clicked the blade open and plunged it into his own neck. His punctured carotid artery spurted an impressive gout of blood that splattered on McGill's shoes. A second later, he fell to his knees on the grass.

The detective was about to step forward to try to put some compression on the wound when his entire body rashed in goosebumps and all the hairs rose on his neck and arms. The frisson was more powerful than ever. A tree nearby was about to go. He scanned the street and saw an oak that had to be a hundred years old in the front yard of a pink house. *Yes.*

McGill turned away from the dying postman and sprinted across the street toward the oak. The trunk was as thick as a car and the limbs creaked low under their own weight. Its hard leaves rattled in the breeze. This was the 30-pound trophy bass of trees. He felt a consuming excitement he hadn't experienced since the night they'd closed in on the Savetier Killer who'd been murdering cops and security guards across the state.

He felt *alive* in a way that he hadn't in years.

Just as he got within a few feet of the spreading canopy, it happened. His ears popped from the pressure change as something like a huge invisible punch rammed down from the sky, and then the *bang!* made him feel as if a 300-pound linebacker had body-slammed him. But he kept his feet, and as he saw the green blur he leaped forward, looking skyward.

And he saw into the hole in the sky.

The vertigo he'd felt before was nothing compared to what he felt now as his mind and vision were dragged in the wake of the tree, hurtling billions of miles into the far reaches of outer space, a distance so vast and cold that no one could ever reach it using human technology.

And in that moment, he witnessed a scene with perfect clarity. A swollen red sun larger than most star systems cast a sullen crimson glare across its galaxy. And silhouetted against that sun was an old god, curled like a deformed, tumorous fetus the size of Jupiter. The thing was more grotesque than a million bloody crime scenes. It was more twisted than the worst dreams of the most debased psychopath. McGill couldn't bring himself to behold it entirely; he could at best focus on a patch of scabrous scales here, a planet-sized claw there. He was sure that if he tried to see it wholly his brain would melt.

The abhorrent god slept in death in the harsh radiation, and yet it was not truly dead, and could never die. Orbiting around the cosmic monstrosity were hundreds of thousands of trees. Some were already desiccated, scorched husks, but some keened silently as they both burned and froze in that terrible airless space.

It opened one vast, star-pupiled eye and gazed back at McGill. And the detective knew its abyssal mind. The god, in its own way, was lonely. It wanted to surround itself with dying things to comfort itself. Trees took a while to die. But the god was older than the star it orbited, and its need was endless. It would run out of trees. And then it would drag every man, woman, and child up into that faraway red desolation to die in terror and torment in its vile, alien orbit.

McGill fell backward onto the lawn as the vision released him. He lay there stunned, weeping, his certainties and beliefs a blasted desolation. This was the first time he'd cried in 25 years, and he didn't care. There was no God but the one he'd witnessed, and it cared nothing for human justice or order or anything else he held dear. The only thing that was real was the certainty of death.

And the detective could not imagine anything more horrible than being dragged away from Mother Earth to feed that cosmic abomination. It wasn't just the agony feeling your flesh boil off your bones and your eyeballs rupture in your skull. It wasn't just the horror of having that monster be the last thing you saw before you died. It was witnessing everything you loved and believed in and had strived for destroyed and mocked by the Universe as you were snuffed out. Billions of people would break and die in that terrible place and there would be no point or greater good or Heaven at the end of it all.

In that moment, the detective wanted to end himself as the postman had. It would be so easy to draw his revolver, blast his own brains across the grass, and be done with it. He'd die in the warm embrace of Earth. And that was the best anyone could hope for now.

"No," McGill whispered to himself. *I have a job. People need me.*

"Oh, my goodness." An elderly white woman with an aluminum cane had emerged from the pink house. She was dressed in a flowered shift and a white shawl. Her slippers were a dingy grey. "Are you okay, sir?"

"Yes, ma'am." He climbed to his feet. "Thank you for asking."

She adjusted her spectacles. "What ... what happened to my tree?"

"Nothing happened to your tree, ma'am. Everything is fine."

He drew his revolver and shot her right between the eyes.

"I'm sorry, ma'am," he told her bleeding corpse. "But this is the kindest thing I can think to do."

He went back to his idling car and headed toward the nearest gun shop. He'd need a whole lot more ammunition for his new work. Someone would stop him, sooner or later. Maybe his partner Gradney would shoot him down. That wouldn't be so bad. It was a funeral suit that fit.

In the meantime, though, he needed to be as kind as he could possibly be.

THE LEVEE BREAKS
by Jayaprakash Satyamurthy

The past is a different country, and besides, the swain was dead. Mostly. For all practical purposes. But past and present were developing an unpleasant habit of overlapping. Trying to keep her timelines straight, Ratna walked down the path that wound between the cottages by the lake, counting down to number 7, right at the corner of a row. The door, once locked and chained, hung open on rusted hinges. She bent under the crossbar, still standing guard, and scuffled into the cottage. Dank inside, dank and dark. Dry leaves blown in by errant winds crunched underfoot. Sound of rats scurrying from her. Damp stains on the walls, furniture rotted and askew. It felt right that this place should be so desolate, so bereft. Ratna smiled to herself. She passed through the living room into the bedroom. The whole bed had collapsed in on itself, the headboard leaning out over the broken-backed bed. Everything was slick, slimy. She opened the door to the bathroom. There, in the tub, a body lay. She stepped closer, eyes adjusting to the dark, to the flickers of spasmodic light filtering in between leaves fluttering on the branches of the trees outside the tiny bathroom window with its glass blinds.

The bathroom was the driest place in the house – unintended irony – insulated from the creeping damp by the tiles. The large, dark figure in the tub resolved into the form of a slumbering woman, hair a wild grey nest, body swaddled in layers of capriciously assembled, haphazardly secured rags. The sleeping woman sensed something, mumbled and shifted in her sleep. Ratna carefully walked backwards, back into the bedroom. For a moment, she had seen herself falling on the woman with vicious nails and teeth, ripping away the foul bits of cloth, rending the flabby, lined old flesh, letting the old, weak blood spill from this sack of drained dreams and shrivelled hopes.

It was an impulse she had acted on before in this place.

Instead, she left the cottages and followed the curve of the lake, all her past selves walking with her, seeing things each with their own eyes. Trees loomed like great towers, settled down to more realistic proportions; some became old and twisted or were felled. Wooden, hand-painted signboards on stores gave way to printed vinyl, streetlamps grew in height and brightness, roads became potholed, were resurfaced, crumbled slowly and started the cycle again. People's clothes changed, dhotis and lungis became rarer, heavy flannel trousers gave way to jeans gave way to cargo shorts and track pants, saris made room for salwar-kameez suits, skirts became more common, and then became shorter.

She reached the old boathouse. It had changed very little over the years. It had already been abandoned and decrepit when she first had seen it. Her grandmother had warned her not to go in there, the boards were old and rotten, she could do herself an injury, maybe even fall through into the water. Over the years she found out that it used to be the private boathouse of a maharaja whose family still owned a massive bungalow near the lake. The bungalow was now a tourist lodge and there were occasional murmurs about fixing up the old boathouse, but nothing had been done about it for decades.

Everything seemed unchanged. Her selves converged, the chatter of memories stilling as she shouldered through the broken door, across weeds and rubble out to the warped, rotting pier. The same old half-sunken boats, the rusted boat hooks, the reeds growing out of the shallow water at the shore, the squelching and creaking. Everything much as it had always been, except for the dark, ominous patch on the boards where she had once lit a fire.

She'd dragged him there, had dragged Ravi there after what had happened in the cottage. Things had been building up for a while. For the last few months, Ravi had been pressuring her to marry him, or at least to have a child with him. She'd hoped a change of scene would give them a chance to reevaluate things, start afresh. Indeed, after the first few days in Kodaikanal, he'd dropped his demands. They had spent long hours walking around aimlessly, not quite trekking, afternoons rowing on the lake – he'd picked up the knack quickly – and a satisfying amount of time just snuggled up in the cottage with only paperbacks, cigarettes and each other for entertainment. Then he'd taken to spending an hour every night by the lake, just peering into the water. He spoke to her of ancient things glimpsed in the depths. She laughed at him, told him it was an artificial lake, put in by the British. She dug around in the library at the Club, and showed him a photograph of the engineer who had overseen the project, a man from the Severn Valley region in Britain. It didn't matter to Ravi. He continued his Narcissus-like vigils at the shore, every night just after sunset. Yes, he'd stopped pestering her about commitment, but he'd also slowly dropped out of their activities, begging off from walks and spending long hours soaking in the bathtub, a quart of whisky at hand, rather than in bed with their ashtrays and piles of books.

Then, he started scrounging around for scraps of paper, tearing endpapers out of books, ripping cigarette packets open, pulling old bills out of pockets and scribbling on them. One afternoon, as Ravi floated in his lukewarm isolation, Ratna collected as many of these jottings as she could find and read them all. She read about the thing that he thought lived in the lake; ancient, wise, vile. Worse, she read that he was convinced he had entered into some kind of pact with this thing. He still wanted a child, still wanted to be united with Ratna in some permanent way, but these natural, even commendable desires had not been in abeyance, as she thought, but had been busily festering into something deeply pathological. She remembered meeting his father, senile before his time, and wondered if there was a history of mental illness in Ravi's family, if the man was crazy, if he was dangerous. She read on, found where Ravi had written about taking her into the lake, to become immortal, to become transformed. They would live eternally in darkness, and she would bear him the child he wanted. She had once, despite her current unwillingness to commit to the idea, thought that Ravi was the kind of guy who would make a good father, had entertained a fleeting vision of them vacationing by the lake, a small child between them. She figured everyone had these kinds of thoughts; unlike Ravi, she was just not convinced that she wanted to act on them. And now the man had built some impossible, obscene fantasy in which he could make it happen.

When Ravi unexpectedly emerged from the bathroom to find her poring over his papers, she was astounded by the force of his rage. Flecks of spittle flew from his mouth, his hands balled into trembling fists and he paced up and down, the cottage suddenly shrinking to doll's-house dimensions against his towering anger. He loomed over her, his soft, paunchy form suddenly grotesque, menacing. He raised a hand above his head. Before she could think what she was doing, she leapt up, grabbed his arm, twisted it behind his back, flung him face-first into the wall. He was screaming at her, screaming obscene threats in an unrecognisable voice. Ratna found all her love transformed into its opposite and she fell upon Ravi with all the rage of disappointed love.

This boathouse, this was where she had dragged him afterwards, under cover of darkness, that same night. He was heavy, but she had found a space of strength within herself and she was not going to let it go. Ratna did not need to rely on the forking of consciousness to see the events of that night clearly. She had brought his bottle of whisky along with her, poured it over him, over the thing that had been him, and set it on fire. He had burned surprisingly quickly and with very little odour. When it was over, she had swept the smouldering residue into the water. There was little she could do to clean up the greasy, burned patch where he had lain, but she did not fear this place being investigated.

Indeed, it looked for all the world as if she were the only person who had been to the old boat house in all the time since that night when Ravi had died, and so had all her old real and imagined selves. She had come here on the bidding of one of those selves. A fond and contented Ratna, sleek with happiness, cradling a child, holding Ravi's hand. She had never met anyone who suited her as well as Ravi, the original Ravi, before he had become that nightmarish, obsessed thing in the tub. Her life was not very bad; it was not especially good. Her life was a big emptiness. She knew that there were many ways that she might have filled her life and not all of them involved Ravi, or marriage, or motherhood. She also knew that all those possible paths had sealed off ahead of her the night she killed Ravi. Nothing new and good was welcome in her life. She rejected it, because any clemency that was allowed her would be tainted by the memory of her crime.

So she sat by the water, sat on the old pier and thought about the things she had never had and never lost. She stared into the water, Narcissus-like. Something may have moved in the water, something may have pulsed and loomed in the depths, something with wisdom and scorn and deceit, something with spiked gifts and ancient promises. Most likely, it had all been madness, madness turning Ravi into something that hadn't really been himself anymore when she had killed him. A kind of communicable madness, maybe. Something that manifested in visions and hallucinations, something that could reach out and claim her from the lands of gone-forever and never-was-at-all. She closed her eyes as the two others slid out of the water onto the old, warped planks. Did not turn as two sets of footsteps squelched their way toward her. She was almost certain that reality had lost its grip on her, but she kept her eyes closed as someone settled into place on either side of her, as a soft, plump hand and a small, slim hand gripped hers, one on each side, and two bodies leant in on her, as something spiked through her and pulled her through.

Wishes are granted, she thought to herself, as all her selves fused into one and were subsumed. *Wishes are granted*, she thought to herself again, as she slipped into darkness and deepness. *Wishes are granted, but we do not know whose they are.*

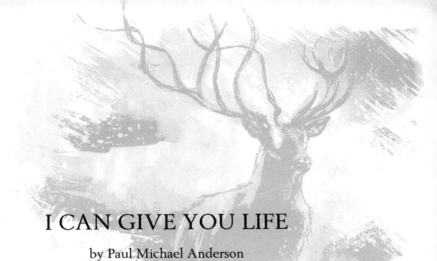

I CAN GIVE YOU LIFE

by Paul Michael Anderson

Charlie was a rookie, so he puked, but he was still a Virginia State Trooper, so he made sure to do it in the woods to the side of the highway, as far from the crime scene as possible.

(how do you know it's a crime scene?)

(what else could it be?)

Wiping his mouth, he stomped back to the road, trying not to trip over an errant tree root. His stomach sloshed with his footfalls, although he couldn't for the life of him imagine what could still be in there. The tree line was a few yards away, the shadows in the ditch beside 526 eastbound deepened by the twisting red and blue lights—

(wait)

There shouldn't *be* blue lights.

(blue lights are county aren't they? this is highway)

He clambered up the ditch with as much dignity as he could manage, stumbling and scraping his left hand against the rocks puncturing the topsoil, wincing at the wire-thin pain. Clips of voices drifted over, resembling beat poetry.

"Getting bad...run the plates...got an idea...exits already closed from Linden to 81...getting worse, is what it is...shouldn'ta run out like that...like that fucking matters..."

The patrol cars—both State Police and Anbeten County—were parked willy-nilly across the closed lanes, framing the configuration of metal and glass in the center of the lane that might've once been a Ford Galaxie station wagon—the extended back was still in approximate shape—but wasn't any longer. The entire frontend had been flattened to the shattered windshield and what remained of the passengers resembled ground chuck, pressed into the vinyl seats.

(how? how does that happen? how is this a crime scene? what does that?)

He approached the officers, grouped by gray or tan uniforms. Most looked up, their faces tight and gazes unreadable; men of varying ages, hair colors, and complexions but sharing enough similar traits—the wideness between the eyes, the thin lips—to mark them as local. He was the only Trooper in Area 13 who hadn't been born in either Anbeten, Frederick, or Warren County.

"Trooper," one of the county boys said, nodding his head slightly.

"Brooks," Harrigan, Area 13's Master Trooper, said, his bushy salt-and-pepper eyebrows drawn together. He didn't look up and his eyes were distant. The other troopers stood behind him, all Trooper IIs; Charlie was the only probie. "You and Trooper Caldwell are going to Schlossen. That's where the folks—"

"Temoin family," a trooper behind him said. He was slightly pudgier than the others, his lank blond hair longer.

Harrigan nodded. "Thank you, Caldwell. That's where they called this in from. They're staying at the Cool Harbor Motel. Go there to get their statement."

He looked up and studied Charlie. His eyes were sharper, but his eyebrows were still bunched. "I'm under no illusions that you expected this on your third day in Area 13 and this is a delicate matter—" The tip of his tongue darted out, wetted his lips. "—and the academy didn't train you for it. Caldwell is lead. Understood?"

Charlie nodded. "Yes, sir."

"Dick and his boys are going to handle this." Harrigan inclined his head to the man who'd addressed him. Dick planted his thumbs in his Sam Browne belt. There were fewer county boys than State Troopers, but they seemed to set their feet more firmly, take up more space on the road.

Charlie's eyes cut back to his superior. "Sir?"

"They'll maintain the road closure until public works has cleaned the mess," Harrigan said. He gestured at a tight clutch of VDOT workers, their orange jumpsuits giving them away, on the far side of the accident. They crowded behind a wiry bald man, his head thrust forward like a strutting cock. His hollowed eye sockets resembled a skull.

Questions piled up in Charlie's head, the questions anyone new would ask and feel stupid for doing so because the answers *must* be obvious, but he looked away and said, "Yes, sir."

Harrigan lifted his chin. "All right, gentlemen. We all know our jobs."

The two groups dispersed—the Troopers to their Fords, while the county boys spread around their sheriff.

(welcome to the illustrious life of a virginia state trooper, charlie brooks!)

And then, a softer voice, a voice he knew but refused to acknowledge:

(isn't this what you wanted?)

Caldwell said, "C'mon, probie," and started for a patrol car, the blue detailing made black in the emergency lights.

Charlie followed. The other officers glanced at him as they walked around the incident—the strange knot of VDOT workers openly gaped at him—but Charlie resisted hunching his shoulders. He was a Virginia State Trooper now; he had his certificate—even if the ink hadn't fully dried yet—and his assignment to prove it.

But he still felt their eyes on him
(*outsider-outsider-outsider-outsider*)
and he hunched his shoulders, anyway.

~

"I vomited my first on-scene, too," Caldwell said. He settled into his seat, kept the cruiser humming at a steady sixty. "This one's at least respectable. Mine? Jack-knifed chicken truck." He shook his head, grinning in the radium-glow of the dashboard lights. "Man, I couldn't eat chicken for two years, and I *like* chicken."

They reached the top of a rise and the Shenandoah Valley spread out before them, heavily sketched in darkness. Route 526 was a black vein running through it. Above, a smattering of stars coldly and indifferently twinkled. The openness made his skin itch. He was from the southeastern coast of Virginia; if people didn't come for the history, they came for the water, and the area had built up accordingly. Here, you might see an errant farmhouse light, but not many. Some homes, he knew, still weren't on public power.

He looked away, down at his left hand. The minor cuts still felt tender.

Caldwell punched his arm, lightly. "C'mon, probie. Relax. We all puke."

"Right." Charlie rubbed the patch of flesh above an eyebrow. "What *was* that back there? I mean, Jesus, it's—"

"—not our problem," Caldwell said, and his tone lost some of its warmth. "We just gotta check on some John Qs and—"

"Why?" Charlie asked. "Why are we *just* going to do this statement? Why was county there? Why was *Harrigan* there? What the hell *was* that back there?"

The cruiser topped another rise and now Charlie could see more pricks of light in the darkness. Schlossen, alone in a sea of black.

Caldwell sighed. "Listen, prob—Charlie. We do things a little differently out here, okay? We might be only a hundred miles west of D.C., but that's like the distance between the Earth and the moon. This is country. Before there was State Police, there were county and town police, and we respect that. We follow traditions. One day, it won't be like that—hell, the state's talking about building an Interstate that runs east-west, like they're doing with 81's north-south run." He glanced at Charlie. "But that's all in the future. We're in transition here. You understand?"

"I'm not going to lie," Charlie said. "I don't."

The lights of Schlossen were closer, and Caldwell cut the Ford down to forty-five. "You're new and we haven't had a new kid in a long time; most cops want to go where the action is—Richmond or Alexandra or Hampton."

Charlie looked away. "That's not any interest of mine."

Caldwell slowed, turned onto Route 17, a regular two-lane black top.

"My point is, just play along," Caldwell said. "Harrigan lets Sheriff Dearborn run Anbeten County because—hell, Anbeten's so small, anyway. One less postage stamp to watch over. We have everything else in NOVA. You understand?"

Charlie struggled not to shrug. Maybe it was the night, maybe it was what he'd seen, but everything seemed slightly off, like a radio between stations and the voices overlaid. He saw the shape of what Caldwell was saying, but he didn't think he was seeing it perfectly.

(or caldwell's not showing it perfectly)

(why was harrigan there? what WAS that?)

"I get it," he said.

"Good," Caldwell said, and the warmth returned to his voice.

~

Crossing over the town bridge—passing a woodcut sign that welcomed travelers to Schlossen and pointed out that not only was Schlossen one of the "Gateways to Skyline Drive" but that it was also "the canoe capital of Virginia"—you were greeted immediately by the grazing fields for cows, followed by a diner, a mechanic, and a small motel. Another farm, and then more businesses. The town crept up on you, putting you in its gut before you noticed.

It was late, and most of the stores were dark, but more than a few businesses had soaped windows, FOR SALE signs. The farms, set far back from muddy and denuded fields, looked dark and foreboding, abandoned monarchs overseeing ruined kingdoms.

"You're staying here in Schlossen, aren't you?" Caldwell asked, turned off the main drag and away from the street lights.

"Uh-huh."

Caldwell pulled into the parking lot of a large, rambling white clapboard building. THE COOL HARBOR MOTEL, the red-and-blue neon sign on the roof said.

"Nice place," Caldwell said, pulling into a parking spot. "I have family here."

He shifted to Park and killed the engine. "It's sad, though. Since I-81 opened up, not enough traffic comes through. The farms are going down—a mixture of bad seasons and not enough customers. This place is a shadow of what it used to be. People don't wanna talk about it, but it's dying."

Charlie couldn't fathom such a thing. People had roots; they stayed close to them.

(except me right of course stop it)

"C'mon," Caldwell said, grabbed a notepad from on top of the dash, and got out.

The older woman at check-in directed them to Room 17, on the second floor. Her gaze unnerved Charlie, although he made sure to keep his face neutral. Her eyes were pale-blue, matching the rinse in her hair, and peered at them peevishly over the top of heavy reading glasses. Her gaze lingered in Charlie's mind long after they left the lobby.

Caldwell knocked on Room 17, two sharp raps.

"Who is it?" a woman asked. Her voice sounded phlegmy, as if she were in the midst of crying.

"Virginia State Police, ma'am," Caldwell said.

A rattle of a chain, a fumbling with the knob, and the door opened to reveal a wraith of a woman, thirty-something going on seventy. Her hair had probably been permed, but it was disheveled now—thick, graying strands framing her swollen and wet eyes.

"You called us, ma'am," Caldwell said. "About the accident on 526?"

Her face squeezed together, fresh tears spilling down her cheeks, but she nodded and moved aside.

They stepped into a cramped double, the bedside lamps turning the floral wallpaper a sickly nicotine yellow. In one of the beds, a tuft of brown hair belonging to what only could've been a boy poked out from under the covers.

The father sat at the edge of the other bed, staring at the small television playing through *Alfred Hitchcock Presents* on the dresser. He had a doughy, sagging face, and the white patches at his temple stood out against his dark hair. He held a bottle in a brown bag and, as Charlie watched, he took a long sip of it.

A girl of what Charlie guessed was thirteen sat in a chair in the corner, knees drawn up and arms encircling them. Her hair hung sweaty in front of her glazed eyes.

The family reminded him of photos of Dresden survivors, expressions reflecting minds that couldn't grasp the destruction they had just walked away from.

"I don't know what else there is to say," the woman said. She studied the worn carpet beside them.

Caldwell flipped open his notepad and clicked his ballpoint. "This is really a matter of making sure we have everything correct, miss," he said.

The father *harrumph*-ed. Charlie glanced over, but the man was still intently watching the television. On the screen, James Donald was helping Patricia Owens find her husband's body.

"I told your dispatch everything we saw," she told the carpet. "Except about filming it."

Caldwell stiffened. "Excuse me?"

She pointed to a pistol-like object on the dresser, beside the television. Charlie went to it—hesitating for the briefest moment before crossing in front of the father's intent gaze—and picked it up to show Caldwell. An 8mm Kodak camera.

Caldwell looked at it for a long moment. "We're going to have to take that, miss."

"Do as you need. It doesn't help us at all. Or that poor family."

"The road ate them," the father said.

Charlie, Caldwell, and the man's wife looked at him.

The father took another long pull from his bottle, his white temples the brightest thing about him.

~

Charlie chased Caldwell across the parking lot. He'd never felt less like a trooper than he did at that very moment.

"Wait a minute, for God's sake!" he yelled, his voice obscenely loud in the night.

Caldwell reached the cruiser and unlocked his door. "A Christing Brownie camera. Goddammit it all. Goddammit it all to hell." He slid into the car, tossing the camera onto the passenger seat, and fumbled his keys into the ignition.

Charlie skidded to a halt beside Caldwell's open door. *"Wait a minute, dammit!"*

Caldwell looked up, as if surprised to see Charlie standing there.

"What the hell was that?" Charlie asked. What had Harrigan said? The academy hadn't trained him for this? Damned skippy.

"I have to get back to the station," Caldwell said, the words clipped, as if talking was a waste of time. "This is important evidence."

"What are you talking about? What about the Temoins? What the hell's *happening?*"

"The county will take care of the family," Caldwell said dismissively. "It's their job, anyway." He gripped the inner door handle. "Listen, you're staying in Schlossen. Think you can find your way home?"

Charlie blinked. *"What—"*

"Welcome to a real investigation," Caldwell said, and slammed the door closed. He fired the Ford's engine with a roar and spun out of the parking lot.

Charlie watched the red lights diminish, then disappear as the cruiser turned a corner. For a moment, not a single linear thought entered his head. He heard no traffic or, he realized, any night sounds at all. Just his breath. Just his heart. The cuts on his hand ached vaguely.

He looked around. The motel's security lights were inadequate, leaving deep pools of shadows around him.

"What in the hell just *happened?*" he asked aloud, but the night gave no answer.

He thought of going into the lobby, calling the station or a cab, but didn't want to see the old woman again. He didn't even want to turn, for fear that she was at the lobby doors, watching him.

Grunting, Charlie started walking.

~

Because of his hike the night before, his feet were already aching by the time he reached Mom's Country Kitchen, a diner set in a low red brick building more fitting for a dentist's office. The restaurant was at the end of a forty-five minute walk through town, past drivers that openly stared at him and businesses with signs reading OPEN but had all the life and vibrancy of being CLOSED.

A bell overhead tinkled as he stepped inside Mom's and nothing so cliché as everyone stopping and staring occurred, but tension filled the air. Backs stiffened, cups of coffee were put down with sharp *clacks* against saucers, conversations stuttered. A clutch of county boys surrounded a corner table and their heads locked into place, looking away from him as he slid into a stool at the counter. At the other end, three older men dressed like farmers—

(then why aren't they out working their fields?)

—didn't have such problems and squinted at him through a grayish-blue haze of cigarette smoke.

"Trooper," a middle-aged woman with bouffant hair said, approaching with a carafe of coffee. Her voice was a lazy Southern drawl, easy on the *R*s. She flipped his mug over in its saucer and filled it. "Need a menu?"

"Yes, please, thank you." He picked the cup up and sipped it, burning his tongue.

She pulled a tall plastic-coated sheet from under the counter. "New, aren't you?"

He sipped his coffee more carefully. "Yes, ma'am."

"How long?"

"Four days?" he said, smiling in a way he hoped was charming.

She nodded approvingly at him. "It's good you're here," she said and moved down to the farmers.

The bell over the door jangled.

"And you're even punctual to our apology-lunch," Caldwell said and sat down beside him. "There's a lot to like about you, probie."

Charlie set his mug down. Its sides burned the tender cuts of his palm. "I was just thinking of what I liked about you and coming up short."

"I'm buying you lunch, aren't I?" Caldwell said, flipping his mug up.

"I had to walk here," Charlie said. "Because, you know, my car is still in Area 13's lot."

"I said I was sorry about that over the phone, Charlie."

(and how did you get my number? jesus i barely know it yet)

"You sure this wasn't a haze?" Charlie asked. "It took me three hours to find my way home. I haven't even been here a damned week, Caldwell."

"No," Caldwell said on a sigh, "that wasn't a haze." He coughed, cleared his throat. "The family last night...the camera...it was important to get it back to Harrigan. It was *evidence.*"

"On a case we're not even running."

Caldwell's mouth opened, but he apparently found nothing there. He shook his head instead.

"Jimmy Caldwell," the waitress said, approaching. She filled his mug. "I haven't seen you in about a minute or so. I was getting to think you were too good for us."

(you think you're better than me boy?)

Charlie squeezed his eyes closed at the memory of the man's voice, but not before—

(the reek of gasoline, the stench of spilled blood)

—momentarily filled his nose.

"Nah, just busy at the station, is all, Dorie." Caldwell raised his mug in a toast.

"Your family still up on Blue Mountain?" she asked, sliding a menu in front of him.

"Dug in like ticks," Caldwell said. He gestured towards himself. "The prodigal son might've heard the call of serving the public, but the Caldwells are inseparable from the land."

A squeak of chairs behind them. Charlie glanced over and saw the county boys standing. They dropped a handful of greenbacks on the dish-laden table, grabbed their hats and moved to the door. They stepped outside, where a weather-worn man in a denim jacket and John Deere cap waited to enter. A few county boys nodded to him. He nodded back and stepped inside.

"Joseph!" Dorie called. "Where in heaven's name have you been?"

The man took off his hat, revealing a luxuriant shock of white hair. "Visiting my daughter downstate."

"Well, come have a cup of coffee," Dorie said.

The man coughed. "Actually, I just wanted to see if Rodney was here. To say goodbye, like. I'm moving in with my daughter and her husband. They bought some land and they need help getting it straight. The good farming's down there now."

Dorie didn't have an immediate reply to that. Charlie looked around. With the county boys gone, what had seemed near-full before now seemed mostly empty. Those who were left had fallen silent, watching.

The man coughed again. "I got nothing going on for me in town and...well, I miss my kiddo, you know."

"We know, Joseph," Dorie said, softly. "We understand."

Charlie glanced at her.

(we?)

"Um," Dorie said. "Rodney's not here, but I'll tell him you stopped in. Okay?"

The man nodded. "I appreciate it, Dorie. Thank you."

"You take care now," Dorie said emphatically.

He smiled and it lit up his face. "You, too, Dorie. You, too." He put his cap back on and nodded at Caldwell and Charlie. "Officers."

They nodded back. "Sir," Caldwell said, in a tone matching Dorie's.

The man stepped back outside. The bell seemed louder now.

Caldwell, Charlie, and Dorie watched through the front window as the man climbed into his '54 Chevy pickup, badly painted fire-hydrant red, and pulled out.

Silence hung for another moment, and then the three farmers picked up their conversation. Dorie drummed her nails on the counter.

Caldwell picked up his menu. "And there goes another one."

~

Charlie paused outside the closed door of the station's big conference room, a Rand McNally Atlas in hand, and cocked his head. Behind him down the darkened hall, the irregular report of typewriters in the bullpen sounded like shots fired by an apathetic army in battle. Conversation was sparse. Two-thirds of the middle-shift was out on patrol.

Why was this door closed? It wasn't even closed during shift briefings.

He opened the conference door and heard the *whisper-squeak-whisper* of a film roll feeding into a projector.

He stopped inside the doorway, frozen. The projector, typically used for training purposes, threw up a silent picture of moving Virginia highway and, distantly, the rumpled red-and-green blanket of the Blue Ridge Mountains against the far wall.

(i told your dispatch everything we saw except about filming it)

The camera lurched, revealing less shell-shocked versions of the Temoin family—father, mother, sister—

(what happened to them did they get home are they all right fuck caldwell took care of the report and i never asked)

(sloppy)

(probie)

—before swiveling back the window. On the far left side of the shot, was a Ford Galaxie booking east. The westbound lanes of this section of 526 were elevated, the median a grassy slope.

The Galaxie was the only other vehicle on the road.

A squeak of metal and Charlie pulled his eyes away. A man sat in one of the seats. A cigarette burned away in his hand.

A flash of color and Charlie looked up. The Galaxie was closer to the camera now.

And then, when the Galaxie was parallel with the Temoins, the road swatted the station wagon. If you blinked at the wrong moment, you would've missed it, and the next frame you saw was of speeding away from the wreckage.

But Charlie hadn't blinked at the wrong moment; Charlie hadn't missed the ground rising up like a ripple of silk right into the Galaxie; Charlie hadn't been spared the almost-frozen quality of metal blossoming outward, glass heliographing the light.

A noise escaped Charlie, a hybrid between a squeak and a throat clearing, and the man in the seat spun.

Charlie hit the light at that moment. Harrigan sat in the seat, wearing the expression of someone caught out, as if he'd been discovered masturbating.

And then the muscles of Harrigan's face were tightening and he stood. The ash of his cigarette hit the floor.

"Brooks," Harrigan said.

Charlie's back straightened. "Sir?"

"Can I help you?"

He remembered the atlas in his hand, raised it. "Looking for a quiet place to read?"

The film reached the end of its roll and the *flap-flap-flap* of 8mm spinning filled the room.

Harrigan moved to the projector, his legs like grey scissors. "An atlas?" he asked, removing the film roll. He stuck the cigarette in his mouth and smoke collected above his head.

"I like to study maps," Charlie said. "Since I'm new to the area, I figured it'd be useful to learn the roads in detail."

Harrigan glanced at him, sliding the small roll of film into a cardboard container. "I learned the roads by driving them."

Charlie nodded. "And I will, too, sir—but I'd rather not get lost on state's time. This just gives me routes to investigate when I'm off-duty."

Harrigan squinted through the cigarette smoke at him. The question—*how much did you see?*—hung between them.

But, instead, he asked, "And you...*like* looking at maps? This is a hobby for you?"

Charlie resisted shrugging. "Since I was a kid. I've always liked knowing where I was. Now, it helps make me more efficient."

Harrigan slowly nodded. "You have no outstanding work waiting?"

"Just turned in all my reports," Charlie replied. "Three tickets on Interstate 81. One speeding, two for bad tags."

Harrigan nodded again. "Good. That's...good." Something relaxed in his voice. You could hear it in the lack of sharpness with certain consonants.

The Master Trooper surveyed the room, then put his cigarette out in a standing ashtray. "Then I'll leave you to it."

He paused on his way out. "I like your thinking," he said, and gave Charlie a clap on the shoulder, but both felt thin, perfunctory.

(that's not what you want to say)

Charlie stood where he was after Harrigan closed the door. His nerves couldn't decide whether to loosen or to tighten further.

Slowly, he went to one of the seats, and opened the atlas on the small desk bolted to the side. He flipped through the pages—topographical maps, blurbs about towns with history, county seats, and roads—before settling on the northern Virginia section.

But none of it made sense; his eyes refused to focus on the page. The final frames of the boy's home movie played in the center of his head and the father's voice recurred to him:

(the road ate them)

Charlie closed his eyes. *How much did you see* had hung between him and the Master Trooper but, now, another question occurred to him: *Why didn't Harrigan react to the footage?*

~

Everything is silent except for the thrum of tires beneath you. You kick your legs in the backseat footwell, boy's legs—shorts in spite of the late season, scabbed knees, scuffed Keds. A Kodak 8mm, a Brownie, is in your hands, its faux-wood decals bright, and it's heavier than you remembered, laden with footage from the trip to Washington, D.C.

(this is a dream you know it so)

You look out the window and the Blue Ridge Mountains unroll to your left, a dull green with hot spots of orange and yellow. You try, as you always do, to imagine people living beneath those trees, far from towns and cities, and can't believe it, but know it's true. The wood people. The earth people.

You look up and the Temoin father is driving, the mother in the passenger seat. The sister sits in the backseat next to you, a Nancy Drew paperback in her hands.

The father points out the windshield, opens his mouth and says,

(you think you're better than us boy?)

but his lips don't match the words, like a dubbed Godzilla movie, and the sound is harsh and slurred, incongruous with the look of amusement on his face.

You follow the father's finger and see a pinprick on the farthest rise— another car. Its windshield reflects the sun, heading towards you in the eastbound lane. You aim the Brownie at it and turn back to your father. He's glancing into the backseat, grinning. His temples aren't white, now.

(you think you can just abandon us boy?)

The mother says something, and you don't hear it, but you hear the father's reply as he smiles at her:

(shut it you nagging bitch)

You look back out the window and the car's closer now, the only other car in sight for the first time in what feels like forever, and it's an aquamarine Ford Galaxie, zooming towards the nation's capital.

Something hot splashes on you and a deafening ringing fills your ears. The father is holding *your* father's Remington 870, smoke pressing against the ceiling, and the mother's head is gone. Gore streaks the passenger side window, the windshield, dots the father's face. He's still grinning.

(all of you nagging me all of you chickenshits fucking UP)

You look out your window and the Galaxie is close enough now to see the family inside—father, mother, kids in the backseat. The back is filled to capacity with luggage.

A boy's voice to your right, thick and hiccupping:

(daddy don't daddy why momma daddy—)

You look and Tim is there, covered in blood, crying and staring at the father with wide eyes.

(shut it you little baby faggot)

The father, no longer even pretending to drive, levels the shotgun and blows Tim's face away. The shot is silent, but the ringing in your ears steps up a notch, and more blood hits you. The smell, like hot metal, clogs your nostrils.

The father's still grinning, but the nose is Roman, the hairline receding into a widow's peak, the color dulling. You know this man.

Out your window the mountains are moving, rising and falling like a flag flapping. The Brownie in your hand is gone, replaced with your father's World War II trench knife, and you grip it so tightly your forearm shakes.

The father's transformation is complete, and he's turning towards you, still grinning, but his eyes blaze and bulge and pin you with a hatred stoked by the fires of hell. As he turns with the shotgun, you lean forward, almost casually, and plunge the trench knife into his shoulder.

The grin becomes a rictus, and he drops the Remington as blood soaks through his white shirt. The dizzying stench of gasoline fills the car.

(this is your life charlie this is you you ain't no better NO BETTER you're NOTHING AT ALL)

Your father bursts into flames.

You look away from the blinding flash. The Galaxie is parallel to you and the westbound lane rises up, liquid as an ocean wave, plowing into the Galaxie, physics driving the front-end every-which-way.

You look away, and your father is still alive, still burning, the flames curling and flowering against the ceiling of the car, but not harming the material.

Through the windshield and fast approaching is the road, rising up to smash into you, to take you along with the family in the Galaxie, and you recoil but your father grabs you by your shirt with a flame-soaked hand, setting it on fire, and it burns, it *burns*. Pulling you towards the flames, you and your dead father watch the road rush to greet you—

~

Charlie sat bolt-upright in his bed, the scream clogging his throat.

He choked it back and swung his legs over the side. Thick darkness filled his bedroom except for the elongated rhombuses on the ceiling of streetlights coming in through the windows. It took him a moment to reorient himself, to remind himself that he was

(in williamsburg)

in Schlossen.

He took a deep breath. The Temoins. Seeing the boy's footage by accident a week ago. Harrigan's shocked expression at being seen. What had happened to all that? It shouldn't nag him, but it did, a meat hook twisting in his brain.

(my point is just go with the flow)

He closed his eyes.

His father waited behind his eyelids, still burning, still trying to take Charlie with him, not in the Temoins' car but back on the farm, where the events of last summer had really happened.

His eyes popped back open.

"Jesus," he muttered, and dry-scrubbed his face.

He pulled his hands away wet. He'd been crying in his sleep.

"Jesus," he said again, his voice furry with disgust.

~

Two weeks to the day that Charlie puked in the woods of 526, he pulled his Studebaker Champion to the shoulder in a plume of road dust and set the brake.

He stepped out and although he felt the slight chill of a morning breeze on his face, he heard no crickets, no scurrying of animals in the underbrush.

He slammed the door—wincing at the sound—and looked up and down the highway.

No traffic.

(not enough traffic goes through here)

526 became a four-lane through Anbeten...but it was empty.

A strange tickle traced the nape of his neck, spread tendrils along the surface of his skull. He looked around, taking in the hillside, the road itself, remembering it washed in confusing emergency lights.

Here. Right here where...

(the highway ripples like a sheet over and over and over again)

Charlie walked down the single broken white-line in the center slowly, watching the asphalt, then stopped a few yards in.

Right here.

From shoulder to shoulder, the asphalt was broken and cracked in a million-different fissures, turning the concrete to pale macadam. Charlie traced the course and saw it continued almost to the horizon-point. Beyond the sides of the highway, rocks jutted like crooked teeth. Along the edge of the woods to his right, the trees slumped back, revealing their root systems.

Charlie hunkered down. That creepy-tickling sensation rippled across his skull again. The area hadn't had a good rain since the accident and, up close, he could see the ghost limning of blood.

"Here," he said, then reached his left hand out and touched one spot, like a religious supplicant. Pins-and-needles tingled across the palm, then faded. "Right here."

He closed his eyes, seeing the film unfold—the road rising and rounding and curling forward, a wave of Portland cement and lime, the Galaxie crashing into its center.

(who were these people?)

He didn't expect an answer, but a random memory bubbled one up:

(inseparable from the land dug in like ticks)

"The land claimed them," Charlie muttered. He opened his eyes and shook his head. Questions filled his mind like helium, none with ready answers, none with easy routes *to* the answers. It'd been his third day on the job, but so much of that night had seemed *wrong*—

(getting bad getting worse shouldn'ta run out like that)

Charlie staggered, the tickly-sensation at the nape of his neck exploding into a fuzzy pressure in the center of his brain. He caught his balance, cupping the back of his head, and looked at the road.

(why did i come here?)

No answer to another question, but it brought another wave of dizziness, more pins and needles in his hand.

(forced)

(that's just silly)

(so's a highway rolling like carpet)

He started back, the click of his Police Issue shoes too loud in his ears, the tickling pressure almost like an internal wind in his mind. Not a single car. Not a single animal. The hillside rose across the westbound lanes, seemed to lean towards him, as if to push him further into the valley at the foot of the

Blue Ridge Mountains.

He slid into his car and almost flooded the engine starting it. When he shifted into gear, the tickling began to recede—enough he could drive, anyway.

Just before the emergency turnaround that would let him head back west, he reached a VDOT depot, heavily screened by trees beginning to feel the autumn burn.

He slowed, peering down the slope through the wide gate. The two garages, the salt storehouse, the woods beneath, but the entire lot appeared empty—not a single personal vehicle in sight.

(today a holiday, or something?)

He sped away, faster than he should've. He already had enough on his plate without wondering about the mysterious road workers. Probably not much work to do on 526, anyway.

He reached the emergency turnaround and took it hard, rear tires struggling to grip the rise, sending out a startled rooster-tail of dust, and the sharp turn west.

The fuzzy pressure, the internal wind, went with him.

~

Harrigan dropped a stack of files on Charlie's desk, making him jump. "Aren't you off-shift now, Brooks?"

Charlie glanced at the wall clock on the far side of the bullpen. Ten after six. His shift was over at five.

He looked around his desk and couldn't piece together what he'd been doing since sitting down at four-thirty. The surface was blameless except for a typewriter, a green blotter, In&Out trays, and a sheet of paper on which he had, apparently, drawn a large descending spiral in black pen.

Around the bullpen, the evening shift had settled in to its routines. He knew none of the people, which wasn't surprising. Aside from the First Sergeant, Harrigan, and Caldwell, Charlie hadn't learned a single other person's name since starting nearly a month ago.

"Apologies, sir," he said. "Woolgathering." This was true. He'd been thinking about the Temoins. And 526. And questions without answers. Anbeten County had the file on the incident, and he couldn't show up and ask to see it without further questions being raised. Area 13 would have the initial call logs, down in the basement archives, but they wouldn't have many answers. Not to the questions *he* had anyway.

(how? what happened? who were the victims? what happened to the temoins?)

"Not much to go home to," Charlie said and his mouth felt numb, barely his own.

"Give it time," Harrigan said, but his tone said he didn't give much of a shit, either way. "What route do you take back to Schlossen?"

"Varies," Charlie answered. "I've been trying different routes from the atlas."

Harrigan poked the files with a spidery finger. "There's a VDOT depot on 526—a little past Schlossen, but within spitting distance, so you won't be too far out of the way." His tone said he didn't give much of a shit if the depot was too far away or not. "They need these files for their yearly budget request. Drop them off, will you?"

Charlie pulled the files close with a hand almost as numb as his mouth. "Of course, sir."

Harrigan stepped back to allow Charlie room to stand. "And I'm going to start pairing you with Caldwell, get you onto more roads with less likelihood of getting lost."

"Yes, sir."

Harrigan nodded. "Then have a good evening, trooper."

Charlie nodded back and moved around the Master Trooper towards the door. Though he didn't look back, he felt the older man watching him.

Studying him.

~

The VDOT depot's orange incandescent security lamps guided Charlie through the open gate. He parked in front of the low, rectangular main office, cut the engine, and got out. He smelled wood burning somewhere.

As opposed to the other day, every available parking space was filled with pickups in varying states of decay, but all the garage bays were dark. A part of him imagined the crew he'd seen the night of the accident standing in them, staring at him with unreadable expressions, waiting...

"Stop that," he whispered. A cool breeze ran fingers up the back of his neck. The fuzzy pressure he'd felt last week had returned, nudging his brains. His left palm, healed, tingled with pins-and-needles.

He made his way to the office door, hand hovering over the knob. Should he just walk in? Knock? He leaned close to the glass, but could see nothing but a waiting room with its tall faux-wood reception desk. Where the hell *was* everyone if their cars were parked?

"Who cares?" he said, and opened the door. The pneumatic arm squealed, and he jumped.

Charlie pulled the door shut behind him, and looked around. Two black doorways greeted him—one behind the reception area, one to his immediate right. No sounds from either, no lights.

"Oh this is ridiculous," he muttered, and rubbed the nape of his neck. The pressure was stronger, sending tentacles down his shoulders and spine.

(*i shouldn't be here*)

"No shit, Sherlock," Charlie whispered and crossed the reception area. He dropped the folders on top of the desk—there; done.

(now i can get the hell outta here)

He crossed back to the door, not looking into either black doorway—

(afraid something's watching you? jesus)

—and nudged it open, trying to avoid that awful metallic squeal again. It was only when he was back outside, that he realized he'd been holding his breath since calling out. He let it out in a gush, whooped in another.

(this is ridiculous)

He said it aloud. "This is ridiculous. It's a fucking depot, for Christ's sake."

A fragile calm built into his chest, but it didn't diminish the pressure in his head, didn't make his shoulders relax.

(can we just say that something is wrong here? this isn't probie newness or something i can just look at askance. something is fucking goddamn wrong here)

"Yeah," he breathed, "but what?"

And then, of course, he heard voices.

An uptick in the breeze, a change in direction, brought the sound to him—a rumble of male voices, incomprehensible, coming from the other end of the depot, where the incandescents didn't reach.

Charlie took a step forward.

(now take one more step, turn left, and get back into your car this isn't your thing)

But he kept walking forward, towards the garage bay. The questions, the impossible mountain of questions, shoved at the front of his brain—

(where is everyone?)

(what is everyone hiding?)

—and were propelled by that internal wind. Even if he wanted to stop walking, he doubted he could. He could no longer feel his legs, or any other part of himself. He was being led.

Something wanted him to *see* this.

Fear filled him—a cold ice-hand clutching his heart, slowing his breath, sending the nerve-endings into a panic. Conscious thought left him.

He came around the side of the garage bays, and the salt storehouse reared up. The rumble of male voices became an indecipherable chorus. It came from beyond the storehouse and the limits of the depot. It came from the solid black wall of the woods.

The remains of the Galaxie squatted behind the storehouse, half-hidden by old oil drums. An equally-damaged sedan and a badly-painted pickup rested beside it. The pickup's driver side door had been punched in, and something black had dried on the inside of the drooping windshield.

(i've seen that truck before)

But his legs kept him going. A buzzing rattled through his head.

He stepped into the woods and darkness swallowed him. He blinked and, off to the left, he saw the flicker of fire. He made for it, not watching his footing but not losing it, either. His body knew where to step, avoiding most of the branches that would've crunched underfoot. His left hand tingled with pins-and-needles.

The first tremor vibrated beneath his foot, but he didn't pause. Up ahead, the men's chant rose to a shout, and another tremor immediately followed, reverberating out from the group. Visions of the Galaxie flashed behind Charlie's eyes, but it couldn't muster the fear of his body being out of his control, of approaching this group of men out in the woods in the night. The tremors continued, irregular in intensity and time. If he'd been in control of his legs, he would've fallen by now.

He slowed to a stop six yards away from the fire. A massive tree trunk provided cover, and he had enough control to get his body behind it. He gripped its bark and the ribbed abrasiveness was the only thing telling him this was real.

The men from VDOT stood in a loose circle around a massive fire pit. They weren't in their orange vests and jumpsuits now, but in jeans and buttondowns, John Deere caps and denim jackets. They stared at a haphazard pile of stones beside the fire, upon which a large oblong book sat, its black-looking covers nearly as thick as the sheaf of rough-cut pages between. The firelight turned their faces red, made their glazed eyes gleam.

One man stepped forward—the bald rooster Charlie had seen before. He held his hands up to the fire.

"This is our covenant!" he called, and the other man rattled something off, slick and guttural.

"You called to us," the rooster continued, "and we called to you!" He didn't speak the way Charlie would've imagined him speaking; his words were clipped, unaccented at all, and deeper than that whistle-of-a-chest could account for. It was the voice of a preacher really laying into the theme of his sermon.

"Our pact was made by both parties," the rooster said. "You signed with prosperity, and we signed with blood."

The men around him shouted, a loose-change-configuration of letters and sounds, like what a dog would sound like trying to form human words. Another tremor rippled underground. The men swayed, but kept their balance. Loose pebbles and stones fell from the—

(altar)

—but the homemade book didn't slip.

"*We worship you!*" the rooster shouted, and the fire seemed to chase the words—licks of flame reaching into the darkness. "*We are your faithful, but you smite us! You condemn us after all our years of service!*"

The men started to chant, but the hardest tremor yet erupted, knocking them off their feet; wood shifted in the fire and sent up an explosion of sparks. The book and the rooster stayed.

Charlie went to his knees, and it was then that he realized he'd gained control of his body again—

(from what?)

(never mind never mind)

—because he started crab-walking backwards, away from the fire and the men and the tremors.

A quick crumple of sound to his right and before he could turn, a thin root wrapped itself around his wrist, twirling up his forearm, and cinched tight. He tried jerking his arm away and the root pulled tighter. His hand went immediately numb.

The hard wind inside his head:

(wait)

(watch)

One of the men barked—at least, that's what it *sounded* like. Charlie turned back and only one person was near the fire; the rest had retreated to the far edge of its afterglow. The rooster clutched the book to his chest.

The man was on his hands and knees, almost *in* the fire, his ballcap askew and his head hanging low. He barked again and a thickish-looking black fluid seeped from his mouth.

(blood)

"You," the man said, around the steady flow of ichor. His jaw worked like what he had said was badly dubbed.

(who do you think you are boy?)

"You," the man said again. His cap fell into the fire. He shivered, a dog trying to shake off the rain. "*You offer...sacrifice for sustenance...*" The last word dribbled away.

The rooster approached. "Yes, lord—we serve you."

"*You...serve nothing,*" the man-thing said. More black dripped from his face. "*You...take...from the land...*"

The man-thing smacked the ground, and the ground recoiled, knocking the rooster down. The other men cowered.

"We give sacrifice!" the rooster said. "We gave you the witnesses!"

A portion of Charlie's already-frozen, already-overloaded brain pinged:

(the temoins he's talking about the temoins)

The man-thing shook his head. Droplets hit the stones surrounding the fire and sizzled. "*Your sacrifices...have been...from others...Your faith...conditional...*"

The man-thing retched—to Charlie, it sounded like a cat choking on a hairball. He spat something thick and black out onto the sodden dirt. This sent off more tremors. Pebbles and loose grit bounced. The makeshift altar fell apart.

With a lunge, the man-thing rocked back, onto his knees, and his face coated in blood. It seeped out of the corners of his mouth, the corners of his upturned eyes, his nostrils. The cords of his neck stood out like cables.

"*Your sacrifices...have gone few...with less faith...less sustenance...you*" *demand more...I demand freedom..."*

The rooster shook. From his position on the ground, it looked feeble. *"We made a pact! We are BOTH bound! We to worship, you to provide!"*

The man-thing turned his head towards the rooster. His upturned eyes bulged, red and swollen. His mouth, still streaming blood, twisted into a rictus grin.

"Your...faithful...depart...leave the church...leave me here trapped...you have angered me."

"WE ARE BOTH BOUND!" the rooster screamed and Charlie, trapped and terrified, had to admire the little guy's balls.

"You...will continue to sacrifice..." the man-thing said, and his eyes were cherry-red now. His hair was lightening, shading towards white. *"With your...deserters...with your faithful..."*

"You will ruin your faithful!" the rooster screamed.

The man-thing looked beyond the rooster, seemed to pin Charlie in his place. In the firelight, the rictus seemed to tick even further upwards.

"I...will have my freedom," the man-thing said, and his eyes exploded with absurd little *pop*s of gore. His hair had turned completely white.

The body went limp, fell face first into the fire. A rush of air, so fierce it rippled Charlie's clothes, bent the bonfire, arrowed towards him. More, he felt the internal wind cycle up, pulling his thoughts apart and away. The world brightened, bleaching out the colors of things, then the shapes, and dimly, he felt the tree root leave his wrist...

~

...and the world resolved to the ceiling of his apartment. He was lying on his back on the floor.

He sat up, wincing at the sharp twinge in his back, the leadenness of his head. Early morning sunlight splashed through the front windows. The apartment was cold; he'd never turned on the heat last night. His breath frosted in front of him.

He was still in uniform, his knees and shoes caked with mud and bits of dead leaves.

He unbuttoned the sleeve of his shirt and jerked it up his arm—a spiral welt traveled the length from his wrist to his elbow.

"That was real," Charlie muttered, and something clenched in his lower gut.

(you offer sacrifice for sustenance)
(we are bound)
(you will continue to sacrifice with your faithful)
(i will have my freedom)

Dizziness slapped him. There was no internal window blowing through the hollows of his empty mind. It was a matter of something too big, too outside-the-realm, to fully comprehend. He tried, and he felt something tilt in his head precariously.

(that was power i saw last night)

(it took me home)

(it controlled me)

The man-thing, looking at him and grinning before the body—

(vessel)

—gave out.

His stomach clenched again and, before he could stop himself, he vomited into his lap.

~

Later, after a shower, he saw that the hair at his temples had gone white. Not *gray*, but *white*, as pure as the driven snow.

(like the vessel)

He could hide the welt, but he couldn't hide this.

(marked)

(i will have my freedom)

Charlie Brooks gripped the sides of his bathroom sink, hung his head, and waited for the dizziness to abate.

~

"I don't recall Chester shaking quite so much," Caldwell said, setting his coffee cup down.

Charlie looked down. He gripped his mug, still sitting in its saucer, and it was porcelain rattling against porcelain. He tightened his grip. "What?"

Caldwell shifted on the stool. "I figure, I'm Matt Dillon, the toughened and nearly-cynical law man of the west, while you're my Chester—partner, friend, semi-deputy—following me to new experiences and lessons." When Charlie continued to stare at him, he said, "Haven't you ever seen *Gunsmoke?*"

Charlie watched the way the nerves in the back of his hand twitched. "I don't watch a lot of television."

A beat of silence.

"What happened to your hair, probie?" Caldwell asked.

"Family curse," Charlie said. He'd practiced this. "It's either go gray early, or start losing my hair. Given the choices, I consider myself lucky."

Caldwell's eyes flicked between Charlie's gaze and the white temples.

(he doesn't believe me doesn't believe)

Finally, Caldwell said, "I think that's the first personal detail I've gotten from you. Got any others?"

Charlie looked away, studied his coffee. "Not really."

"Really? Everyone's got something. Hobbies. Interest. A girl."

He shook his head. "Not really."

Caldwell looked at him with lidded eyes. "Nothing, you say."

Charlie shrugged. "Not much of a reader, not much of a jock. I..." He moved his jaw, as if words were dice and he was rolling them around before shooting them. "I always wanted to be a State Trooper. I thought it would, y'know, fulfill me. Personally."

Caldwell considered this. "And did it?"

"Not sure yet." A soft voice, a woman's voice he'd known:

(isn't this what you wanted charlie?)

(the minister at the lectern, looking down at charlie and his bandaged hands)

Another beat of silence. Then, Caldwell asked, "Got a lot of family, then?"

"Not anymore," Charlie said, feeling like he'd stepped from one mine field to another. He spoke slowly. "I'm from the coast. When you live on the coast, you're naturally transient. My aunts and uncles moved off, had small families—if they had kids at all."

"You're the last?" Caldwell asked, for the first time appearing genuinely curious.

(he was always curious you're paranoid)

"As far as I know," Charlie said, and, in his mind's eye, he saw his father, a Roman candle about to burn out, between the bodies of Charlie's mother and Tim. "And I'm no different—I left my hometown, too."

(when the burns healed)

Caldwell shook his head. "You'll never see that here," he said, sipping his cup. "I'm nearly a heretic for coming down from Blue Mountain. Around here, people don't leave the land."

(because it eats you)

(we are bound)

Lunch arrived and Caldwell tucked in. Charlie's eyes wandered. A scattering of farmers-who-weren't-farming at the back tables appeared to be staring at him, and he avoided looking back there. The traffic out on Commerce Avenue was listless, barely two cars passing each other at any given time.

At the edge of the counter, he saw the town weekly—*The Anbeten Sentinel.* The above-the-fold headline read, LOCAL MAN'S TRUCK DISCOVERED. Beneath, the bullet read, *Authorities speculate victim got lost in the forest.*

The picture below was of the red pickup Charlie had seen at the depot. He'd also seen it outside the front window of Mom's when Joseph had come in to say goodbye.

(people don't leave the land)
(we are bound)
(because it eats you)
(i've been marked)
When Caldwell asked if he was going to finish his plate, Charlie pushed it over without a word.

~

Charlie was signing the patrol car back in when Harrigan's office door opened in the hallway behind him and Harrigan's voice barreled out: "What do you expect me to *do*, Dick?"

He stiffened. In front of him was the bullpen, in that state of transition between shifts. The secretaries were closing their desks down for the day. Men coming on shift were chatting with the ones about to punch out. He still didn't know anyone's name.

"I expect you to understand the gravity of the situation," Sheriff Dearborn said.

He heard their approaching footfalls.

"You think I don't?" Harrigan said, lowering his voice. Charlie still held the pen, poised above the sign-out clipboard tacked to the wall. "We're all together on this."

"You're not *there*, Jeff," Dearborn said, matching Harrigan's volume. "It's like you're standing outside the church, hearing only parts of the sermon."

Charlie resisted shivering at that.

"I can't direct traffic that way," Harrigan said, a firmness in his voice. It sounded like they'd stopped at the mouth of the hallway. Charlie's back began to sweat.

"And you know that," Harrigan went on. "The depot boys probably told you the same thing. It takes funds and personnel to do what you're asking, and the state watches those things."

(would you finish signing in already jesus they're gonna notice)
He scribbled something on the clipboard sheet, and slid the pen into the holder. When he turned, Harrigan and Dearborn were right there.

"Brooks," Harrigan said.

"Trooper," Dearborn said.

They both looked at his temples.

"Sirs," Charlie said, feeling his uniform shirt cling to the sweat.

"I had Trooper Brooks here drop off the file requests for the depot boys," Harrigan said. "For their budget. The fact that they requested it *tells* you that the state is watching."

"I understand that, Jeff," Dearborn said, studying Charlie a moment longer, then moved into the room. They paused at an empty desk a few feet away. "But it is a dire situation we're in."

Charlie turned away, standing in the mouth of the hallway, in front of the men's room. Caldwell had ducked in there when they'd come back to Area 13, complaining about his stomach and leaving Charlie with...*this.*

"I know that, Dick," Harrigan said, his voice lower than ever, but now Charlie's ears were tuned. Everyone else's conversation fell to a low rumble. "And I can appreciate how serious it is by the fact you came all this way, but you knew the answer before you got in your car."

"It's taking us, Jeff," Dearborn said. "Eddington thinks that it'll just whittle us down until *that* frees it from the pact. We need outsiders. You don't have a congregation if the faithful—"

Charlie closed his eyes as a dust-swirl of dizziness swept him.

(we are bound)

(he's talking about the fire the man-thing the book)

He leaned against the wall, trying to make it look nonchalant by crossing his arms, but it was the only thing keeping him on his feet.

"I'll see what I—" Harrigan began, but then Caldwell stepped out of the men's room. Caldwell's face was flushed and cheesy; a sickly sweat clung to his forehead.

"Oh, buddy-boy," he said, "we should *not* have had lunch at that roadside."

Charlie winced. "How bad?"

Caldwell's sick eyes rolled towards him. In a lower voice, he said, "I feel like I shit out my entire intestine. Thank Christ it's the end of shift." He shuffled forward and clapped a hand to Charlie's shoulder. "You're flying solo tomorrow and this isn't snoozing through a speed trap on 81. Think you can handle it?"

They'd spent the past four days out on the roads and Charlie had seen more routes than he had in the month prior riding the roads alone. With it came a sense of place—a rough map in his head, with Schlossen in the center. His first night-time impression of the town was right—the dying town was all alone, nestled in a valley, connected to the world via secondary routes that were losing place in favor of I-81. In towns near the interstate—Stephen's City, Middletown, Front Royal—new businesses were opening and traffic was heavier. In Schlossen he saw FOR SALE and FOR RENT signs popping up like crabgrass in an indifferently-cared-for lawn.

"I think I can handle it," Charlie said.

"Good, 'cause you ain't got much of a choice."

He shuffled into the bullpen and Charlie turned.

To see Dearborn and Harrigan staring at him.

~

Area 13's First Sergeant was a gray, bendable straw of a man by the name of

Bulloch and, standing in the front of the conference room the next morning, he looked like a sacrifice.

Charlie sat in the back row, feeling the emptiness of the seat beside him. Bulloch read through the outstanding news from the overnight, the assignments needed to finish those up. The Troopers—Trooper IIs and Senior Troopers, all local boys—zoned through it. Grayish-blue with cigarette smoke hung above their heads. Backs only straightened when the First Sergeant got to the day's routes.

Bulloch said, "And Trooper Brooks, with Trooper Caldwell ill this morning, you're assigned to Route 526, from the Shenandoah County line to the Fauquier County line."

Charlie stiffened. The space between Shenandoah and Fauquier was Anbeten County. He and Caldwell hadn't been assigned that route yet— Charlie hadn't heard *anyone* assigned to it. As Caldwell had pointed out the night of the Galaxie, the State Police tended to let Dearborn and the rest of the county boys run the roads in Anbeten.

Harrigan, sitting in the front with the other Master Troopers and Sergeants, had turned around to stare at him. Harrigan often handled the morning rotations.

Harrigan and Dearborn, staring at him yesterday

Charlie made his head nod. "Yes, sir."

Harrigan turned away slowly, and even after he showed Charlie his back, the man's unreadable expression lingered.

~

Two things told you, when driving on 526, that you were in Anbeten County: the small rectangular metal sign that said ENTERING ANBETEN COUNTY at mile-marker 12 (when going west, from Shenandoah), and the complete drop-off of traffic.

Charlie would add a third: the pins-and-needles tingle that seeped up the nape of his neck when he crossed over the county line. It crept along the nerve-endings and skin, pushing into the soft meat of his brain.

He wanted to turn the AM high, but didn't for fear of missing broadcasts from the dash-mic, which squawked and spit with cross-talk. His hands slid over the steering wheel, unable to fully grip and get comfortable. He felt Caldwell's absence.

The highway, still a two-lane this close to the county line, was barren. Charlie passed turn-offs for 55, 37, 340, 522, 11—as if, even without the aid of the interstate, highway planners had tried to steer people away from crossing through Anbeten County.

(because it's fucking cursed)

(we are bound)

526 ran across the top of Anbeten's pear-shaped territory like a stitch

across the Frankenstein monster's forehead. It ran for twenty-three and a half miles.

Charlie checked his odometer. Only nineteen to go.

He took a deep breath as eastbound and westbound split into separate two-lanes. He rolled his shoulders as he passed the turn off for Route 17, which would take him home to Schlossen—although, since the night of the fire, thinking of "home" and "Schlossen" in the same sentence left a queasy feeling in Charlie's gut—and he felt the absurd urge to take it. Go back to town—

"—get off the road," he muttered, tucking his chin down, as if the road would see his lips moving.

(it's not the road but the ground itself)

"It killed that family in the Galaxie," he said. "Killed that old boy—Joseph." He swallowed a sudden knot in his throat. "Killed the Temoins."

The tingling in his head ticked up a notch, and that internal wind began to blow. For the first time in days, the welt on his forearm throbbed.

(it's all in your head all in your head stop it)

"Easy for you to say."

He passed mile-marker 28 and realized he'd passed the spot where the...the *whatever* had taken the Galaxie.

He checked his speedometer. Pushing seventy-five. He eased up on the gas until it hit sixty-five. Like seeing the turn-off for 17, the urge to just floor the Bel Air's gas came to him; burn through the remaining miles until he reached the Fauquier County line, cross over, then sit and count the hours until he was off-shift. Dearborn handled Anbeten; Charlie's superiors couldn't honestly expect anything to happen during his shift, could they?

(harrigan does)

A shiver zipped up his spine at that. *I'll see what I—* Harrigan had started to say, and then Caldwell had come out.

—can do, he'd probably finished.

And now, look—he was assigned to 526, alone, when no other Troopers were ever assigned to it.

The tickling pressed into his brain, making him shake, making that internal wind blow harder.

(i had trooper brooks here drop off the file requests)

(eddington thinks that it'll just whittle us down...we need outsiders)

(eddington's the rooster eddington's the rooster)

Dizziness began to tilt through him, and the Bel Air drifted into the other lane.

(they knew i was there)

He bit his lower lip and corrected the drifting car. "Goddammit—*stop that!* You're fucking paranoid!"

The interior voice sounded like his father:

(prove me wrong)

He crested a rise and, at the top of the next, a sedan sat on the shoulder.

He braked instinctively. Then reasoning reasserted itself and he hit the gas again, albeit slower than before. He flicked on the turn signal and pulled in behind the car. It was a blue Dodge Royal Lancer; he'd known a kid in high school with one and that memory caused a clench of homesickness he hadn't known he possessed.

No one stood around the car. He saw nothing trampled down in the field to the right to show someone had walked through it.

Charlie killed the engine. He glanced at the dash-mic, but then turned away. Investigate first, then call it in.

As he got out, the tickling in his mind came back stronger. His shoes gritted over loose pebbles, impossibly loud. His patrol car ticked to itself. The morning breeze brought the smell of pine and soil from the woods at the opposite end of the field. But no birds singing, no crickets.

He walked up the driver side of the Dodge, hand on his holster. The interior was clean. Keys dangled from the ignition.

The internal wind blew.

(charrrliiieee)

Charlie looked around, but of course nothing was there.

He walked to the front of the car and placed a hand on the hood. Warm, and it was still early enough that the sun couldn't have done it.

(call this in now call this in)

He walked around to the passenger side, gripped the handle, and tried it. It *clunk*ed open.

He paused again, looking through the window. Unlocked car, still warm, keys in the ignition. No sign of people.

(the road ate them)

(charrrrliiieee)

Charlie winced, shook his head. His mouth had gone dry.

He debated opening the door the entire way, reaching in and pulling the keys. Instead, he slammed the door closed again—the *chunk* echoed out into the field.

(call this in)

Instead, he stepped off the shoulder, to the top of the small hill that descended into the field.

"Hello?" he called, and his voice rolled out and into the woods. The tickling increased, the internal wind grew, dizziness nudged itself more into the center of his brain.

(what are you doing?)

"I don't know," he said, and his mouth felt numb, not his own, as if he'd just paid a visit to the dentist. He stepped into the field, and his legs matched his mouth—used by someone else.

He spread his fingers across the tips of the grass, felt their furry heads. They stung his left hand, which began to bleed along the shallow cuts he'd gotten his third night on the job.

(but those cuts healed weeks ago)
The welt on his right arm throbbed in time with his heartbeat.
(charrrliiieee)
"I'm here," he said, and his voice was a sleepy growl. The dizziness was a cap over his mind, the wind blowing through the hollow chambers beneath.
(this is what harrigan wanted oh yes he wanted it dearborn eddington caldwell caldwell? yes him as well all the local boys they need the outsider they need to keep the congregation full can't sacrifice the faithful)
A wind came up from the woods, a hollow roar in his ears.
Charlie kept walking, still feeling the grass tops, leaving bloody dobs on the left. A brightness appeared above the woods, a limning of white over the treetops, and Charlie was not surprised. The brightness thickened, seemed to reach toward him—
(charrrliiieee)
—and the wind blew harder now, both inside and out—
(charrrliiieee)
—and the dizziness came hard—
(charrrliiieee)
—and he kept walking, but he tripped over a hidden rock and—

~

—he goes to his hands and knees and the soil is different—thicker, richer, muddier. More alive.
Charlie lifts his head and the woods have zoomed forward, the treeline bare feet from him, but they are different, species he's never seen before—or never seen outside of biology and geography textbooks. Tropical.
The grass here is higher, too, and sharper; he pushes the blades aside and they slice his palms. He hugs his wounded hands to his chest and feels the sweat course down his brow. It's hotter, more humid.
Around him, strange, unseen animals scream and call out. The sun boils in a molten-gray sky.
And then the ground shakes.
It's a small tremor,
(i've felt this before)
and then another, and another, another-another-another, until the word is meaningless and it's a constant vibration under him, a grumbling of the earth that obscures everything else.
Something blots out the sun. At first he thinks it's cloud-cover, but he blinks and, no, he doesn't know what it is. What is covering the sky is gray and roiling, but it isn't just the sky—it approaches across the earth, hiding the mountains (higher and with sharper peaks than the Blue Ridge Mountains). It's a cloud, a

curtain of rain, a solid. All of these things and none of these things. It hurts his eyes to look at. He senses a shape behind *the shape—the structure's* true *form, a darkening in the center of this massive thing—but his eyes can't or won't unlock it. It's like his brain knows the truth of what is in front of him and won't let him see it.*

The shape approaches, bigger than anything Charlie has ever seen, but he cannot move. His body shakes above the low-earthquake. His hands burn. His head throbs. His heart is a solid lump of unmoving muscle in his chest.

The shape pauses. It takes up Charlie's entire view—this gaseous, liquid, solid thing. Its black center is directly in front of him.

(it sees me)

And then the shape dives, plummets into the ground, and the low-tremors become a full-scale earthquake. Around him, trees splinter and crack and explode. Rocks and boulders fly. The mountains crumble, rise up, crumble again. The ground beneath Charlie splits in a million directions. Rocks and roots shoot through the gaps. One wraps itself around his right forearm and something pops *in his head—a game-show* ding!*—and suddenly he sees with his mind's eye images of other grayish things, all around, this younger world—going into the sea, into the mountains, into the ice. Burying themselves.*

(we call them gods and to us they are gods but they were just here first they are older than gods)

The root tightens and breaks skin and the sleeve of his uniform becomes sodden with blood. It pulls and Charlie is dragged, down into the ground—

—and, lands, standing, onto 526, but it's a 526 as constructed on a movie set—artificially built, in a black soundstage. He cannot see where it ends or where it begins. Hidden spotlights shine on just this section of the highway and it is crammed with cars from the 1950s, 1940s, 1930s—going so far back to show carriages and horseless carts. They are side-to-side, nose-to-nose, stretching into the darkness. He sees traveling sacks, made with animal skins, crafted weapons like spears and tomahawks.

(all the sacrifices all of them the ones its claimed on its land)

He sees no people. No skeletons or corpses. They were sacrificed.

(the family in the galaxie the temoins joseph)

The root still grips him and it tugs at him again, into and out of darkness, and onto another black soundstage. He sees a dozen men dressed in ways he'd only seen back in Williamsburg, at the historical sites. Colonists. They stand in a loose group and one holds open a large, thin book with rough-cut pages. The man holding the book, Charlie sees with no surprise, is the rooster—Eddington, or someone who looks remarkably similar to him.

One by one, the men cut their fingers and dribble blood upon the open page. With each offering, Eddington's ancestor says in a doggerel that is, nevertheless, perfectly understood by Charlie: "It will be honored."

And then the voice of the man-thing Charlie had seen that night out at the depot, booming as if from hidden speakers: "This is what has damned us all."

The root tugs him again, into and out of darkness, and it's 526 again, but emptier. He sees the Galaxie, Joseph's pickup, a half dozen others, scattered and damaged, but the contrast to before is apparent; the sacrifices have slimmed, become violent. Charlie thinks of all those turn-offs before 526 enters Anbeten County.

From the darkness at the opposite end, Eddington approaches, walking the center line. Under the spotlights, his face is shadowed, eyes mere sockets and nose a blade.

He stops and opens his mouth and blackish-blood falls out.

"This is the end of the pact," Eddington says, in the voice of the man-thing.

Charlie blinks and now it's Caldwell standing there. "This is the end of my slumber and my acquiescence."

Blink and it's Harrigan. "I seek my freedom."

Blink and it was Charlie, his hair milk-white. "They seek your death as supplication."

Charlie screams, but the root does not pull him back into the darkness. Instead, the Charlie-thing approaches. "The pact must be broken, or you shall die and I shall be condemned."

The Charlie-thing stands before him. He smells of soil and pine and iron-rich blood. "They must pay for their arrogance, but not with you. You did not sign with blood. You are not of the faithful. Only you can be a vessel and grant me freedom. You will be marked, but you will live."

His eyeless face grins at Charlie, blood seeping from between his pink teeth. "Break the pact and all will be well. Fail and you will die in ways you have never imagined."

The Charlie-thing raises his hands, dirt covering corpse-pale skin, closes them into fists with the thumbs out. The nails are long and sharp.

"Break the pact," the Charlie-thing says and tilts the thumbs to jam them into Charlie's eyes.

~

He was screaming in the driver seat of his patrol car.

It took him a moment to get himself to stop, and even then, he couldn't stop shaking; his nerves thrummed with delayed reaction, made his teeth chatter.

Through his windshield, the Dodge was still there, but the sun had moved to the other side. It was afternoon—late afternoon, by the look. The sun was behind him.

His right arm burned, the skin tender against his uniform. He looked down and saw the sleeve of his uniform shredded and stained. He pushed it up—his hand aching and tacky with old blood—and saw a fresh welt, freshly scabbed over.

Charlie slumped in his seat.

(real it was real all of it)

(we are bound)

(break the pact)

(you will die)

"They sent me here to die," he said and his voice sounded like he'd been gargling dirt.

(harrigan eddington dearborn)

(break the pact)

He thought of his family and, for the first time, didn't shy away—his home in the big house on the outskirts of Williamsburg. His father trying his hand at farming, then assisting on other farms, then whatever odd jobs he could scrounge; his mother, too traditional to ever say a word, just picking up the slack whenever she could. He and Tim, trying to find their own places. Tim found it in football. Charlie studied atlases and dreamed about law enforcement, of being a State Trooper, of having a *place* and a *home* and getting as far the hell away from Williamsburg as he possibly could. Home wasn't on the outskirts of a tourist trap, never seeing the same face twice, watching his father devolve into a surly paranoid. Home wasn't slowly building debt and madness and transience.

(maybe it was maybe it is look where you ended up)

Half-dozing, his body more exhausted than he could've ever imagined, his brow furrowed.

Look how it *had* ended up—his mother and brother, dead on the yellow grass outside the weather-battered shack that was supposed to be the family barn, their faces blown off; his father, stabbed and burning, falling to his knees and still reaching for Charlie. Charlie had sustained second-degree burns on both arms and hands, but he had survived.

He had *survived.*

(you will be marked but you will live)

The squawking of the dash-mic brought him back: *something-something-526-something-something.*

He straightened in his seat and reached for the mic. He caught a glimpse of himself in the rearview mirror. His hair was bleached-white, the sockets around his eyes puffy with bruising.

(the charlie-thing tilting his thumbs to blind him)

He shook his head and grabbed the mic. "This is Car 19, out on 526. Copy."

He let go of the TALK button and listened to the ghost-static, the distant murmur of other voices just outside of the channel's range.

Dispatch came back, but the voice wasn't who he had heard before. "Car 19? What's your twenty?"

Charlie tried to recall the last mile marker. "Near Mile 36, Dispatch. Witnessed an—" He tried to remember the ten-codes from the Academy, the list of numerics that kept CB-radio jockeys from spying into police business.

Looking at the abandoned Dodge, he said, "Witnessed an 11-96, but nothing was suspicious. Just abandoned. 10-24, copy."

Another long pause and then dispatch's unfamiliar—but *recognizable*—voice came back: "Car 19, you advise a 11-96? Is it an 11-99?"

Charlie closed his eyes, thinking hard. *11-99* was code for...for...

He opened his eyes. For *officer needs help?*

"Dispatch, be advised," he said. "This is not an 11-99. Suspicious vehicle was abandoned."

The response was immediate. "19, we have patrols 11-76. *Stay calm.* Anbeten County's 11-77 is roughly ten minutes." A *click*, and then: "All units, be advised. Patrol has a 10-31 out on 526. 10-53 all exits leading off and on. *Do not engage.* Anbeten can be there quicker."

Charlie tried to keep track of what dispatch was spouting.

11-76—cars are enroute. Anbeten County's cars.

11-77—estimated time of arrival of personnel.

10-31—crime in progress.

10-53—block all roads.

Anbeten County was responding to a crime and the State Police were to block all roads on and off of 526.

For the first time since waking up, his heart was racing. "Dispatch, *10-22* that assignment. 526 is *clear. Clear*—do you copy?"

Dispatch came back and he finally recognized the voice over the speaker. Harrigan. "Trooper Brooks, stay—"

His fist bashed into the dash-mic once, twice, three times—snapping plastic and denting metal. The pain was fantastic, a gruff-roar that made the paper-cuts from the prehistoric grass seem like pinches. Harrigan's voice cut out in a scream of static.

Charlie hugged his bleeding knuckles to his chest.

(they're coming for me)

Dearborn and his county boys would be here in ten minutes.

Except, their station was over fifteen minutes away, in Schlossen itself.

(they were waiting for me)

Eventually, most likely after dark, someone would've driven along 526 and found his car. His body would've either been reduced to something you could put into a shoebox or missing altogether. He was supposed to be sacrificed. He was an outsider. Not of the congregation.

(now they're coming to make sure i am sacrificed)

He grunted and, leaning across the bench seats, popped open the glove compartment and grabbed the First Aid kit. He pulled out the gauze and wrapped it around his right hand. The fingers weren't broken, but the knuckles were enlarged. He found aspirin packets and choked two down.

He straightened and took a breath. His brain kicked along, thinking of the next few moments. He felt no tickle or dizziness.

(of course not i'm already marked)

He checked the rearview and the sun was setting fast. It usually did in the mountains. He saw no emergency lights. Not yet. How long was ten minutes?

What did he want to do? He could stay, he supposed. Allow himself to be the sacrifice they so desperately needed. This home had turned out no better than what he had escaped from in Williamsburg; his survival *there* had only led to this. Maybe this was fate. He could give in. This wasn't his fight. He was an outsider. Everyone agreed on that—both the people and the god. He could stay and wait for the end.

Instead, he turned the engine over and the Chevy roared to life. An emergency turn-off came up and he took it, barely touching the brake before twisting the wheel. The back tires skidded and screamed and he roared up the incline, jostling into the westbound lanes and arrowing down the highway. The sun had fallen behind the mountains, the peaks barely highlighted with autumnal yellow.

His best bet was driving forward, see if he could shoot through their net, then figure out the next step.

(break the pact)

But how? *How?* What could he do and how would he know he could do it before it was too late?

He thought of his father, turning the shotgun towards him with the air still ringing from gunning down Tim. Charlie had grabbed the World War II trench knife from the workbench inside the shack, but that was as far as forethought had gone. When his father had kept coming, Charlie had literally fallen over the gas can. It was only that and his father's lit cigarette that had saved his life.

Charlie had to hope for the same blind luck.

(not the best plan not at all)

(better than nothing)

(survivor)

He drove over one rise, two rises, and still no sirens. Everything before his eyes popped with the most vivid crispness, not quelled at all by the thickening shadows and softening grays of evening.

He came over the third rise and there they were—a line of patrol cars, two rows deep, barreling down both the east and westbound lanes, lights throbbing. For an instant, Charlie was something akin to flattered—they were doing this for *him.*

Everyone braked at the same time and over the shriek of rubber on asphalt, Charlie faintly heard the *clunk* of cars rear-ending each other. Vehicles rested at crazy angles, blocking all lanes. Charlie stopped a bare six yards away, the headlights blinding him.

He heard the sound of car doors opening and figures made black behind the headlights appeared. Charlie rolled his window down.

"You might as well come out now, Trooper," Dearborn called. "You're not getting through and we got an easy two dozen weapons aimed at you."

(but you won't shoot me you can't if you want a sacrifice for your god can you?)

For good measure, he revved the engine and Dearborn, still talking, immediately shut up. The figures all blended as they hunched and flinched.

Charlie grinned, but didn't dare look into the rearview mirror, terrified he would look how he felt—a grinning death's head.

"We just want to talk to you, Trooper," Dearborn called.

(right after you tell me how many weapons are aimed at me)

"This doesn't have to be unpleasant," Dearborn said. "But some things need to be settled and I can't yell all night."

(he has no idea how much i know)

He revved the engine again, but it was half-hearted and the figures didn't flinch. The sun was completely gone now and everything behind the lights was a black blob, but Charlie could see there was no getting through that line. All he'd do was get a lot of people killed, including himself.

(if they have their way i'm dead anyway)

But he thought of the gas can, he thought of blind luck, he thought of

(a vessel)

(break the pact and you will live)

His hand and arm, burning, burning.

"I'm coming out!" he called through the open window.

The engine still running, he opened his door and took a step outside, one foot still in the car. The headlights washed over him, blinded him.

"I want to talk to Harrigan!" he called, because he felt he should call something out. Anything to stall until the proverbial gas can appeared. "I want him to explain it!"

"Oh, he'll be here," Dearborn said, lower than before. "You're his boy, and all." Then a sound like a chuckle. "This didn't go exactly according to plan, but it's plain obvious you've been touched, boy. Oh my, this might actually work. Eddington was right."

He heard the footsteps too late; he started to turn and a rifle butt came crashing down, right into the center of his face. A bright flare of pain, and then he was gone.

~

Charlie's burning father looks up at him. His face is a melted candle. His eyes are gone, leaving running, glowing sockets. When he speaks, he's easily heard over the crackle of the fire killing him, and his voice is the voice of the man-thing.

(you'll know the way)

he says,

(and you can break the pact charlie but you have to wake UP—)

Charlie opened his eyes in the backseat of a patrol car with his left hand burning and the ache in his head a leaden bell forever tolling. The car hit a bump, jostling him, and he bit his lip to keep from screaming.

The interior of the car was pitch-black. Two men sat up front, poorly lit by the glow of the dashboard.

"—Eddington be ready?" Harrigan said from the passenger seat. He spoke in a low voice.

"Old pecker was about pissing his pants when I got him on the horn," Dearborn said. "He and his boys will be ready. You'd think he was almost *glad* things didn't work out the way we talked. He wants to *see* your man back there."

Another bump and Charlie let his body go limp, let it roll a bit. He had to keep biting his lip to keep from groaning, and the sucking-pennies taste of blood filled his mouth.

Harrigan nodded and the two men fell silent. Charlie rested his head on the vinyl seat. Through the window, the night sky stared indifferently back at him, the scattered stars like pinpricks. He thought of driving away with Caldwell, seeing the Shenandoah Valley open up when they reached the top of a rise, with Schlossen a tiny alienated cluster to one side.

"What do you think happened to him?" Harrigan asked.

That awkward chuffing sound again. "I think it liked him."

Charlie didn't need to wonder what *it* was.

"Then why not take him *then*?" Harrigan pressed. He shook his head. "That's why I sent him out there, for Chrissake. You'd said it was getting unpredictable and Brooks would be good bait. Why not take him then?"

"Getting cold feet, Jeff? Been a few years since you seen a god at work?"

Harrigan's head turned towards the Sheriff. "Our families go back far enough, Dick," he said.

Dearborn shifted in his seat. "Who can know the mind of a god? He's obviously been touched, and not like Eddington and them other boys. He's been *prepped*." He paused. "You sure he doesn't have family? We had relatives of those people who recorded what happened to the Whitneys, coming around and asking questions. Handled them, but it made a few of my men sweat a little."

Harrigan shook his head. "No. Family's dead....he killed his father."

The car swerved a bit. *"What?"*

"Father had battle-fatigue, according to reports. World War II vet. Killed the mother and brother. Brooks stabbed him and set him on fire."

Dearborn whistled through his teeth. "Jesus Christ."

"Something feels off about this," Harrigan said, and sighed. "It took the Temoins—after the Whitneys and Joe Ratigan—but that wasn't enough. We have to give it Brooks."

"It's about appeasement, Jeff," Dearborn said. "It wants out of the pact. Those Temoins of yours used to be regular course for it. Now it goes after the Whitneys. And Joseph Ratigan. And Marla Mullins. And anyone else who wants to leave the service before the sermon's done." Dearborn shook his head. "Your boy's just supposed to be a stop-over until we figure things out. Him being touched...that just made us all feel better."

"I'll feel better when it's over," Harrigan said. "The state—the *Colonel* of the *State Police*—is going to be looking at us after this."

"You'll figure it out," Dearborn said, and the car went into a turn. Charlie's head thumped against the door and it sent another toll of agony through his skull. He groaned before he could stop it.

"He's gonna wake up before the party," Dearborn said. "Good."

Charlie saw Harrigan's head turn to look back and, although he knew the Master Trooper couldn't see in the darkness, he lidded his eyes, made them appear closed.

The car jostled more and more—they were off pavement now. Charlie caught a flash of light, a porch light, but it was gone before he could make out anything else. The spitting-burn of his hand intensified slowly. A pulse began to beat in his head, rising in slow but steady increments from the back of his mind.

(break the pact break the pact break the pact)

A rumble of something beneath, like a run of stones in the road, and then Dearborn brought the car to a stop.

"Told you they'd be ready," Dearborn said, and Harrigan nodded.

Charlie could smell wood burning, and soil, and pine. He closed his eyes—

(break the pact)

—and saw the eyeless Harrigan, the eyeless Caldwell, the eyeless Eddington—

(break the pact)

—the eyeless *him*, grinning death's head.

(they seek your death for supplication)

(break the pact)

Dearborn and Harrigan got out of the car. "Lemme get some of the boys to help me," Dearborn said. Charlie heard the crunch of leaves underfoot, dwindling away. The rumble of many male voices speaking came to him—a guttural chant with many parts and, when put together, it sounded like the revving of race car engines.

"*Mi him eck torch. Grrritch eck torch. Eck torch!*"

It chilled his skin, made his burning hand seem that much hotter, wormed into his head and nestled there, finding a friend in the steady beat already at work in his brain.

On the passenger side, he saw Harrigan walk to the backseat to look through the window at him. He lidded his eyes again, but the Master Trooper's expression, half-lit by the fire, was stone. One eye gleamed like half-buried quartz.

Crunching leaves, growing louder, and the door behind Charlie's head opened. Charlie let his head fall, fully closed his eyes.

"*Jee-zus*," one man breathed. "What the hell happened to him?"

"Nothing compared to what's going to happen," another man said. "C'mon—grab an armpit."

Hands reached in and gripped him roughly under the arms.

(break the pack break the pact break the)

The men took a breath, one of them going, "One, two, *three...*" and then they yanked him from the backseat. He felt his ass leave the vinyl, but the weight distribution was off— all three toppled to the ground. One man's foot caught Charlie along the side of his head as he fell and the scream peeled out of him in a banshee's shriek. He hit the dirt, feeling the coldness beneath, smelling the minerals.

(it i'm smelling it)

The chanting paused, but did not stop, and Charlie heard the rush of people approaching as he got himself to his hands and knees, every muscle rippling as if trying to run away from his bones.

The soft voice, the woman's voice, his mother's voice:

(isn't this what you wanted? isn't this what you wanted charlie?)

Everything hurt, everything was wrong, and nothing was his own anymore. He had been chosen, but he was a vessel, a meat puppet, and all he could do was shake and shiver on the ground like a sick—

(father)

(vessel)

—dog.

(this isn't what i wanted this isn't what i wanted)

(the Presbyterian minister at the lectern beside his family's coffins, saying, "and we turn to psalm 107, verse 9: 'for he satisfieth the longing soul, and filleth the hungry soul with goodness'")

"What the *fuck* is wrong with you?" Dearborn hollered.

"He *feels* wrong!" one of the men replied.

"He's been touched," Eddington said, somewhat far away. "He's been with *It*." "Get 'im on his feet, goddammit," Dearborn said, and Charlie heard a twang in his words, a little quiver, he hadn't noticed before. Scared. He'd been giving Harrigan shit about seeing gods work, but in the end, the Anbeten Sheriff was piss-terrified.

"Do *not* do that," Charlie barked, his head lowered, and he hadn't even known he was going to speak. His voice sounded like he was gargling dirt. "Stay *back* from me."

More crunching leaves, and the men around him were muttering. He heard more twangs.

(me they're scared of me)

(vessel)

(filleth the hungry soul)

And then the voice of the man-thing and the voice of his father spoke up, a choir from hell:

(they will not stop and you must not either)

"Get him," Eddington said, sounding the calmest of everyone. "Get him and bring him to me. Now."

A moment's hesitation, and then rough hands grabbed him, lifted him, his head facedown and swinging like the clapper of the bell tolling in his head. They handled him awkwardly, as if unsure how to hold onto him. One man hissed. "Christ, it's like holding onto snakes."

"He's responding to the words," Eddington said, "the calling."

(vessel)

(mi him eck torch grritch eck torch eck torch!)

(filleth the hungry soul)

(eck torch!)

They carried him away from the car. Charlie could feel the heat of the approaching fire, see the wavering afterglow on the ground. His hand burned hottest of all.

He looked up, and the fire was five times the size of the one he'd witnessed before, blazing high above everyone's heads with what looked like tree trunks in the center. The VDOT workers were there, mixed with the county boys and Harrigan's men, wearing heavy robes of rich cloth, cinched tight with silken ropes. Country-rough faces with too-widely-set blue eyes, studied him with mixtures of fear and anticipation. He didn't see Caldwell amongst their number and felt good about that.

Eddington stood waiting by a large lectern built of rounded stone in front of the fire. In his left hand, he held a Bowie knife large enough to gut a deer, but it was the open book in his right that Charlie's eyes locked on. The beat in his head grew adamant.

(BREAK THE PACT BREAK THE PACT BREAK THE)

"Bring him close," Eddington said.

They did and the fire seem to reach for him.

The VDOT workers, joined with the police, began chanting louder as Eddington looked down at the book. "We bring You this meat," he intoned, "in honor and worship for the gifts You have bestowed upon us, and in hopes that You will continue to bless us. With our left hand we bring it."

"*Mi him eck torch!*" the workers chanted.

Charlie's body spasmed, the nerves spitting through his muscles, but the officers held him tight. His head whipped this way and that, white hair flying, sweat hitting the hot stone and sizzling.

(BREAK THE PACT BREAK THE PACT BREAK THE)

"With our right hand we touch Your face with love and trust," Eddington said, his voice rising to a preacher-shout. "With our left hand we feed You the blood and meat of the worthy. *We renew our pact in blood!*" He raised the Bowie knife and the firelight slid along the honed edge like liquid butter.

"*Grrritch eck torch!*" the VDOT workers chanted.

The fire in his hand was excruciating. The pain in his head was a memory owned by someone else in the face of such agony. He was no longer Charlie Brooks. He was the vessel.

(filleth the hungry soul)

"*Keep us in Your thoughts!*" Eddington cried. "*Keep us in Your thoughts and remember the pact our fathers made with You!*"

"*ECK TORCH!*" the VDOT workers bellowed. Charlie bellowed with them, an inarticulate howl.

"*REMEMBER US AND OUR HANDS REMEMBER YOU!*" Eddington screamed and stepped forward, the Bowie knife held high to plunge into Charlie's back.

Charlie jerked and his left hand was momentarily freed. It knocked the others off-balance and suddenly he was falling, but not before he saw the cuts on his hand glow orange. Flames poured out of the wounds and consumed his hand, turning it into a fisted torch. A glimmer of Charlie's consciousness remained and he thought of his father, reaching for him.

Charlie hit the ground and it trembled beneath him. Eddington staggered. The VDOT workers stopped mid-chant.

Charlie got to his knees, then to his feet, hunched over, favoring his burning hand. It did not touch his flesh. Now that the fire was freed, all he felt was a comforting warmth.

He turned towards Eddington and the rooster flinched. Charlie opened his mouth and it was not the voice of a man-thing, but the voice of a god, a sound that had never been twisted into human speech; the crack of tree trunks splintering in a high wind, the rumble of boulders crashing in a landslide.

"*Our time is done,*" It said with Charlie's mouth.

He heard the click of guns, but when he turned, Dearborn and the other county boys were already faltering, their faces draining of expression, eyes widening. Some dropped their guns but didn't move their hands at all, as if they hadn't noticed.

He turned back to Eddington and the rooster was frozen to the spot, the Bowie knife still held high, the book still open.

"*Who grows weary of your tired faith?*" It asked, approaching. Blood dribbled from his mouth. "*I do.*"

He reached towards the book and saw the thin pages were ancient, more animal-skin than real paper, and written long ago with heavy inks. Rust-colored blotches covered the bottom portion.

He laid his burning hand on the page and it erupted in flame. Immediately the ground trembled beneath him and something inhuman roared within his head, a bellow of triumph.

The flames slid from his hand—pink from the heat but otherwise blameless—feeding the fire. More flames tasted Eddington's robed arm, found it good, and consumed it. The VDOT leader couldn't move. He stared at Charlie, his eyes vacant windows to an empty house.

"*The final sacrifice,*" It said with Charlie's mouth, "*is all of you.*"

As if that were the order, the fire took Eddington, consuming him and pulling him down. The man screamed, once, a thin, tea-kettle sound, and then fell flat on his face.

The ground erupted around them, heavy cracks zipping in all directions. The pyre spilled beyond the safety rocks, catching some of the faithful. Harrigan and his men plummeted into a gap that yawned beneath them and then were squashed when the ground moved the opposite way. Few screamed. Few had time to.

Charlie fell and hugged his patch of still-solid ground, his throat a ruin, the shaking earth blessedly cool against his cheek. All around him, the ground tore itself apart. The entire night was alive with the sound of destruction.

(just hold on hold on we will get through this it promised)

And then something crashed into the back of his head, driving his face into the soil, and Charlie Brooks knew no more.

~

Birds called him back.

He opened his eyes and did not immediately know who he was.

He got unsteadily to his feet. His body was one huge knot of bruised muscle. His uniform was destroyed—burned, caked with dirt, torn. His exposed skin was pink and blistered. He touched a hand to his face and his eyebrows were gone, his hair a crisp stubble. The back of his head throbbed, but it didn't necessarily bother him. In an odd way, the pain was fairly pleasant, a part of him glad to be feeling anything at all.

He looked around and saw nothing but leaning trees rising out of a morning fog, exposed roots like frozen tentacles, stones like the worn teeth of ancient monsters poking from loose soil. The breeze, carrying bird morningsong, was cool and blessed against his new skin.

For some reason, he expected bodies.

Hugging his midsection, he walked in no particular direction. It began to come back to him. His name. Who he was. His family. Most of what had happened to him. He tried to remember what had led to this and the only thing that came from the blackness of his memory was of a voice, deep and loud and not even remotely human, intoning, "*Our time is done.*"

The sun rose, but could not pierce the fog. It remained an ill-defined yellow disc that he used to set direction.

Eventually, he found his way back to 526, or what was left of it. The crumbled edges rose twenty feet above him, with a steep hill of loose dirt and stone the only way up.

It took him an hour, but he did it. When, finally, he pulled himself up to what remained of the westbound lanes, he turned and looked back.

"Jesus Christ," he breathed.

A massive crater, too big to see the far edges of, had taken Anbeten County—and, he assumed, a fair chunk out of Shenandoah, Fauquier, and Warren, too. The distant outline of the Blue Ridge Mountains, rising above the fog nestled within the bowl of the crater, were slumped—more foothills than mountaintops now.

And he heard no sirens, no people. Just the breeze. Just the birds. He might've been the only human being in all of Northern Virginia. He knew that couldn't be true, but, looking out, it seemed possible.

Hunger gnawed into his gut, but he ignored it for the moment, instead sitting down on the edge of the ruined road and staring out at the destruction. He'd seen It come, in the vision that had touched him, had made him a vessel, and, now, he'd seen It leave.

(to where? where would it go? what would it do?)

He assumed he'd find the answer eventually, when he reached civilization or whatever remained of it, but, for now, it seemed enough to sit here, to look at the work a god had done and know that it had been done through him.

(for he satisfieth the longing soul, and filleth the hungry soul with goodness)

Now the land was alive, but empty.

Like he was, still.

ACKNOWLEDGEMENTS:

This book wouldn't exist without the incredible array of talented authors and artists who brought their absolute best work to the table for this project. I appreciate their efforts more than I can possibly express. I'd also like to especially thank Jennifer and Sera Wilson, Jon Padgett, Mike Davis of the Lovecraft eZine, Michael David Wilson of This is Horror, and Michael Denham of Signal Horizon for all of their hard work in helping in any way they could to get this project off the ground.

I'd also like to thank our backers. Without the hundreds of folks who came together to support our Kickstarter, the same above-mentioned lack of existence would have been inevitable. Every person who donated to our campaign has my deepest gratitude. Thank you all so much:

A Bear
Adam Carter
Adam Rains
Alex Shvartsman
Alexander Pyles
Alicia Hilton
Allison Dickson
Amanda Niehaus-Hard
Amanda Nixon
Amy H. Sturgis
Andrew Foxx
Andrew Hatchell
Andrew Hurley
Andrew Koury
Anna Klein
Anonymous
Anonymous
Anonymous
Anya Martin
Arne Handt
Ash Quarterly
Barb Moermond
Barbara Matzner-Volfing

Bear Weiter
Benet Devereux
Benjamin Widmer
Björn S.
Bjorn Smars
Boudicea Coviello
Brad
Brennan Willingham
Brent Clark Esq.
Brian Fortune
Brian Lesmes
Brian W. Horstman
Brock Wilbur
Bruce Baugh
Bryant Durrell
BUDDY H
C. P. Dunphey
Cameron
Candace Wiggins
Carlos Ernesto Mcreynolds
Carver Rapp
Cat Wyatt
Chad Bowden
Charles Rat
Charles shaw
Chris Basler
Chris Gomes
Chris McLaren
Chris Mountenay
Chrissie Booth
Christophe Pettus
Christopher Duncan
Christopher Stephen
Christopher 'Vulpine' Kalley
ciak
Claus Appel
Cliff Winnig
Connie Brentford
Crosley Parrott
CW Rice
D. J. Hayes
Dagmar Baumann
Dan & Emily Alban
Daniel Moore Hinton

Dark Regions Press
Darren Fisher
Dave Agnew
Dave Behrend
David Bjorne
David Busboom
David Edelstein
David Ploskonka
David Sharp
David Thirteen
deadpoolica@gmail.com
Debbie Crookston
Dickie
Doris Wilke
doungjai gam
Dr. Greg Conners
Earl P. Dean
Edward Drummond
Emily Lutringer
Emma Clark
Emmanuelle Cunningham
eric priehs
Erik Odeldahl
F. R. Michaels
Fiona Maeve Geist
Frances Rowat
Francis Burns
Fred Cardona
Fred Herman
Fred Isajenko
GeoffM
Geoffrey Young Haney
GMark C
Governmentality
Greg Stockton
Gregory Martin
Guest 1775514789
Guest 487283372
Gus Butler
H N Springford
Hans Bolvinkel
Henry Lopez
Henry Weisenborn
Holly Iossa

Isaac Chappell
J Dinges
J. P. Wiske
Jaap van Poelgeest
Jake West
James Fallweather
jason duelge
Jason Seymour
JD Hetland
Jeff Hotchkiss
Jeff Narucki
Jessi Stone
Jessica Hilt
Jessica McHugh
Jim Coniglio
Jim Gotaas
Jody Rose
Joe Kontor
John Claude Smith
John Linwood Grant
John M Gamble
John Paull Fitch
John Stewart Muller
Jonathan K. Stephens
Jordan Reyes
José Pacheco
Joseph Gustafson
Josh King
Karli Watson
Karolina Lebek
Kaye Reeves
Keith Lowery
Kent Corlain
Kevin
Kevin Holderny
Kevin Wadlow
Khanavis Kruel
Kimberly Mitchell
Klaus Hiebert
Kory
Kris Majury
Kristin Centorcelli
KT Wagner
Kyle Callahan

Kyle Johnson
Kylie Corley
Lee Dong-Hyun
Lesley Conner
Lorelei
Lysette
M. V. Ho
Mabel Harper
Maggie Doane
Marcheto
Martin Buerger
Mary Ann Peden-Coviello
Mason Mustain
Matt Brandenburg
Matt Cantrell
Matt Henshaw
Matt Kirchhoff
Matt Neil Hill
Matt Taylor
Matthew Aronoff
Matthew Carpenter
Matthew Jaffe
Matthew Robinson
Maverick Keene
Max Booth III
Maxwell I. Gold
mcstravick.s@gmail.com
Melissa Davis
Michael Adams
Michael Hirtzy
Michael Patrick Hicks
Michael Picco
Michael Sawecki
Mike Boreal
Mike Shema
MorganScorpion
Nancy Lambert
Nathan Blixt
Nathan Blumenfeld
Nathan Rosen
Nayad Monroe
Nesa Sivagnanam
Nicolas Courdouan
nikolaos sotiriadis

Nina Shepardson
Noah Green
Occulted Sound
Oliver Isbell
P Byhmer
Pamela Durgin
Patricia Root
Paul Leong
Paul M. Feeney
Paula Limbaugh
Pedro Alfaro
Peter DiCrescenzo
Petr
Philip Gelatt
Philip R. "Pib" Burns
Phufmeistr
Pip
Q Fortier
R. B. Wood
Richard Salter
Richard Thomas
Rob Voss
Robert Claney
Robert Killheffer
Robert Osgood
Roberto "Sunglar" Micheri
Roger Venable
Ronnie Ball
Ronnie Smart
Ross T. Byers
Ryan Lelache
Ryan Walz
S. L. Edwards
S.E. Casey
Sam Cowan
Sandor Silverman
Scarlett R. Algee
Scott Desmarais
Scott F. Feighner aka Scoot
Scott Kemper
Scott Valeri
Sean Ford
Sean McCoy
Seth M. Lindberg

Shane Burley
Shannon Giglio
Shaun Higgins
Shaun Jacob Cobble
SignalHorizon.com
Stephan Imri-Knight
Stephen Ballentine
Steve Tillman
Steven Wynne
Susan Jessen
Sydney Dunstan
Tasha Turner
Taylor Grant
Terence Merkelbach
Tess Grover
The Lovecraft Tapes Podcast
The New Nonsense
Thomas Corrigan
Thomas Schryver
Timothy Evan Paul
Todd Keisling
Todd Quinn
Tom Alaerts
Tom Fenton
Tom Galazka
tom reed
Tracey Bloomfield
Trevor A. Ramirez
Vivian Hall
William DeGeest
William Rieder
William Root
Yaah'nosh
Zach Bartlett
Zack Haskin